IN SEARCH
of the
RABBIT MAN

In Search
of the
Rabbit Man

A Novel

By

Jon-Michael Hamilton

Copyright © Jon-Michael Hamilton.

All rights reserved. No part of this book may be reproduced in any form or by any electronic or mechanical means, including information storage and retrieval systems, without permission in writing from the publisher, except by reviewers, who may quote brief passages in a review.

ISBN: 978-1-63649-246-9 (Paperback Edition)
ISBN: 978-1-63649-247-6 (Hardcover Edition)
ISBN: 978-1-63649-245-2 (E-book Edition)

Some characters and events in this book are fictitious. Any similarity to real persons, living or dead, is coincidental and not intended by the author.

Book Ordering Information

Phone Number: 315 288-7939 ext. 1000 or 347-901-4920
Email: info@globalsummithouse.com
Global Summit House
www.globalsummithouse.com

Printed in the United States of America

Special thanks to

Vickie Boo, the Rock of our family and her own

Bazaar and family

Mean Dean and family

Pookie and family

Sgt Maj. and family

Mom & Dad living life long together

The editors and production team

And

Countless others

With many names

And many thanks

PROLOGUE

1968

The body was found on a day not unlike other days, when spring was in full bloom and there was a time when the sky was soft and humble. This had been Texas and Dallas as far back as the sky had settled on the renaming of the land. This happened as long ago as the heroes of the state made their marks, and writers lived to spout and scribe and illustrate with long tales of boasting, or with soft whines or whispers.

These were the few days before summer when the sky was filled with short puffy clouds that crawled across, giving the sky a quiet blue—not the shouting blue-and-white cumulus of March and early April that could be seen in the Midwest or the East. This did not happen every day in spring, just a few days. It was said that it always predicted a hot summer, maybe, but that was what the Wisdom Wiser women of the black community had always said.

The Wisdom Wiser women were the wise old black women who watched the gray clouds and stated the gray attitude that had elevated to become the ruling thought in a community that just wanted to do what was right. It wasn't easy to get to that level of authority by years of foretold reasoning. This took being right at times of indecision, and that had to resonate with the present. It gave the reasoning of right and wrong to a community. It traveled within and defined a black community. And in turn this was what the old wives had said throughout the years. They were and are still looking for that good time before the bad, and for what went around to come back. Those wives, those mothers, those young girls who told their brothers who had listened to their fathers, who had probably told their wives who had told their daughters who had listened to their mothers and on and on and up and around and no one knew why...because it was Texas. Maybe it was just learned behavior from tribal ways and the designs of family from a time they were forced to forget, or maybe it was just the whites. But maybe it was just the religion that everyone agreed upon, and they told the old wives that the good are paid when they inherit the earth. In the bad that is also Texas, a God-fearing state, the bad shall reap the inheritance of the sun.

And it was just another seasonal sky with years of predecessors moving back and forth in the silence of selfish memory that would expel the memory of other skies and seasons and days. It would expel Christmas and Easter and other such holiday seasons only because those days signaled the approaching last days of the school year—or ever more quietly, the last days of elementary school for the small children.

These were unique days to the participants of those days, and there were the days that every participant had known or would know. It was the beginning of the new, of past times that really became past times. You grew up and looked forward to what was denied because it had been put aside until you were older. No one knew when it would begin, but only when it could end.

Perhaps it would begin right after the New Year's holiday, when young people rushed in after presents and the cheer and the promises that no one could keep because they had never experienced the alternative. Some just called it the Christmas hangover. Or it could begin right after Easter, when all the holiday candy had vanished and the toys were old and you had mastered your studies and responsibilities for that age. This is what made those days different from Christmas or Easter, or other such holiday seasons. But then, it was within those days when the police found the body.

The Highland Hills and Bishop Heights neighborhoods were separated by a ruddy creek of running water that flowed from north to south in a trickle in the right season and a gurgle in another, through overdeveloped bush and woodland trees of moderate height. "Moderate" was between two and four feet. The neighborhoods were essentially black American.

The year 1968 was the time when it was in vogue to be called black, when black found a voice, when black was beautiful. Songs pronounced it. Singers sang about it. James Brown said it best: "Just say it loud." The newspapers reflected it, and the televisions documented the proud and beautiful struggle of civil rights marchers in their black pants and water-drenched white shirts. It was okay to be called black American, or just plain black instead of *Negro*. It was in vogue to say "those blacks," or "these blacks," or "Black people, please listen." Anything was better than the previous. And in Texas, people slowly began to listen...but slowly. The reality was that Texans were just Texans and that was it, or maybe just Texans only whispered about differences.

Stretching through the neighborhoods were the major streets that acted as the traffic arteries of the community. Bonnie View Road was a winding street that paralleled the ruddy creek and went north and away from the Bishops Heights elementary school. The road crossed over the west-to-east intersection of Simpson Stuart Road and continued on north through the major environs of the Oak Cliff neighborhoods, which were the earlier developed neighborhoods for black families. Simpson Stuart Road crept from another woodland area, named Singing Hills in the future, and cornered off the Highland Hills cul-de-sac and crossed the train tracks until it connected to the 310 freeway that reached north and south to the interstate.

Highland Hills was the neighborhood that was named for the flowing hills that the homes, sidewalks, and streets stretched across. They didn't just sit on them, but more or less straddled the hills as if they were clinging to an incline. The hills weren't striking, even if you could compare them to the smaller hills of the state. But if you tried to compare them to the hills in the *John Wayne* movie *The Quiet Man* or any golf course in the white areas, you could have an argument for the hills coming up short and unimpressive. But when you compared the

ix

hills to the flat streets of Bishop Heights, the hills could become the great hills of Texas—but this was just from the eye of the adolescent.

Both neighborhoods were among the housing developments that seemed to pop up more and more in the southern extremes of the city. Both were very clean neighborhoods. Both were 100 percent black. If added together the number of people was fewer than a thousand, counting children and pets. In Dallas in the '60s, there were a lot of neighborhoods beginning to set up that way. Some few were the neighborhoods where all the blacks with families and friends were found. The already nicely developed neighborhoods were the white or southern Texan neighborhoods. But back in 1962 there was a push for black home ownership and everyone was trying to get out of the projects. This was consistent with leading the nation with fairness and had nothing to do with the illumination of the civil rights struggle on the television news or its national print exposure. Or it was just an attempt to quell a perceived envy. This was Texas and men could really be men. Texas was a fair-weather state in 1968.

The exact report said that the Dallas police found this particular body near the newly developed community of Oak Cliff, an offshoot of South Dallas, in an underdeveloped field that was obscured from curious passersby occupants of cars—or walking black eyes—by a sprouting of young oak and maple trees, other brush, wild weeds, and a jagged running creek that gurgled underneath. The body did not have identification or clothing save undershorts, and reeked from weeks of water running over it and from mold, fungus, and other such scavengers as well. It had so much decay that one could not tell at first glance if the body was a black person or white, but the undershorts gave the identity of a male.

Water kept the skin moist and lazy and brought big clumsy fruit flies, great giant wood rats, and other parasites that eat and gnaw and harvest rotten flesh. The buzzing and stench from the decay hovered around the trees that surrounded the body like a thick cloud of putrid waste that you didn't smell every day. Above it circled big black crows that sometimes sat on the telephone wires that stretched above and along the streets or the trees. Those wires were temporary for the crows because more often than not craved the flat quiet isolated landscapes of weeds, tall grass, and vegetable growth..

Some elementary children had reported the body because they were exploring the trail that ran through the brush like a jagged lightning bolt. This biblical reference that the parents used helped to keep some of the children out of the woods. But not all of them. The children who lived in the Highland Hills community, had used the trail to walk to school every day since the school in Bishop Heights had opened some five years ago, in 1963. The school was about a quarter mile away from Highland Hills, and the body marked the spot on an imaginary dividing line in the creek. But where the trail crosses the creek is where the children from both neighborhoods had pushed back and forth over territorial lines. The Bishop Heights children would walk their friends from Highland Hills to this point. They would stop short for the apparent reason that both were remembering the boundary lines. The Highland Hills children would continue, some briskly and some not, on to their homes and return using the same route in the mornings.

After days of trying to avoid the stench, someone had finally investigated—because that was the only way you could find that area of the creek. You had to really want to go down and in there. The children had finally given up and gone home and had told their parents. The parents had finally called the police. But the body was in the deepest part of the creek, and the police used specially trained dogs that were sensitive to the odors of dead bodies. Four officers and two dogs went back into the deepest part and brought the body out, covered by a blanket, and on two six-foot planks with a big heavy potato bag connecting the planks. It was April 11, 1968, and the week after Dr. Martin Luther King Jr.'s death.

It was immediately afterward when the rumors started flowing about the body through the grapevine—a singular voice that filled every neighborhood. Rumors flourished that the body was a young man who had died with a frown on his face and strange marks on his eyebrows, nose, and throat, and had been there for more than a month.

Rumors swirled about an old man's body with the same deep scarring on the face and scrapings down to the bone. Rumors ran wild about animals that happened to have escaped the zoo or were dropped off by angry zoo attendants between the newly developed neighborhoods, and the animals were said to be sought by the police and game officials respectively. Other rumors abounded about the wild animals that already lived in the fields and defended the creek area to protect their threatened homes—animals like crazy night owls, lost coyotes, and rabid angry squirrels and rabbits. But the most frightening rumor of all was about the half-man half-rabbit with white hair on his neck and back, who needed a taste for something other than grass or carrots.

Skin color was never clearly communicated about the body, at least not to the community at large, and that gave it an ominous effect of dread nonetheless. It didn't matter that the most interesting and alarming rumor had not yet been confirmed, but it brought attention and common thought to both neighborhoods. And when the people who didn't live in the neighborhood heard the rumor, they would judge. This was the biggest fear by far in both neighborhoods: the hidden fear that others would judge this new, clean, freshly populated neighborhood by the body that was found in it, like what had been done in other neighborhoods in the past, and that nothing would have changed and this new beginning would just be a new ground for the old, painful, meaningless, reactions.

The rumors festered into the neighborhoods, the schools, and families like the dark serpent that ran Adam and Eve out of Eden. The clerks at the new Five & Dime store repeated and reinforced those rumors. The store sat on the left of Simpson Stuart Road; if you were driving to the interstate you would pass by it. The clerks at the E-Z Shop reinforced the rumors as well. That store sat on the right of Bonnie View after you crossed Simpson Stuart, and if you were heading north and into old Oak Cliff you could see the big red letters identifying it from five blocks away.

The cashiers knew nothing about the rumors except what they had heard. They didn't know if what was repeated was true or not. That

xii

was not the crux of the dilemma. The clerks just responded to their customers and their customers just responded to their friends. And no one could fault the cashiers for continuing to pass on rumors when they were the face of authority for the business interest in the community. Because while the blacks lived there, they didn't really own much, save their homes. The community really belonged to the businesses that serviced it. That's the way you had to look at it in business. Who would want to travel miles for goods when the store was right down the street? That's why it was called a convenience store. It's just the way you do business in a neighborhood that you don't live in. Plus, it's best if you try to know your customers. You should get to know their likes and dislikes. You should know their courage and their fears. Based on what the cashiers repeated and what the people who listened to the cashiers believed, the stores reacted and began to close early, a little after sunset. No one would show up anyway.

For days the rumors became a message that was passed on to the young children. This was the information of a community that thrived on information. Because of the newness of the community, the people felt they were privileged to live in a place that was shown in newspaper advertisements as a new beginning. It was a new neighborhood, and this was something that the parents reacted to, even though they never said why. This was the information that was overheard or whispered or gathered in bits and pieces. This was the information that was passed on from the eldest to the youngest and everyone thought about protecting the other. This was the protection for the community's self-imposed curfew. This was the protection that brought the children home by sunset. This was the protection that made no one want to go through the trail at night. This was the protection that fell like a shadow and made the streets all but empty in the neighborhoods after sunset, and everyone was inside of their homes unless you were coming or going to work. Official information stopped and rumors continued, and no one knew if the case had been solved yet. That much became apparent to the kids growing up within the shadow of uncertainty.

This shadow of society would never show as a catalyst toward the normal behavior of the community, but it really was a reflection of an attitude for the children to absorb while they lived in the Bishop Heights–Highland Hills area. In fact, in the 1960's the normal behavior for children who were growing up in the infant stages of the protests and the new civil rights struggle had almost just afterward discovered that their childish indiscretions were being considered as delinquent or militant behaviors. But 1968 was moving fast. A lot had already happened with Dr. King. A lot had happened before him and a lot was happening after him. A lot of things were changing. The voice of the community said, "We've uncovered a truth, now we must do something about it."

And by the same turn, there was a voice to suppress change. "Be aware of the race-mixing and free love and free spirits from these hippies and radical left-wingers that talk about changing our American politics and foreign policy."

The silent cry of the community was finally found, and rested in the soft murmurs of the funeral parlors that began sprouting up like weeds—so silent, so still, so familiar, so comforting that they were soon respectfully called second homes for the colored people.

I

The Sighting
April 13, 1968
Saturday

On the surface, Michelangelo Malone, named by his mother, but called Mikey for short by his friends and family, was a typical sixth grader growing up in the new community. If anything, he was the typical American twelve-year-old with all the toys and dreams that were available for a boy his age and this was something that has father felt was important and fought hard for. His father, Big Teddy Malone, did not want his family to feel any differently from any other American, or Texas family growing up so he purchased as much as he could to give them the same comforts.

Mikey spent a lot of his time, like all the average American boys, playing make-believe in his room lying on the floor on a large brown rug playing G. I. Joe. He would place the figures atop and through the middle of an empty grocery box that he often played with. He had tried to construct a transit bus with the seats streaming down each side and sunlight gleaming through the windows, but had seen the design of the interior of an airplane in a *World Book* encyclopedia and had constructed that instead.

The figures were large, about twelve inches high, and plastic, posed as models of the American military fighting men and even in the uniforms of the services that they represented. He had three separate ones: an army infantryman with a helmet atop the head and a green fatigue uniform; a sailor poised in a crouched position, which seemed almost neutral but both hands were ready to grip a weapon if need be, and—the one that Mikey put in charge of all the other military men— the one in the blue air force uniform. This uniform looked so much like his father's uniform that this G. I. Joe had to be in charge, just like his father. These were his first loves, where he could relive great military and Biblical battles, or scenes from television shows or western movies, or solve some of the minor problems of his life. And the best thing about his G. I. Joe scenarios was that they always won.

Mikey's other prized possession was his electric football set. It was his father's favorite as well. They would play together when his father, Theodore "Big Teddy" Malone, an average sized man with big arms, light skin color, short hair and a thinly trimmed mustache, had time on the weekends. The figures were small, about one inch high, and plastic, posed as models of the professional players of the era and placed on plastic pedestals that were smaller than one inch. They even had the uniforms painted over all the padded equipment that was underneath, and helmets atop their heads. There was one poised in a crouched position with the hands near the knees waiting for something, either blocking or catching the ball or making a weak tackle. Then another one crouched over with both fists in balls and placed underneath the shoulder pads and against the chest. This was the blocking form for the professionals, and the tiny models had a sense of reality for the game. There was one that had one arm forward with the elbow bent, and the other arm bent in back, which gave the model a look of running. Finally, there were two with the arms spread out and at the sides with the hands palms out, waiting to touch or tackle anything.

The uniform colors were of the champions of the previous year, the Green Bay Packers and of course—a big insult to the football city of Dallas—the St. Louis Cardinals. The general attitude of those who knew best, the Cowboy fans, was that the '66 and '67 big games were the NFL championships between the Cowboys and the Packers, not the Super Bowl. Even though 1968 was the start of "What is This New Super Bowl Thing?" it was just another way of putting Texas lower on the ladder of best. "We are the Biggest! We do things bigger! And the Cardinals have never ever won football, only baseball!"

Of course, everything that Texas knew about baseball was heard from St. Louis. Men would listen to anything that had competition and winning in it. Men would talk and drink and gather in bunches and talk about sports. In the fall, football is in bloom and everyone talks about the Cowboys or any college team that is near the city. But in the spring, the air is cool and the girls have to go home, and baseball is heard in the evening air—when you really can't dance, but you still want to win.

But they could move, these figures, straight ahead on a green tin sheet that was a makeshift football field. When you turned on the electrical power the tin field shook with mild violence, and the men moved back and forth and up and down the long green field. It was the latest in improvements of sports game designs in 1968. Mikey loved it. Mikey cherished it.

The team plane was not a manufacturer store innovation. It was a shoebox from a department store, and its construction was very simple. Mikey had taken his school scissors with the round edges and the big finger loops, and slowly, painstakingly, folded angles for the wings, then cut squares for windows on both sides and in front, and on the right-side front, a door that folded outward. He would slide the figures in and to their own imaginary seats without removing the top of the shoebox. That was the task. He would use his small fingers first, and then later a ruler from school, to align them perfectly side by side from front to back. Sometimes he would take the top of the shoebox off and align it. But he would never use the team plane windows for the alignment of the players. He knew that when they rode on the plane, no one was allowed to touch the players through the windows. Although he didn't have glass windows to fortify the construction, no one else would touch these players through the windows either. He knew that real players rode on the buses to and from the game, because his father, a member of the transit company, sometimes drove a professional team to and from the game. One time his father had taken him on the bus when he was younger, maybe seven or eight, and he had sat with the players in awe—small, still smiling, but very silent. His father was always sharing things like that with him.

From Big Teddy's job as a starting point, it made an easy transition to the important sport of the day and the state, which was football. It was not uncommon for Texas citizens to visualize and refer to each and every day as a football day. It was in the fall or spring and of course summer when football would blend in with the water and the air of each and every day. No one was immune. The store clerks and the managers and the builders and bankers would combine with the hearts of the teachers and the officers and the law clerks each and every day to breathe football to the few that first watched and then joined. When men watched football, they became like gods or the coaches or the controllers. To Mikey, it seemed that the more they watched, the more they began to tell the players what to do. They would shout and curse and swear and cry in the late afternoons at the Cotton Bowl, and then take their wives and children home to Sunday supper. But of course, if the players actually did what these particular men had requested, then the men would send their families home and strut and drink throughout all hours of the night.

Big Teddy was not immune. First, he would bring home the newspapers, particularly the sports page and the news about them Cowboys, because that's what they were called around these parts: those Cowboys. Them boys. Every healthy city has something to cheer about. When boys play games and winning is an expression—no, a measurement of self, of life, then everyone has one.

For Mikey, it was a kid's-sized football uniform with the plastic shoulder, knee, thigh, and waist pads included. Holding those pads in place were the pants, white and bulky with a white cloth belt that laced across the waist and adjusted to the size of the individual. Mikey thought it was a beautiful red jersey, with thin white strips that raced across the shoulders like the speed lines of a race car that undoubtedly invoked speed. And he was fast. He could run fast.

Well, he could have been a fast runner if it had not been for the helmet, or maybe that helmet. It was a large round plastic covering with two white plastic bars circling across the mouth from ear to ear. It was like a silly clown smile, thought Mikey. And it had a smaller strap that circled underneath the chin and snapped onto the helmet. He could not run fast in that helmet. It bounced up and down and side to side and made Mikey try to balance it when he was standing and pointing it in the direction in which he was running, but it was always there. The effort was there as well. The helmet, the jersey, and the pants from a large department store catalog were the unmistakable ensemble that kept the historical accounts of his physical efforts.

Mikey was in a hurry. Since his first steps, whenever he would go anywhere, he would move with a purpose, as if there were some importance in his destination. It was strange, his mother thought, that he could move with such purpose now when he had taken the longest in the labor of childbirth. That's what she called it, "the labor of childbirth." Hours and hours of pushing and waiting until it became apparent to her that this was an abnormal mental challenge between herself and her unborn child. This labor of childbirth was different from her other three children and she even had time to discount because of the child's gender. Girls were different from boys, is what she had been told from her five sisters. Boys you carried more between your hips, because they were ready to arrive into the world. Girls took their time in delivery, but never this long. No child took this long. Mikey's mother had said so because her validations were the five boys, she had help deliver in the housing projects where they lived before moving to the new home.

Mikey would not walk or talk or assume a name until he was ready. When it was all over, finally, his mother had given him the name Michelangelo, regardless of what his father had suggested. At that time, she often confused the Archangel with the Italian painter, but at the same time gave credence to divine intervention for all of their accomplishments and her own. This name would bestow greatness on him one way or another, she had thought, since he almost didn't make it and she had almost given up. The name meant more, and how could she let him forget it?

"Mikey" was the name given by his oldest sister when his father introduced football to the entire family and he was large enough to hike the football to him. To hike the ball is to straddle sideways over center, which is to stand aside the football and lean over with one hand and pass the ball backward to an awaiting passer or runner. He had done this in his younger years and the name had stuck. Somehow "Duke" had become "Little Duke," and then back to Mikey. It was from his insistence. Mikey was twelve years old and moving in a hurry at seven in the evening.

Underneath the surface, Mikey had a passion for knowledge, and not just book education. He asked a lot of questions and searched for answers. Now as he pulled on his Rocky the Flying Squirrel cap and moved from his bedroom to the main family area, the television and dining room, he was on another quest. He tried hard to move past the sofa where his three sisters and mother were gathered. Except for his mother, they were all staring intently at the movie that flickered with blue light and occasional blaring musical and vocal sounds. It was a new color television set and it was always turned up loud. It was his father's latest purchase. It was the family's constant indoctrination into mainstream society. It gave them the news in color, weather, sports, and information about the Cowboys. Whether it was the football Cowboys or Gary Cooper or John Wayne, the indoctrination blared and brandished the news of the day. Mikey tried to move through them as quickly as possible by darting under the vision of the television. He didn't quite make it.

"Michael, where are you going at this time?"

His mother, Maxi Malone, a big woman with high cheekbones, brown skin and long black hair, never took the luxury of calling him by that nickname. She never did and she never would. Her tone in her words always sounded like an order to him more so than the actual words.

Te'ah Malone, his older sister by two years and his favorite sister, and more in the image of her father, stopped him as he tried to move past them.

"Mom, you know Mike is just a busybody. He's probably just going to the trash cans." Te'ah always called him Mike to his mother but Mikey when she talked to him.

The trash cans were in the backyard against the fence, facing the alley. Everyone knew that Mikey hated this area and never ventured there, but Te'ah knew better than all. She was his favorite because she was just perfect and she never gave up. This was evident at least to him. Even when the relatives came over, she was perfect. Palmer Malone, the next sister, two years younger than Mikey, was always almost perfect because that is what the next sister in line has to be in Texas, was there as well when the relatives would come by. And everybody knew that "just perfect" is better than "always perfect" in Texas. The majority ruled over the singular minority with sound rational Texas judgment, because the always-perfect strived to be like the just-perfect to get the attention of the majority. And history says that Texas knows this best. Texans always try harder.

"I hope he doesn't smell a body like his friends did," said Palmer.

"Look at that hat," said Dottie Malone, the youngest. She was four years younger than Mikey and just like Palmer, was more in the image of her mother. Both were already tall for their age. "It probably does smells like a dead body."

Te'ah said nothing.

"Michael," his mother said. "You know it's close to eight o'clock and your father will be calling. You had better stay in shouting distance, and that does not only mean your ears. You'd better be at arm's length before the second call."

On the surface Mikey was just like any other twelve-year-old, but underneath he was entirely different. He didn't try to show how he was different from the other students, but it came out in his everyday adventures. Outside was Texas at its best in the early days of April. After the spring showers, the bloom of the flowers, and the smell, the smell of a sweet memory of some endeared remembrance beckoned in what is now when brave men speak, a romantic inference of a time when the land was bold and could be seen as far as the horizons end. In the past,

Mikey remembered the Sundays after church when he would run from the front yard to the backyard, a Texas testament of freedom; running wild and free over the land, in frantic machinations of destinations and mischief, which led to curiosity for a young sprite of seven. He could carry this on for years, and he did so at least until he found something that he considered a fact. But as soon as he found a fact, it created another question.

In Dallas there were maple trees and spring mimosa, and in Mikey's backyard the seasonal rosebushes, plum trees, and apple trees. In the daytime this gave Mikey his springtime hobby. Wild insects were frantic for the greens, the reds, the soft fragrances, and the blooms that permeate through the spring air; they not only signaled the blooms, but also the buzzing, darting, and ducking of the seasonal prey. Mikey was not prey, and although he learned the word later in life it was a posture, he was unaccustomed to. Mikey would learn later that prey were the victims that he had seen on the "newfangled"—his Dad's words—television set whom the detective, police, or hero had to avenge or rescue from danger. Mikey was not prey.

Mikey used his insect net, another of his creations, made from an old pair of his mother's stockings. It was cut from the leg but not too high up, because even he knew better than that from his mother and his friends who had heard from their mothers. Mikey used a clothing hanger from his dad's closet, bent into a circle and a handle to the right specifications as well, and stalked in the daytime after school and in the evenings after dinner. He was brave enough to capture honeybees, blue wasps, and the dreaded yellow jacket wasps with the stingers that he was allergic to. In fact, he was allergic to all bee stings. He had found this out at a young age when he was stung by a big bumbling yellow jacket and his arm and face had swollen up to itchy, tight proportions.

But that wouldn't stop Mikey. He would sneak up behind them every so often, ever so quietly, and swoop down with the net over them. Then he would place them above a jar filled with rubbing alcohol where the fumes would mercifully subdue some and drown the rest. He would take them out afterward and stick pins through them and place them on white board paper like the ones he had seen in his science class. The alcohol smelled like the doctor's office where he had been for his vaccinations. From his first vaccinations to his later visits, Mikey had associated that smell with clinical accomplishment. The nurse at the office would rub his arm with alcohol from a bottle and a puff of cotton and say that the alcohol would make everything clean, and to be still while she poked him with the needle.

It was no surprise that he would use the alcohol later. It was such a visual experience. He would know and not trust. He would scour for other insects over the grounds and the grasses and the big sand mound that his father had had delivered by a brown dump truck from the alley to the backyard. But this was an expansion and not a personal present. This was for the future of his children and not for growing the grass in the backyard. This was Big Teddy's plan. He was a man who felt the inadequacies of the time, but planned for the future. So, he had three girls and one son. He could make the most for the future. This was Texas.

Mikey would collect more for his display. There were moths, beetles, caterpillars, butterflies, earthworms, and fireflies all stuck on the white board paper. He would cut them open, not from revenge but curiosity, with a single-edged razor that he had collected...had had donated... well, had absconded from his father's shaving bag, and begin to look inside them. He had to do it quickly and delicately and within the first six hours, or they would dry out and the insects would be too brittle to investigate and would have to be thrown away. This made his search inexhaustible. He was always looking for more. He was always looking inside. He was always asking why.

It was the night sky that was the biggest attraction for Mikey. This was the time when the fireflies would bumble and buzz and flicker. It was always the night that held the cool April breeze and a hint of moisture that saturated all of the green leaves and trees and bush of the yard. For him it always smelled fresh. When the roses closed at night and when the buds gave off a fragrance from the friction of closing tight, the air would hold a mixture of deep green grass with a scent of soft powder. This was the makeup of the Malone family backyard, and Mikey would be there from after school and until sleep and never consider the interests and needs of his siblings for the inside.

"Why do they like to be so close together inside?"

He had said that before to his friends, and to his small G. I. Joe military men. The girls domain was always the interior. The living room, the dining room, and all the bedrooms were what they protected. His mother had defined a role and his sisters had reinforced it. Inside was for girls and outside was for boys. And while they were comfortable with the cooking and cleaning and the entertaining, Mikey and his father were more comfortable outside with the grass and the trees and the cars. Little Mikey and his father would cut the grass, trim the brush, and wash the family car: a 1964 Plymouth Sport Fury. Outside was where the sports were. Outside was where the hunting was. This was where Mikey would find the insects and hunt like the other men, he had read about in his history books. Men like Davy Crockett, Daniel Boone, and ol' Sam Houston at the Alamo, who were the great staples of Texas and Frontier history. Outside was where they had found the body.

Mikey walked out to the backyard step. He liked to stop here and smell the night air. He would take a deep sniff and hope for a cold night air to cool his nostrils, his mouth, and his insides. This was the way that you brought the outside to yourself. His father taught him that. "Take in the air and look around. This is Texas."

He looked from the back porch to the furthest corner of the backyard where the yard ended and the metal fence enclosed his father's home off, separating it from the alley that surrounded the homes where the backyards faced. The house was of the new design where brick and wood merged and created the jagged lines in the backyard corner. This was an "L" shape, or a straight "Z" shape that Mikey could use. He moved back to the bottom edge and reached with his hands and pulled his body up. The jagged lines had the standard four-inch brick overhang that gave ample space for hands and feet. He was a lean kid, but a little over five feet tall and it was easy for him to reach things. He had hung the longest on the top middle bar of the crazy transparent building called the jungle gym, a collection of bars forming squares atop squares. And he had also held on the longest on the monkey bars. This was to the "ah ha" of his classmates at Bishop Heights Elementary.

Mikey reached to the next ledge and pulled himself up. Here he was an arm's length from the roof. He reached around and held on to the roof overhang and pulled himself up that as well. After safely on top, he walked as softly as possible up some ten feet and to his routine perch. At this position, he would try to look out to the trail and up and out to where the body was found. Sometimes he saw light from that direction. Sometimes he didn't. This, as always, was the birth of curiosity. He had found this birth of curiosity when he was much younger, when he would see the people on Sunday mornings putting their hands onto the morning offerings and taking change out. And at night he would look at the stars with the other kids, waiting for the occasional falling star and seeing something with more ramifications.

Every summer the neighborhood kids were entertained in the summer nights. Everyone believed that the first one to see a falling star could make a wish and would have good luck, so everyone looked. This was the birth of curiosity. His curiosity. It was the sowing to a young seedling. It was the urge that gave Mikey, a seedling, the strength— not of being strong, but a strength indeed since he had never had the strength before—to climb to the top of a mountain. Maybe this was the mountaintop that Dr. King had envisioned, although it held a sense of irony that was beyond Mikey's years.

II

Doing the Part
April 15, 1968
Monday

That morning, Mikey got up from his bed and off to school as usual. With freshly cut grass and smells as sharp and refreshing as newly dropped rain, and fresh sounds of early morning birds and dripping leaves and dripping rooftops and dripping drainage, and April clouds and finally sun, these days marked the cry of the spring season. It was a morning of beginning and new with dripping and so much early gray. The morning was fresh with happiness and moist with sadness.

Doing his part, Mikey brushed his teeth, washed his face, and wore the clothes that he had selected for himself for the day. His mother, Mama Maxi, had said that "the word 'selected' only meant 'used' in the mind," but really these were the clothes that weren't too dirty or weren't worn more than twice in a one-week period. Mikey's selection only meant what had been the least used as well, and by far the least expected—or so he reasoned. The clothes just happened to be the blue jeans and white shirt, white socks, and black Converse sneakers that Mikey had become accustomed to wearing.

And while they were the clothes of a routine born from necessity, he concluded that it was just a coincidence that when his mother chose for him, she had always selected as close as she could to the same colors as the civil rights marchers. She was very religious and felt that all her children should do their part however small.

From their perch on the sofa, the family gazed to the black-and-white television that sat on the makeshift television stand—a converted bookcase with books underneath and squandered Christmas cards that covered the first shelf underneath the television, that gave the family's entire history—and watched the figures that fought in muted silence.

Mikey's family was silent. Mama Maxi shushed everyone into silence. She watched with intense eyes and taut bitten lips. If she had her hands on one of the children, she would not let go until the broadcast was over.

It was the silence that became the sound that was really heard. It filled the family dining room while the television showed the streaming tide of the firemen's hoses, the barking snarling dogs, the policemen carrying shields, and the stoic national guard.

It was just a coincidence that Mikey's mother had continued to select them. Even now, a week after Dr. King's death and the televised riots in the cities like Chicago and New York, she persisted in her own personal efforts to follow Dr. King's example. That meant the style of clothing for her only son. So, to keep in step with the family wishes—his mother's wishes—he did his part.

It was always normal for him to do his part in the family. Just deciding on the way to do his part was sometimes the question. While he helped with the home cleaning duties or the grass and trimming duties of the trees and flowers, he was helping. But when he was attending to his experiments and his collection of information he was also helping, and in his own way.

Mikey continued through his morning routine with this in mind, but not drawing the alarm that only seemed to have an effect on the older men. With their warnings of Cassius Clay and Jim Brown and others, he could surely feel the difference. Why were his father and uncles different? What made it different? Maybe doing their part was different from his part. It should be because they were much older, he reasoned. Mikey stopped and thought about putting those questions in his book and writing a full paragraph that would explore the questions and possible answers. This would take minutes away from his morning preparations and doing his part. He continued his morning grooming, and continued his part.

He challenged himself to remember to put it into his book later. After all, two big parts of the morning were avoiding his sisters for the fear of disagreements, and writing in his book. Both would take time. His sisters always wanted to use the restroom and move him out of the way. And if they got there first, they would never leave, and that would take time. Mikey would have preferred to write in his journal at school; if he began to scribe at home, he sometimes lost his place for the bathroom, and then he lost his place in his writings. He always prepared to get it over with early in the morning and before everyone stirred. And if he were lucky, he would be out of everyone's hair and out and about before anyone knew it. He had places to go and people to tell of his latest observations.

If everything went correctly, he would write in school. School was his safest place for reflection. Of all the places he could be, school was the place that he felt he could make good on his own merit, and not because he was the only boy or his father's son, but because he had the best idea. After all, his father was "only" the second black American to work for the transit company in Dallas, and the only one for a long period of time. And driving buses was a good thing. It was giving back to the country, just like the postmen and the teachers. Uniforms and giving back to the country were the general preferences of the community.

And Mikey always thought of this fact, but in a different way. He only stayed up at night a long time because he had his own way to think about and his own things to do the next day and the next. The night before, he had been experimenting and writing in his journal until his mother had told him to go to his bed late in the early morning. His journal was a series of tablets. There were three of them, and they all had green covers. Mikey's father had given them to him. Mikey's father had given him many things that had been left on the bus or had come from the company. One day there were comic books, first editions brought home by his father. Another day there were golf clubs, a set of long hard irons that had all the assorted clubs and even a wood driver.

Mikey's father had worked for the transit company since Mikey was five years old, so there were a lot of things in his journal that Mikey, in his age, called "stuff." One tablet held all the science stuff. It was a combination of math and science stuff, which, unfortunately, he was good at. Good in the sense that he could follow the numbers and remember the names and somehow remember the colors. Colors were good for science with its green and blue and brown. The next tablet was the book of people. Mikey would jot down tidbits of information about the things that people would do. Sometimes they were little things like how many times Te'ah would comb her hair in her bedroom mirror, the bathroom mirror, and the living room mirror. This was accompanied with the times, days, and occasions.

When Mikey was outside, he would watch what he thought was the North Star, the guiding beacon for all sailors in times of troubles. Ever since he had read that it had served as a beacon of for those travelers, he had looked to its mystery as salvation. He could use something like that, a salvation from fear, especially the fear that covered the neighborhoods like a blanket. He didn't know if he had the same troubles as the past sailors that he had read about in school, if they had dead bodies found where they lived, but he continued to look out. He could see a comparison with his feeling of lost and theirs, and their feelings of indecision now new but familiar to him. He would not write about the comparison, the human element. He would only document his findings, his observations, and his own opinion. He would do that until he was called in for his sleep. His mother had seen to that and Te'ah had made sure of it.

Mikey did not really sleep long, only four or five hours or so. He had admitted to Te'ah a long time ago that he was afraid of the dark and had gotten the sisterly smile and pat on the head. He had told his father as well, and gotten no real sympathy that he could interpret. He had admitted that he watched in the dark until the dark became light. And he had done this at an early age. He had watched when his eyelids were down and he began to see his eyelids. First, he saw the red of the eyelids and the blood that coursed through them. Then not long after, and with practice or continued staring, he began to see light, a lighted figure that floated and circled and pushed at his face. Maybe it was his imagination.

The living room was off-limits for kids during the week, so Mikey walked through the back door of the house and around to the empty front driveway. His father had long since departed for work, but his rules still existed. *Don't walk in the grass. Use the back door. Take out the trash if there is any. Be polite. Smell good. Comb your hair. Tie your shoes.*

These were all rules that Mikey respected. These were the rules that Mikey looked for in a person. These were the rules that his father looked for in a person. These were the foundation of marriage, and the rules that his mother expected from all her children because his father respected them. That was the upside of marriage, his mother had told his sisters. She smiled because she felt it was the upside of a commitment. Doing and expecting. Mikey expected the same in every relationship because his sisters would practice for their impending marriages and it was just too many to rules for them to complete. Te'ah once asked, "Why not fool them and not do the same?" But Mikey was too young to discern the difference in her question. Not following the same rules in a marriage should end the marriage, he reasoned.

Mr. Ross, the next-door neighbor, stood in his yard doing an early watering. He looked really chipper in his postman uniform. That's what the television commercials had said. The short pants and long grayish-blue socks gave the entire postman a unique quality, and in turn gave the neighborhood a unique quality. It was part of something big, or just being a part of something that gave the optimism. It was the uniforms that gave the optimism. On Mikey's street there were three more postman families, one more from the transit company now, two from Frito-Lay, and maybe two teachers. And on the adjoining street where Michael Daniels and Michael Washington lived, there were three postmen, two teachers, and the women of Texas Instruments. It was black people in uniforms that created the normalcy for the neighborhood. The homes were of uniform design, the autos were all of recent years, and the working people represented their employment.

The neighborhood reacted to the dead body in its own fashion. As good hardworking people in America, in Dallas, in south Oak Cliff, in the Bishop College area, they reacted as docile professionals—if there is such a thing. Some professionals who had worked in earnest and felt an indebtedness to the country for their jobs, perhaps from a World War II residue or just an entitlement of class, would then complain of the discomfort that the uncertainty would bring. They would feel the obligation and the right to voice their discomfort. But the people of the Bishop Heights community were professional public servants—which is what all professionals are, only servants of a community to provide a service. They didn't see the alikeness, the sameness only separated by perspective or land value or distance from the server. They could not see the delineations of distance that defined the ego that co-defined the identity of the persona. They could not complain. They would have to wait until someone took care of the problem and look as innocent as possible. They would wait from habit for the authorities or the governing body to answer the questions. But there were a lot of questions to answer. The primary one for the professional blacks was not how but why kill Dr. King. As Dr. King was the silent cry, the body only lingered in some same sound of heart and misery and many whispers of dread: "If they killed King…" "It is there for a reason and…" "We should just be quiet and not make…" The echo was a constant deafening murmur. But seconded was the damned dead body.

Mikey grabbed toast, bacon, and a spoonful of strawberry jelly from the dining room table and walked out the back door with a napkin surrounding his makeshift breakfast. He went around to the driveway and finally stopped to wait by the curb. His mother would kill him if she knew he was eating food by the curb, or "on the street," as she had called it. He was waiting for Michael Daniels and Michael Washington, the dudes who were both his age from the next street over. They would all walk to school together. They made up the newest editions of the safety patrol boys. They were all just typical American boys.

Michael "Fee Fee." Daniels was the first to arrive. He was called that because the first time they had played basketball, Michael Daniels had passed gas with a sharp frump sound and everyone had laughed and screamed out, "Daniels, Daniels, tarts, and tarts." This phrase quickly evolved to "tart" and "tart farts." The patrol boys would never say "gas," for the sake of decorum. So, Michael Washington called him "Fee Fee" to rhyme, and the name stuck in mixed company and in the classroom in some of the strangest occasions. Like, whenever there was a flash card contest between the boys and the girls and the excitement and a rush to congratulate, then the name would be blurted out by both Michaels. And Daniels would respond. Even in the moments of excitement civilized decorum could be forgotten.

Daniels was shorter than Mikey and had dark brown skin and bushy black eyebrows and hair. He walked downhill from where the street curved from another crossing street that jutted out and east into the next neighborhood. It was east to the northern parallel of the main street and everything that went north and south and into the vanishing horizon. The street where Daniels and Washington lived was named Silverhill Drive.

"I watched *The Invaders* for the third straight week," he said as he walked side by side with Mikey. *The Invaders* was a television show that depicted an alien invasion among the American inhabitants. Daniels was shorter than Mikey, and wore blue jeans and the latest cotton striped shirt. He had a short brow that showed well with a wrinkle when he would get excited or frustrated over the smallest things. Mikey knew it was something serious to talk about when Michael Daniels's brow grew somehow darker, and his eyes held distance as if in deep thoughts. As they began to walk down the sidewalk to the school, they talked about the adolescent things that gave them mystery and supplemented their fears.

"I watched, *The Science Fiction show.*"

"You always say that. Didn't you watch, *The Alien Invasion show?*"

"It's just television. Who has time? Plus, I don't want to think about people from other planets as sneaky. I would rather see them up front." Mikey didn't want anyone to know that his sisters ruled the television. Anything scary or mysterious was out of the question, except *Science*

Fiction. Somehow, watching shows about space was okay. But other than *Science Fiction* it was always cartoon shows, or *Daniel Boone* or *The Wonderful World of Disney*, until the Sunday night movie came on. And then look out—it was always some type of love story.

"*The Alien* show could be the real thing," said Michael Daniels. He stood back and looked away to his right. It sounded like an aside.

"Black invaders from space?" said Michael Washington. He had walked up from the left as usual, from the connecting street Silverhill, without either Michael watching. He would always walk up alone, and always after Daniels had arrived, to maintain the air of surprise. He was the same height as Daniels but with very light skin and wore oval wire rimmed glasses. His teacher always teased him as looking like a scientist or poet. This added to his quiet demeanor. "I saw them on the last episode," he said. "The aliens took over their bodies as well.

"Eventually there will be black people in space," Mikey said. He greeted him with a smile. Washington only looked to Daniels. He glared quietly and then looked away.

"Could they really be up there in space?" Daniels said and pointed up to the blue sky overhead. The sky had become pilfered with wisps of thin-stretching high white clouds. Daniels smiled with a glint of boyish dishonesty, made an eerie sound, and then moved closer to the group. The boys laughed.

"Did anyone see my Tippy running down the street?" Michael Washington asked with a hint of urgency "Or running down the alley?" Tippy was the family dog, which in reality was his dog, which translated into the day-to-day chores of feeding, watering, and never letting anything happen to the dog. Tippy was a small bumbling gray-and-white terrier that stood a few feet above the ground. The dog would run and hop from inside the house to outside, onto both the front and back yards. "Someone left the gate open and Tippy ran out again."

"Did you get into trouble?" Mikey asked.

"I didn't leave it open, no matter what they think!"

"So, who's to blame?" Daniels asked. He began to move away from Washington. He tried to smile but it came up short, and slowly his smile faded away. "But you know you're not to blame. So, you're not in trouble?"

It was their routine for the guys to act this way. While Mikey sat back for the discussions and observed, Michael Daniels would show guilt or too much concern, and lately Michael Washington had the problem. The roles had been reversed; this aloofness, this guilt, this anger was always discussed with this routine of shielding pain and coming together in the end. It served all parties well in private as well as under public scrutiny in front of their siblings, because Michael Daniels had a brother two years older and Michael Washington had a sister three years younger. This gave them their identity as a group, but blurred it as well.

They had been together since the first grade, the three Michaels, and had always competed for the highest honors. It was early in their adolescences that Mikey emerged as the inquisitive one. Whether it was a result of a larger family environment because he had more to contend with, or just good old fear of the dark that made him pay attention and remember everything, Mikey always showed the benefits of memory but he never thought that way. He always felt that it was preordained. And maybe it was. In a large family, siblings always feel that all happenstance is preordained. And he always used it. At school Mikey's mental benefits would always be sought out for answers to situations inside and outside the classroom. It was not as simple as something lost or "Where did I leave my cap, books or lunch?" but more "Why did this happen?" Mikey looked at things too much, too often, and for too long. With this practice he always saw too much.

When Michael Daniels tried to play this role, he would always come up short. Memory was tiresome for him, or just room for another argument. Someone would always have a different opinion, and this would always make him feel like he was under attack and he would take a defensive position with his stance and attitude. His brother always had a different opinion from him and so would his father. This seemed like it happened for as long as he could remember, and made it natural that he should never want to be the decision maker until something affected him. He always wished he could have the answer, but he could never talk to his family. He was more comfortable talking to Mikey. And this played into their roles and made them less interchangeable.

Michael Washington, the quiet one had the ability to sneak up behind the boys or girls at school and sometimes the adults that he wanted attention from. He liked to do things like that. He was quiet just like his dog, a tiny, tan, tail wagging snippet of a terrier that never barked in anger or at all. He was very close to his dog, and that was a good thing since he had the responsibility of caring for it. He must have learned this from his parents, who were very quiet as well. In fact, the Washington home was the quietest home in the neighborhood. There was never any music or sounds from the radio or kitchen with pots or plates, or loud shouting of people to come over or to come home. It seemed right that Tippy, Michael Washington's dog, was a quiet little animal as well. If not for the soft pitter-patter of his little paws, he was practically soundless. He never growled, probably because he was always like a little puppy, and if his wagging tail made any noise it would be the loudest body part that the dog possessed. If he yelped or yapped, then he would be silenced quickly by one of the family members so often that now the slightest movement in the direction of the dog would cause silence. It was no wonder that it took a while to find him missing.

The boys pushed and jabbed and continued walking to the school. They would always arrive early in the morning and stay a little later after school, performing the duties and responsibilities of the patrol boys. All three walked in same step with, white shirts, blue pants and black shoes. This was the unofficial Patrol boy uniform. But was still from the typical American elementary school wardrobe.

Bone Girl
April 15, 1968
Monday

Yolanda Jackson lived in a quaint red-and-white brick house up at the bend of the street where it stretched into a circle and then extended and connected to the adjoining Silverhill Drive. She could be seen standing on her porch or in her yard after school, holding her black Labrador retriever and taunting the boys as they walked past her to Silverhill Drive to play street football. What the boys didn't know was that she would go inside after they passed. All they knew was that she was not there when the games were over.

She didn't think much of the body that was found in the woods near the creek. When she first heard about it, she had told Mikey that day at school that "it's normal for things to pass, and that is what's up to the nature of things to decide. The body in the woods near the creek is normal since this is where we live." She knew things would pass and she felt it was something you could not control anyway, so do everything that you need to do, everything that you want, and whatever you want before it comes.

Yolanda was old for her age, and that could mean a lot of things. It started with her thinking of older things. Things like boys liking you and flirting with them and having your way around the school were some of the first things she learned. And although rail-thin she was seemed that she was physically taller, stronger, and closer to the features of a young woman than most of the girls her age. This gave her another edge. And because of the way she looked it also meant that her mental age was way past the mental age of the boys in her grade. She was thought to be closer to the mental age of the Wisdom Wiser's, a group of mentally superior older black women in every community where blacks lived and communed. This was a good thing and aligned with her future ambitions.

No one in Mikey's group, the three Michaels, knew for sure what the answers were, but they all knew of such a person in the community who had the answers. It started within their own families where, if they lived in the same proximity, they fell victim to the council. And the thing that made the council so great was because they believed in specialization before specialization became American. This came from the teachings of the Bible. The Wisdom Wiser's believed that their opinions were from the one person, usually the oldest, who could see with clarity in times of chaos, and this was all that was to be accomplished. True, chaos had been in existence a lot longer than the Wisdom Wiser's had been, but if the ladies knew words or where to find them and were worldly in terms of their thinking as in historic significance to those words, those events, then their words would measure up to any task.

But the greatest commodity was found in the spoken word. The stories were passed down from generation to generation and from family to family in Negro spirituals, and lessons learned about families and by relatives to relatives while living in or moving on to other communities. The tales of personal tragedies and successes entwined within the Christian religion were the talking points; the repeating points and then the ability to discern the lessons learned from them as rote behavior in any situation was the counsel given by the Wisdom Wiser's.

The women were particularly relevant with information and opinions when it came to Jim Crowe and the ways of men. Things like how Dr. King felt about the black communities and what he was trying to do for them were interpreted in detail on cool Sunday evenings on the outside patio of every patio home in black communities and some details taken with hope and some taken with fear. When he died it shook the entire black community and the church community, but the Wisdom Wiser's were steadfast in their outlook. They felt the loss but didn't feel that all was lost. After all, Civil Rights was a new thing for everyone and there was always comfort in the old way of life.

The introduction and accessibility of the radio and LPs in the communities made knowledge and therefore feeling more accessible and coming from different impartial sources and voices brought new opinions. These voices began to compete with the importance of the Wisdom Wiser's in the community. They tried to adapt with some moderate authority about the importance of the Black Panther Party, and to some extent the good of LBJ and the hope of the Kennedys, but the Vietnam War and the hippies and the political suggestions of the new music found them missing the relevance of the emerging young black community. This went hand in hand with the diminishing importance of the church in the community and the always illuming presence of the Rabbit Man. Young black men wanted action. Young black women wanted to live. And deep within that need was pull for immediacy and the push toward the irrational. The Wisdom Wiser's held fast their arrogant stare of certain failure from within their years of credibility.

Yolanda took this in stride as well. She continued to give advice and her opinions whenever necessary or when the opportunity occurred. If anything, the lesson she learned was the need for more information about everything.

All everybody knew was that Yolanda was the meanest sixth grader in the school. And she wore glasses at a young age but that did not hold her back. No one would call her four-eyes more than once. Mikey just thought of her as Wonder Woman because when she took her glasses off then she meant business. it was the distinction that Mikey had learned from his Superman comics but he kept it from the others. Maybe Yolanda knew or maybe she didn't but she meant business when she took her glasses off. In reality, Yolanda was more. She was closer to the equal of a man than anyone at the school. And in spite of the glasses, black rim, cat eye, or wire rim, she was still cute. She had long fluffy black hair tied into two side pigtails that gave her a horned look. But when she would take them off, which was often you could see her in the real light. She had soft features, brown, and pouted lips and fire-blazing eyes that took in everything with a sternness that forced the truth from anyone that they fell upon. And although she dressed in pants like the other girls after school her school dresses and skirts were just a little bit more celebrated in style, color and fabric.

From Mikey's mother's side of the family there were four uncles and on his father's side at least eight uncles that he knew of and they all had the same old opinion of girls. From his mother's side there were things that girls could not do, like cars. Hot Rods and a '57 Chevy and, of course, the '67 GTO were the tools of separation. There was racing and red cars because brothers were doing it in Texas. That's what they called it. And it was cool with the whites as long as it was in the black part of town "because it was 1968, man." From his father's side it was religion and women had a special subservient place in it.

South Dallas was meant for blacks, with its sprawling green landscapes, trees, and horizons, the wood-frame homes and some brick homes. To the extreme was the state fair and the Cotton Bowl. This was where the Cowboys played their home games, and the state fair was held where students and families from all over Texas would attend. During this time was also when the big Texas vs. Oklahoma football game was held every year, where fans and alumni from Austin and Oklahoma would gather and root for their favorite team.

It was also a great time for service-related jobs. The booming influx of money and people meant more cars to be parked and washed, more people and bags in the hotels for toting and shoe shining, and more dishes, pots, pans and waste to be disposed of. Anytime you looked to the south in Dallas you saw natural landscape and hope and thriving commerce in the fall. In the north there were the buildings, hotels, innovations, the banking buildings, and downtown Dallas and northern mystery and yellows and light colors.

This was Mikey's father's influence. Because all buses used the downtown area as the hub of transportation, all buses had to migrate downtown and drop off just about every passenger who was working in the city and the surrounding suburbs. Downtown was also the center of banking, hotel business, restaurants, and all kinds of clothing and book sales. After all, five years earlier President Kennedy had traversed through this sprawling epic center that gave Dallas its identity in those days, and he had felt quite welcomed. Nothing really happened until he left it, but he had been through there. How many cities can say that the president has traveled through their downtown? It was still an attraction and this translated into interest for everyone.

Five years later it was still the melting pot where black maids and golf course gardeners were in walking transit with young downtown lawyers and young bankers and hotel clerks. It was still the young upwardly mobile white briefly intersecting with the working-class black. It became the natural and ideal Jim Crow example in microcosm, with economics as the determining schism. The blacks in their working clothes and jackets would pass by the whites in their black or blue Brooks Brother's suits and ties and wingtip shoes without a glimmer of recognition. Some of the blacks had to give walking way to the whites who, somehow, never changed their direction when walking towards the blacks. It was the hierarchy of person. It gave downtown Dallas the starkness of identity for itself within Texas and in the United States.

A lot more came from his mother's brothers, his uncles. It meant that Mikey had a lot of influences on his upbringing. Because it was Texas, there were sports firsts like the first black football player was gonna play in the Southwest Conference this year. Sure, there was Jim Brown, and the Cowboys had a few like Bobby Hayes, Mel Renfro, and more, but college football was something different. The Southwest Conference was notoriously white only, with the Texas Longhorns leading the charge of "No black players in the SWC."

When Mikey was six years old, his introduction to sports was professional football on Sundays and the Dallas Cowboys. Later there was baseball where the '64 Cardinals were the news. Baseball came from his mother's side because of his mother's father. She would the read the commentary and the box score to her to her father, and swore that was how she learned to read well. She would read the newspaper before Mikey's father would. She would read the meanings of advertisements from the television commercials and magazines and simplify announcements of human needs to one basic choice: "Do you really need that to be happy?" or "My mother can do that; she taught all of us!" or finally, "Your father can do that, and you will be able to one day." And Mikey's father was a naturally talented man with wood products and painting. At one time he actually attempted to paint a portrait of Christ for the family. His father had everything correct except the face. He left that blank. So, the picture was left that way, perfect, exceptional, and unfinished. Mikey wondered about that, so he asked his mother. Her reply was simply that, "Man is not supposed to copy the face of Christ."

Religion came from Mikey's father side. Of his father's nine brothers, six were Baptist ministers, which was a good profession for a black man in the '60s. Mikey's father's two older brothers had their own churches and were successful with large congregations of at least one hundred members, and the other four were either working in their brothers' churches or learning from other ministers.

It would seem like the family tradition started with Mikey's grandfather, the elder Malone as the leader and first to obtain the position of minister, but Mikey's father broke from that vocation. He was more inclined to move toward the direct services in life so he had become a transit operator, a very noble profession for a black man in the '60s. When Mikey's father started, there was only one other black man driving with him. Of course, the others were all white. Mikey's mother took up the slack. Every Sunday she marched the family, minus her husband, into the church. She even began to play the piano in the services whenever possible. She played by ear and never tried to read music.

While the women of both families loved the music, the men moved to a different motivation. His father and his mother and his aunts and uncles, there were a lot of them, they all loved music. They could see the meaning of music beyond sex and violence. They could hear the overt action within the suggestion.

What did it all mean, anyway? Mikey would find himself asking that after a confrontation with Yolanda that had ended with her smile after his victories. She was always an attractive girl with a lighter skin tone than the other girls, and long hair that was tied into pigtails on the sides. Sometimes she would use them like ropes to hit people when she turned her head really fast. Again, she would smile. She always had that smile, the blinding smile that never said defeat. Mikey knew it and felt right then and there that she felt it meant more. She was about the same height as the boys, and that was normal because girls developed faster than boys, but she always wanted to be right. She always knew what was right and she fought tooth and nail to see that the right way was the way that things were done. This had been going on for at least four years and there didn't seem to be any let-up.

But she was always second to Mikey. She always tried to be right and this started in the *Weekly Reader*, the weekly journal about world events that was issued to the Bishop Heights students from the third to the sixth grades. Back in the fifth grade she had predicted that Russia would invade Czechoslovakia and Poland and no one knew why she had said it. Then it was the multiplication table, the decimals, and the state capitals. She was always right in reading and writing and sixth-grade things to do. But she was always second. She just couldn't play football.

Later, when everyone became familiar with her, they began to call her Barbie because of the dolls. She had a lot of them. No one said anything about the fact that they were all of the Caucasian skin color, but Yolanda must have taken it that way since she had a lighter skin tone than the other girls. And no one said anything about the time back in the summer of last year when she painted the first Barbie, that she had received on her ninth Christmas, brown with the oil paint during art period, but no one called her Barbie anymore. She would do such a thing and it was true, the fact that whatever she had, she had the right to own. She just had them and they were hers and that was that. Her mother had given them to her or maybe an uncle had, or maybe she had just found the first one.

Her world was Mikey's world, but with more restrictions. And since she was a girl, Yolanda really had more freedoms or less worldly responsibilities. The women didn't have to speak out about anything that was wrong and it was as if they thought the men should, but the men didn't say anything because they tried and failed and eventually learned to ignore or just endure. The women in the '60s had lives but started to speak out for their rights. Old mean-ass Yolanda Jackson was learning rights and although she would cry for that which wasn't right and she fought on in some way, anyway. She was a lot like the opposite of Betty Boop, who was the cartoon heroine that always got into trouble. Yolanda preferred Betty Boop to Olive Oyl. While other girls would think it normal for two men to fight over a woman, Yolanda felt that being along and independent proved your strength and worth, regardless of the mishaps that you could encounter. At least they were of your own doing, she reasoned, and after all, Olive was eventually going to marry one man or the other. Yolanda felt she would never get married. Her spirit came from her mother, a widow with two small girls. Yolanda's mother was a professional bookkeeper who never complained about the absence of a man in the lives of her daughters'. And while her late husband had left her an insurance policy, she continued to rise every morning for work and expect the same from her daughters.

Yolanda was at the school waiting for them. Her mother would drop her off without a second thought and was aware that Yolanda would try to make friends with the boys. What her mother didn't know was that the boys would not wait or walk with her, but they would always talk to her on the schoolyard. To get back at them, she would always hide somewhere on the campus and wait until the boys began the flag raising, and then approach them. This maneuver helped only so much, but magnified her feeling of separation. She felt this and didn't understand what it said to her for a long time. She didn't understand the difference between boys and girls when it came to school and education. She really didn't know what she wanted to do, but she couldn't stand for the boys to always be right at school. If that was the way it was, then why did she have to be in school in the first place? It seemed that someone was really trying to challenge her and it created a quiet anger in her. For some reason the other girls did not see this or feel this.

Yolanda first noticed this anger in the flash-card and spelling competitions. It started in Miss McGregor's class in fourth grade when she won the spelling competition for three straight weeks. It was against the children in her class, but Miss McGregor had promised to let her compete against all of the fourth graders at the Bishop Heights Elementary. Miss McGregor was a proud young black woman of about thirty, with dark black hair that was so straight it looked like it was from a white girl. She was buxom and round and wore riding skirts that swayed when she walked, and had big ideas for a school with only fifty-five fourth graders. She was from an all-girls' college in McKinney, Texas, which was a smaller city than Dallas. It seemed that Miss McGregor wanted more for all of her girls, and she would stress the proper etiquette, walking style, tone of voice, and how much eye contact a young lady should reveal. She would always say, "Girls, watch your staring!" or "Girls, try not to act too proud!"

Yolanda would try not to giggle when her fellow classmates were caught, but later began to resent the admonishments from the teacher. It tended to grate on the fourth grader and she would become quiet for that moment, just waiting to voice her opinion. Even now as a sixth grader, Yolanda remembered Miss McGregor's instructions about presence as something totally opposite to how she felt when she won in the classroom contest.

Tell it Like It Is
January 15, 1967

Music was a tool used by the masses to give, to find some meaning in their lives, from the larger society, and for also a useful discovery about their own considerations. When it was used to document the event within a life, the events of that season, or the hopes of the state or country, then it would create an emotional bond that could unify the citizens. Even the great composers found that music was a tool to be used to bring people together, if just to listened. If it was used as a profession, then the money received was used to feed and clothe the ones they love—if they indeed loved other people. It became a job. Or if it was just the music that they loved only and could not help to create, then the money would celebrate and affirm that conviction or affliction. It was how they gave back to the music. It was also how the music became interwound with drink and revelry, or everything that came from the adulation that could be received from the creation of music. And if they didn't have it before then they made the music to receive it. And so, they lived to enhance or destroy life because that was always the fight within it. The people who created it really could not enjoy their own music the way so many others did.

That was the saddest element of the phenomenon. The ones who made the music could only use the music to live from and not live by, because their own lyrics or their own performance of their instruments should not give them the direction in their lives. If so then they would become a priest, a prophet, or a soapbox preacher on a street corner, who only use for music was as religion, and that was a no-no for the religious south. It would became blasphemous and a hypocrisy for a pop artist to live a life from his lyrics because it was too close to the ego, too close to being a leader of people, or too close to God's word. It could never change their lives like it had changed so many others who had listened and lived by the meaning, the emotion of the music, because the only ones who could enjoy their own music and live by their own music were the ones who indoctrinated the sound like a religion, like the old Negro blues, or the Country and Western music. Those genres had words and emotions to live by, and so much sadness, and were the only ones that existed where you could practice what you preached. That was until the '60s. Then music became a performance of happiness, of direction, as well as something to initiate a change in life.

This was the contradiction that Officer Kenneth Milton Conway experienced, even though it evolved into a contradiction within a contradiction. He first grew up with music from the late '50s. There was gospel on Sundays and early pre-Motown on the other days of the week. He really loved Smokey Robinson and the Miracles, and there was Little Anthony and Otis Redding. Now he only used music to determine behavior and habits. His problem was that he was caught in the middle in his life and the inflexible dichotomy of the music of the past few years, which was a reflection of his dilemma. Music now commented, directed, and pronounced on a political and recreational level, and now reached more and more people of differences who found that central vein of agreement.

Kenneth was one of the first of three coloreds hired to the Dallas police department. That was a big thing for Dallas and the coloreds who were able to watch, like the few colored ministers who were aligned with the civil rights movement and the liberals who migrated from Wiley College and settled in the communities of the new black middle class of Dallas. But being one of the first coloreds on the force wasn't a big problem because his home was Chicago and he had been in the city for two years. He did not know many of the coloreds who lived in the city because he was a policeman, he was new, and he had to trust his fellow policemen—and that was invariably the crux of the problem. The Windy City with its aggressive civil rights momentum was a fledgling memory and all but absent from the bounding flat landscape of Dallas.

It was never more evident than in the stratified demographics of the city. It was not just the large white North and the lower colored South. It was not just a poverty line and below in the colored east and the equally unsatisfied brown west. On the outskirts of the Dallas neighborhoods were the white townships that were not quite suburbs yet, but were country landscapes that had their own schools and housed farm animals as a norm. And if the center was thought to be a safe haven, that was a misnomer. Downtown, the hub of the business district was filled with its own stratified demographics of merchants and bankers and businessmen, and of course the lower-waged service aids. It was then that Kenneth realized that gone were the vertical screeching housing projects of Chicago that stretched ten and thirteen floors up from poverty and crime and black angst, because the word "colored" was obsolete in Chicago, against a gray skyline. The only housing projects in Dallas were three floors up at a max and housed two families per block.

Kenneth first saw this as a possible living advantage for the coloreds in the projects. The fewer numbers must have meant more freedoms for the people, because more space meant more areas to grow and live and laugh, right? It also meant fewer people to watch out for against theft and vandalism. That's what he thought, until he started his first tour in the East Dallas projects. The fewer numbers actually meant that it was easier to identify the male and female troublemakers because they were all black. That was the reasoning that his counterparts used, and they also reasoned that there was just as much crime here as in the Windy City. Of course, he didn't agree. They had never lived in the projects on the south side of Chicago with gangs and police brutality going hand in hand against the innocent. He could not understand how his white counterparts could identify the behavior of the troublemakers before they got into trouble—or, better still, how they could still remember the troublemakers and where they would be at a certain time of day or night. Even more curious was how they could discern the difference between the law abiders and the lawbreakers. "It's all in the training," is what they would say. "You'd better get your colored ass used to it."

Kenneth became more accustomed to the type of law enforcement used there, and that was what bothered him the most with his first assignment. In the East Dallas projects, there was not a complicated strategy for law enforcement. Even with the smaller numbers, it became just like Chicago where anger festered and the police force waited for the reaction or initiated the action to get the reaction. At least that's what was rumored to be happening in Chicago even right now, about the police causing all the problems in the projects, mostly with black people.

Kenneth was at his East Dallas assignment for one whole year of anger meeting anger and despair going without consoling, and he never questioned his role in the equation. He was the black face in uniform in the community that was used to make everything more digestible, if actual enforcement against crime could be. If criminals were going to commit crimes for the sake of crime, then no one could make the punishment for their wrongdoings more acceptable. But if people were committing crimes because of a need against a personal condition, then they would need consoling, and Kenneth was the right face at the right time—or so he thought.

He was tall and thin as a pole holding up a yield sign in the middle of streaming traffic, and with shiny orange-brown skin the hue of a discarded leaf in the fall, he an attractive figure that women responded to and men admired. Some were even jealous. He had a sparkling smile and eyes, and gained praise from the older ladies of the projects about what a fine young man he was and how they wish he was their son or son-in-law. The captain felt that this was the best weapon for the new era in law enforcement. If people responded favorably to the patrolman, the enforcement of the law was more voluntary than mandatory. That's why the uniformed patrolman must look immaculate at all times. It was a plus that Kenneth was a patrolman of color. It made law enforcement of his people easier. And it made sense.

In Search of the Rabbit Man

That is, until the effects of the assignment had taken their toll on Kenneth. Now his eyes held a dull stare that could never betray the emotion or consideration of his thoughts, which he kept hidden behind dark mirror-reflecting shades. His voice, which before was filled with mirth and glee, was now filled with force and intimidation even when the words were just a greeting. Now he could make "hello" seem like a threat. The effect was a young man who held back his true feelings and therefore his true self, and was fast becoming old before his time.

He had come to Texas seeking some way to make a change. He wanted to be different, or at least different from his contemporaries. There was a change in the air for his generation, and Chicago was fast becoming a national flashover point for everything that was happening in America. In New York, the Harlem stories about the radical musicians were abundant, and more musicians began to sing radical songs against the Vietnam War. In Detroit, Malcolm and the black Muslims were crowding the headlines with rights for the black man and were catching on all over. In the South there was Dr. King and the civil rights movement that was catching on all over. In the West there were the Black Panthers and their aggressive agenda for the black man that was catching on all over. And so, it seemed to Kenneth that from the time of his high school graduation to his admittance to the Dallas police force in the fall of '66 that everything was moving too fast. He wasn't overly ambitious. He just didn't want to get swept up into something that everyone was seemingly becoming attached to, and he needed to see more for himself before making any decisions.

The Texas summer were as hot as hell, and for the first time he saw heat streams rising up from the afternoon in streets and from the windows. It was so dry sometimes that it seemed that the air that he breathed would burn his nostrils and lungs. In the beginning of course he would have problems with the physical police training, until he got used to the sun or the training was nearing an end. He couldn't decide which the reason was. All he knew was that the training was over, summer was ending, and he was used to the running and the repetitious exercises. He moved from the training with a sense of accomplishment for himself, but not a sense of trust from his fellow officers, and he was told not to expect it. In fact, he was told that he would have to work harder to earn their trust because he was one of the first colored Americans to be allowed to join the force. He was also told that he hadn't earned the trust of his instructors. In fact, one in particular, a Norman Truitt, a tobacco-chewing, spitting-everywhere-he-walked and spitting-every-time-Kenneth-would-ask-a-question, tall, lean, country-and-western piece of wood (his own words) gave Kenneth hell from day one till the day he left. He even spit on the floor when Kenneth got his badge. But those were the good days.

Kenneth's first partner, Patrolman Herman T. Ross, was a heavyset warm but extremely opinionated officer. He had notions that were framed and perfected from as long ago as his father's father childhood, and no one was going to change them. He was comfortable with those notions because the logic was hard to argue with. In his notions, everything had a place and there was no reason to change anything. He had a big laugh that would fill the car and rock the windows, and he had a genuine honest way about him as long as you remembered your place. The East Dallas projects suited him well because this was the place for these types of people. He was comfortable being surrounded by poor, dirty, raggedy black people around his job. He loved to see the running disheveled children roaming through the trash from the knocked-over cans and the ravishing stray dogs. In the first couple of weeks, the hardest thing for Kenneth to get accustomed to was, when there was no trash, Patrolman Herman T. Ross would make some. He would toss out food wrappers and empty soda bottles, and would sometimes knock over the trash cans himself. Patrolman Herman T. Ross's reasoning was that he was there to enforce the laws and not make a cosmetic change to the projects, and even trash had its place.

And although they were one of two patrol cars that were stationed in the area, Patrolman Ross never found a reason to interact with the other patrol car, save a hello or maybe an offhand comment about an episode of *Bonanza*. Of course, nothing happened in the daytime. Most of the children were in school, and the mothers who were at home doing the housekeeping and babysitting usually stayed inside or only traveled in large packs of babies, toddlers, and preschoolers to the corner store for milk, rice, macaroni, or beans. There would never be any instances for crime in the daytime, so Big Ross—which was what his fellow officers called him, more because of his size and loud voice than the fact that he had the most seniority in the unit—Big Ross would only drive to one spot and linger. He would speak to the old men who were sitting outside in the shade in their rocking chairs and stools, and then move to another spot and speak to the old ladies who were sweeping off their porches, and then move back to the corner store and wait for the mothers who had forgotten something or were just the second wave of customers.

Then there would be lunch in the car at the Good Luck Burger drive-up or maybe takeout from a Luby's restaurant, which was never too far away. They never sat in a restaurant together, and that was okay with Kenneth. He really didn't know how he would react if he was the only black person in the place trying to eat with his mentor, or if he was sitting with the only white person in the place regardless of the uniform. Or to have lunch in public with people who always seemed to forget his name, save for "boy." He always called everyone else by his or her name and he never forgot a single one, so this was something that Kenneth had to become accustomed to. In Chicago, black men were trying to erase the degrading term of "boy" as a label for a full-grown adult and "colored" as an identification of a race of people. It was rumored that in the South, no matter where you lived or how old you lived to be, you were still a boy in the eyes of white America. This minor inconvenience and the saturation of country music that filled every daytime street corner was the extent of the training for Kenneth in the first six months.

The second six months were different, beginning with Kenneth being assigned to the second shift, the four o'clock to midnight shift, and was teamed with Patrolman Ernest Rebo Parnell. From the start, Kenneth knew that not only did the time change for his assignment— which sometimes meant a layover to finish up some paperwork for booking or disorderly conduct—but the attitude on the watch changed as well. Just some four years prior, the Dallas police had suffered its worst hour. It wasn't enough of a tragic smear that the President of the United States was assassinated in the greatest state of the Union and in the heart of the city that Sam Houston helped to establish, but while the nation watched, the assassin had been gunned down while in the custody of the Dallas police by a patriotic club owner. This was enough to make the average patrolman feel that there was more than a little something to live down, but Patrolman Parnell was different.

Having been a patrolman for just three years in November of 1963 and realizing that the downtown assignment was a special task for a young ambitious patrolman, Patrolman Parnell had tried to make the most of it. When the alarm sounded and all chaos ensued, he saw it as an opportunity to gain respect and prestige. In the manhunt for Oswald he had found himself surrounded by very serious and experienced officers who knew the gravity of the event a lot better than he did, and sneered at his tagging along. He wanted instructions, but was confined to car duty and crowd control until the assassin was contained and incarcerated. Then he was relegated to crowd control in the front of the downtown station.

He thought he remembered, while standing on the sidewalk, seeing an official-looking man in a gray suit walk past him and into the parking lot of the station. He only caught a glimpse but he couldn't stop to look because he was engaged with a group of black women who were crying and carrying on and asking for information and distracting him from the very important duty of crowd control. Why were black people here, anyway? They weren't with the press. After the parking lot melee with Ruby shooting Oswald, Patrolman Parnell told his superiors about his crowd control experience with the black women and the official-looking man in the gray suit moving past him to the parking lot. No one confirmed whether it was Ruby or not, but the silence that ensued whenever he walked into the room was evident.

Even though the criticism toward the Dallas police department was unwarranted, because the most desperate people can do the most desperate things at any time, they carried the burden internally longer than their accusers or critics would have hoped to have accomplish. In the measurement of a decade of national chaos, the Dallas police were among the tops in city law enforcement, and save for the assassinations the city was considered a very peaceful place to live with few if any out-of-the-ordinary crimes. This was attributed to the goodwill of the people, the great state tradition, and the efforts of the patrolmen at large.

But Patrolman Ernest Rebo Parnell was never satisfied. Maybe if it were definite that the official-looking man that he had let get past him was Jack Ruby, then things would have evolved differently. Maybe if he had maintained the trust that he felt he had lost from his fellow officers, then he would have been a different person. Maybe if those black ladies hadn't ever approached him with their tears and their whiny voices and their proclamations of doom for the end of the world, then he would have felt better about black people. He was from Kilgore, Texas, a small town maybe an hour away from Dallas, and the black people there never approached him or talked to him about world affairs. If they had stayed away then he would not have been in the situation he was in or felt the way he felt. How was it possible that people could change just because of a few tall buildings or a transit system or a few hundred thousand more people? Maybe they thought they had changed and times had changed because of the movement from one location to another, from one part of the state to another, from one year to the next, but it hadn't and never would; he would see to that. He hadn't changed. He was still the same shy, honest farm boy from Kilgore who loved country music, and if he hadn't changed, then the black people hadn't changed either. They just needed to be reminded that the conditions and attitudes of the South were just as strong and resolved as they were before that war a hundred years before and he was just the patrolman to remind them.

At the start of 1964 and his reassignment to the East Dallas projects, he found plenty of people who needed to be reminded of the way things were. He had started out with Big Ross, just like everyone else, and was not pleased with the easygoing attitude that surrounded him everywhere they went throughout the day watch. Big Ross was trying to be friends with the blacks that lived in these hovels of government appeasements. He even called some by their first names as opposed to "boy" or other familiar racially derogatory labels, and he even smiled at them from time to time. Big Ross was not looking at law enforcement with the same seriousness as Rebo—or, for that matter, acting like a true disciple of the Southern manners and teachings.

The year 1964 crept by slowly for Rebo. He had several arguments with Big Ross that prolonged his patrolman elevation. The result was an extra six months of riding in the same patrol car with Big Ross, and he hated it. When he finally left in the spring of '64 he felt he had suffered enough embarrassment to last his family a lifetime. His parents, his uncles, and brothers were bearing the brunt of the ridicule in Dallas and Kilgore to last a lifetime. His youngest brother William Parnell had left the state and moved off to Montana, which was a lifelong dream for him, but Rebo took it as more evidence that his shame had some consequences. His non-acceptance by his fellow officers created problems and arguments within his family, and he slowly lost contact with them altogether. He worked harder at doing the right thing on his job, but a twenty-four-hour by-the-book patrolman is a hard man to live with. He lived alone. He had a sweetheart in Kilgore but had gradually moved away from her in both physical and emotional distance until it was more comfortable for him to have her memory than her presence. He was alienated from his fellow officers, and further exacerbated the alienation with his stiff demeanor and short temper. No one would spend time with him and there were not many people that he would want to spend time with. He didn't have a pet, a place to be, a place to go, or anything to do after work but think about work. He would stay around the substation when his shift would end and he would criticize the off going shift—or the ongoing shift; it didn't matter. He was most interested and happiest when he had input for the job. Unfortunately, his input went by unnoticed. His fellow officers ignored him with a numbing silence that droned to incessant increasing screaming. He heard it when he was ignored. He heard it when there was a disagreement with any decision that he would make that involved his job or the people that surrounded him. He heard it from time to time, sometimes a lot and sometimes never. But it was always there.

Few people can manage to keep their lives away from the influences that others impose on it. Few people can withstand criticism from the people that move within their spheres and form the essences of their world. Life is fair in the way that everyone uses everyone else for one thing or another and always, always, the strongest survive. It wasn't fair for Kenneth to have to team up with Rebo after Rebo had become disillusioned with his place on his job.

In January of '67 and the start of the longest year of Kenneth's life to that date, Kenneth began patrolling the East Dallas projects on the second shift with Ernest Rebo Parnell, with Motown in full swing with the progressive movement in the civil rights struggle and with Dr. King's momentum. Of course, Rebo still felt that time stood still, and sometimes he remembered the downtown streets of 1962, but for the most part he was too active policing and performing law enforcement Rebo-style. It was the norm to have some type of confrontation with the citizen and project dregs every night. Rebo did not make a distinction between the two. He really wasn't biased when it came to his brand of justice. Both shared the same pain, disappointment, and brutality with equal measure. If you were black, after dark, and not smiling humbly, then you were accustomed to slow scrutiny from the patrol car, which sometimes included shining the light, blaring the horn, or whining the siren. And heaven help you if Rebo had to stop the car and walk out with his nightstick and teeth snarling and come toward you.

During this period, life became a succession of ballads for Kenneth, but because he wasn't of his own self-reflection the ballads became the sad country lyrics that engulfed his co-workers and their explanation for the behavior in the East Dallas projects. If he had used an awareness to analyze his role in the drama that continued to unfold night after night then he would compare himself to a character in a German opera, loud and shouting with closely squinting eyes. The inhabitants of the projects only expounded on their plight with varying degrees of explanations that ranged from "my woman left me and that's why I'm drunk" to "I'm just drunk enough to kill that mutha for messing with my woman or car or dog or something…" It didn't help that the economically segregated and self-confined only had two stores, and while both had plenty of secondhand food, both profited most from monies earned from the revenue of their liquor sales. The young men in the projects drank from sundown until curfew or until someone shooed them away. The women drank until they got into shouting matches with other women or men, and then they would skulk away unbridled or unluckily with a mate for further, more secluded fighting in the night. The music was loud sometimes, and as long as it was the blues and not some '60s flower-power integration revolution music then Kenneth noticed that Rebo didn't really have much to say. But let it rock 'n' roll with some drug music or some James Brown "black and proud" music, and this was a cause for alarm and scrutiny. This meant that instead of drowning in the sorrow of their plight the inhabitants were listening to a choice within their plight, and that could mean trouble. This was the training that Patrolman Parnell offered to Patrolman Conway, and he had better remember it.

"I'm only gonna tell you this one mo' time. Da surest sign of trouble is the sounds that you hear. You gotta' learn to know wha'ta listen for," said Ernest Rebo.

They were slowly cruising through the projects one day in '67 in the last of the winter and cursing each other, Kenneth doing so silently and Rebo whenever the occasion called for it.

"Ya listen up, you fucking po' boy rook, 'cause if my life depends on it ya better hear me. Ya better be a policeman at all times, an dat don't mean 'cause you want to. Ya better back my play at all times, cause if I'm left hanging then I'm gonna have your ass."

And Kenneth understood that Rebo's play could be anything at any given moment at any time of the shift.

Tell it to The Rain
February 23, 1967
Monday

An evening in the East Dallas projects in a winter without the sun was a sight to stop and remember, but of course that depended on the margin for expectation. Some people saw it as an extension of governmental goodwill originating some thirty-five years earlier by a daring young Texas politician who was now the President of the United States, but back then was on his way to bigger and better things, and saw the projects as filled with security and hope for a better tomorrow. There was a fairness that permeated the one-hundred-building establishment that sat under a February gray sky and it started with the small percentage of the occupant's income as cost for the dwellings. From a high income of fifty-five dollars per week to the low of twenty-two, all were welcome to the same living conditions based on the income and the same percentage value requirement from every family. This was a good starting point to gain a foothold on tomorrow, and the occupants tried to make the most of it. The ambitious lot shopped modestly with an eye for thrift and saved up for a home that personified the American dream. For the most part, life was clean, the homes were clean, and the tenants kept the lots clean. Often in the summer you could see the fathers pushing behind a push mower, its wheel-turning action rotating the cutting roll that lay parallel between the two wheels. The evenings were filled with grass chipping away with a crank and a swish and a soft-tip sound as it came to rest behind the mower.

But other expectations from those who passed by or noticed from some advertisement or found the topic in the many critical conversations about the progressive movements from other places that were comparable to the city landscape saw it as a place for projecting their anger toward a homogenous haven of slovenliness and laziness. They always took the chance to say "those kinds of people," and "those types are pests and they bring roaches and rats with them." They would not change, could not change, and refused to change because of the way it was, the times, the attitudes, the money. And while the prevailing Texas middle class counted their blessings in response to the absence of the hippies or Muslims or Black Panthers or any other blotch of radicalism that seemed to mark the decade, they could still frown on any attempt of morality within change. After all, this was still LBJ country, and they did pay good money to city officials and employees to make sure that their area remained the same and the same attitude was in place for the liberal legislators who would try to move the area in too rapid a change. There was no room for radicalism in this part of the world, and the eyes of state would not permit it anyway.

The buildings were red brick like distant gingerbread homes, because of the white trimmings of wood and concrete that framed the windows and doorways and edges of the flat roofs. The streets were gray-white concrete streams that glistened white-gold under the afternoon sun, as if the designers had that scene in mind. The facades were pure with the smiling-face dimensions of two top smaller bedroom windows and wider bottom dining and living room windows trimmed in white on a vertical line congruent to the baseline and a porch that seemed to flop down just in front of the doorway and trimming in white for the nose.

They were in rows of four sets of five family dwellings that stood back to back in parallel to another row of four that established the street blocks that made up the cross streets. In the back, lots were separated by softer concrete that created an alleyway of convenience or security contrivance because fences were illegal. They were filled with trees that stretched out and across the thick black conduit of wires that ran above the telephone wires and all up high and reaching out to towering poles that housed the electrical units. The telephone lines were heavier and black with tiny silver wiring, but at the furthest end of the street, the street that led out and away, there was a junction just above the electrical conduit and those wires continued with the electricity and the thoughts and dreams of the inhabitants going out and into their homes without judgment. Underneath the telephone lines was life in motion.

Behind the homes and in the lots were circular clotheslines shaped like large but thin white kite frames of four metal poles with wires tied together by their tails. They could revolve and were shared by the two homes that made the unit. There were two silver tin trash cans with the tops supplied by the landlord and two picnic tables shared by the unit, which had been brown earlier but were now a grayish brown because of the peeling paint and the wood decay from weather erosion to the original construction in 1955. They were good for folding clothes from the drying clothesline, or changing cloth diapers of baying young children, or toys and lunch for the before-school-age children that were abundant throughout the area. But a lot of times they were used by the mothers for congregating with other mothers, or just resting in peace from the grind of a happy existence.

The greatest majority of inhabitants of the project, unlike those of other cities, were those of the average family as a family of three school-age children, and very seldom were any in their late teens. The growing feeling was that four were delegated to areas of more expanses and farmland was everywhere. Sharecropping was still as popular in the furthest rural areas regardless of the Alabama and Mississippi stories of uniqueness, but the term had been changed to "renters," because of the growing number of people settling in the state, forgetting that western pilgrimage to California, and settling for being black. They had been that way from their history, making it so much easier to accept the untold precept of labor without ownership. But here in the projects the inhabitants felt differently, with the dream of Ward and June Cleaver, or *Father Knows Best,* or Ozzie and Harriet, or something else that the black father has been taught and now provided insight for his children. That meant money, education, happiness, and just moving away from the fighting of the rural areas just hadn't caught on with the rest of the poor blacks, because what was being enforced was not in the schools and not said aloud. Or maybe they just haven't had the fourth child yet.

In February the weather was cold and wet and sometimes white with snow or socked–in with rain; it depended on the dominant weather patterns. Dallas was at the bottom of tornado alley, so it felt windy, but not as massively or demonstratively every year as the other members of the alley experienced, even in the tornado season. Other influences gave it the hue of nature that was hue to man. The Gulf Stream brought moisture, but even it had to yield sometimes to a cold flow from the Arctic that had the priority of a jet stream; it might share a Pacific flow and maybe relent to a southwesterly system. But still, if Mexican weather were meant for the state, it had better be from the Texas-end of Mexico.

The people were bundled in winter attire and they liked it, especially the children with red scarves and the English-fashioned double-breasted tan coats and beret hat—a much cheaper, '66 version of the Mood-Twiggy-British look—and the all-weather yellow rain boots. With the handle of a red wagon in one hand and a lollipop clinched in the other, the children were like a page out of the Christmas edition of the Sears Roebuck catalog. The boys had the small blocks that they used for almost every purpose, such as loads for the wagons little truck stops for the toy trucks, or steps that moved up and alongside the porch. And while the girls had their rain gear on display, the boys always had their cap pistols and holsters for display and wrapped around their waists, with white cowboy hats sitting proudly on the backs of their heads—or, if the hats were black, tilted down over a brow and shifted to the left or right side of their heads.

The mothers always had a new coat or one that was put away for special occasions like going to church near Christmas Day, and if the day didn't fall on Sunday and the parents found something else more elegant and relaxing to do, it was always the same for New Year's Eve and New Year's Day. These special occasions meant going out to a movie that you could walk into, or walking into a restaurant that you could dress nice for, or even going to the Dallas Symphony Orchestra under the baton of conductor Donald Johanos for a brisk evening of music, when everything was quiet save that full and lusty music from Dallas's best musicians. January was filled with the payoff effects of scrimping and scraping and sacrificing for layaway plans of one and two dollars per week starting as far back as last January, which was one of the benefits for the patrons of the Sears Roebuck department store. A good Christmas started immediately after the one that you just scraped for had finished, and four to six dollars a month was a good start.

Pride abounded in the moving traffic of shiny cars, old '57 Chevy and Ford trucks and a Galaxie 500 every now and then. If the police weren't around and if you were lucky, an out-of-place Mustang or Camaro with a happily employed young man behind the wheel would crawl through and filter a memory onto the cold surface that was wet from dew, and for the first time there was a hint of green grass. And you could see the American steel, the American thoughts, the American design, and the American weed—a resilient plant that was never welcome, but seemed to show up wherever dirt was cultivated and became fertile. The weed can grow alongside anything that lives, and if life and this time period adopt a mascot then weeds are the symbol of existence for any struggling family. And if you are a budding young black kid who has actually purchased a car that has a future of shin and shim and speed, because that is what is valued by a young man who wants the respect of his elders that he trusts, then you are a weed and don't even know it. Even if the speed limit is observed, a weed is out there trying to do more or grow more, or just trying to survive like everyone else and trying not to hurt anyone.

Solomon Davis was one of the lucky ones, or one of the ones who seemed like everything turned out right for him. He had a new '65 Mustang that was sent to him by his grandmother, his father's mother who lived in the East somewhere. The down payment was a high school graduation present that everyone wanted for him, and when it arrived by transport truck at the projects it created a mixed stir of envy and pride. What no one knew was that he had received a violin, the present that he wanted most, from his grandmother weeks before the Mustang arrived. When the fathers and mothers of the neighborhood saw the car, they all thought that this was a young man on the rise, and if things went well for him then they should surely go well for their children. Things were looking up. The many grandmothers who lived in the dwellings were just as proud as if he were their own grandson moving up and beyond. He was months away from his twentieth birthday and looked like the musical artist Stevie Wonder with clear brown skin, the thin mustache over his lip, and the white shirt and tie and brown sweater and slacks—brown or blue, dark green, or black, but always slacks for his job—and the black-framed glasses that complemented the thin angular frame and short-cropped hair. This created a more appealing sight for the older women to linger on and they would set their eyes on him and see the calm strength of honesty and conviction of attempting to excel in spite of the obvious opposition to his success. The young girls only saw the Stevie Wonder in him. He was first and foremost a famous musician who was in their midst. He made their days more memorable and their nights more enchanting.

Not many young black men carried themselves the way that he did, and it was for a good reason, but he seemed to rise above it. He was respectable and would help almost anyone. He had some college, about a year and a half from the downtown two-year college a few blocks away from the infamous book depository building and grassy knoll, which few young blacks had the opportunity—or, for some, the inclination—to attend from his neighborhood. Those who did never came back to the area. Solomon could live almost anywhere with his earnings from the warehouse, but he stayed in the projects to help his mom and his four young stepsisters who were an energetic jumble of arms, legs, and hair and a bountiful handful for her single-parent capabilities. He stayed behind to help with the discipline. He stayed behind to help with the caring. He stayed behind to help with the rent. While government funds would help Mom to some extent, Solomon's job at the warehouse office of Sears Roebuck a couple of blocks away from the department store on Lamar was a godsend and a boost to the many needs of the family.

Solomon's days were filled with filing, sweeping, and sometimes lifting and helping out on the large warehouse floor where the department store items would come in "in bulk," and he would always look forward to that day when perhaps there would be overtime, even for him. It was no mistake that most blacks thought that the Sears Roebuck Company in the Dallas area was owned by blacks, or at least didn't really mistreat them, or were more tolerant of the black inquiries about payment. There were a lot of city jobs opening up for black men, like the post office, and the bus company, and the various metal, wire, and dye companies, and then there were some opening up in the large factories like Frito-Lay and Proctor & Gamble, but none seemed to cater to the black community like the layaway plan at Sears. Sears even had male black sales representatives in the men's section and black females in the women's section.

But Solomon's biggest flaw was that he never thought of true competition between people as gradients of color, and if so, he never showed any difficulty with the interactions between his co-workers and the other tenants of the projects. The treatise of race relations as survival of the fittest never entered into his mannerism. And while his work demeanor was equally respectable for both white and black, he continued to hear the comments of "Who do you think you are?" or "You keep forgetting your place," and finally, "Boy, that black ain't gonna come off no matter how hard you try." His reply was a smile and a nod and a brisk step in the same direction and on to his destination. It wasn't that he was afraid of confrontation; it was just a lot easier to walk past it.

That was before the boss Mr. Lemon hired a new secretary. Dawn M. Patten was everything Texas, but was not born or raised in Texas. Even with the long curly brunette hair and the long shapely legs and trim body like an athlete, that wasn't the true definition of Dawn. It was her attitude that gave her personality. It was bright and trusting, almost to the level of childlike innocence. This should have made her movements jerky with curiosity, but she always moved a beat slower and took a breath slower, which gave her time—which became every man's time, and that was just like a Texas woman. She was a harsh yellow flower in a swollen lake of pain that carried the plains and the needed sunset in her eyes and the hope of every person with a dream. She was the far snowcapped mountain to the west and the cool wetness of the deep gulf coast down south where the gulf breezes brought coolness for the season and the still clear quiet of a starlit night. She was the best end to any fight, and just listening to her soft twang about fairness and girl things and scattered treats was something that every man should listen to at least once, not only from his mother's lap of singsong comfort but in his life to balance the sterile coldness of a man's wants as a cold fact of life. The grim contradiction that she was a white girl with curly brown hair from upstate Maryland without a firsthand clue of Texas politics should have been enough to make her options limited but clear. In reality, she was Maryland where race relations were never as strained as they were in the South, and this made her presence and her awareness a difference from the norm.

Dawn talked to all the men at the job and gave them equal importance, but was drawn to Solomon because he was polite and clean. She thought he would have looked more like Bob Dylan than Stevie Wonder if he'd only worn his hair longer. The natural fashion would have given him a Jimi Hendricks look, and she would have been no less interested, but he wore it short. She wasn't a Beatle girl anymore, and she responded to poetry as always a struggle against the norm. She heard the Dylan lyrics as poetry and a cry of subtle outrage. She also liked the symphony, and that's where she first met Solomon. He was there in his best Sunday black suit and a tiny black tie and a smile, standing in a corner during an intermission, alone, like he didn't belong—or worse, that he worked at the place. But she saw in his eyes the recognition of the string work of a Bach overture that had preceded the intermission and knew that there was something more to the man than working diligently and patiently as an intermediate between the office and the warehouse stalls.

Although Texas was firmly entrenched in the civil rights movement to support President Johnson's finally passed legislation, pushed through by hook or crook, there were not many places Dawn and Solomon could be seen together. They would meet at an outdoor park around the symphony hall. He would have his violin in its case and take it out and play, and in dark-shaded glasses would blend in like the out-of-town artists that were migrating down south toward Austin or west to California. She would come to their table and sit across from him with her violin in its case, left shut, and a music book standing straight up before her face as her eyes stared dreamily to him from behind large dark white-rimmed butterfly shades. She had fun with the arrangement and the disguises, and suggested a change for their appearance as often as possible. Her favorites were from her recent fantasies of doing her part in leading the way to women's equality. She had felt this way for a long time. Back in her early childhood she aspired to be June Cleaver or maybe Lucille Ball, but after her entrance to college and learning different expressions and impressions, her days became occupied with many different arguments on race and sex and choices for life issues. These arguments started early but seemed to blossom from '65 to '66.

When Dawn was alone in upstate Maryland, the days she would show up in old jeans and a large secondhand shirt tied around her waist with an old discarded tie made college seem to open the world for her. She realized that for the first time in her life, her appearance could say something beyond words. Now clothes could convey an attitude beyond the quiet little girl or the fast girl or the popular girl or the doting mother. Clothes could make a political statement as much and as strong as the silent protest of the civil rights marchers. She would complement this look with as many sunflowers as she could find and stick them into her hair. And while the University of Maryland wasn't necessarily a radical college, more students were moving away from the Beatle days and more toward the folk commentary of Bob Dylan.

And then Dawn realized that she was not alone. That was her biggest validation. And that she wasn't like her mother was only the beginning. What she wanted was far different from what her mother had wanted. What she needed, she felt, was different from what her mother had needed. And when she finally talked to her mother on the day when she told her parents—who were forty years older than she, that she would not complete college and would find other things to do, they were both disappointed. Her mother cried. Whether they were tears of sorrow or of joy was never quite discernable because her mother never disputed Dawn's decision, only nodded her head up and down in animated affirmation.

Solomon sometimes wore dark jeans and an African dashiki shirt with a flower headband tied around his head. At other times he would wear his Sunday best of black suit and shoes with white shirt and thin black tie, and try to pass for one of the mentors for the symphony orchestra. He had resisted Dawn's advances or as long as he could, but the happiness of the challenge beckoned. It wasn't a challenge to be with her for the sake of an argument per se, and that was the constant challenge put forth by both cultures at that time: to keep or try to establish an argument for the equality of the status quo, but more so to snub and challenge and communicate to both cultures on the levels of shared weakness. It would be a slap in the face of both cultures from both friends if they didn't understand the message. This is when she urged and he consented to walk through downtown with her on Saturday afternoons when both cultures were there to shop, the blacks on Elm Street and the whites on Main Street.

They would walk up and down all of the downtown streets on those afternoons, with Dawn leading Solomon because he would wear heavy dark shades across his eyes. Even when he walked, his face was up and staring out as if he were blind. It wasn't long before she had found a cane to complement his wardrobe. In fact, this was her challenge; she would create many such scenarios for excursions into the city consciousness. When they passed older white women who were busy with their shopping at the big Sanger Harris department store on Main Street or the patrons at the Zales jewelers on Elm Street they would stare, and some would sympathize, and some would stare at the strangely dressed white woman leading a black blind musician around the downtown streets. He would agree with her wishes for the sake of adventure and friendship—because that's all it was for him—and so he would wear as many different disguises as she could create and try to play the many parts that she suggested.

Her true strength was found in the reasons for her make-believe. She used it to protect an untouched innocence that started when she escaped from the unpleasant times in Maryland when her parents resisted her whims. She had started to use it back when she was a child at the orphanage with the only doll that she had ever owned, a Raggedy Ann doll that she had found discarded in a corner. Later in her preteens and teens, all alone in her spacious bedroom in Maryland when she was alone and the rejections of friends—first, "don't play with my dolls" and "don't come to my house," and boys later—allowed the memories of the orphanage to creep up and touch her when she least expected it. Why it started was the secret that she hoped no one would ask because it was at her core and it would make her vulnerable, and she would never allow that so she wasn't telling. She only knew that she was good at it because she had to be—in school when she had to pretend to be a respectable student that was willing to learn but deep down she could care less, and at home when she had to be the doting child who loved everything that her mother and father prepared for her. Someone, a teacher or minister or even a nun at the orphanage had told her—and she remembered what was said and almost who had said it, almost; it was fleeting and always at the furthest reaches of her memory—that she didn't have a mean streak in her at all, but she realized that people wanted to be better than other people in this country and she had a survival streak that she should use at all times. The person said this when it was found out that Dawn wanted to win, and did win the Maypole dance, the gymnastic tricks, and the puzzle games. When Dawn entered high school, her home economics teacher told her that her time was coming and she would begin to live in that time, but this teacher only saw her potential in sewing and cooking and etiquette. Dawn saw the future as a time when she could relax and truly trust the people that she had accepted in her life for the first time.

VI

The Beat Goes On
March 17, 1967

The second shift began in a damp heavy air of an evening glint and sheen. March was usually a cool month with an evening breeze that would cool off the day, but some days, like this one, the air was still and hot and heavy with humidity and needed the breeze. For the first time in a repetition of first times, Rebo had a moment of self-doubt with his purpose and with his decisions in his old yet young life. His attitude, which was an insistence on neutral compliance, was created primarily from what he had gleaned from his early experiences; it could be called his mental awareness if he had read the latest *Reader's Digest* instead of an *American Farm* magazine. But he wasn't well read in the least, so he had to rely on the simple principles first like the choice between pain and not pain; those principles later conformed or evolved into the premise of success over failure. That maturity gave him what he now felt was the confidence to determine what was needed in the outcome of any situation. It was stored in a reservoir of youthful experiences from the time when he was young, but now he used it as a man. A policeman.

This was the way he approached the first day of every week, starting on Monday until this day, a Friday. If anything, he wanted consistency within his routine and within the routine of his few subordinates. He thought about becoming a sergeant one day, with all of the authority and respect that accompanied the position. It was the reward for living the way of the policeman. The unselfishness of giving. The way things should be when the world is right. But the position eluded him for one reason or another and he couldn't understand why. He stood in the parking lot that looked more like an underground train station, with heavy shadows and with its gray walls and cold gray concrete floors, than a place of official functions. He stood next to his black-and-white cruiser and directly in front of his probationary partner.

He made his partner stand by the patrol car, and then he began the inspection. It was a humiliating process that complimented the red-yellow glow of the flat landscape in this part of Texas. He walked a straight line to the patrolman and invaded as close as he could until he was the only object in the new patrolman's field of vision. Then Rebo sniffed the air around him. Finally, he exhaled and Kenneth could smell the rank Wild Turkey on Rebo's breath and in his lungs and blood, as the soft cloud of rankness always circled both of their heads. Rebo could never smell the rankness, but always found satisfaction in the discomfort that performing this soft ritual would achieve. It was the way his father had taught him to act, because that was the same way you had to treat the land and everything close to you. You had to fight the land, weed the land, break the land down, and then damn near drown the land if you wanted the land to grow anything, and because that was the way it was when you wanted to make land grow. His father taught each of his sons this golden rule of life, and treated them all the same way in work, love, and religion. Religion in Texas was sometimes political, the right Baptist and the wrong Baptist religion in those parts. When said often enough and remembered long enough, it was one and the same with politics. Rebo, being the smallest, always tried the hardest but always came up short in his father's eyes, he felt—but it was the same for all of the sons. Everyone tried their hardest and always came up short. That was his father's way.

"Smells like neck bones and shit, boy!" Rebo said to Kenneth. Although Rebo was only five years older, he preferred to call him "boy" as opposed to "rook" or his given name, because not only did it remind him of but continued to demonstrate that the separation between Kenneth and himself was much more prominent than age. It was something he had become accustomed to relying on. "I guess that's normal for you people, huh, boy?"

After the inspection both patrolmen entered their vehicle and rolled out of the downtown garage at a comfortable speed, heading to State Highway 30 by way of Interstate 45. They had been riding together for two months, but Rebo still held the disproportionate formalities as a sword over the head of his probationary rookie. While Rebo would be vulgar, discriminating, and insulting, Kenneth was still restrained to the highest protocols of rank. He addressed Rebo as "Officer Parnell" and "sir", and was not allowed to look his training officer in the eye, which was normal within the ranks. This was the routine for the two months.

Although Kenneth felt he had taken some strides toward being treated like a fellow officer when he was partnered with Big Ross, he knew from rumors, the passing treatment, and looks from him that teaming with Rebo was a step in the wrong direction. He always had the feeling that he was under some type of hammer, and that it would fall and his good fortunes and his plans would be lost. This was the way everyone at the station had treated him lately, and that made him feel bad, but with Rebo it was worse because he had to spend so much time with him. With everyone else he could walk away but with Rebo he had to ride and walk and be with him. Rebo insisted that Kenneth say to him "sir, yes sir," loudly and in public and that was every day. It was more than the initiation that was expected. It was the fear of losing his job at any moment, because that was the way it was in the world that gave him his agreeable posture and his mindset and made him compliant. But it had been more of an impending dread lately. The whole thing was wearing thin and he wondered how long he could last. People were changing and times were changing, and there were civil rights marches in Chicago and a lot more opportunities for young people with experience. He would wait for now and take it but would always try to look ahead.

"Country music is the music of good hardworking white people. All this new hippie, race-mixing stuff is from people who want to take over the government. Leave it to them long-haired pot-smoking fools and we would walk right out of Vietnam and let the commie slant-eyes have everything. I know the Japs are behind this kind of horseshit, and we ought to drop another A-bomb on their asses."

Rebo's daily political spiel was consistently directed toward non-Christians as well as blacks, and was as routine as his insistence on driving the patrol car every day. Deeply rooted in that spiel was his true inner character. He believed that you had to kick the enemy when they were down and that the Japanese were still plotting revenge for the Hiroshima and Nagasaki bombings. He believed that all Asians were alike, all blacks were truly Africans and non-Christians and had only become Christians because they didn't want to be whipped during slavery, and all whites were the same. He felt that in the end all things were going to be the same regardless of the new music, the new clothes that people were wearing, the new words people were saying, and of course the drugs that caused the new attitudes.

Rebo wasn't good with women because he didn't understand them, nor did he take the time to get to know them. He felt that women needed men, and because of his job he would always be desirable for any single woman. And he wasn't far from right. The opportunities for making a living were still scarce for women and their best bet for the future was marriage to a man with a good job, and better still if he were white. That's why he couldn't understand the new attitudes and music and those so-called hippie parties that were rumored to have sex between people who were just friends, and with people of other races and with people of the same sex. Not only did he not understand it, but the latter made him angry beyond reason. His anger was so intense that he could see white lights flashing in his eyes.

The traffic was sparse in a straight direction away from downtown, but building up going into and beyond downtown. Many cars were moving from the south and heading north for the night. They made good time in moving to their first location in the East Dallas projects. As was his fashion, Rebo seem to loosen up from being the stern mentor and became more of a partner and leader of the watch. He loved to give advice to anyone who would listen, and this was a contradiction in his prejudices that he just could not control.

JON-MICHAEL HAMILTON

"When you work long enough, you should get you a big fat woman and marry her. You know, one of those that can cook really good neck bones and pig feet and knows how to buy a good watermelon, and goes to church every Sunday and sings loud and sweats rivers down her cheeks," said Rebo, laughing at the singsong image he had created.

"Thank you, sir. I know your concern is for me," said Kenneth. He tried hard to keep the sarcasm from his voice, but it crept in nonetheless so he tried a different tactic.

"Where would I find a woman like that, sir? I mean, I can't just walk up to one while we're on duty, and we work so hard that I don't have any time off to go and look for one. Where could I find me a woman like that?"

"Boy, you talk too much. I tell you one thing, and you go ahead and tell me your entire life story. How the hell would I know where to find a fat black woman? It seems that every time we are near that laundry place by that church, there are about three or four of them walking with bags of clothes. Go there. You have to wash your clothes, don't you? Well, when you go there, pick one and tell her 'you'b is a poe-lice-man,'" he said in a mocking tone. "That always works; it works for me. I don't think you have any brains, boy. You ask me everything."

"Well, yeah, sir. I don't know what to do unless you tell me how to do it."

"And if that doesn't work you need to go to church and sing with them and catch them when they fall." Rebo laughed again at the image that he had created. "Ha, ha, that would be a sight."

"Yeah, sir. That would be a sight."

Rebo quickly looked to Kenneth suspiciously. It seemed that what Kenneth was saying or how he was saying it was familiar, maybe said once or twice before, but he couldn't be sure. Days and people were becoming a blur to him. More often than not, he forgot and attributed it to a lack of importance; he remembered the important things, so it was that and not the drinking. The drinking was a good thing in its own way because it was a way to wash out the memories and recent experiences that were bad from the previous nights. Maybe someone had said the wrong thing to him, and bumped into him or had just taken him for granted. Then that would have led to the long stare or the short stare or the look; it would depend on the number of instances that you saw the person walking or talking or both.

It was soon after the assassination of Kennedy that Rebo found the way to find his way to his way. This meant having his way at any cost, or just finding a way to feel in control in any situation. He had accepted killing at an early age because animals were needed to live on and man was on this planet to live from something. That was the reason that you were hungry. His father had told him that and he would always remember. It was somewhere in the Bible, and that made it right if you looked at it the way you were supposed to. Rebo needed to look at it his way again. He hunted for food and for revenge when he was young, with his brothers and sometimes his father. Even if young Rebo didn't kill it personally he knew someone had, and it had to be done so man could live. Animals provided food and sustenance like even clothing and tools, and someone had to survive from it. Young Rebo felt that killing was necessary, and even though the movies had people who killed because they wanted something, Rebo saw no difference between killing for food and killing from danger, because food was survival. But he had actually killed later for the fun of it.

They turned right on Hazard and quickly passed by a flash of tan and white brick and wood, which was the Hope Well Baptist church. It was the largest church in the East Dallas project area, and where practically everyone went on Sunday who actually practiced religion. It was the center of the community for the churchgoing people, and was more than just lines and angles and windows for black people. It was the hope of a better time, and actually had gained more prominence with Dr. King and the civil rights efforts. It served many purposes. It helped the needy, consoled the inconsolable, and communicated to the new civil rights activists. These were the strong young mothers and wives of the many service workers in the city. These were the brave young seniors from Lincoln High School, the only high school in the area. These were the churchgoing men who also served in the church as deacons and trustees and with their community voices were the closest thing to black politicians in the state. A few of the parsons had questioned the feasibility of such an organization for equal rights when all the efforts were being ignored or threatened to be stamped out by one senseless act or another. Other more radical voices mused that it was a place of fear for the weak and a target for the weaker.

The car pulled over to the side of the road and the front of the church. It was a large building with stilted peaks in the ceilings that stretched up to the amber sky. This was a usual Friday spot for the beginning of the shift. Usually Rebo insisted that Kenneth remain in the car, but this time he instructed him to enter with him. Inside, the church was impressive with the rows and rows of tan pews forging an aisle down to a big dark-brown pulpit that was centered and looked like it could harvest all the attention of an anxious congregation. Behind the pulpit was an impressive tan stage that was elevated above the floor and bordered by dark heavy curtains.

The church was empty, save a few people milling together in small groups and in separate secluded corners. When Rebo and Kenneth walked in, they attracted as much attention as a small fly flying aimlessly in a place where it knew it didn't belong. No one from the groups looked to them or acknowledged them. As they proceeded, Rebo walking proudly in front and Kenneth following stiffly, a small man dressed in a white shirt and blue-jean overalls moved away from the nearest group and to the center aisle. He walked up the aisle and met them halfway and in the center of the church.

"Well, preacher, I see you're at it again on a Friday night," said Rebo. The intentional slight in the reverend's title was always the way that he approached the people that he felt were less a man then he was.

"Yes, officer; we're having Bible study, just like we do every Friday evening, and choir rehearsals and other meetings later tonight. You are welcome to come by for cake when it's all over," said the reverend.

Both men stared at each other eye to eye first, and then looked up and down to size up the other. Then after a quiet beat where neither man moved, the reverend smiled a full smile and then laughed quietly.

"It's always good to see you, Officer Parnell. I hope you've been well." The reverend said it slowly and with much effort and composure.

The reverend was one of the few people to call Rebo the name that was etched on his nametag. Rebo enjoyed the reaction to his street name and at the same time enjoyed reluctance from the others officers. Rebo liked it because it showed hope for this old preacher who felt that some good comes from nothing. The reverend actually thought that Rebo had some good in him. He knew about some of Rebo's history and how he was the only officer who felt that he had let President Kennedy's killer's killer walk by before making the killer face the anger. He reached out a hand to Rebo, who ignored the handshake.

Rebo continued his stare, a constant, probing assessment, which was meant to neutralize any emotional transference.

It never worked with Reverend Robinson. "Rev" is what his congregation called him, or "the right reverend," or the kids would call him "Reverend R.", He was the kind of man who could see the good in everyone. This was not from his vocation, but from his demeanor and his early personality makeup. He grew up in the Jim Crow era of the state and harbored no ill feelings toward the way things just happened to be. It was who he was and what led him to his calling. He was in his late forties, but had his calling to the church in 1940 in the midst of a great national turmoil that always hit black people harder.

"I know you're planning more, preacher man, and I'm just coming by to remind you that I will always be in the area. Hell, I just might catch my own Dr. King here in East Dallas. What do you say to that?" Rebo said with a threatening smile.

"Well, I'll be mighty proud if you caught me and confused me with the Reverend Dr. Martin Luther King Jr. Lord knows we believe in the same God. But officer, you know we are all God-Fearing and respectable folks. We won't be breaking any rules now."

"You know, if I look long and hard enough, I'll be able to find something that's wrong in this place. I don't think this place comes from hard honest work, and I can look around and find something that is wrong. And you know how I love to find things that are wrong."

"Yes, officer, we all know how much you like to find things that are wrong."

Reverend Robinson stared pleadingly to the officer, who met his stare with an added intensity.

Throughout the exchange Kenneth stood quietly behind Rebo, until he remembered his officer training and begin to look for a threat to his fellow officer. He looked to the first group of people who were huddled to the right of the two men and sized them up. There were four elderly women with Bibles, deep in scripture. The other group nearer the stage sitting adjacent to a rear exit door was five middle-aged black men all in blue-jean overalls, two with trucker ball caps. At first glance it appeared that the men were reading their Bibles in quiet whispers, but with closer observation it was apparent that they were watching the reverend and Rebo intently. While not moving, they were poised with their shoulders hunched and ready for some type of movement. Whether it was to move forward toward the reverend and Rebo or sideways to the exit and freedom was a mystery left undiscovered, because the conversation between the officer and the minister had finally run its course.

Rebo turned and walked briskly out of the church doors, followed by Kenneth with the same pace. Outside the evening came alive with the sounds of a restless community in need of change, but struggling to stay afloat. In the distance there was music and laughter, a few horns blowing, and the general noise of busyness. You could hear people moving, heels of shoes clip-clopping, playful children screaming, a trumpet blaring, and mothers calling out the dinner call. Rebo and Kenneth moved out and into that movement of life with different purposes. This was similar to Chicago for Kenneth, but so different. In Chicago he saw the despair from living on the poverty line from payment to payment, from paycheck to paycheck, from handout to handout. This balanced with the fact that the denizens were living in one of the largest, historically significant cities in North America. Living in Chicago, the city of "Big Shoulders" is a prize in itself. This fact also motivated the young people to grasp whatever opportunities were available, to move out and away for their parent's cultured tameness, and into the rewards and freedoms of the big city. The people of the East Dallas projects were straight from the farms, for the most part, and grateful and somewhat content in their squalor. Kenneth didn't personally know anyone who lived in this area, even though he was familiar with the usual people who showed up on his watch.

On his daytime watch he had known the women who nursed and fed the young children and made sure they didn't run out into the street in front of passing cars. These were the same women who washed the clothes at the local laundromat and hung the clothes out to dry. He didn't know their names or remember them if they told him. It was the same for the second or evening shift. He would see the young women home from work from cleaning one place or another, shopping at the food mart for dinner for their husbands who would be home from one lifting or pulling job or another. He would see those same men stagger back to the brick placements, beaten and exhausted and ready for sleep. And he would see how they would all change on the weekends, on the Friday nights when they could finally unwind and allow some freedom of expression to enter into their demeanor and this is where he and Rebo came in. He had found this out in his training. When the drinking and music starts, the confusion is not far behind.

They rode quickly to the Five and Dime, and by the time that they arrived there the soft veil of night had dropped like the turning of a page from a *Life* magazine, from clean and erectness to slouching and slickness. Rebo liked this stop because it marked the beginning of the night routine. It was where a large number of male residents would come by to do their daily portion of *Pork Rinds* and Falstaff beer.

1968

VII

The Patrol Boys
April 15, 1968
Monday

As the boys turned the corner and walked up the inclined road that led to Bishop Heights Elementary, a slight breeze blew and then picked up in intensity as it flowed down the incline and blew into the faces of the boys as they moved up. It blew clean and fresh and cool. The boys leaned into it as they approached. It blew and Mikey could forget the rain of the night before, but it was always present. It seemed that lately something would always happen new with the weather in April, and all of the nights before could be forgotten. It was the way spring always began with a promised change of scenery and sound and smell. It blew and would blow the flag that the three boys were rushing to run up the school flagpole. To have the patrol boys run up the flag had become a new tradition for the school over the last three years, deriving from support of the Vietnam War efforts and the new patriotic spirit that infused most elementary schools around the state.

It had probably started a long time ago in hometown USA during World War II when all the men were away and only the women and children were left in the neighborhoods, but not much in the black schools. If there were a tradition of boys with the responsibility of running the American flag up the flagpole, it would go unnoticed in the rural and improvised black communities. There was nothing especially noteworthy about the rustic rural sharecropper homes of the South or the congested brick facades of the inner city where most blacks lived during and after the Depression that could personify the American dream. In fact, progress all but stopped during the war, with more concentration on supporting the war effort. But the '60s were different. Now there were black homes and neighborhoods going up, and elementary and secondary schools that reflected the civil rights efforts, the patriotic traditions, and new media services to document the changes.

From the classroom Mikey often thought he could hear the flag as it flapped in the breeze. They were the school patrol boys, the few students in the sixth grade who had a bit of elementary school authority. They wore their yellow waist belts with the shoulder strap crossing their hearts and over their shoulders. The patrol boys would always keep vigil, watch for the elements, and be there to advise the other students. They were the conduits of communication from the principal to the teachers to the students. They became closet weathermen and crossing guards and wondered what elements or inclement weather would affect the raising of the flag—or, for that matter, the school or the student body. They were also in charge of afterschool street and intersection crossings. Since there were only three intersections leading to and from the school, the boys were assigned one each. This was an added responsibility: protecting. Making sure the students crossed the streets safely on their way home. At least, that was what Mikey felt. Although he could acknowledge the responsibility of protecting, he did not recognize his importance in the scheme of things. And this alone gave him the freedom of seriousness and at the same time, a sense of selflessness. He was only doing his part for his community, his state, and his country. He could do no less. History had no real impact on his efforts or demeanor.

The school block was the latest innovation in the newly formed neighborhood. It consisted of the senior high, John F. Kennedy; the middle school, Milton K. Curry; and the elementary school. All the schools were constructed of fine brick and concrete with stunning walkways, cleanly cut grass, and windows that shone in the sun. The senior high school where Mikey's older sister Te'ah attended had a sparkling new and surprisingly competitive sports program, with football and basketball leading the charge. To complement the program, the football team would practice at the school's field but played their home games at the local Bishop College stadium. The basketball team had their own gym and home games were filled to capacity from the growing neighborhoods.

The middle school for grades seven and eight was one huge two-story building with twelve classrooms on the top and eight on the bottom. Both schools had their own cafeteria facility. The elementary school, Bishop Heights, was two parallel gray brick buildings that housed five classrooms on each side and was separated by interior hallways. In turn, the buildings were separated by a concrete walkway that had a big awning that draped over it. The first building housed the first through third grades with three classrooms for each grade, and the second building did the same for the fourth through sixth grades. Behind the second building was the play area, a large grassy area where the boys ran and played football and the girls would play hopscotch and jump rope. There was a combination lunchroom–auditorium connected to the first building, which housed about one hundred and fifty students, and the principal's office. The attendance office was adjacent to it. Facing the street were the front grassy area and the flagpole.

The patrol boys entered the principal's office and retrieved their patrol belts and the American flag. The flag was large for two students, but easy for three. A broad and clean six feet by four feet, stars and stripes that still gleamed from newness by the manufacturer. The boys exited the principal's office and moved out of the building and over to the flagpole. Mr. McIntire, a tall dark-skinned principal from Howard University, had always wanted two boys to handle the flag while the other patrol boy ran the flag up by the rope after the first loop was attached to the hook. After watching Mr. McIntire's example, Mikey tried and mastered all three positions and the other two Michaels followed suit. Initially this became routine and was subject to the whim of the person who had mastered it first to be the leader and decide who would have the choice of positions. This changed quickly, after everyone became familiar with the task, to a fair and more honest rotation. This morning Mikey held the rope and attached the first loop, while Daniels and Washington made sure the flag did not touch the ground.

"This should not just be a job for boys!" said Yolanda. She had quietly moved behind the boys and stood and stared with a scowl.

"Oh boy, just go away Yolanda," said Mikey. "You know you're not supposed to interfere." He liked Yolanda and had known her since the first grade.

"Yeah, interference…pass interference. You're getting too close." Daniels joined in with the football jibes. It was a normal practice for the boys to talk football around the girls when they didn't want them around. It was normal for boys in Texas to mention football as often as possible. It was all around the state and in the air and in the water. And although Mikey loved baseball, he joined in with the football spirit of things. He found a smile that had been hiding.

"And you know you're too skinny to do men's work," said Washington. He looked to Daniels, then look to Yolanda with a big smile. Daniels joined with the smile and they both chimed at the same time. "Bone Girl! Bone Girl, Bone Girl belongs on another world!"

They both smiled and looked to Mikey. He did not return the smile, but tugged on the rope harder and it pulled the flag up without attaching the other loop. Daniels lost his balance and stumbled, almost going down on the grass. He released his end of the flag as he fell away from the group. Washington had to scamper forward to keep both edges off the ground.

"Hey, wait!!" shouted Daniels.

Yolanda laughed a great screaming laugh and walked away to the school entrance. "That's what you get, always trying to hog everything. Oink, oink. I didn't want to do it anyway. I'm glad you're doing it… and you'd better do it right."

Daniels quickly recovered his balance and stood up, making the trio complete, again. This time all three boys shouted, "Bone Girl, Bone Girl, belongs on another world." And then all three laughed and continued their task to completion.

Inside the classroom there was a bustle of energy. The walls were decorated with mathematic equations, various writing samples, and colorful drawings depicting the life in the neighborhood. There were pictures of mothers in their gardens, in rose patches, and under peach and pear trees with babies and lunch baskets; and fathers washing cars, pushing lawn mowers, and trimming hedges and trees. This surrounded the twenty sixth-graders fresh from the weekend who sat in four rows of five desks, and were now talking about some of the events that had happened in the previous three days. There was talk of cartoons and touch football and leftover Easter candy. There was a general exuberance until Mr. Campbell entered the classroom. He had a stocky build and could have easily been a blue-collar worker or even a football player. The boys often debated on the position Mr. Campbell would have played if he did play football. Mikey always argued for running back primarily because it was the most celebrated position for blacks, and Mr. Campbell often complimented him on his own quarterbacking skills in the touch football games that they would play against the other sixth grade classes during recess. Daniels and Washington always countered with lineman; offense or defense did not matter as long as his number was in the fifties. Today Mr. Campbell addressed the class with more-than-usual seriousness.

"Before we get to the spelling exercises, I want to announce that we will have an assembly in the cafeteria before lunch," he said. "Some policemen would like to talk to you about certain things. The assemblies have already started with the younger grades, and since we are the sixth grade we will wait until our time."

"What will the assembly be about, Mr. Campbell?" Yolanda asked quickly, before being acknowledged by the teacher. Her quick mind was always ready to get to the point, whether she was welcomed or not.

"We'll find out when we get there, Ms. Jackson. Now you're going to make me regret telling you if you're going to continue to ask questions that will be answered later. We are old enough now to use patience and good judgment. Isn't that right, class?"

"Yes, Mr. Campbell," was the response in chorus.

Yolanda reluctantly relented but still had a scowl of dissatisfaction on her face. Somewhere she felt that this was another example of where girls weren't important enough to have the information, and she envisioned that the information would be for the boys only. In this she was alone because the other girls in the classroom were considering other things. Jackie Simpson, Patricia Price, Gail Payne, and Barbara Curtis were all easy to manage. These few girls were watchful of how to be a young lady. That included how to dress and sit and bat their eyelashes, and also how to make a request with a soft sweet twinge of a plea in their voices when they were talking to adults and boys. The normal way young girls tested and honed their persuasion skills was on their fathers and grandparents. Yolanda's father was no longer with her. He had divorced and remarried and had started on his other family—with two sons, no less. She had never learned those persuasion skills and had no real use for them. Her way was different.

Yolanda's voice moved from monotone to an octave higher for urgency, and sometimes bordered on a scream depending on the demand. Yolanda's request always appeared to be a demand. This went unnoticed by her. She only felt the need for answers or results, and it didn't matter how she got them at this point in her life. How she could arrive at her quest at this moment was something new, and it was as if it were the first time, she approached the problem that way. With all of her other qualities that abounded—her quick mind, her thirst for intelligence, her strong will to not be ignored again, and her desire to win—her most cherished quality was her short memory for failure. She began to ponder with a smile on her face. Surrounded by her dangling pigtails that she had done by herself, she quickly began to look to her hands. These were the extension of the power in her gender and her people.

In 1968, not many blacks had jobs that did not call for using your hands. All Yolanda knew were teachers and preachers, and they still used hand gestures. For women, there were telephone operators, food servers, and typists, and the men were mechanics, plumbers, construction workers, gardeners, and everything to do with hands. That's why the Black Power sign meant so much, she concluded. Holding up the hand

In a closed fist was an argument for not working with your hands, and was somehow being better than the hand or field workers. Everyone that she saw using the sign didn't work with his or her hands. They were mostly the students from Bishop College, an all-black college down by the 7-Eleven on Simpson Stuart Road in Highland Hills, or by people that frequented the Record Shop at the small group of stores that connected to the grocery store call the E-Z shop. Some others attended the same church that she did.

"Also, after the meeting, the officers would like to meet with the patrol boys. And I will say that you guys are doing a great job. Everyone is commenting about your professionalism," said Mr. Campbell.

"Black Power," shouted Yolanda. She raised her fist in the air with the salute. This stunned the entire class. There was complete silence. Yolanda's girlfriends turned to her with stunned faces. Michael Daniels, sitting away from her and two seats forward, held a tight smirk. He knew something was wrong, but exactly what, he did not know. He only knew that Bone Girl had done it again.

Mr. Campbell stared at Yolanda and held the silence for a beat longer before moving to his desk. Yolanda was not so defiant, but had to appear to be so when she held his stare. She was looking for some type of reaction, whether affirmation or condemnation. Neither was forthcoming from Mr. Campbell. He opened his roll book and began to take attendance. Mikey looked to Yolanda and caught her eye. He nodded in affirmation when he saw a glint of a tear in her eye. He wanted to let her know that she had done nothing wrong.

"Should we wear our patrol belts?" asked Mikey, breaking the silence.

"Yeah! That would be a cool thing," Daniels added.

With the tension broken, the classroom turned back to its usual exuberance until Mr. Campbell tapped his desk with his ruler.

"Okay, let's settle down and prepare for today's spelling test," he said. "And guys, I don't think you will need your belts, because I am introducing you to the officers."

This rest of the day was special. There was a lot of energy lingering from the safety assembly that the entire school had attended in the cafeteria before lunch. When the sixth graders finally arrived, they all sat at their individual lunch tables and received the same basic information from the elementary school principal, Mr. McIntire. He had the same basic position on the stage behind a highly shined brown podium, but it seemed his message was delivered with a more solemn tone. This could be attributed to the dead body that had been found in the trail a few days ago. Although no one mentioned it, it was still a mystery that hung over everybody's heads.

After he finished with his speech, Mr. McIntire introduced the policemen who were newly assigned to the fire station that stood adjacent to the trail. It seemed like it was overnight that now the fire station also served as a police substation with at least two officers on duty at all times. Previously the officers only came to the school for the safety meetings at the beginning of the twenty-week semesters, in August and January. And where they had come from, no one at the school ever wondered or cared. The fact that it was April and the police substation was in the community conversation coming from parents and older teenagers, and the officers were here on the campus now, was something that left a pall of apprehension in the community and the school.

In the pause between speakers, Mikey noticed that everyone reacted as if they were uneasy about what was to follow. One officer, Officer Morton, was older and white, and had brown hair and used darting eyes to look at the students. It seemed that he was looking at every student. He was stocky and looked like he was always holding his breath. The other officer, a young black man, was thin and wore glasses. His name plate that perched above his left breast pocket said *Conway*. His hair was cut short like the fathers in the neighborhood, even though he appeared young enough to be one of the students at Bishop College and could wear the big Afros or naturals or braids like them. Mikey saw this as interesting. The students were told to watch and report any strange person who visited the neighborhood. Everybody nodded in anticipation of the ending to an uneasy assembly, and most could not wait to ask questions to more familiar people in more familiar

In Search of the Rabbit Man

surroundings. But as usual, Yolanda had questions and she made some good points. Her questions were as probing as they were relevant.

"What exactly do you mean by strange, officer?" she asked.

"Morton. My name is Officer Morton and that is a good question. I guess you could say any person that you haven't seen before or you are unsure of. You see, we're trying to make your neighborhood as safe as possible."

"What about the ice cream truck man? I never see the same one twice and no one knows where they come from or where they go," she continued.

"Well, the ice cream man is harmless. He just brings refreshments to you kids. Isn't that correct?" asked Officer Morton. He was trying to reason with the young girl she he used a soft and consoling tone in his voice.

The ice cream man was not affiliated with any company. He was usually a white man, which everyone took as a businessman with a truck that had a large refrigerator unit attached to the back, which kept everything frozen like a freezer. The truck had Popsicles and cone advertisements decorating the sides and prices penciled in below the advertisements.

A smattering of *yeses* and *rights* gradually grew to looks of scorn toward Yolanda. She was undaunted, took her glasses off, and held Officer Morton in her stare. Sitting adjacent to her and two tables down, Daniels tried to get her attention. He wanted her to shut up so the patrol boys could meet the policemen. He felt that she was trying to prolong their moment of their impending adulation. The rest of the students begin to quiet down when they noticed that their stares had no effect on her.

"I don't take ice cream from strangers, but so what? Should we notify you when we see them coming into the neighborhood, so maybe you can check them out?" she asked with a stern voice.

Officer Conway took a step forward. He could see a familiar distress in the young girl's eyes. It wasn't fear. It was more a cold unblinking anger from a place of wisdom and experience. For a moment he remembered that stern look from his elders. The look that was older than the child's years.

"Maybe if you have more questions, you should ask your parents and they could decide if it is okay," said Conway. As soon as he said it, he knew something didn't go the way he had anticipated. It was in the way she smiled…her unexpected smile that told him. He saw just a glint of white teeth and the crinkle in the corners of her lips that told him that more was coming.

"Well, one day we were driving, my uncle was driving me to the new department store in North Dallas and the police stopped us and asked us where we were going and why did we want to go there. I think the same thing should be done to the ice cream truck drivers. No one knows where they come from and some of the trucks are dirty and my uncle's car was very clean and nice and the police stopped us. It should be the same…"

"And this is not the time to bring that up, Ms. Jackson!" Mr. McIntire said this and moved forward beside the officers. It was his intention to stop the debate that Yolanda was leading to. He had been the principal for three years and had witnessed, first hand and second hand from her teachers, the growing impatience in Yolanda's comparisons. He also heard that she liked to argue about civil rights treatment. This came from her fourth-grade teacher Ms. West. It was rumored that Yolanda's commenting on the marches and why there were not any planned in Texas was always a daily topic for discussion. While Mr. McIntire looked stern, Officer Morton was left with a questioning look, as if searching for a more satisfactory answer. Officer Conway stood with a puzzling and distant look that left his face with a bland and vacant expression. Yolanda relented with a smile and placed her hands flat on the table, content with her point. With her back erect, her chin down, and her long hair in pigtails framing both sides of her face, she began to look like a beacon of youth and innocence. It was her victory posture. She could hold that position and not move a muscle and not blink an eye. This was something that she had first practiced at home at the dinner table when her mother grew tired of discussing the points that Yolanda brought up in their talks. Her mother could never stay angry with her when she would take this posture. She perfected it in the classroom when she defeated the boys in flash cards for mathematics or state capitals or any other contest of memory. At first, it would be a cause for alarm but later as her classmates became used to it, they would expect it when she felt she had won at something. Some would try to ignore. Washington would become intimidated and shy away. Daniels would become angry and usually try to distract her. Mikey admired it. Then she placed her glasses back on the tip of her nose and before her eyes and it was over.

The officers exhaled and concluded the safety presentation without any further interruptions, and every other class except Mr. Campbell's class returned to their classrooms. While his sixth graders remained patiently at their lunch tables, Mr. Campbell beckoned the patrol boys to walk with him to the stage where the officers and principal stood.

"Okay, that is the last of them," said Mr. McIntire. "I guess everything went well. I want to thank you for coming to our school at this time. I didn't think there was a call for alarm and you officers handled it nicely. I don't think anyone should be nervous about anything now." He moved to shake the hands of the officers in turn.

"This is a nice school and very quiet. These schools are really getting better now," said Morton. "I like the way you have them under control. Do you live around here?"

"No, I don't. I am from Chicago, so this is a change for me as well. Here comes the teacher I was telling you about. Mr. Campbell, this is Officer Morton."

Mr. Campbell walked up with the patrol boys following. He shook the hands of both officers. "Good to meet you, and these are the patrol boys for this year."

The patrol boys smiled with pride. Daniels was especially impressed with the shiny shoes and badges, and the highly pressed dark blue trousers and shirts. Mikey noticed the handguns. He admired weapons of all makes. His uncle in Tyler, Texas had a beautiful Remington shot gun and a cowboy-type Winchester rifle. He couldn't wait until next

Christmas when he would be closer to thirteen and receive his first B.B. gun. But these was handguns. Both officers had slick black pistols with brown handgrips placed tightly in black holsters and wrapped just as tightly around their waists. Up close, the matching creases in the trousers and shirts that traced down from shoulder to shoe and the striking black leather waist belts with handcuffs on the opposite side of the holsters and the snug belt buckles gave the uniform the appearance of animated royalty. No matter how close you stood to the officers, if they didn't move, they didn't seem real. They appeared as immobile mannequins with the posture and indecipherable breaths to match. They seemed so unreal, Mikey thought. Did they feel? Did they have family?

"So, what exactly is their function on the campus?" asked Morton. He addressed the question to Mr. McIntire, who in turn gave way to Mr. Campbell.

Mr. Campbell beamed with pride. It wasn't often that he got a chance to reveal something of importance in front of the principal. It was just a matter of respect. After all, regardless of their different origins, neither was from Texas. One was from the North and one was from the South, and they both shared the love of teaching. And Mr. Campbell was helping. The patrol boys were his idea. It had fumbled at first, three years ago, but this group was good. Mr. Campbell had hopes for the program. The patrol boys were the way to show responsibility and dispel the rumors and negative generalizations of a black township of lazy, dumb, and ignorant individuals, not knowing how to take care of themselves, and never getting better. These were the generalizations that he was tired of hearing in his home town the proud city of Mobile, Alabama. That's why he moved to Texas, to dispel the rumors in the land of opportunity and change, for a man with ideas.

"They are the reminders of safety on the campus," said Mr. Campbell. "If anything is necessary for safety and these young men see it, they can try to resolve it or bring it to a teacher's attention."

"When you say safety, you mean hanging on the monkey bars too long or maybe pushing the merry-go-round too fast?"

"No, Officer Morton, sir. I mean after-school safety..."

In Search of the Rabbit Man

"Officer Morton, I can give you a list of their responsibilities, if it's that important," said Mr. McIntire.

"We'll need a list of a lot of things at the substation, but it is best if we got it from the people responsible. We are just trying to keep everybody safe, and if that means knowing everything about everything in this and the adjoining neighborhoods, then we will know."

"We are not the ones who are hiding things," said Mr. Campbell, a little too fast. "This school and the parents that live in the area are doing what they can to make this a good place to learn. Our record proves that the right things are happening."

Morton looked to Mr. Campbell for a beat while Mr. McIntire began to take a step closer. McIntire didn't know what was going on, but he felt his input should have ended the inquiry.

"Do you live in the neighborhood, Mr. Campbell?" asked Officer Morton. He could see just over the heads of Campbell and the patrol boys. The young girl with all the questions stood and began to move to the stage.

Yolanda wondered what was taking so long. She thought it would be a couple of handshakes; maybe the patrol boys would get honorary badges or medals. That would just be too much to endure. Daniels would be so happy. Washington never did anything anyway. Mikey helped everyone cross the street by walking out in the crosswalk with the stop sign. The cars were at the official stop sign anyway. These were just parents coming to pick up the little kids and the kids who lived too far away to walk. How hard could the job be? This was talking too long. Yolanda stood and began to move to the stage. She felt she was right again.

"No, I don't live in the neighborhood, but I am looking to move in when the new residences are completed," said Mr. Campbell.

"Well, when you do you will see the list we will have collected. We plan to get to know every parent in the surrounding neighborhoods, and yes, we plan to talk to the mobile ice cream vendors in the areas and make sure everything is legal in that respect." Morton smiled for the first time and looked directly at the approaching young girl.

83

JON-MICHAEL HAMILTON

The patrol boys, Mr. Campbell, and Mr. McIntire turned and watched as Yolanda walked up. Daniels thought, *Oh boy, here comes Bone Girl again*, and Bone Girl stopped in midstride when she heard Officer Morton's pronouncement. She turned and walked away with a swing of the pigtails and a brief smile. She knew then that it was okay to go back to the classroom.

VIII

The Grasslands
April 17, 1968
Wednesday

The best time of the day was the after-lunch recess. Even with the sky overcast, the day would be good. This was the time when the Bishop Heights elementary students got a chance to exert all of the energy that they had stored away while reading and writing and doing math calculations to running and laughing and playing. Mikey and the rest of the patrol boys would get their class together and play touch football against Mr. Robinson's sixth grade class. This was sometimes the combined members of the remaining two sixth grade classes because there were always only three classes and it made the competition more competitive, more Texas. Even together the other sixth grade classes were not an intellectual and therefore not a physical match for Mr. Campbell's class. Led by their daring quarterback, Mikey, and the other two patrol boys assisting with blocking, catching, and running, the games became more frustration for some and affirmation for others. The games were played without much fanfare or observation, until frustration overcame the other team and roughhousing ensued. That's when Mr. Campbell would tap the glass of his classroom window or Mr. Robinson, providing supervision on the grounds, would blow his whistle and the opposing team—led by Ronnie Stringer—would either back down or issue the challenge to move to another location for a game of unsupervised tackle football. Tackle football was something that was strictly forbidden by the principal, and this was reinforced by the teachers and echoed by the parents. After all, clean clothes were a priority at the school.

The game started the usual way, with Mr. Campbell's class throwing the ball off to the Robinson/Ronnie Stringer team. Throwing the ball made it a lot easier to control the direction, as opposed to kicking the ball as the normal starting or after-touchdown kickoff required. Once the ball was kicked atop the sixth-grade building by Marvin Gooden, another of Mr. Campbell's brainy students. Thinking was his specialty because he was so enamored with Mr. Spock of the television series *Star Trek*. Marvin was always reading his dictionary, or any dictionary available, in his spare time and on study time in the classroom in order to build his ever-enlarging vocabulary. Whenever there was a classroom opportunity to recite or make speeches, or even to respond with his opinion, he would try his best to use one of his newly discovered words. This was a good thing that the guys acknowledged, but even though he was tall for his age the only bad thing for Marvin was that he was so uncoordinated. In simple things like using his reflexes in games of speed or reacting to flash-card games he was just average, and below some of the girls. Then when it came to football his status diminished even more, because running, catching, or even covering a receiver was hard for him. When the class played the game, his job was usually centering the ball to the quarterback for the team and maybe moving into the way of oncoming rushers. With that he made the most of the opportunity and felt the kinship and camaraderie of the team. And Mikey liked him best because he could play chess. No one in the sixth grade played chess except Marvin and Mikey. Others tried to learn, but Marvin would beat them so badly and it made Mikey want to beat them the same way, so they were the only ones left. And Mikey always beat Marvin.

It was a disadvantage for Ronnie Stringer's team to play against Mr. Campbell's class because Mikey could throw the ball farther than anyone in the sixth grade. And he was usually protected and sought after for that reason. He could linger back and away from the action and watch and throw touchdowns just like Dandy Don. That could be the end of it if he wanted it that way, but he really liked to do his part. He tried to throw the ball to everybody on the team, even the guy who hiked the ball, and everyone liked that about him. On the kickoff he would throw the ball high and rush down and usually would be the first man down to make the touch below the belt on the opposing runner. This time Mikey threw the ball high while his team rushed down to touch the runner. There were feint moves and push blocks and shoves and finally the runner was subdued about five yards from where he caught the ball. This was how the game began.

While the boys played their stupid game, the girls would sometimes watch, but mostly they would move off to the side and talk about hair and things and pretend to be adults. Sometimes Yolanda led the group. Today, while still reveling in her quiet victory at the assembly, Jackie Simpson, Patrice Price, and Gail Payne followed behind her as she walked, talking about a new song. The girls began to walk toward their favorite tree. They were busy talking, and all faced each other with Patrice and Gail leading.

Jackie Simpson was the shy one. She was shorter, with dark brown skin and even darker hair. Her mother always decorated her hair with red bows and pink barrettes at the ends of six small tufts of hair—two on the top, two on the sides, and two in the back—that were carefully twisted after brushing. It made her eyebrows seemed to be pulled back and gave her entire face an upward appearance. She wore the same knee-length dresses or skirts that the others wore, and they all had either loafers or black-and-white saddle shoes. Gail was taller with lighter skin and a fluffy ponytail adorned with a blue ribbon. Patricia was more of a heavyset youngster, with long braids that streamed down the sides of her head. She was the most outgoing and prettiest of the girls, with thick eyebrows, long lashes, and full pouting lips.

"I can't wait until seventh grade. My mom said she might let me wear an Afro," said Patricia.

"And maybe a miniskirt too, huh?" asked Jackie in disbelief.

Patricia laughed and placed one hand on her hip. She started to rock to a silent tune. Around the school there were streets lined with homes, but in the recess area and behind the school there was undeveloped land where large trees and high grass and a bubbling creek were located that ran behind the high school practice field all the way to the community park two miles away. The girls continued walking toward the trees.

"Why do you care so much about what the boys do, Yolanda? It makes them think that we care about the and that. they are better than us," said Gail.

"They would think that anyway, so it only means that we let them know that they are wrong. We should be able to do anything that they do," said Yolanda.

"That's why she wins all the spelling and flash-card tests."

"But she just started winning after Valentine's Day. I think it's because she didn't get the right person to give her a Valentine's card," said Gail. She smiled and then the other two girls smiled in turn. Yolanda did not smile, but tilted her head and rolled her eyes at Gail. She took a deep breath and then frowned.

"What is that rotten smell?" she asked.

"Yeah! Something really smells like bad meat!"

The girls looked around as if noticing the smell for the first time and now realizing it made it overbearing. Gail was standing closest to the tree but with her back to it. She sniffed in the air and walked closer to the tree as if following her nose. She got to the tree, then leaned and peered around behind it. Then she jumped back and screamed a loud, skin-curling scream and ran toward the buildings. With her jump, Jackie jumped also and screamed as well and followed. Patricia ran to catch them and screamed also.

"A body! A body! A body by the tree!" screamed Gail. Jackie and Patricia joined in with the screams. Yolanda stayed longer and took a look around the tree. Abruptly she turned and ran as well.

The girls ran back to the buildings, with three of them screaming loudly. Mr. Robinson heard the screaming and turned toward it while blowing his whistle for the girls to stop running. He thought this was another one of the running games that the girls played for entertainment. The only running on the campus was for football or kickball, and this didn't look like kickball. He continued to blow his whistle until the leading girl, Gail, came abreast of him. He saw the fear and tears in her eyes and thought better about stopping her. He looked to Mr. Campbell's window and saw that he was now aware of the excitement. With the moment of eye contact made and understood, Mr. Robinson allowed the girls to pass him and go on into the building.

The entire playground had stopped moving. The football game stopped. The jungle gym stopped. The hopscotch game stopped. The double Dutch rope jumping stopped. Everyone looked around for guidance. The words that resonated the most were, "a body," which translated to another body and the unresolved fears and suspicions of weeks before.

Finally, what seemed like an eternity but was really three minutes later, Mr. Campbell walked from the building and signaled with his hand to Mr. Robinson. Then Mr. Robinson blew his whistle one long blast and beckoned with his hands to the students. The recess period was now officially over and everybody began moving back into the classroom. There were some groans from the students at the jungle gym, and a few from the football players, but the rest of the students were overcome with curiosity and a twinge of fear. A few had lingering stares out to the tree where the young girls were running from, and that's when they noticed Yolanda walking briskly from the area.

"Look at Bone Girl take her sweet time about everything," said Washington. He was a little upset about the shortened recess and took his disappointment out on his favorite topic of criticism. He was promised a touchdown catch today from Mikey, and this had interfered with his plans. "I knew she had something to do with this."

"Yeah, well, how can she have anything to do with a body?" asked Mikey. "Let's just go into the classroom and find out what really happened."

"This was my day. You promised me my day, Mikey. She always seems to be in the middle of something good for us."

"Let's just go."

The patrol boys led the way back into the classroom. The other students followed close behind. No one was talking. The air around the school felt heavy with gloom as a large cloud floated silently and obscured the sun.

Inside the classroom, Jackie and Patricia sat quietly. Gail was missing. Mr. Campbell stood by the door and allowed everyone to enter.

"Please, everybody sit down quietly," he said. "Don't ask any questions."

After everyone entered, Mr. Campbell closed the door. Everyone sat in their assigned seats and faced the front of the classroom in silence. Washington wanted to ask the question, any question that would break the silence. Why was the recess cut short? Why does everything happen when it's his time to have something? He had lost his dog and it was his fault. Everybody in his family said that it was his fault...

Abruptly, the door opened with a creak and Yolanda entered the classroom with a stoic expression and straight posture. She wasn't even out of breath. She moved to her seat and slowly sat down. All eyes watched her. Daniels began to get angry. He felt that every time something happened and she was there, she would be the center of attention. She had a way of changing everything around.

"Mr. Campbell, I've found out what is going on. I know what it was that Gail saw."

"How do you know?" asked Washington. He said this with a twinge of anger in his voice that he could not hide.

"I'm sorry, Michael. But someone is going to tell you this sooner or later." Yolanda's voice grew strangely soft. No one had ever heard her talk this way to Washington. This captured everyone's attention more than the preceding events. Yolanda had just been almost nice to Michael Washington, and that was something new and somewhat alarming. Washington heard this and recoiled. He could sense something wasn't right, and maybe Yolanda would strike him or try another way to cause embarrassment for him.

"Okay, let's settle down, young lady. There is no reason to cause any more suspense today." Mr. Campbell could sense that something was askew as well.

"Where is Gail?" asked Jackie. She looked up from her embrace with Patrice for the first time. Both girls had been crying, but more for their friend than for something that had directly happened to them. Neither boy had looked around the tree.

"Someone should go out there and confirm the identity of the body," said Marvin Gooden. He had thought about this ever since the recess had been called short, and it was a chance to use his new vocabulary words. "It is the logical thing to do."

"Let's not jump to any conclusions," said Mr. Campbell. "Mr. McIntire has been notified and is doing what is necessary. I'm sure he will let us know what we should do."

"There is nothing to do. It is not a person's body. It's a dog's body," said Yolanda. After first looking to Mr. Campbell, she looked to Michael Washington.

"It's something you should know, Michael…"

"Both of you…come up to the desk," Mr. Campbell said. "Yolanda, if this is another one of your shenanigans, then an apology is going to be necessary and that will be for the entire class."

Rising from her desk, Yolanda said, "This is not a joke. It's not a person's body. It's a dog. It looks like Michael Washington's dog, Tippy." She walked to Mr. Campbell, and for the first time today looked like a sullen little girl. Gone was the arrogance and pride of being right all the time; it was replaced by a genuine expression of empathy. Mr. Campbell knew at that moment that she was telling the truth.

"How does she know for sure?" Washington cried out. He stood, and instead of walking to Mr. Campbell's desk, he bolted out of the door and down the hallway. He was making his way outside when Mikey and Michael Daniels stood and began to follow him.

"Boys, come back! Sit down! Everybody stay in your seats!" Mr. Campbell said and then moved out into the hallway and after the patrol boys.

Even if he wasn't the fastest runner in the sixth grade, Washington kept moving at a faster pace than the rest of the boys. It was hard for the other two patrol boys to gain any ground. He would get there first and he knew that. He wanted to get there first to confirm his worst fears. After being accused of leaving the backyard gate open and the garage door open, when Tippy never returned for dinner he could only dream of the worst possible thing to happen. And it would all be his fault. He knew he left the garage door open just a tiny crack to give Tippy some fresh air, and if Tippy did go out in the yard for his business he would have returned. He did not remember if the backyard gate was open or not, but he knew he didn't open it—yet there it was on the morning of Tippy's leaving, wide open. He couldn't argue with his parents because his father was busy working at night and his mother was always angry from the prank phone calls that she received at night. And she was always so angry with him after it happened, he would spend more time in the quiet of the garage with Tippy, his best friend. This could not be his dog like ugly Bone Girl had said. He ran faster.

Mikey turned the corner from the building and rushed out behind Washington. He could see him making good time running to the tree. Mikey began to run faster. He wanted to get to the tree before Washington. He knew some of the turmoil that Washington was going through with his family; after all, best friends talk to each other. He knew about the distance that existed between Washington and his father. He rationalized to Washington that it was the distance to his job and all the working at night and his sometimes being too tired to come home at night. It was the second job and the nature of the hotel business. Sometimes Washington would cry in anger about his mother's way of projecting her sadness toward him. How she wanted him around always. How she always wanted to know where he was every moment of the day or night. How he felt so alone with only the patrol boys and Tippy to keep him company. Mikey ran faster because he wanted to get there before Washington.

Michael Washington finally reached the tree and abruptly slowed to a timid walk. After the urgency he became hesitant, as if he were avoiding the discovery, and it was now like walking through broken glass. There was sweat on his face that ran from his forehead to his cheeks and mixed with the tears that dripped down his face in dirty streaks. His heart began to slow and his breaths became slower with each advancing step. When he reached the base of the tree he moved around to the back and out of sight.

Mr. Campbell trailed both students and tried to increase his pace as best he could. If anyone were watching his actions it would quell the argument of whether Mr. Campbell could play running back or lineman. He trudged forward and began to realize that he had on the wrong shoes for this type of activity. There were dips in the ground that, when covered with grass, would mislead the first-time traveler. Mr. Campbell quickly found his spontaneity a disadvantage. To his benefit, his slow pace made it possible for the custodian, Mr. Jordan, to catch up with him. Mr. Jordan was carrying a shovel in one hand and a medium-sized box in the other.

"You better slow down, Herman. You're going to fall in one of dem holes," said Jordan. His movements were awkward because of all of the materials he was carrying.

"Hurry up, man. I've got to get there before that kid."

"It's too late for that now. He's a' ready to the tree. This makes the second such critter I'm gonna have to scoop up in the last month."

"How do you know it's a critter? I didn't hear anything about any critters! When did that happen?"

"Maybe you'd better ask the principal, and if this keeps going on maybe you could ask him to tell the grass cutters to do this stuff. This has nothing to do with mopping and cleaning."

Mr. Campbell didn't listen. He began to tune Jordan out and concentrate on the two boys who were up ahead. He saw Michael Washington slow down, walk, and then finally vanish. At the same time, he saw Mikey slow down as well. Mr. Campbell began to increase his walk almost to a trot.

"Wait boys...Wait...Don't go there!!" Campbell shouted. But no one listened.

Mikey saw Washington vanish behind the tree trunk and immediately begin to slow down. He felt a dread in his stomach and somehow felt that the silence that surrounded the moment was normal. He didn't consider that his walking added to the silence or how anticipation blocked out everything. He hoped to see Washington return from the mystery with a smile and a sigh of relief. He walked closer and could hear for the first time the soft crying that now crept into the silence, and then the other sounds of cars passing, Mr. Campbell shouting, and then louder sobs and crying. Mikey slowed to a walk now, and with each step he took he knew it would take him to his friend's sadness. It was obvious now that the animal was Tippy, the happy bumbling little gray-and-white terrier that was Washington's most loyal friend. Why else would he be reacting this way?

Washington finally appeared from behind the tree trunk. He was slumped over and his face was haggard and streaming with tears and sweat. He walked stiffed legged, almost robotic and slow. His pants were sagging and covered with mud from last night's showers and the beginnings of red droplets that began to stream down his front pockets. His shirt was wet from sweat, and now a smear of blood showed above his belt buckle. In his arms he carried the small terrier whose eyes were still open and looking up to the overcast sky. The dog still looked playful, but there was noticeable blood tracing down the middle of its ribs and stomach. Mikey stopped and tried to make eye contact with Washington, but his eyes stared out toward the school building and remained unblinking as if he were in a daze. Mikey begin to tear up as well, but gained control when he heard Mr. Campbell and Mr. Jordan approaching.

"Son, put the animal down!" ordered Mr. Campbell. He was thinking of a parent's reaction from a child coming home with bloody clothes. The longer the child held the animal, the more there was a chance that blood would flow down to his clothing.

Dropping the shovel, Mr. Jordan came up from behind with the box in both hands at waist level. He moved toward the child in a slow but steady pace.

"Just bring him to me, son...Just bring him here so we can rest... Just keep walking so we can rest..."

Mr. Jordan continued walking forward and now pointed the open end of the box toward the child. The closer he moved, the softer he talked. Washington continued to walk forward and stared out in a daze to the building. He followed Mr. Jordan's voice as if he was in a dark cavern and now approaching light. He held the dog loosely now, and the closer he moved to Mr. Jordan the closer Mr. Jordan moved the box underneath the animal. Finally, Washington reached Mr. Jordan with the dead animal still in his arms. Mr. Jordan moved the box completely underneath the animal and then began to lift the box up and under the child's arms.

"Just let it rest son…Just let it rest…Its okay, just let it rest."

Mikey and Mr. Campbell watched as Washington removed his arms from the box and released the animal. He let his arms drop down to his sides and continued to stare at the building, and now past the building to the sky.

Mr. Campbell put his arm around Washington as Mikey and Michael Daniels walked behind them back to the building and the classroom. Mr. Campbell would take Washington to the principal's office and then make arrangements for him to go home.

Mr. Jordan was walking slower. He was looking around for some sign of how the animal could have been dropped off near the schoolyard. He saw pieces of a green bandana caught in some of the grass leading out to the street.

IX

Hercules McElroy
April 19, 1968
Friday

The days began to pass quietly and quickly. For Mikey it was a blur, starting when Washington vanished from school. He was missed in the classroom with his quick smile and just as quick temper, his constant struggle against Yolanda, the Bone Girl, his energy and enthusiasm on the football playground, and his steadiness as a patrol boy. Mikey went home on the first day that Washington missed and his mother said that he needed rest. He was not allowed to see Daniels either. Mikey told his mother what happened and she purchased a card for the students to sign and to give to Washington. Mikey did so and brought it to Washington's home the next day, and Washington's mother accepted it but did not give out any more information.

Everybody looked at the death of the little dog differently. Mikey's mother said the world was coming to an end. She said all the signs were there, starting with the Vietnam War and the terrible pictures that were shown on television. And then there were the assassinations of JFK and MLK. She had always said in the past that the television was the devil's machine, but she would still look at selected programs because she wanted to know what the devil was doing. She said it was not right to show everybody the violence of the war as well as the civil rights struggle, and it would lead to people trying to do the same thing on both sides and probably at the same time. She felt that some people were supposed to do certain things and some people were supposed to do other things, but not at the same time. She would often wonder aloud what would happen if the devil's thing and the Lord's thing happened at the same time and if it does, then that is when the world is gonna end. Just like Revelation says.

"Never in my lifetime has anybody been able to stand up for black people and it is just not right...it's in the Bible with Moses and Pharaoh. It is not right. The world is coming to an end..."

Then she would go and play the family piano for as long as she could. Mikey would like it for a while, but he and his sister found other things to do on these times and she would continue. Mikey told her about Washington and it was not a good time, those thirty minutes when she preaches and then predicted the future. "I'm really sorry, baby, but the world is coming to an end."

She had good reason to believe this. Her world and education were limited to the barren scrapings of a rural childhood. Her small town was really uncouth and country, as the city saying went when she was trying for her jobs in the city. The Bible had a big impact on her life. She dropped out of school in the sixth grade and married Mikey's father, but still wanted to read. So, she read the Bible and played the piano, and worked and raised her children and watched. It helped to some extent that Big Teddy, who was three years older, was the son of a preacher, even if he was the opposite of one.

Mr. Campbell chimed in with Yolanda's theme of loss by saying, "Everything that lives will die, eventually. Michael Washington will get over it..."

"Who will take Washington's place on the Patrol Boys?" asked Marvin Gooden. "Someone will have to do it until he feels better, and I volunteer myself."

"Why do the patrol boys have to be boys? Why can't they be girls? I'll bet everywhere else in the world the patrol boys are called patrol people." It was Yolanda speaking, of course.

"Yeah, Mr. Campbell there is such a thing as meter maids."

And that's how it went on the days that followed, the quiet dog Tippy, and the mysterious death. The dog was found to have had a large gash from its throat down to its stomach, which no one could explain. And no one had any explanation how the dog could wander five blocks away from home for the first and last time of its tiny precious life.

The evenings were filled with forecasts of doom and destruction for the whole world with the downfall of America, and Mikey tried to fill the nights with plans and hypotheticals of helping his mother and his friends solve their problems. That is what he felt he was: a problem solver. He was a person who could help and use his abilities for their best use. He had done so in the past. He had helped his mother with finding her father's shoes and socks. He had helped his father with lawn care and grooming. He had done his part with reducing the insect population around his home with his capture and collection efforts. He had helped out at the school with the patrol boys and leading the sports and academic teams. He had done his part. Only now did he feel useless. For the first time he felt the emptiness of being unable to help Washington or his mother or his community with their pain or fears.

On the third day Washington came back to school sullen, withdrawn and with very little to say. Mr. Campbell didn't push him with questions or ask for his missing assignments, and talked softly when he was near him or had to address him. Even Yolanda was hesitant with her interactions toward Washington for the most part, but that was in the morning sessions. When it came to flash cards her zeal returned and she won hands down over Mikey. Marvin Gooden had taken over Washington patrol detail while he was out. Marvin was energized until Washington came back and then he experienced the first contradictory emotions of his life. Would he argue to retain his newfound position or willingly relinquish it to Washington upon his return? Should he give in and offer the position to Washington, or wait until he was told to? If he kept the position of patrol boy, how happy should he feel about it? Prior to this quandary his life of twelve years had been more or less decision-free. His clothes were prepared by his mother, his transportation to school provided by his father. The school provided his meals. Mr. Campbell provided his assignments and invariably his likes and dislikes. And his position on the football team was given to him by Mikey. Gratefully, Mr. Campbell provided the solution and announced it to the entire class.

"Until, Mr. Washington feels better about things, Mr. Gooden will be a new member of the patrol boys and assume all of the responsibilities."

"Why can't a girl be the replacement?" said Yolanda. She said it more to get a reaction from Washington. There was a long beat and then Washington looked down to his hands that were on his desk.

"It's too dangerous for girls," said Michael Daniels, seizing upon the moment that Washington had missed. And then it was over, that moment, that chance to regain normalcy again.

On the night of the third day Mikey decided to take vigilance on the neighborhood. He waited until everyone was sound asleep, and then he crept out of his bedroom and moved to the dining room. He could hear the snoring of his parents in room farthest away from the dining room. The deep throaty snores of his father and the high wine of his mother were easy to determine, so he knew they were fast asleep moving toward the eleven o'clock hour. His sisters were a different story altogether. He gave a slight self-reprimand because he forgot to check all the sounds in the hallway and had to return to their closed door to listen. His sisters slept soundly, with the only indication being the steady breaths that he heard muffled through the door. Satisfied with his secrecy, Mikey moved past the dining room and out the back door as quietly as possible. His destination was the ledge in the back of the house adjacent to the backyard. He would take his position and give vigilance to the night. He needed this time to reflect on his emotions. He could not shake the feeling of helplessness and wondered what could be done.

* * * *

On the fourth day, Washington was closer to his former self than in past days. In class he found his voice on the occasion when Yolanda, who continued to pick at the Patrol Boys, found a streak of arguments from boys' sports to boys' cars and carried the classroom discussion with zeal and vehemence. Daniels quickly rebuffed her points with the usual labeling and rhyme and Washington joined for the first time in what seem like a long time.

"Bone Girl, Bone Girl...comes from another world."

There was a hushed silence and then a nervous applause. Even Yolanda smiled briefly and then resumed her argument. Mr. Campbell had to stop the discussion and move the class lesson to the topics that were prescribed.

When Mikey returned home from school, he felt happy for the first time in days. His happiness stemmed from Washington's return to the touch football team on recess and his gradual unwinding from the previous days' events. Mikey still felt a sense of helplessness from his inability to actively alleviate the tension and pain that surrounded him.

Mikey stepped outside and began to walk aimlessly around in the front yard, nonchalantly looking at the bank of rosebushes that traced the front facade of the home. This was the place where he would find insects and hummingbirds and other seasonal life that shared his family's space. In the distance from Silverhill, the next street over, Mikey heard the faint sounds of music. Although early, it could only be the ice cream man's truck. The usual time was closer to five o'clock when the parents were home and could pass money to the children.

Mikey discarded the thought of purchasing ice cream from the ice cream man, but quickly reflected back to the assembly of last week. Yolanda had asked the policemen what could be done about the strangers in the neighborhood. He wondered where Bone Girl was, anyway, and if she heard the music that was now getting louder and coming closer. Would Bone Girl take this opportunity to prove her point about the disparity in the police interest? Sometimes Bone Girl was a real problem, but sometimes she was irreplaceable, he thought. He smiled because he knew he would never tell her that in front of the guys, but maybe he could compliment her in another way. He would stop and investigate the ice cream man and tell the guys later. He knew she would hear about it and hold her head upright with her pigtails drooping down and just savor the moment. That was the way she had done things in the past. He would wait until the truck came around the corner and stop it and investigate the driver. It would be his first step in helping in the neighborhood.

The sound grew louder from around the next street. Mikey could make it out now, so the truck must have turned on his street, La Grange Drive. He heard music and a speech. This must be a new type of ice cream truck. The words were probably the types of bars or cones that the truck was selling. The words became clearer now.

"He walks…He talks…He can stand on his head like a spinning top…He's incredible…He's superhuman…He's unbelievable…He can put his finger in the ground and stop the world…"

The music was a strange instrumental number that sounded familiar to Mikey, but he couldn't place when he had heard it before. He remembered the music from the radio and the music from church, but this wasn't from neither of those. He remembered the music from *Popeye the Sailor* and it sounded closer to that than anything, but even that wasn't a 100 percent match. It wasn't *Underdog*, or *Mighty Mouse*, or *Star Trek*, but it was familiar.

The music came around the corner and rolled downhill toward Mikey's home, and he could see its source for the first time. It wasn't a truck at all. It was a white convertible with two black men in the front seats, two more black men walking on the sides by the doors, and then one man sitting in the back but not in the seats. He was sitting atop the seats and on the trunk. For a moment it looked like the news report of the president when he had ridden through downtown on that fearful day when the whole neighborhood cried. That day was different from the day that Dr. King was killed. People became angry that day. On the day of the president's death everyone cried, if not aloud, then just a little.

Mikey watched in awe as the big white convertible rolled alongside his home with the music blaring just as loudly. The men who stood by the doors were younger men dressed in black pants with black leather jackets and had on black berets and dark shades. They continued their chant. The man driving the car was an older man and had on a white suit with white gloves and dark shades also. The man on the backseat was young, probably the youngest. He was maybe twenty years old with light skin, curly hair, and a curvy smile. He had on blue jeans and a red T-shirt that was cut around the shoulders and stomach, revealing taut muscles and a named tattoo. The name on the tattoo said *Hercules.*

"He walks…He talks…He can stand on his head like a spinning top…He's incredible…He's superhuman….He's unbelievable…He can put his finger in the ground and turn the world upside down…Hercules McElroy…Hercules McElroy…Hercules McElroy…He is the first and only black hero…"

The car stopped. The chant continued. The men on the sides started a little dance and then stopped abruptly. Then the music stopped and there was silence, except for dogs barking. From somewhere, a baby cried.

Mikey walked closer to the car. At closer inspection he could see that it was not as clean as he had thought it was. The tires were a dingy gray from traveling on highways and back roads and fields. The underbody of the car was smudged with mud and grass and some dried blood from an animal that hadn't moved very quickly.

"What's up, little man? I bet you're wondering what brings us here. Let me introduce myself. My name is the one and only Sam Smooth and this here in the backseat is the one and only Hercules McElroy." From the driver's seat, Sam Smooth spoke quickly, almost sing-song-like, and had a gleam in his eyes that shone underneath his shades. "Hercules is the greatest hero in the world, and Hercules McElroy is his distant offspring. I guess you don't believe me. I guess you think it is unbelievable. I guess you might think he is darker than the television Hercules. Well, let me tell you, little man, Hercules was a Greek with tanned skin and curly hair—as you can see, Hercules McElroy has curly hair. But you still don't believe me. Hercules, show him."

Hercules McElroy stood up on the backseat of the car and began to stretch his arms up high above his head. After a few attempts to reach up to the sky he spread his arms out horizontally and stretched until one hand almost reached the front window and the other hand reached almost to the edge of the trunk. Mikey had never seen a person with such arm length. Hercules McElroy was six feet four inches with muscles, and when he stretched his arms and retracted them, he made his muscles in his arms, chest, back, and neck pop and pulse with exaggerated sheen. He looked like an average guy but bigger, and when he stretched, he became larger, as if a mythical giant was growing right before his eyes.

Other people were coming out of their homes. From up in the circle, Ronald Turner, a sophomore at the high school, must have heard the music and started walking down to the car with his classmate Jarvis Walker. Two homes to the left of Mikey's home lived Mr. Freeman Adams and his wife. Mr. Adams worked at night at the postal service, so when Mikey had heard the music, he must have heard it as well. He came out of his front door and stood in his driveway with his car behind him. He gazed out as well.

"What's up, Cool Cat?" shouted Mr. Adams. This was the name he had given to Mikey when Mikey and the other patrol boys rode their bikes down the street and into La Grange Circle. The street circle jutted away in an oblique to a patch of homes that encircled the widening street. Mikey didn't answer, but only looked to the face of Hercules McElroy.

By that time Mr. Adams had walked up from his home and stood in the street with the other onlookers. Mikey moved closer and watched the face of Hercules McElroy, and saw for the first time the strange look on his face. It was then that he didn't look so young. He looked much older, maybe thirty. It was when the high school kids started doubting him that his face changed. All of a sudden, he looked kind of sad.

Other onlookers were gathering around, so Sam Smooth opened the car door and exited out into the street. Now standing everyone could see his full white suit glistening in the sun.

"Now watch what he can do," said Sam Smooth. He took out a small box of double-edged razor blades and plucked one out. "Hercules McElroy will now show you what no man will show you. He will show you how tough he is on the inside."

Sam Smooth took the razor blade and placed it in Hercules McElroy's hand. Hercules closed his hand on the blade and took two large breaths, then three large breaths. He moved two fingers to his mouth, placing the razor blade into it. He began to chew, making crunching sounds first and then more fluid motions, as if it were meatballs or a small sandwich in his mouth. He chewed steadily for about a minute and then stopped.

"He didn't chew that," shouted Turner.

"It's still in his hand somewhere," shouted Walker.

"If you don't think he hasn't chewed the razor, then you don't know Hercules McElroy. We have been all over the country with people not knowing him when we drive up, but when we leave, everybody knows his name. This place is so new and off in the boonies that no one has heard of anything here." Sam Smooth said this and then directed his comments to Mr. Adams. "You are older than these young kids; have you heard of Hercules McElroy?"

"No, I can't say that I have."

"Do you want to bet on what Hercules can and can't do?"

"That would be a dumb bet."

"I say he didn't chew that," said Turner. "I'll bet the three dollars."

"Yeah," said Walker. "I'll bet my money too." He began counting a dollar, a few quarters, some nickels and dimes and pennies. "I have a dollar eighty-nine, man, and that is a bet."

Sam Smooth only laughed. "People come from around the country to see Hercules McElroy. No one pays us three dollars and eighty-nine cents to see his incredible, and I say very incredible exploits."

Sam Smooth looked to Mikey, who had never taken his eyes off Hercules McElroy. In fact, Mikey hadn't moved an inch closer or away throughout the bickering, and neither had Hercules McElroy. Hercules just stood there with his mouth closed and his eyes staring past the top of Mikey's home.

"You've been watching the whole time, huh, Cool Cat?" asked Sam Smooth. He was quick to pick up things and when he used Mikey's nickname it brought a brief but disarming closeness between them.

Mikey exhaled, nodded his head and smiled, but never took his eyes away from Hercules McElroy.

"Then you deserve to see the true and awesome incredible power of Hercules McElroy. And when we show you, we will show everybody else around here. Hercules, show them your power. Open your mouth."

Hercules waited a few beats after Sam Smooth had given the order, as if waiting for a drum roll. His eyes returned to normal and his face seemed to change from stone to lifelike in the blink of an eye. He opened his mouth and showed tiny bits and pieces of the razor blade. There were some pieces on his tongue and the inside of his lips, but when he lifted his tongue you could see that the majority of the blade had vanished down his throat and into his stomach. One of the men walking outside of the vehicle gave Hercules McElroy a bottle of red soda, which he had retrieved from the front seat. Hercules popped the top with the palm of his hand and threw the cap into the backseat of the car. He took a long and hard drink and finished the bottle with one long swallow. All the onlookers gasped with disbelief.

"Son, you'd better eat a loaf of bread," said Mr. Adams. His voice cracked just a little from emotion but he could not hide the fact that he was impressed. "Bread will wash everything down and make sure everything comes out all right."

"What do you know about Hercules McElroy?" said Sam Smooth. He jumped a little toward Mr. Adams and showed a few front teeth. He looked like a snake ready to uncoil and strike.

"Settle down, son. I don't know that much about anybody, but what I do know is that razor blades cut hair and skin and it can't be a good thing to have them floating around in your stomach," said Mr. Adams.

He wasn't backing down, but he was trying to show the genuine concern he had for the young strong man. Mr. Adams was like that, and in that he showed a likeness to a generation of older black males who had a concern for the up-and-coming generation.

Sam Smooth did not accept the concern. He did not accept any curiosity for his person or his companions from anyone, especially older black men. He had heard doubt enough in his life.

"You should mind your own business, old man. I'm the only one who is concerned with Hercules McElroy and you should just keep your big mouth shut," said Sam Smooth coldly.

That was when it seemed that everything stopped: the birds that were chirping, the inclement April breeze that would trace the trees and clotheslines, the occasional radio and television sounds from the surrounding homes, and lastly, the breathing of all the onlookers. The two black men in shades seemed to freeze to a coiling posture as if ready to strike. Mikey saw this and didn't know exactly what was going to happen, but nonetheless felt helpless when the mood changed from happy and frolicking to the tension that now existed. On an impulse he shouted.

"Do you think Hercules McElroy could beat the Rabbit Man?"

Sam Smooth stared at Mikey and held the moment for a beat more, then seemed to release it. "Hercules McElroy can beat anyone. Hercules McElroy is the greatest man living, black or white. Hercules McElroy has the greatest strength, speed, skill, and brains. No one can beat Hercules McElroy. No one on this planet."

The guys in shades began to move away from the onlookers and moved back to both sides of the car. Hercules McElroy hopped over the doors of the car and back to the backseat. When everyone was in position, Smooth opened the car door and returned to his position behind the steering wheel. He turned the key in the ignition, and as soon as the engine caught the music began to play again. Mikey watched in awe with his unanswered question lingering in the air. Could Hercules McElroy beat the Rabbit Man? He pondered this as the car drove away, and from somewhere in the reserves of his young mind the tune that was playing in the car finally had a parallel recognition. It was a tune that could be heard at the state fair or a circus. It was a tune that spoke of happiness and adventure.

In the Beginning
April 20, 1968
Saturday

"So, you told him that you didn't think he could beat the Rabbit Man. I bet he took that with some salt, huh?" said Big Teddy. He laughed loudly and winked an eye at his son. The family was sitting at dinner. This was in the family room reconstructed for this occasion. Mikey and his father, Teddy; his mother, Maxi; and his older sister Theodora had lifted the dinner table from the dining room and brought it into the family room as they had on previous Sundays. The television was turned off and the room was cleared of all magazines, newspapers, and shopping brochures. The only things that were left in the room were the family sofa and the bookcase that Teddy had created from the wood, sandpaper, varnish, and finish that he had purchased after he was given encyclopedias from a patron on his bus route. Teddy was handy with his hands and had also constructed the long dark-brown dinner table primarily from memory and imagination.

After everything was prepared, the family washed while Maxi finished the final touches to the family meal. When it was time, it was Mikey and his three sisters, Theodora—called Te'ah, then there was Dottie, and Palmer, and Mikey's mother and father, all sitting down and enjoying a Sunday evening roast beef with macaroni and cheese and black-eyed peas. It seemed like all Mikey's favorites were at the table, with corn bread and apple pie for desert as the coup de grace. In the afternoon sunlight, the room had a wispy homely feel when rays of sunlight cut through the windows and glinted off of the silverware and plates and touched some of the family portraits that were positioned in the family's fancy living room. This was the only time the family would have a chance to dine together, and it became as sacred as a religious event and no one was excused from it.

"No one has ever really seen the Rabbit Man, Daddy," said Te'ah. "All my friends say that it is a big fib that people tell the young kids to keep them at home."

"Don't talk to your father like that. If he says so, then it is so in this house. Your father provides everything for us, and if he says there is a Rabbit Man, then there is."

"Don't tell her anything, Mac; she'll find out for herself." Big Teddy used Maxi's pet name, which was a signal that the conversation should not be taken as seriously as his daughter Te'ah had mistakenly introduced. "She'll be walking around with her buddies who have those Afro hairstyles and her miniskirt friends and one day come face-to-face with the Rabbit Man. But I'll always be there to help you, my Te'ah Boo, because that's what men do; they help make everything better for the people they love."

He smiled a big smile, then drank from the big glass on the table that was filled with Coca-Cola and ice cubes. He was the only one with soda; the children and his wife had water. He had always told Mikey that it was the man's privilege to drink the strong stuff on the weekends, and Coca-Cola fit that description. Mikey's mother sat down quietly and looked to her plate. She neither agreed nor disagreed with her husband when it came to the women of the '60s and their newfound roles in society. She left all of the decisions of the roles for the children to assume to her husband, partly because she didn't want confrontations and partly because she didn't want the children to see husband and wife in confrontation. And lastly, her husband had more interactions in the city with his city bus driver job. He could see and hear more of what was going on in the world than she could, so she relented to his judgments.

"And so, them little buggers came driving down the street with that circus music playing and telling everyone how great they were, and they expect everyone to believe them," said Big Teddy.

"That's what it was," said Mikey. "It was circus music. I knew I heard it somewhere before."

"When did you ever hear circus music?" asked Palmer.

"It must have been at the state fair," said Mikey.

"No, it was from that movie that we watched, Mikey. It was about the circus and the man who played in *The Ten Commandments* was in it. And Jimmy Stewart was the clown. You remember, Mikey."

"Yeah, I remember, Dad. It was the movie with all the elephants. Yeah, now I remember. Oh boy, that was some good music."

"Mikey really likes circus music, Mikey likes circus music," said Palmer. This is how the teasing began. The girls would always find something that Mikey liked and then make a singsong about it.

"Stop, you dummy...You know, Dad, he looked a lot like Muhammad Ali. He had light skin and long arms and really big muscles."

"Yeah, and he probably talked a lot like Clay, telling everyone how great he is, and now looked at what happened to him. People have to learn how to be quiet and listen."

"No, Dad, he didn't say anything. It was the other man. He called himself, Sam Smooth. He was doing all the talking."

"Hercules McElroy, huh? Probably just a made-up name that anybody can use. You should wonder why he didn't change it to some Muslim name like Kyambogo Eli. Now that's a name he could have used." Big Teddy started laughing again, and this time begins to clap his hands.

"Muhammad Ali says that the Muslim religion is the religion of black people and that Christianity is the religion of white people," said Te'ah.

"That's hogwash. Your grandfather was a Christian minister and he was definitely a black man. My father used to say this and you should remember it as long as you want to be religious: 'It's not the religion that matters, it's the people behind the religion that matters.'"

"What does that mean, Daddy?" asked Te'ah. She was slowly becoming angry, and when this happened, she would pout. It could last for hours, like the one occasion when she was ready to wear her hair like a young lady and not a child, but was refused; she pouted for days into the second week. Afterward, when she finally got her way, she went back to her normal demeanor.

"Theodora, it means that it's up to the person and not the name that determines how a person act."

"Daddy, when you call me Theodora, you really make me want to run and hide. Why don't you just call me Te'ah like everyone else does?"

"Your father thought long and hard for your name," said Maxi. "He even read those old dusty encyclopedias that he brought home from work. He just told me in the hospital after you came that your name was Theodora."

"And he didn't give you an explanation, Mommy?" asked Te'ah.

"No…no, he just told me that we would be proud of you one day and that you would live up to your name."

"And you will, Theodora. I know you will."

"It sounds like I was named after you, dad." Te'ah reasoned.

"Theodora, show some respect for you father. He trying to do good things and wants you to do the same.

"Daddy, you're always doing great things, but why did you give Mikey his name?" asked Palmer. She loved to sit at the dinner table and listen to these types of conversations. Even though she didn't know the full extent of the conversation, she felt it was great entertainment. She was a bright third grader and usually asked questions to prolong her enjoyment.

"You ask that question every day, Palmer," said Mikey. He knew the answer that his father would give. He would defer it to his mother's wishes that he be named after the great Michelangelo, a great artist and inventor.

"That was all your mother's idea, little Palmer-pooh. She really knows how to get her way when she wants to."

"I think Michelangelo is the greatest person that has ever lived. My mother's mother always talked about artist in her family's life and it got me to thinking about art. Well, in my fifth year of school they gave us some old art books with pictures, and I remember Michelangelo's pictures," said Mikey's mother. Her grandmother was Native American mixed with black, and she always had tales for her grandchildren. All of Maxi's children had some of the features of the Native Americans, with the high cheekbones and proud noses and the impressive height and body definition. The children got everything else from Teddy's side of the family: the hair, which was all curly and brown; the skin tone, which was very light colored for blacks and even called high yellow; and the curiosity and creativity, which was an offspring of curiosity and envy. Both parents were musically inclined, singing and playing instruments. Big Teddy played the guitar and Maxi played the piano and helped out at the church services.

"It seems like every other boy is named Michael at Mikey's school," said Palmer. "Especially in his class. Don't you get tired of all of the confusion?"

"I think it is a good thing, and we are all friends. It makes it easier to get along. It never comes up, and we go by last names all the time," said Mikey. "And we all make up the patrol boys, except for Marvin."

"You mean that really smart boy whose father is a principal?" asked Teddy.

"I guess he is smart," said Mikey.

"I'll bet he is not smarter than Mikey," said Dottie with a small voice. She was the youngest. She was in the second grade and could easily be ignored at the dinner table. She found out at an early age that she had to do certain things to garner attention. Sometimes she would play with her food until her father encouraged her to finish her meal. Oftentimes she would side against Palmer, whenever and whatever the situation. Since they were separated by only two years, they were forced to spend a lot of time together. In Palmer's case the time was used for an irritating companion and in Dottie's case for a playmate. There was a difference.

"I guess you boys keep a lot of things going on at the school," said Big Teddy.

"We have a lot of fun," said Mikey.

"What is this new patrol boy situation?" asked Big Teddy.

"We are supposed to take extra care and watch out for strangers walking or driving near the school, and be ready to tell Mr. Campbell or the principal whenever something like that happens. Everybody thinks it's a good idea, especially Mr. Campbell, but Yolanda says that it's nothing. She thinks the police should stop the ice cream man and ask for his license and things."

"That is one smart girl, isn't she, Maxi? I bet she thinks of everything, huh? What was that name you guys called her?"

"They call her Bone Girl because she is so skinny," said Palmer.

"Sometimes she is right," said Mikey. He began to get serious for the first time. "Like when she talks about the body on the trail. She says it is normal for things to die, just like it is normal for things to be born."

"What do you think about that, Michael?" asked his mother. She would use a portion of his full name when he became serious. She would use his entire name, Michelangelo, when he was lazy or needed some additional prodding.

"Well, I said she was right sometimes, but that doesn't explain how the body got there and if the Rabbit Man did it. So, I guess she doesn't have all the answers."

"No one has all the answers, son," said Big Teddy.

"Then did the Rabbit Man cause the body, Dad?"

"No one knows for sure, son. The best thing to do is to let the police find out, and stay away from the trail."

"No one has ever seen the Rabbit Man, Daddy. It's just a rumor about a half-man half-rabbit thing that bites people for the fun of it," said Te'ah.

Big Teddy took a big bite of roast beef and chewed easily. He seemed to ponder the statement that Te'ah had presented. No one had really seen the Rabbit Man. It was something that had been put in place by the realtors when Big Teddy had asked about the areas that surrounded his home. After all, he had children that he wanted to see raised the right way, not running wild in the wind and trees. He saw the area and asked, and the realtor told him this with a smile—but not a sincere smile. It was a smile that Big Teddy had seen before when it was accompanied by the word "boy." It was the smile that white folks gave coloreds when they wanted them to mind their own business. It was then that he knew it wasn't a real half-man half-rabbit living in those woods. But it was also then that he realized that he didn't want his children traveling through that area alone. And so, he repeated the misinformation and all was fine—until the body turned up, and then the rumors and then the fears. He finished chewing and took a big swallow and then washed the remainders down with the Coca-Cola.

"Maybe there's not a Rabbit Man on that trail, Te'ah Boo. But whatever is there is no concern of ours. We should just do what we are supposed to do and nothing will happen badly. If you girls continue to go to school, and me and your mother continue to work, and Mikey continues to throw touchdowns, then we will be okay."

"But Dad, there was a dead body found in the area where the kids from Highland Hills used to go home. Somebody should do something, maybe call a meeting..."

"And do what, Theodora? Maybe march down the street to the E-Z shop, or maybe further down to Bishop College, or maybe just keep walking all the way down the highway to downtown."

"No, Daddy; how about the churches or the PTA meetings? Anything is better than nothing."

"Maxi, what about the PTA meetings? Do you ladies have time for marching somewhere because a dead body was found in some trail?"

"No, hon, most of our time is spent trying to find more ways to get books for the classrooms."

"Well, Mom, don't you think that finding a dead body in the trail makes it harder for people to find money for books?"

"Hell, Theodora, it's probably a tramp or drifter who died from hunger or something. Just let the police handle it."

"How do we know the police did not do it?"

"Where do you get those ideas from? Maxi, we have to watch the people she's been talking to. She is picking up some bad ideas."

Big Teddy said this with his conviction wavering. He had lived long enough in Texas to know that anything was possible. He had dropped out of school in the eighth grade, married, and come to the city to work and make money. He started out by shining shoes at the bus station and doing odd jobs for people with money—which meant white people—and learned to toe the line and smile and be humble in the face of anger and danger. He had a family to think about and not much had changed. He was still in the city making money, with four children now, and a home and a new car, and he still had to toe the line and smile and be humble in the face of anger and danger. Public servants had to learn this, and the good ones did. The great ones mastered it. He had witnessed for himself the success of the great ones moving in a colorless society where the only color was green, where there were some black men who had gotten along so easily with white society that the color distinction and tension brought on by that distinction was nonexistent. He could be like those men with a little more effort, a little more time, and a little more patience. That is what his supervisor, Mr. Johnson, was always telling him. Mr. Johnson said that all the blacks who were interested in moving up should have patience, regardless of what the popular music said.

"Well, Dad, there are some people who say that the police don't take the interests of black people seriously. That's what all the college students are saying. That's what all the people walking in the rallies are saying. That's what the civil rights marches are about, and Dr. King," said Te'ah.

Her eyes began to tear up. It was hard for her to watch the television coverage and listen to her teachers, and then come home and hear her parents act like nothing was happening in the world. Sometimes she was afraid to talk to her friends about the conversations that her family had about the civil rights movement, and sometimes she was just plain jealous when her friends told her about the anger that their fathers felt and the freedoms that applied with the anger. There were instances like homework problems when her friends could blame them on the teachers or the school board or the education system if they came home with low scores. That didn't happen in her home. Or there were times when notices were sent home about misbehavior, and her friends' parents would side with them against the teacher, the principal—or, if situations would occur like jaywalking or littering, even the police. It was like the civil rights movement bypassed her home and only stayed at the school with her friends and teachers, or on the college campus, or was confined only to the small box-covered television.

But what could Big Teddy really say? Sure, he could put everything in jeopardy by missing work and going to the rally meetings, but what about his family's future? He had worked hard and loved hard, and he could not lose everything when things were just beginning to move up. When the football season started again, he would be driving the Dallas Cowboys to the games on his bus, and that was nothing to take lightly. The prize assignment on Sundays during football was taking the Cowboys to the game and watching the cheering fans surround his bus. It was hard to throw that away. He could not think about losing his new home of eight years with its spacious backyard. He had thought about converting his own patio, pouring his own concrete, and placing his own brick. He had even planned to create his own brick barbecue pit with a grill and chimney. It would look just like a smaller version of the brick smokers that the Smokey Joe's and Hardeman's restaurants used in their business chains. But this was his firstborn with tears in her eyes, and it touched his heart in a way like nothing else could. He remembered what his father, the great right reverend, would say about this time: "God gives you these moments to test your soul, and if this is not enough, he will test you again."

"Theodora, honey, everything is going to be all right," he said to her softly.

"What about the dog that was found at Mikey's school. The police didn't even show up for that!" said Te'ah, persisting.

"The police have more things to do than to find out how some dog died in the neighborhood. I would think the janitors would have more to say."

"But it was a dog from Silverhill that was found, and it was Michael Washington's dog."

"Michael Washington probably left the gate open and the dog probably followed him to school."

"But that doesn't make sense! Mikey, tell him what you told me."

"There's not much to say, Dad," said Mikey.

"Son, just tell me everything."

"Well, Michael Washington said he knew he didn't leave the gate open, but when he left for school in the morning the gate was open and Tippy was gone. That was two days before we found him."

"So, maybe little Tippy just wandered around the trash cans and stuff. He was a little dog and maybe it took him that long to get to the school. Had Washington ever taken him to the school?"

"Yeah, I think so, maybe once or twice when he was really small. But it was on a Sunday though."

"So, there it is. He probably wandered for those days, forgot where he lived, and remembered the school when he saw the children walking toward it. What do you think, Maxi?"

"Who knows what dogs think? That little dog could've done anything. Maybe followed some music or some smell for food and got lost."

"Yeah, your mom is right. Dogs don't have good sense," said Big Teddy.

"But that doesn't say how he died," said Te'ah.

"No one cares how it died. What's dead is dead and there's no one to call to ask about it," said Big Teddy.

"So how do you think he died, Mikey?" asked Mikey's mother? For the first time there was a hint of defiance in her manner. Michelangelo was her only son and she always listened intently while not trying to show too much favoritism toward him.

"It not a he, it's an, it," said Big Teddy.

Mikey paused for a second, conflicted between alliances for his mother or his father was normal when decisions were made for things out of the ordinary. And when questions came up about "how do you feel?" and "what do you think about that?" He was always encouraged to tell the truth about his feelings and his thinking, and sometimes it would make his father happy, but it always made his mother happy.

"I don't know how he died, but I do know what he looked like. I was right behind Washington when he found him and I was running really fast. Mr. Campbell and the custodian were behind me, and everybody was telling Washington to slow down but he kept going. Yolanda never should have told him that it was Tippy, but she always wants to know and say everything. She told us when our lunches had gotten wet from a leak in the closet in the classroom. She tries to know everything."

"And she probably knew how the dog died," said Maxi.

"I don't think anyone knows how it died, but I know what it looked like..."

"Well?"

"It was opened down the middle and some of the parts were hanging out. Washington tried to push them back in but they kept falling out and covering him with blood. He was crying and crying and I felt really bad for him."

"Well, Michael, the only thing you can do is to be a friend for him," said Maxi. "He needs a real friend now."

"But did the Rabbit Man eat the dog?" asked Dottie.

"I'm not sure, but I know that the police will find out what happened," said Big Teddy.

"I thought you said the police had more things to do than find a dog killer," said Dottie.

"Young lady, you shouldn't use that tone when you talk to your father like that," said Big Teddy.

"Someone has to do something; things are dying..."

The tiny second grader began to cry softly, and when Palmer chimed in with more frightful whimpering sounds the Sunday afternoon mood changed to one of dread and despair. While Big Teddy had to show strength, deep down inside he was crying as well. It always hurt him when his girls cried. He did not want this to happen to his family. It was one of the reasons why he had moved to the new neighborhood and away from the hustle and fear of the East Dallas projects. Life was supposed to be simpler.

"Everyone just be quiet; there is nothing that is going to happen to this family. We just need to stay together and remember that we are safe if we talk to each other. Remember our deal, no secrets," he said.

His voice was soft and reassuring. His manner was calm. He had a glint of a smile in his eyes and a creeping smile under his mustached lips. Dottie and Palmer stopped whimpering with a sniffle. Te'ah slumped her shoulders as if to release. Maxi quietly sipped her glass of water. Teddy looked across the table to his son and finally let the happiness he kept inside for his family leak forward in a smile. It was a gleaming smile that illuminated the once-again happy room.

"Mikey and I won't let anything happen to anyone here. Isn't that right, son?"

"I'll do my part, Dad."

The doorbell rang with a crackling ring of immediacy from the outside world and broke the family bond of Christian unity. Big Teddy got up and looked out the window. He saw a police cruiser parked outside blocking his driveway. He opened the door and saw one officer on the porch and another officer standing behind him.

"Mr. Malone. Sorry to bother you on a Sunday, but we need to ask you a couple of questions. Would you come outside, please?"

"Yeah, sure. I'll be right there."

"Just come on now. It won't take that long."

Big Teddy walked out without another word. He closed the door behind him and followed the officers to their car.

XI

Northbound Lights in the Clouds
May 19, 1967

"We could ride south as far as we can to the edge of land, and see Galveston and eventually make it down the gulf. Even though it's not the ocean you'll get a chance to see the water and maybe some sand or whatever, and all the cool air that comes off the water that you can bear," Dawn said.

At times she was as poetic in her life as she was beautiful. She was sitting on the passenger side of the twin bucket seats of the Mustang, smiling at Solomon with a crooked smile that seemed a little off-center. That kind of smile always belonged to the person who could see things quite differently and askew from everyone else. And in her bright yellow sundress and large straw floppy hat, Dawn could shield herself from the imagined and prying eyes of judgment and be honest about her whims. She knew Solomon had never seen the ocean. And she knew how to spur his curiosity for an adventure. That's what she liked about him, but it was hard to determine if it was the fact that she knew him well or the adventure that followed with them that spurred her affection.

"It will be just in time for the ending of the school year down in Houston, and there are so many things to do there. We could mingle with all the college kids who are taking a break from learning before they go home for the summer." She meant this more with an implication of the past than of their present. She knew nothing about the Houston area but being near gulf, the ocean, was the biggest attraction for her.

JON-MICHAEL HAMILTON

She had almost lost her soft Maryland singsong musings, but they were still there and she said the last part with a twinge of maybe something missed. She had felt the need for education at a very young age and it had become a part of her personality ingrained, and second nature in her movements. She felt that need to be appreciated in a different way when she thought about her own college experiences. It had been something that she had wanted and not something that was forced on her. She knew that now, and it had become something of a natural acceptance in her life, even though there was only the one year of her attendance. She reasoned that any one of those kids could have been her, whatever they were doing, and it was 1967. Things were happening now with great music and all the new clothes and hairstyles, just like the people on the television show, *The Happening*.

This was the time when you could make decisions from so many new choices, and Texas could never change that. She was like everyone else of the mod time who thought differently about marriage because there was no rush for anything. There was always so much to do in life before becoming too old. Too much had happened. The country had discovered nuclear energy and floating satellites and television. There was a lot more to do in life, especially if you had the money to do it. But she didn't see it that way all the time. She was still getting an allowance from her parents—her father, really—and money was never a consideration in her life. Of course, she knew her limitations and it was well within the boundaries of what it was she liked to do, but it was still the connection to another and she knew she was never alone. She had a job and she rented a room from an elderly lady, so she was really alone because she wanted it that way. That's all that was wanted from life at this time.

Life was easier her way. In her way there were fewer people to disappoint, or fewer people to disappoint her when they didn't know everything that was going on with her and how she was feeling, or how she liked sunsets and trees and quiet places because they never disappointed. They were always the things you could count on. She liked to see the last glint of sunlight spying and taunting the horizon before the sun finally set, as if a daring lover were waving good-bye and beckoning a reunion at the same time. She was interested in the little things like budding flowers freshly adorning the sunlight in a short-cropped grass backyard. In Maryland, where she was from, the grass was always green for yards and yards and filled with tiny blades that fought the sun. This gave her the opportunity to see and explore her new need to empathize with the lives of other people, like her mother with her quiet dependence and acceptance. Afterward, she could easily imagine herself in another person's life. Somehow this gave her information about the way people wanted to live and what should be important in life, and she found comfort in that.

"And you think that can make everything work out just right. Just being around people who are learning things. They still have their parents' home training keeping them wanting the same things. I'd just as soon stay here in town where everything is where I know it. At least we know what to expect and where from. And I still like playing your chauffeur when we drive. It's been good," Solomon said.

"But just think how much fun it would be to try our life in a new city. And we need the practice if we want to be good when we go to San Francisco."

"You really want to go to the West and be a poet, don't you, Dawn?"

She said in her singsong tone, "Everyone should try something that makes them feel good. We can both be something different. It's not any harder than what we've been doing, plus it's easier than fighting. It's like in *Rebel Without A Cause*, when everyone has to find out how to trust each other. We've just got to always remember to trust each other. That is the most important thing in life, Solomon."

In the past, Solomon had heard a lot about girls like Dawn. "Crazy white girls" was what was overheard in whispered groups that moved by him from high school and now in the college circles. The truth was that they were the type of girls who were going to the colleges, listening hard, finding different meanings in the music, watching the news, and always trying to experiment with things because it was in their nature to help and care, but really it was the way their mothers were before and

123

during World War II. Just finding a way into a man's world. And during the war when they found their way it was hard to go back when it had ended. After World War II with their first yawning of independence their mothers passed that breath of industrial independence to them and gave to them the same helping and caring nature that they had shared with all women, plus the independence of a working, confident class. This helped the girls immensely because now they could see more of the world with their new independence. It was like stepping outside into the sunlight and actually having an effect on what was moving outside of the home. Only now, the people really had to listen to them.

Earlier in their friendship Solomon wasn't as cynical about life as he had become in the last two months, but maybe it was always there. It grew from the vacant and mean looks, the slurs underneath the breaths of people passing by, and finally, being stopped and questioned by perfect strangers when they were walking together was where the renunciation of it had come from. It had started at work, or rather they had started at work with the make-believe. It was easy to play along with her. When he was cornered and alone in a narrow place at work by either the black or white men, he would play the role of the quiet youth whom all the whites felt was harmless as long as he didn't show any bravery, or the role of an innocent optimist whom some older black men felt was his overly religious side. The few young men whom he felt he could trust and needed to impress what they thought were the wild and bewildered militant and needing advice. He began to gain confidence when he realized that these weren't just games, but chances to win in his life. And it was then that he became serious in life. He found out that this gave him certain freedoms in their relationship. Even though these freedoms could never be expressed in public, this was okay with him. It became second nature within his established roles at work and was a very simple transition to offset the prying eyes of the Southern public. It didn't matter who, because black people are just as prying as white people and are just as judgmental about who was with whom. And it wasn't that he didn't care about the social mores and what they were about. The truth was he was using it as a way to compete with her in the game of survival and keeping their friendship close. But in solitary moments of bewilderment he often wondered how he had come to this point.

Initially their friendship was just a new thing for him, an out-of-state girl from the East who saw things differently. This was a girl who was untouched by Southern politics and who actually had become his friend. But now the friendship was becoming something that he could depend on and something that he could trust. She was dependable for him, but she had always given the air of innocence. It was like she didn't care what people thought about her choices. He had realized a long time before he had gotten close to her that strangers should never know about your choices, so he almost misinterpreted her curiosity and confidence. In fact, she was well-liked just as he was. The differences were night and day. But it was inevitable that the same uncultured eye would see them as products of the same choice that gave those positions over them. These were the college kids working around them who were not doing as much physical labor as they were.

It was rumored and later confirmed that Sears, Roebuck and Company was bringing in college kids for the summer months and Christmas break. The workers were first instructed to stay away from them, but if they were picked then they should teach them just like the other temporary workers that had worked with the company and then moved on.

There was a deep chasm that separated the workingmen from the bosses in the suits and from those who had never done manual labor. After the Second World War, communism's always-evident stare filtered down and intermingled with the American dream and the social consciousness. Something in the American dream where everyone had the right to a good life meshed with the socialist message of "everyone is of equal value and deserves an equal amount," which translates to the right to a good life. But remnants of this message filtered down to the warehousemen in the form of instructions and short messages about things that did not concern them, and time was never taken to explain it to them. The banks that were predominantly downtown had the air of money in every crease on the highly polished floors that led to corners and angles of the floor. In this light, people responded differently to the common laborers than they did to the people who were dressed like they didn't want to or couldn't afford to get dirty. And it seemed to this working class that this was the true evidence of the separate classes and the disparity of the American dream. It all boiled down to what you could do and whom you knew to get ahead in life, the capitalist dream—the dream that wasn't on television.

"I have a map in my bag. I'll take it out and take a look."

She reached to her side, but there was not enough room to free the bag that had become wedged between the door and the seat. It was a big clunky thing, yellow like the straw hat that drooped over her eyes, and to free it she had to open and exit the car. She moved in frills and swishes but always came to a definite stop, and this gave a seriousness that people mistook for an air of authority about her. With her looks, no one at the warehouse would challenge her. After all, being white and with some college was all the entire blue-collar Southerners needed to avoid any confrontations. Most of them thought, "Why bother? The way things are going, someone will say something to her someday."

She stood outside the car and pulled the map out with one hand while looping the purse straps over her shoulder with another. She fluffed the map out like a pillow casing and guided it down to the hood of the Mustang. It was a two-sided map, one side the state of Texas and the other side, Dallas and Fort Worth. But the state side was what Dawn was interested in. She traced her finger down the long creasing line of the interstate that ran from Galveston to Wichita and hummed a bird song, which she did unconsciously when she was happy and busy.

"How long will it take us to drive there and back?" Solomon asked. All the months they had been friends, they had never been away overnight—or, for that matter, been out of Dallas. Solomon thought that this adventure could become more trouble than mystery. It was the newness of the suggestion, the distance from home, and always the meeting of strangers—some friends, some not. He wasn't reckless, although the older black men at the warehouse had whispered as much and he had heard them, but he never quite knew what to do about it.

126

IN SEARCH OF THE RABBIT MAN

There was always some criticism, but few suggestions seemed helpful. What he could remember was always the reminders of staying in your place and staying away from the white man, as if the civil rights struggle did not exist in the warehouse where Solomon worked, or in the city that he now looked to with a different curiosity because of Dawn.

And with that he softened to her. She was different, or what he wished everyone was like. He didn't know for sure, because he could not stand it if everyone was like her. He would be wrong.

"How long will it take us if we left right now and stayed for the sunset like you're taking about doing?"

"It wouldn't take long," she said in singsong. She kept her head down and continued to look at the map.

"I just don't want to be caught in a strange place and not knowing anyone at night."

"Yeah, I know," she said with some indifference, while hiding the distance in her voice as if she were searching or had just gazed on a distant point. But it wasn't directed to him. He knew that. This was her way of sorting things out. Where she would find the simplest answers to the hardest questions and say quickly that they were the simplest problems to solve. He had seen this quality or habit or same glitch in his grandmother mannerisms and how she moved to decisions that weren't ever considered a wrong choice but something that was inferred, a confidence that was easy to trust. No one knew what quandary they saw when they looked back to the distant point because it had become quiet in the point of their clarity.

Solomon walked around to the driver's side of the car without another word, and in the routine of silence he opened his door and sat in the car, and then closed the door. Dawn opened the passenger's side, sat down as well. She closed the door, and reached into the glove box, and pulled out the SEARS placard. Solomon started the engine without looking to her, and pulled out of the parking lot and onto the street.

He drove in silence. Without the music, you could hear the swish of the wind against the slightly parted windows as the car streamed east from the warehouse and finally through downtown. The day was sunny and smelled new and clean. Dawn's soft lemon fragrance from a shampoo joined with the whiff of pine and maple and gave the day the memory. Solomon could see himself both in the car and from above in the car, and the two planes of reference gave him his movement through this gaze of resistance and attraction and it felt normal. It was like the way he felt in the city with his job mannerisms and his collegiate demeanor, and the juxtaposition of work and the idea of aligning within an intellectual class.

Solomon drove straight on Lamar and passed by El Centro, and could see the students interacting with the downtown working traffic. All were moving to the transit or through the transit, the students with a rebellious exuberance and newfound independence, and the workers with a melancholy chorus of exhaustion. Each looked to the other in a suspicion that was new and not easily overcome.

He turned left on Main and headed through the downtown area. Main crossed the interstate, and this was where Solomon was headed. The little '65 slicked through the windows of downtown stores and held the reflections of a young black man driving beside a pale shrouded figure under a big floppy hat and dark shades. The dichotomy was the piercing honesty and the just-as-piercing deceit that the image infused in the American conscience when the people who were passing by saw a clean and honest Stevie Wonder–type black man with dark shades driving a relatively new car and sitting beside a stoic shrouded white female. Some saw this as a sellout to the black movement. Some saw this as a harmless subjugation image, because they had seen Stevie playing music in the beach movies with Frankie and Annette and his image was harmless. Some saw a familiar fork in the moment of delicacy when one saw familiar servitude and one saw lust. The figures were staring straight ahead in indifference as if they were strangers, and the drive was a task and not a pleasure for either. This indifference was contagious because everyone in passing was either walking or riding and ignoring the figures on their trek.

Solomon edged the Mustang through the Friday evening traffic and the occasional red light and took the north on-ramp, not the south, on the 75 and moved into the northbound traffic. Dawn's suggestions were for another day. Who could make it there and back without an overnight? She didn't want that either. It would be something unexplored for her as well. It would be something that she would have said to hell with if she were in Maryland, where everything was familiar. But she was in Texas, where everything that was right was said in that way, and she would have to get used to it like he had done a long time ago.

Moving away from downtown and into North Dallas was immediately different. Even closer and in the dying evening light, it was apparent that the northern parts of the city had more lights, and used more silver that glinted and gleamed in the light regardless of the time of day. You could see the new car dealerships off to the right and the rising northbound city in the distance that did indeed rise up and above the ground. And to the east, nestling in green trees, was Greenville Avenue and its restaurant areas to the furthest right. Three weeks before, in the beginning of Solomon's first journey into North Dallas, he had marveled about how everything looked so clean and white and brand new. He had taken Dawn there in her innocence and his absorbed reservations from generations before him of open Jim Crow and a reason to walk away, or maybe it was the echoes of Jim Crow and being around expensive places in the wrong way.

The streets that led to Dawn's home were cluttered with new and shiny expensive cars, green lawns, and gray-and-white brickwork. There was one street with homes that had white brick furnishings and long stone draping buntings, and homes with two garages in back that were done in some of the most fantastic ways with fountains in the lawns. Another street with the same motif had smaller but just as beautiful homes, with quiet sprawling life reaching up or standing above.

The place where Dawn rented a room from a friend of her parents was an old quiet wooden structure made with the wooden columns echoing the homes of the antebellum South during that period when everything that was right was said that way. The columns were complemented down below by a small protruding porch. The elderly widow, Mrs. Beatrice Perkins, who rented the room to her was a nice springy Southern belle with a head full of gray hair and still had some of the zest of her youth. She loved to sit on her front porch and laugh at the changes that dared to invade her neighborhood, and spike her afternoon tea with a touch of country bourbon. She was wiry and strong and opinionated, and followed up her opinions with a sassy profanity fill tirade that left all interlopers off-balance and stunned. Dawn loved her, and she had seen a spark in Dawn that wasn't unlike the spark an elderly lady had had for her when she was Dawn's age a long time ago in the gaiety of 1920s. Mrs. Perkins thought the spark was the dare for change against the norm, or how she had learned it before while watching so much justice from might, and that uneasiness from her that changed into curiosity that was learned later as the break against the storm. Mrs. Beatrice Perkins, or Beebe to her friends, had it in her as far back as she could remember during the time of prohibition, smoking for women, and dancing and dating different men. She saw this spark in Dawn as foreshadowing a wave of newness, of interest, of difference, of change in some way with transistor radios and different music and passions without reservations. She was no dummy. Her connections to community life were the limited number of people who surrounded her and breathed the same leaf-filled air and enjoyed the same sunshine in the way that they walked as she watched them from her porch with their happy smiles and frowns of life. She knew that she had grown larger throughout the years, but not in stature. It was more in her knowledge of the human narrative; after all, life is just stories of the latest wave of dances or drugs, or just something from the government. There were just enough people who saw the need to document whatever happened. She smiled a lot in her old age, and she even said this to herself, but she did remember the jazz age the age of sound, which was in her formative years.

The little '65 edged straight ahead and through the terse stillness of the quiet evening. The sun was settling for a lazy orange-yellow glint that shimmered through green leaves and trees and blue and brown dust. Solomon felt the calm of an old confidence buried deep down in every living thing that has enjoyed the free will of a breeze. The calm is

IN SEARCH OF THE RABBIT MAN

second nature, and when recognized for the first time, is a moment of clarity for the animal. When it is reacted to is when the animal reaches the maturity of knowledge through understanding.

Solomon was in a different neighborhood from his East Dallas projects, and it seemed to him that it was more than just the paved streets and the white houses. It seemed that the attitudes or dispositions of the people were more carefree and beyond the normal economic concerns. He saw this from the items that were clustered around the homes like ornaments that were half-hidden, or decorated in such a way as to seem normal when surrounding the central status. There were two and sometimes maybe three shiny new cars or a truck adorning the driveways and garages—always garages attached to the front of the house or in back with a driveway leading to it. But then the whole image of carefree somehow changed and became one of pups feeding from the mother's teat and the power the mother has over her brood at that moment. The house and its ornaments and this image attempted to provoke and prolong, but failed and changed again into inanimate memories not unlike trophies. The material possessions became cold and persevered like trophies when lingered on and scrutinized, because trophies are at their very best when remembered.

Dawn liked this street more than the streets leading to her home, and not only because it led to the house. It was the picturesque journey, like a downhill tunnel where the sound would leave, and if sound came back then it would lead to a cozy and piercing silence. She saw the street as a quiet place, quaint at times, but at the same time kind of gaudy, where the neighborhoods in Maryland seem to be older with much more history. She saw the Texas accomplishments as efforts and the older Eastern accomplishments as just predetermination, since they were so old. Her opinions would not change very often, but in moments of quiet disappointment she could switch over to the opposite of her own opinion and see the purity of the reasoning in creating something new. She had found that place of irony in her understanding of 1967 where the old was still dominant because it was conservative and the new were in opposition in catching up, which became a change in views, values, and attitudes for the new. The Southern likes and dislikes would never change, and it wasn't just the war. She felt the South was only holding up progress. Race was still an up-front and topical issue in the South. This variation of her opinion led her back to the piercing silence. As if the silence was a place of contemplation where she used it when she wanted distance, and she used it when she didn't know she was using it.

She saw her relationship with Solomon in that light, and in the same different light that seemed to be dominating her altogether. She saw no difference when talking to him when she realized his patterns. He had a rhythm to his life; from the way he drove his car to the way he walked when he delivered the mail to the offices. His posture would be straight up and he would never stumble in his steps, even if someone walked directly into his path. He would step aside adeptly and continue on his way. He could create the distance and he could find the way to get closer in the distance as if closing it off. She was in the middle of too close and far away because this was the rhythm of her life—a numbing silence that she could control. But Solomon would smile at her like he would smile at everyone, and his effort was an opening up of himself and a closeness. She liked it. It was warm. It pulled her in and it kept her away. His smile had a hint of strength and at the same time a pathetic weakness. His smile was 1967 on every level. The duality of his smile was complete with the sparkle of innocence and optimism and a budding dullness from an absence of affirmation. This was where she could blend and see life from every angle at that moment of indecision. With the pull from both sides, she didn't know why she was so comfortable there.

The tiny gray Mustang silently pulled up to the home. Mrs. Perkins sat at her porch chair corner under the house's front awning and looking through the morning newspaper, finally read after her day of excursion into the city. Her face was half hidden underneath a big matching sun hat and a shadow from the awning, and you could only see her chin and the smile lurking in the corner of her lips. She saw the city as a tinted blue in the places on the horizon and green closer in the distance. That was the beauty of the land. The distance that always brought the

IN SEARCH OF THE RABBIT MAN

newness. The closeness that always brought the familiarity. She saw the Mustang pull up and she felt the same smile and then frown.

The newspapers were filled with the war and the city's feeling about the war. The morning news spoke for everyone and everyone else was an outsider. The newspaper was dominant, the lifeblood, and the narrative. Twenty, twenty five years before and after that was radio, or maybe it was just life that never recovered from the '20s. Mrs. Perkins liked pictures, and they were in the magazines and sometimes in the newspapers, but there were more on the television and she liked to watch the changing pictures just to marvel on the change. She was like that a long time ago and she was like that now. She wanted to know that what she had felt was her own decision toward change that heckled and laughed and gave her a life a long time ago.

Dawn got out of the car and moved away from it. Solomon stared straight ahead. Dawn walked up the steps with her bag and her sun hat and opened the screen door with a long low winching sound, which is the sound of screen doors after the evening mist has started to drop. The mist like life settled in places that were thought protected but betrayed the silence that it evoked like the silence of a moment gone.

Dawn walked through that moment but not beyond it, and carried it with her into the home as if in expectation of an outcome and always an expectation of an outcome. It was always there, that dingy push-away feeling that she found always in front of her face and her nose when she returned to her home. It was returning home without a sense of satisfaction that bothered her lately.

When she first got to Texas and started to work, she went home with a sense of satisfaction, that sense that she had earned her way and now could rest. Now it seemed that it was always too much to do but with not enough time, so what was done was good. She felt it was what she had settled for. The day would end and then she would have dinner and prepare for tomorrow's work and sleep. The day would end with her return to her home and it was quiet and it was hers.

Driving out, Solomon felt a familiar silence, an odd silence, and a soothing silence. The little Mustang retraced its previous trek, back through the sea of trees that appeared to loom over each street and gave still shadows a name, and back through the same inviting homes now startling from the early street lamps and seemingly slowing of the air as the noise of cars and people and the daylight faltered and the neighborhood closed in slowly like a dying rose. Dinner in this neighborhood, in this part of Dallas, was a time of silence with family and the cool quiet of affirmation that brought a warm ending to the day. Back in the 1940s and 1950s and even now, the only sounds heard outside—because everyone was inside by this time—would be the silent squeaking footsteps from the thick black-soled kitchen shoes of the maids moving away on the sidewalk and to an artery of bus lines that led back to the remaining three points on the compass. Solomon could see a few dark women and brown women, some big if they were lucky and thin with some beauty if unlucky, coming out of back doors and through the side gates and walking on the sidewalks with their bags loaded with scruffs of clothing handed down and leftover lunch and early dinner samplings carried casually back to their own families. This made the traveling easier. There was a normalcy in black faces moving away from the white homes as if a working life were leaving and giving way to family life, and the fruits of rewards were now enjoyed from the efforts of the working life. He was in that working life and there was pride in that, so he could relax and lean back into the seat and follow the street back out to downtown and the interstate.

But education and Dawn were changing him. He didn't feel like the working life. The realization of this feeling made it harder for him, and the traveling became harder, but not because he wanted to stay there. It was more because he wanted the place to change. Dawn had that kind of effect on him. In so many ways, when he was away from her, he could feel himself moving forward without her in their life, or life with her and his life without her. In those times she would grow distant while he would grow in the clarity of the movement of his life.

The dayworkers were striding out to the bus stops and sneering back at each other in sly liberation of the moment that was moving to the next moment. Solomon drove past the male car attendants who were attentive to the large luxury Cadillac and Lincoln town cars that needed attention the next day, who would be scrubbing from the previous day's waste and see some purpose, if nothing more than temporary satisfaction.

He moved past this in the little Mustang and saw clarity in his purpose, and at the same time, an absence of clarity in the movement of the day. He heard, as if hearing it for the first time, the deep echo of sternness, the sternness of hesitation that pulled him and gave him the dark fear of a repeated remembrance and then a new cry shouting out with music and lyrics in opposition as negative forces to positive forces brought the light and gave the day a fleeting imbalance. Then Solomon saw the light of the way out of the tunnel, and there was clarity in his destination.

Respect
June 13, 1967

"So, all that civil rights colored boy shit is just that horseshit that people didn't step on and now want to pick up when they want to cause trouble. You hear me. Horseshit. And it's got everybody looking at you guys different like things have changed so much. There is nothing anybody here wants to hear about these civil rights, King shit. We got some of yawl in jails and some of yawl in good jobs just like you and old Bubba, and that seems equal to me. Yawl just wants to gets the chance to be different!"

Kenneth was stoic and trying to show as few movements as possible, but Rebo's reasoning tried to offset the balance. Kenneth was sitting upright in the passenger seat of the cruiser with his left hand on his knee and his right hand alternating from the door handle to the bottom underside on his seat. When he looked away through the passenger window of the car was when his eyes glossed with anger. When he looked straight ahead, his eyes were more passive. He had learned from his time with Rebo that when the word "colored" came out of Rebo's morning whiskey-scented mouth, it was his way of keeping things in the order that he knew. It was a generalized way, but was his way in which everything was black or white in the city. The lines that crossed the city and the lines that separated the city were black and white, so the decisions in law were black or white.

Yet Kenneth remembered his first intertwining into white society where black was scary and associated with the dark night, mystery, and wrongness and the absence of light and knowledge. But then white was right because of the associated stigma of light and dark and night and day, and the people of Chicago and their contradiction and their will to survive in their own black and white struggles.

There was nothing like a cold wind blowing across a frozen Lake Superior in a menacing unrelenting freezing chill that forced your shoulders to hunch and bunch in a meaningless effort to keep your neck and your back warm, especially if you had on your body all that was warm that you could find, or could just get your layers on your hands because everything you had was used and flimsy, then you would learn that right from wrong was different when you had to survive.

Someone had equated that equality meant sharing that pain a long time ago, but it resonated more now with the civil rights movement and that black wasn't evil anymore or worth the servitude role. That reasoning after decades of struggles begin moving closer in whispers and finally to the 1950s in the Baptist churches that sprouted up in the growing black communities.

In Chicago Kenneth had learned things as well, when he had been growing up where there were more people who needed more and he had listened. He had seen the animosity of need push through the neighborhood and keep people huddled with darting eyes and looking for an advantage and how it made black-on-black so easy. Some people organized like the Vice Lords, the Rangers, and the Disciples, and their purpose and their altruistic effort was to reach out with their own sense of direction.

There were a few more black officers working in other neighborhoods, and a few were working traffic duty downtown, but Bubba Mack and Kenneth had been seen together from the first beginning. Bubba Mack—or his Christian name, Roger Lee Jones—was one of the other black policemen on the force. He was a football player from a district champion school, and his hiring was at the same time as Kenneth's because Kenneth's hiring was considered an out-of-town favor if

Chicago and Dallas had any kind of connection besides football. The Cowboys and the oil money were reasons to consider Dallas as a place to trade if you were a city that was long civilized before the cow-town high jinxes and the long stares from the feeling of vast sunsets without people. If you got close to people and still saw the sunsets, then you owned the sunsets and someone had to fight you to take them.

"Bubba Mack" sounded like a Southern nickname, so Kenneth equated the name with the amount of sophistication and intelligence the person must have been exposed to, but Bubba had always received the most attention. Kenneth had finished high school in Chicago and had one year of community college there, and he felt the Texas blacks, who lacked the education, were lower to him. If not, then what was education good for? The Bubba Macks and the Herman Leroy's and the Wendell Johnny boys were more accustomed to agreeing with the things that they didn't like in order to live in the reality of their perspective of the moment.

It was hard for Kenneth to accept these blacks as someone wanting the same thing in life as he wanted, when they acted so differently and talked so much like the whites with the same country sayings for happiness and sadness and speaking with the same twanged accent as the whites. But he wouldn't tell Rebo that. In fact, it was hard enough trying to find someone here in the city that he could say anything to. After all, he couldn't just talk to the other policemen or tell them what he was thinking, and he never saw Bubba Mack. It seemed like Bubba Mack was always at a west station, or on the new south side communities of the city. Bubba Mack knew the city. They really did love football in this city and in this state. But what could he say to the big country brother anyway? Maybe it was for the best.

Kenneth had faced this one question of resolve often enough to himself, and it had begun to ring true. In a way he felt unique to be the only black officer in the east substation, but it was the kind of uniqueness that was lonely and everyone knew it. Then again, who would say anything? It was noticed and commented about in sarcasm, and that became the good times. If it was laughter and snickers then it became bad, and they ignored him then and all was normal, which was what he accepted as not as much an intrusion on his values. He wasn't the same as Bubba Mack, or he felt strongly that he was not. Kenneth had heard from higher-ups when there was a meeting downtown, or someplace, that Rebo had picked his name at random like a sampler portion at Luby's. Kenneth had heard it enough what a good old boy that Bubba Mack was. "I heard he could really run that ball."

Kenneth was alone in Dallas and isolated as well, because it was so different from what he had left behind. He felt that. He clung to that. Because if he didn't have that, then what was going through this discomfort all about? He had become accustomed to travel. It was a sense of freedom. But he had to hang on to what he remembered because it was what he felt and what his own values were based on. It was who he was and who he wanted to be.

Things had changed on the patrol. The patrol routine had been concentrated on the East Dallas projects, and this was a comfortable place for Rebo because he could focus his opinions without any opposition to his intelligence. It was good for Kenneth because he was black, but didn't consider himself as that black because he was a cop and he knew more than the Texas blacks, and had seen the Midwest and the snow and the open corruption and that made him better than those Texas blacks. Times were better for both officers and for different reasons, but now the location had changed. Downtown Dallas was different from East Dallas, and if he had heard the word nigger anywhere else in this godforsaken state, he would've ignored it because it would not have been directed toward him. But of course, if it was said to a Texas black or any black person who was suspected of a crime, then this became a matter of police discipline to find the same values on the force and to find the same respect in the ranks. It was the vocabulary of enforcement over the inhabitants of an area, most likely an area where blacks were as common as stop signs or mailboxes. Because it would always take control of a situation, this alikeness gave him a sense of belonging. But he could turn it off when he was away from the job and around other blacks, or try to conceal it because it was unnecessary for them to know the truth. He had little success with the people in the black community. He didn't know many people and he was reluctant to talk to the black women of the community. He knew the best black women were still up in Chicago.

"Civil rights" was an unsatisfied dream in Chicago in 1967, and the south side ghetto wards stretching to the sky gave the city a value within a value. Just because it was low-rent high-rise doesn't make it clean. It made Kenneth question whether he could take the Chicago value to a land of desolation. In Chicago the women seemed to live faster because there was an urgency that was unforgiving, and Chicago on the South Side is merciless from the weather and the people. The value of success was measured differently in Chicago. The money from shipping and receiving freight from trains and ships and the amount of people surrounding the hub and breathing and feeding from and into the city meant real business opportunities for blacks. Hell, even the crimes seemed more sophisticated. At least that's what Kenneth had always thought from his time of listening to his uncles and the older boys in the apartment building. The women were hard on the outside but soft on the inside, and at least giving. His mother was like that because she had to know that way from putting up with and eventually discarding his weak and broken father.

The car was moving at a steady pace, and for the first time Kenneth realized that they were leaving East Dallas. Downtown and the hub of the city skyline beckoned with each bouncing curve of Haskell Avenue, and he could again feel the uniqueness of his position with each car that passed by and the occupants' reactions. Some would stare long and hard, and some would stare in incredulous disbelief or mirth, and then others would stare hard with pride. The pride was primarily from the windows of the buses that transported the night cleaning labor to downtown locations and beyond.

"So, we are going to drive to the Holiday Inn and provide backup, in case you have a minute's worth of brain and wonder why we're not on the beat." A minute's worth of brain was something Rebo remembered his father saying to him when he was out of his element and with the privilege of being with him. His father would say, "Get in the truck" and that would be enough; Rebo would follow and jump in the passenger seat.

In Search of the Rabbit Man

"If it's to be that marching and singing, I wonder how you gonna act. Are you're going to throw off your blues and jump in the line? Am I going to have to use my stick on you? Ha, ha! What about if they hose you from a hydrant? You going to be able to swim? Boy, I can't wait to tell everybody the news. We lost a rookie to the damn King cause. Ha, ha!"

Rebo's laughter bounced around the windows of the cruiser. It was ironic, lighthearted laughter when it could have been worse. Rebo had learned that the greatest strength to mean spiritedness was when it was unpredictable. Once, he was riding with his father to get the usual supplies for the farm, feed for the chickens, flour and cornmeal for the family, and thread—his mother always needed thread for the mending and making. He knew this, and his father knew the purpose of the trip as well, but when all was gathered his father would send him away from the truck for something obscure, like the price of a new feather pillow, or a spool of fabric for his mother, or something else. He would always run fast to complete the task, and he would always return to an empty space where the old truck had been.

Kenneth felt that the Texas blacks thought more in terms of submission as opposed to ambition. He weighed their responses to their perceived life humiliations toward the type of humiliations that he shared from Rebo and the rest of the officers. Where would the flash point start that he had learned from his training? In every hostile situation where there were differences between people, there was a solution of action to solve the difference. He knew to always be aware of the social stations of the people, as if someone had said it from a government slogan. But a Texas translation was more direct and to the point, like a hammer on a protruding nail that wasn't like the other nails, all balanced and in their places. When would he flash over to a likeness with the Southern black? For that matter, when would the Southern black flash over to a likeness with him? After all, his station was higher than most Texas blacks, or so he had learned. He would often wonder where were the similarities beyond the stations in their respective lives. When did he become just like them? He answered his own questions. He was a policeman. That is what the man had sold him on when he came to the college campus on that cold day in November. The future of the world was in his hands. "You could be like Jackie Robinson." But at the same time, he often heard, sometimes with the same urgency, "Who do you think you are? Some damn Jackie Robinson?"

The cruiser swayed from bad suspension on the bounding curves and turns along Haskell and through the Fair Park area, and then merged with Interstate 30 and the westbound traffic. During sunset, downtown Dallas looked like a thin veil of yellowish-red tint that had been stretched across smooth gray concrete dreams of white-collar ambitions. The amber tint from the sun bathed and reflected on the cold concrete and the glass and the newfound dreams, the shadows coming in from the east giving the city its duality. Rebo saw it all. The bankers and the important men, the restaurateurs and the hotel barons all lumped together in an old memory of family teachings. The city that he loved; the city that he hated because it hated him. From I-30 to the northbound 45 it was an easy right turn merging, and the northbound traffic was more frantic, unrelenting, and even for a police cruiser. Rebo gave way to northbound drivers as if it were a normal maneuver. His face and body took on a passive awareness that was a full shoulder back, chin down, eyes avoiding contact, and wide-eyed staring meekly and straight ahead. He reduced the speed of the cruiser and let the northbound traffic have the right-of-way, and almost caused an accident with a lawn truck of an ambitious black driver and son who were looking for work on the north side of the city. As the truck—an old black Ford with two gasoline mowers on the bed and an old push mower for emergences if the gasoline was hard to come by, and two trimming shears tied loosely and bouncing up with the truck's decelerations—moved alongside the cruiser, the driver of the truck took that passive look from Rebo in a moment's recognition as if something was given and accepted. Rebo, who replaced his look with angry eyes and a contemptible curl to his already-pursed lips, looked with a pent-up anger convincingly to the driver, who gave way to the police cruiser. "Conservative civil rights," he said loudly.

Rebo regained his composure, his posture of the leader, and his confidence, and he accelerated in front of the truck and two more cars. He made the difficult left merge from the right and then followed the off-ramp that curved left and underneath the swirling northbound traffic, and then took the exit to downtown Elm Street.

Kenneth had thought that driving was the least important task in the job of a policeman. His training instructors had harped so often on the benefits of horseback versus the mechanical, attention-needing cruiser that now was the staple for a patrol officer in his assignment area, that he had been led to believe that the horse was superior. There was perhaps an area in the city where patrolmen were on horseback, and he knew that if he wanted to move in that direction then he would have to learn to ride a horse. Cars were soon becoming the embodiment of the person that drove them, so the Chicago part of him willingly diminished the superiority of the animal for a good Ford or Chevy that would respond from the accelerator and not the squeezing of the knees. When does a horse take on the personality of the rider? He just didn't know enough about his new environs. It was a proud job, but he also was not told enough.

Kenneth's first impression of a policeman was what he thought was the most important task: to uphold the peace to the point of becoming the parent in any situation. This was before his training had begun. He had learned a long time before that upholding the peace was a question of age and position, and having the confidence to hope that the age difference could discern the difference between right or wrong. His early childhood was when a parent would have the last word and the last opinion that had to be followed by everyone younger. The South Side was like that. Black people were like that. It was usually a mother who had the last word. When he got older it was strength that made everything right. Men were like that. He had learned that from his mother and everyone older than him. Men had to be stronger.

He witnessed this in his fourth grade of schooling. It started on the playground when Jerry Pitman, a bigger fourth grader, forced one of the smaller boys to give him his place in line for lunch. It was smooth. No one saw it happen but Kenneth, because the teachers were not looking for something like this. It had never happened in the previous three grades. Maybe it was because when they were in line someone always watched the students. Maybe it was the way the teachers were taught and they expected the same from him. Kenneth would make sure that if it happened to him, he would be ready. He lived in this way for a long time and he had benefited from knowing what people planned to do before they thought to do it. He also learned how to profit from the situations and whether to get in the middle or just stay out and wait. He had learned the value of voice and the value of silence, depending on the advantage of the situation, and he had learned it at a price that was high without question of any insight or knowledge of previous prices. His father had left him at a young age.

The cruiser continued on Main past Harwood and Rebo begin to feel a deeper kind of competitiveness. He didn't know why or how he felt this way, but it had started with the assignment. It was a deep twisting hunger that came from shame and the incompleteness of acceptance. It was this same incompleteness in life that stemmed the creation of highways and towns and buildings and everything that was good to this point. But it was also the same incompleteness that could be rebellious and demanding and narcissistic. He had seen some of this sameness in himself. It was just a fighter standing up for what he believed and trying hard to make it that way.

"We should be using the cruiser over on San Jacinto where the First Baptist of Dallas is and not over with these communists, but I just follow my orders. That's where the real religion is, and ain't nobody talking bout race mixing and rights shit," said Rebo. "That's where they really read the Bible."

Rebo knew that the First Baptist Church of Dallas had a belief along those lines. For the most part the church's membership reflected this philosophy from the one active voice of the sameness in human nature. All he knew was it was back to Macon, Mississippi, where his father grew up, and the quiet Jim Crow life that kept the fear away by dominating what was there.

Kenneth ignored Rebo's periodic testament about religion and the First Baptist of Dallas, and looked out as they rolled passed the H. L. Green's department store. The store straddled the entire end block of Elm and Main and provided a soft walkway from one street to the next. The store looked too ordinary to have anything of value in it. Kenneth's impressions of what he felt the store could be had been confirmed when he had walked through the store on an off-day. He had hoped to meet a girl worth talking to. Someone had told him that this was the place that black people shopped when they were downtown. He had thought it would be a start to meeting people away from the station.

He had put on his Kango, jeans, and brown leather jacket. With his pace and his beat and he had found out that he was out of step with the way he was used to doing things with girls. He didn't find anyone there that he could talk to in the store. In fact, he felt it was a just another joke from the white officers to tell him to go to that store before he realized that those officers didn't know what he liked or really wanted in a woman. In fact, he felt that they didn't know what he really wanted or who he really was, and maybe that was not a good thing. After all, they did suggest the store and there were women there in the normal sense. It wasn't like meeting women while you were in uniform when you hadn't really learned how to act. You were just learning how to do the job and wear the uniform. So, who could fault you?

The uniform was blue trousers and a blue blouse—not just blue, but the deepest truest midnight blue that almost crossed over to black. The lines were straight and taut and were always required to be straight from the cutting leg creases that split the knee and the ankle and crinkled on an angle across a highly shined black shoe, straight from the back pockets and straddled the heel. The blouse was sharp like creased envelopes off the shoulders, with two sharp chest creases tracing down the middle pocket from the shoulder to the belt that made the uniform almost complete. The uniform carried the pride of a unit of men who shared a likeness in uniform and gender and purpose and walked the same way and had a prescribed way for their behavior in all the situations that could arise from wearing the uniform. "Women will come to you in your assigned patrol," which was the East Dallas projects, "and expect more" from the man in the uniform. This was just like every place else in the city. "People expect more nowadays, especially from people who worked for them, but our job is to enforce the law."

The cruiser pulled up to the hotel with a squeaky squeak and up-and-down near the other parked patrol cars. In the dim sunset the sky was still and quiet, more than had been predicted, but the hotel had streaming black figures moving in slow solemn reverence of a simmering reflection of light from the silver and chrome and the dying window gleam of progression. Rebo felt a contradictory twinge again, and where he sometimes found himself as neutral and inactive to the pull of the day and the push of it, as he had been as a growing teen, he knew that the times had changed. At the hotel, everything looked as different as the growing city and the progression of the times, and that movement in time was the point of the push and pull.

Rebo saw her sitting in the Mustang with a large floppy hat that tilted up on her head to show the light against her forehead and her large shades flirting like dark oblong blanks against her eyes. She looked absolutely tan or pinkish tan, and her nose was sharp and proud. She had brown curly hair underneath the hat and her lips held a soft pucker of top lip over her grin. She sat quietly against the pull or push of her own wind opposite a colored boy who was sitting in the driver's seat, and Rebo felt that twinge. She was a hippie or an alternate lifestyle individual, but she had the confidence in purpose that he had seen in his own mother's eyes. That moment of identification was the moment of contradiction, of hesitation, of a breath of hope for a quiet place. He had witnessed his own father's manner toward his mother and he did not understand the distance that they had shared that was always cut off in splurges of anger and then more distance. He wanted the same and he wanted the opposite. She was a fleeting moment in his memory that he had always wanted to chase and find the meaning of, but the present was all too current and there was never enough time. She emerged from the car on the passenger side and moved away from him and he felt it.

Be Sure to Wear Flowers
July 4, 1967

June nineteenth was a day more than two weeks prior to the Fourth of July, but it was as much a Texas holiday as the Fourth was a national one, for different reasons. For all the written historic reasons, both holidays had significance, but that distance between the two days was an ever evolving-plane as the difference between the races. Texans liked to blow things up on the Fourth and see the pieces of clutter ignite from the orange dancing flames and then settle back down in a silent christening of fluttering confetti. They liked the loud bang of a good shotgun blast, the clang of iron on iron from an alarm bell, and the long whoosh of fireworks that came from a distance in the night. The sounds brought the awareness and the familiarity and to a people who were no strangers to hearing things and then listening to far-away sounds of life and survival it was a normal part of their life. Everything had a certain amount of distance, and as far as you could still see in some directions. Distance meant time and everything moving at a certain pace, like watching things grow and ripen, like things being moved in their own inertia and movement in its own season. But more satisfaction for this pace is found in the gratitude of love of watching things grow and evolve or stay the same, and that became part of the inertia of give-and-take and keeping things down that were boiling up in many areas now. The whole place was great for hunting, and everyone learned and loved and honed those traits and instincts, and their perception of movement grew keen with the distance. This awareness of movement is what is primal in the distance.

Dawn was familiar with distance in both ways. She was primal and mental, and that was from the impasses in her youth. She could breathe in the distance in her lungs and her toes and her fingers because it was her familiar comfort, and she could feel the confidence in knowing that there was the distance that she could create first within and then without. She could bring the things into her world that she cared about to diminish the normal distance, but became what was her distance. She had learned from the orphanage about the need for distance and how to make the most from what was there. There wasn't much space then, and she had to learn to value the small things. She had taken that same perspective to her later days, as things now were smaller but meant more. Like a good happy smile from Solomon that could be brought in and into her distance, and Beebe, of course, as she tinkered and scolded with a gleam of bribery as she was always in movement and never still. The final contrast was the clean smell of sky and fresh sheets blowing from a breeze under a milky cloudy white-and-blue sky. All the varying degrees of distance that she had become accustomed to having and not having, and now that there was a choice in variety. She could adjust her pallet to accept what was there at that moment because she had chosen the moment. Dawn wasn't selfish. She was just protective of herself because she was accustomed to being alone and she was particular in what she allowed herself to care about. She liked the stillness that she could control that came from the distance when she demanded her distance. She would stay in her room sometimes on times like today—a Texas Fourth was not a Maryland Fourth—and tinker with her objects like her trinkets and shiny girl things and enjoy her distance, despite Beebe's urgings to come down and watch the new color television that Dawn herself had purchased from the liberty of her employee discount from Sears.

It was the afternoon of the Fourth of July in Texas, and Beebe needed things to be the way that she had had them as before, in the latter years of the '20s in her spring of awakening and dying in the dying spring of abandonment. There was nothing to care about but the moment and the movement that begat only the next day, the fall of times like in old Rome where everything was complacent and no one looked past tomorrow. It was more a European way of doing things to try and pull direction from the past than the younger American way of doing things and establishing new traditions. But the '20s saw the recovery from the First World War, and as after every war the realization of life's limitations leaves you open to suggestions. There was an overall sense of gaiety, but with a strain more of serious celebration since the stakes had been revealed through film and newsreels and there was a seriousness for a larger purpose: a nation and the confidence it brought you with winning and the arrogance that came with it. There was more conflict and emotion in the newsreels that were shown before and between the movies than the silent movies could ever capture. The larger cities were formed from the need for imports and the ocean that brought trade from the Canadian and California gold rushes. It was inside of Beebe, from her beginnings of what had kept her alive, this urge to give Dawn the realization of the quaint fullness of tradition as important as it was to a man and was man's tradition in the sense that it dictated the behavior of men toward everything of conquest, including women.

Beebe's life began in Los Angeles and her most important and adventurous days were in the year 1928. This was the place that she had learned the meaning of distance within the segregation of the neighborhoods.

Beebe had always been a strong person, or at least she liked to think as much. At seventeen she had always idolized Louise Brooks, and that in itself was advanced for her age. Most of her classmates wore bobby socks and sweaters, but Beebe was different. Her idolization of the silent film star was a natural transition to the imitation of her look, with the same cap of jet-black hair cropped short with Roman bangs and a falling shag that draped loosely above her neck and covered her ears. She was gray-streaked now with that same cap of short hair, but not in spirit, and time had been nice to her body and her mind. Her eyes could still sparkle far beyond the thin wire rims that held the slender posts of her glasses across her Irish cheeks, and her lips stayed taut like unmoving lines above and beyond an equally thin and strong chin. She was still thin and firm with angular shoulders and arms that had never held her own child, and held a listless longing that was heard as soft breezes would crease through her unrestrained elbows. It would give her a chill at the worst times from her youth until now, because her own mother had preached the bondage of flesh: "When you give it its breath, then it belongs to you," and vice versa. But Beebe remembered her mother, and something had forced her to be different. She did not want the same things of value that her mother had valued. Family was obviously missing, and a mate; a best friend was good enough to pass the time for her. She had not always been alone, but she was alone now.

Beebe's home interiors were as incompatible to her exterior and neighbor's home exteriors as a row of same striking rosebuds closed up at night contrasting in red violence with a stream of long yellow petals and long green-stem gladiolas breaking the symmetry. While sometimes contrasting the lush green of nature with the glory and white morality of the facades in some rooms, Beebe's interiors were a separate product and of her own personality. The living room, the entrance room, the greeting room was large enough for a sofa and loveseat and wood complements like end tables, and was swarming with relics from the long-gone 1920s. Here were some of her greatest treasures like the cultivated movie poster of King Vidor's *The Crowd* encased in glass like a museum picture and an assorted number of old movie magazines with portraits of Garbo, Valentino as the Sheik, and Fairbanks as The Gaucho. These were as much collectables as was more longing memorabilia that garnished her entrance room and represented Beebe's time of innocence. Time that was just like those long-gone years of the '20s when innocence was not taken but given in abandonment and then lost.

The family room was now a room with a television, sofa, soft print pillows, a coffee table, a bookcase with books, and a lemonade cart. The room was more '60s than anything and she couldn't wait for the broadcast of *The Mike Douglas Show*. This was a daily routine that happened around two o'clock. *The Mike Douglas Show* seemed as if it had the window to the world of New York and California, and that was where the movie and television stars did their work. Beebe had always liked the movies. In her teens in the '20s she was adventurous, and with that she saw more and was smart enough to learn from her experiences.

Beebe had seen death caused from the callousness of neglect. At first it was in the speakeasy joints and dance halls that she would sneak out and attend at a young age when the nights of Los Angeles would shimmer with excitement. She was drawn to the shimmer of light against the cool cloudless sky, and a waft of moist air from the ocean that gave her nights the mystery of danger that was most like the movies that she loved. There was so much fun in those days, and the liquor was boundless. She was a child of adventure who soon became a young woman of adventure in the span of four years with an appetite for the pace and movement of the blink of an eye. Even with death, she saw it from the overexposure of the intoxication of the moment, and it was still like the blink of an eye because the next thing was always happening. This made her more aware, and the more she learned the more she became careful. In reflection, those days seemed like a haze of intoxication from some bad and illegal intoxicant.

Dawn entered the hallway from her bedroom and went to the stairs. As she walked overhead, she saw Beebe sitting on the sofa and watching the television. Television was the greatest reflection that the times had changed, and Beebe gave it her fullest attention and in her most serene moments of reflection. She continued to marvel at how things had changed lately in the ways to communicate with people and what was said, and gave the people what they wanted as well as what you wanted. Everyone was somebody and everyone had something to say; the blacks wanted rights and this coincided with the young girls who were extended the rights that their mothers had first experienced during the Second World War. Some wanted work, but some wanted the love that was always taken for granted with the infrequency of communication and the new escape from liquor and life with drugs. All of this had happened before, but was becoming available for everyone through an everyday report on television of how things were happening in the daytime or at the immediate like the movies. Beebe reasoned that the reports had to be current because at first glance the reports were so light in color like daylight. Even she knew movies had everything in color now lightened with the almost-realistic hue of your eye's interpretation and had everything to do with color, but the seldom-seen old black-and-white films still had the urgency of violence or immediateness and in what was real and what was Hollywood from the lighting. You received it free through the airways of your antennae, so it had to be the truth. And, of course, it was backed it up by the newspapers. Only on Sundays did you see color pictures, and that was maybe if they decided to run the page on new homes or the comics, or just pictures of importance or of the city functions.

"What are you watching now? You've been watching the same thing all morning," Dawn said as she walked down the stairs to the lounge room that the big television seemed to hover in like a flower with buzzing, burping sounds. Beebe sat on the sofa watching, with her frail form that brought all of the light and the air to her. She knew how to dominate a room.

"*The Mike Douglas Show* is about to come on, or I think it will. I can't find my *TV Guide,* but I hope he has some great movie star on the show, like Gregory Peck, or Gable, or Lana Turner or someone. I don't know about the holiday schedules or if they are going to air the program or not. But if not, I'm going to watch something."

Beebe always felt that words heard or actually seen spoken always meant more from television then when they were firsthand from the usual platitudes of discourse. Television gave everything certain credibility. For her it started with the advent of sound in movies. She felt it gave the medium more meaning. Even though movies were made the same way with scene-by-scene precision the final production, the actual sound film had a deeper meaning. To repeat a word was to give it more urgency, especially when words were repeated, coded, whispered, or rumored from a point of trust. The ease-dropping or voyeuristic effect is always a stimulation for creativity, and both Beebe and Dawn shared the news hour as a ritual. Dawn saw the news as information sorely needed to give her some explanation or validation of the times. The news was also in the music, or in the reality the music commented on like the war and the protest, the peace movement, and the other events and that were the most unique and magnificent phenomena of the times. There was Bob Dylan. That's what everybody in Maryland was saying. The songs had a message that was not just about love or dancing or moonlight like the songs in the '50s, but something more dangerous and louder and angry.

Beebe saw the news as a changing expression of the times. She marveled at the technology and the realism and the immediacy of the storylines. She enjoyed the dramas because they were so convenient and compelling. Sound really changed the medium.

"Will he say something about the war?" Dawn asked. She was sitting, now beside Beebe, with a sleep-filled sullen look on her face.

"It's not that kind of show. Mike has entertainment, and you know that entertainment is the strongest thing in the country."

"If you believe that, then you are out of touch," said Dawn, in a light-heart tone.

Beebe looked to Dawn for a second and then turned back to the television set with a tight smile. "And that's another thing, these new phrases; what does it mean to be in touch or out of touch? What am I really touching besides what is in front of me?"

"Now, you're being unrealistic. You cherished those silent movies and those musicals that you say touched so many people. I've heard you say that. I've heard professors say that the movies changed everything. Professor Stacy said that Hitler used movies to back his cause and change the German people, and that's just one example."

"Yeah, well, I don't know about that, but what has that got to do with being out of touch? It sounds like an insult."

"It's just an expression."

"It is noise, and too much of it. I accept your apology. Now shush because the program is starting up."

The music started and the show began to take life. The announcer, Charlie Tuna, with a proud lusty voice rattled off the names of the guests: "Marty Allen, Engelbert Humperdinck, Steve Rossi, and the beautiful Adela Rogers St. Johns." The camera cut to Mike Douglas sitting at his table in his classic blue blazer and floral-print tie. He began with his greetings to the live audience as well as the viewing audience and quickly started talking about how great the New York weather was. He soon recapped the names of his guests and then the show paused for a commercial break.

Beebe showed her disappointed with a minor frown that creased the side of her face. "These are the same guests that are always on the show. Couldn't Mike have found someone new for this holiday?"

"Maybe no one wants to work on the holidays," said Dawn. She was quickly approaching the humor of the situation.

"That's the best time to work. That's when you can get your biggest audience, when everyone is off of work. You should be able to get the most people looking at you."

"I don't know about that. I think it would be the best thing to enjoy yourself with your family. Maybe sit at a party table and talk about things that are important. How could anyone sit and watch television like we are doing?"

Dawn had never heard Beebe speak about her family in any way. She smiled lightly to the side and tried to keep a neutral tone, but could not hide the growing humor in her voice. "Admit it; you've never heard of any of these people before, have you? You always react this way. Every time there are new guests you always say you really don't recognize them. Except Leslie Uggams. That's all you take about. It's like you only recognize her."

"She's a colored girl."

"And that's how you know her?"

"Not many coloreds singing on television now, are there?"

"But she can sing, too, or can't she?"

"Well, that's probably why she's on television."

"But you know her because she is a black woman."

In Search of the Rabbit Man

"Well, that is the first thing that I noticed, and it is the thing that I remember most. The colored girl on *The Mike Douglas Show*. Now be quiet."

She let out a high-glee giggle, and then there was a quiet that was always there when Beebe sounded like old California or old Texas or old America. "And if it's not Jack Benny, it shouldn't be on television. He knows where the coloreds stand and he will never let them forget it."

The true beauty of Dawn was in the way she could hide what she really felt within the layers of her personality. She had started with her own sense of self in the orphanage to fill the void that the sense of loneliness brings you and you realize that there is no one specifically for you and you have to fend for yourself. She added to that the layer of family found at an almost-too-late age. A time when mistrust had already festered in a cold young cleavage in her heart. If anything, she had learned to say things with an even or almost disarming quality that could get her point across without offending. It was another one of her defense mechanisms.

"Well, Jack Benny did just the opposite. I've heard people say that if Jack didn't put blacks on television, they would have never been there. The one writer in a black magazine said that." She responded more from anger than from rationality, but her tone was measured. Beebe could sense the change in the atmosphere, and without looking to Dawn she responded.

"You've heard people say!" said Beebe, in mild mimicry. "How often have I heard that? You could run rivers from what you've heard people say. What about Shirley Temple and that black fellow that was dancing with her?"

Beebe was drawing from one of her many favorite Western characters. At times it was Marlene Dietrich from *Destry* and on other occasions it was Doris Day's Calamity Jane. She could always have a powerful notion and would not hesitate to find some means to fulfill it. But it was just a character, a character that she admired and wished she had the opportunity to perform on film. The next best thing was to give her audience the full range of her hidden talent. She would try a Lana Turner or a Virginia Maya or Ingrid Bergman or a Piper Laurie, but never a Katherine or a Betty or Joan. She was more suited for the latter with her dark hair and slender frame, but she preferred the aforementioned with the blond hair. It was something about the fatality in the roles that the characters played that she found a rooting for the underdog.

And while Beebe was comfortably hidden away in her machinations, the world continued to change around her. She was a child during the First World War and a woman in the second. She was a struggling actress and chorus line dancer in the silent era, and a silent investor urged by an old lover and friend when sound took off. This left her comfortably living in Dallas, where she had moved after the assassination and could stay for as long as she wanted. She had noticed a change in attitudes lately, and she was secretly frozen in front of her television during the news hour to listen to the growing outrage of people who had the chance to speak and act but did not have the experience to make this social comment with any sense of responsibility.

"It's the hairstyles. It's the long hairstyles," Beebe lamented more to herself then to Dawn. She could see something in the hairstyles that brought the races together. She had seen that same sort of phenomenon taking place when the 1920s were going well. All the women were dressed as flappers and the men were so groomed and stylish, and everyone was laughing and happy and drinking and wanting the same thing and looking the same. But that was what she thought was the downfall. Everybody wanting the same thing at the same time could not be a good thing. And the races were different, separate. She remembered the blacks in shades of brown or gray with ragged dingy clothes and passive postures. How could they want the same thing as good white people? She could not even remember when a black person had ever looked her in the eye. How could they want the same as whites?

"You can't tell the girls from the boys, and sometimes you can't tell the blacks from the whites. And all the intermixing is going to cause everybody to start looking like everybody."

"And what's wrong with that? It might be a way to stop all of the violence that is happening in the world!" said Dawn, with a twinge of passion bubbling up. "There would be no more Vietnam War, and our soldiers dying and killing other people."

"You are in a dream world, girl! There will always be fighting other people. That's the way it was, that's the way it will be! You should just be concerned with yourself and your next meal and your next day's rest! You young people care about things that you can't do anything about. If it's not Vietnam, then it would be another country or another place or another people, and so on and so on."

"You make it sound so hopeless. There has got to be a way to change things."

"It's not hopeless. It's the way it is. Maybe you should try to enjoy things the way they are and stop looking for trouble. I can't even enjoy my show with you creating all this noise."

"This noise is what it's all about. Maybe this is what it will be."

"Well not today. And not during *The Mike Douglas Show*."

They grew quiet, and the only sounds were the murmurs from the television set. Beebe never mentioned Solomon, and her withholding gave Dawn the freedom to think that it was okay to be around him. She felt it was strange that Beebe never said anything one way or the other, especially with her comments about blacks. Dawn would not change anyway. She could not see the differences in the races. Not in Maryland and not here in Texas, so it would not have mattered anyway. She could still move out and she could still enjoy her freedom.

They sat there through the evening, and then Dawn left when Solomon came by to pick her up in the Mustang. The evening fireworks at the Fair Park would be the greatest display in the state of Texas and she did not want to miss it.

Chasing Rabbits
August 24, 1967

The biggest change in Solomon's personality, his manner, was first noticed in his dark brown eyes. They held the same deep autumn sun scald that had the smolder of burned satin deepening and stretching and becoming lost with the cold and the cool wind that promised winter. This change was more noticeable for family members, friends of family members, churchgoers, and the older ladies in the projects from him having the softest and most caring eyes ever seen on a young man to the blazing anger that was now. They would often wonder out loud at what he had seen before and what was on the inside, before, that made his gaze so tender, and why they could not see the world that way. They saw that same tenderness and concern mirrored within his actions, and there was an air of comfort whenever he was in the room because nothing seemed as bad or could be as bad, but they never saw what he saw. It was in the respect that he showed them and must likely have felt that gave his movements a veneer of clean as in thoughts and actions. It was the optimism he felt for his life, his friends, and his future that ran deep in his heart like a permanence of faith and not fate that gave him the confidence to comfort and give.

He believed in a cause as a way to walk the right way, as infants mirror those same movements for moments to build on in their own brief lives like walking to food or loved ones or just plain adventure. These movements, just like any infants, are strong and confident and always clumsy with unprepared steps in many directions, never following the beaten path and often accompanied by that first such entrance of pain within the destination. Therein were stumbling blocks to overcome, and sometimes just a single stopping point to look for in some explanation as in school when the explanation was spoken out loudly and explained.

It was unfortunate for him that his eyes also betrayed the brief and meager experiences of his life. Or maybe it was the knowledge of those experiences that people at one time or another had experienced for themselves, that recognition that had clouded and betrayed the valued optimism that glimmered in his eyes with every fresh encounter of something new. His experiences had been quiet and uneventful to this day, he thought. His choices so far had been choices directed from request, with some consideration for the origin of the request. But there weren't any major decisions that he could say were life-changing. Even his experiences with Dawn were innocent. He had to admit that to himself among his normally inquisitive peers. He didn't know that many females—only the few at school, a few from high school, and maybe one or two in the projects—and not many that were life-changing. He didn't talk to that many males, maybe the few at work and a couple at school, and sometimes Melvin Hillyard, an old high school chum who was a day student as well. But not anything out of the ordinary. Yet he had gotten arrested.

And it wasn't that everyone had been arrested in the city, but the recognition in his eyes that was shared was from everyone's understanding of at one time or another how it was to have your privileges denied. It seemed like jail was always a thing coming, waiting to happen and to hopefully avoid in his life. He had been diligent in playing by the rules, first to win by the rules because it seemed like the right way to keep good Christian values, and then in turn avoid jail time. The problem he felt was that the reality of disapproval in a city that boasted of approval for everyone who was Texan made it hard to avoid. This was truly the first time that he had felt the feeling of unworthiness and a worthlessness with no way to convince his way out with his good deeds.

That jail cell was so damn cold. It had very thin air which had a cool clamminess to it and where sound carried freely on the inside but silenced the sound echoes of the entire outside, the life, the living, the much cherished vibration of free movement. He was not alone and the other men there and in all of them he saw the same alikeness of defeat in their eyes. Some protected that defeat with hard angry stares and with mad-dog breaths that snapped at you if your stare lingered, while others tried to share in that defeat with the spiritual eyes of understanding the misfortune and finding the strength to overcome. The eyes were loud and clouded out into the silence of movement. The heavy-footed clanging to be heard, the shuffled stepping briskly from side to side like scraping on eggshells, and the soft padded grated sounds of feet that dragged any grime that was bound underfoot, the sure sliding step, the coward with music, the one to watch more from creeping up behind you. There seemed to be more of them now. Within all of the marching and the speaking and the rights arguments, there were more imprisoned convicts with the same melody of revolt, regret, or opportunity and some with downright bewilderment. Those were the loudest that he noticed. The ones without a plan.

He was sitting alone in the student lounge nearest the front doors of the college at the end of a mini sofa with a perfect view of the bookroom and the main lobby leading to the elevators. He sat alone because he wanted to, and he felt fortunate that he was even sitting in the lounge without the many whites who challenged him in one way or another for sitting in the area. The girls gave hard stares or just held their noses up, and the guys walked closer than they were supposed to near his shoes, his shoulders, or his eyesight. He sat deep as if invisible in the foam and imitation suede that sort of flanked adjacent to a picture of LBJ that was facing the stairway entrance to the above floors, and the elevators and classrooms.

Solomon pretended to gaze through a few pages of a neglected textbook while hoping to catch his professors either leaving to or coming from one of the three walkways and give anyone—it didn't matter, whoever would listen—the explanation of for missing seven days or one week of school days. The Sears manger position was a memory now. He had to start all over on the night shift in the receiving area, which should have been a good thing considering his one week of incarceration, but he still felt a quiet humbling frustration of wasted effort. But he believed he didn't feel the same humiliation that the other men in his situation had felt, no matter how hard they had tried to make him feel that way. The experience had told him something about himself and he had changed in his values somewhat. He didn't want to go there again or feel that way again or be in that situation again, not being able to speak up for himself, and this was something that he had learned. He didn't know if it was determination or a defeated fear, but he would fight to avoid it and that was the good fight. And it started with the small steps, like talking to the professors and trying a face-to-face. His professors were never impolite and never too personal, so he didn't know what to expect.

The lounge was picking up with other students coming in for the day, but it was not as busy as a lunch or break between classes, so for the most part Solomon sat alone. Passing through were professors with the appearance that their academic discipline had modeled for the clientele to perhaps speak to the same of their breed. There were the science professors with active yet casual blazers or sweaters with khaki pants and loafers, or the business professors with a blue and gray suits and ties and the same flat black brogans or some kind of oxford or garibaldi. Some of the professors wore the look as a medal of achievement. The language professors were all of a type, with the unifying element for males and even females being found on their oftentimes upturned noses of concentration for the temporal illustrations of language. They all had that same pair of black-rimmed glasses resting or in close proximity to their noses, as it was obvious that they saw more or something different.

Those were the three types that Solomon was hoping to promise to convince with his actions today. His three classes were of those disciplines. One Science, one English, and a Business class were on his schedule for the fall and had proven to be difficult with work and night classes that could only be harder in the daytime. He wanted to talk to at least one of his professors before he talked to the registrar's office.

He reasoned that first an explanation to someone who knew him could ease his transition to day classes and hopefully curtail further inquiry or inspection. After all, the professors must know each other from their meetings or something.

But his mind and heart was still there, in that place where he didn't know if he was charged with anything or not. There were the threats in the initial interrogation, and the police did not like his explanation about the ownership of his car. So, they had kept him and the Mustang in the downtown impound until his mother could finally retrieve the original ownership paper from his grandmother, who lived in Houston. This was something that the police stipulated that got him out, but the car was still theirs until the fine for the towing and storage was paid. And if it took more than two weeks to pay, then more of the fine would be added to it. He was lucky that he had the money though, with some of his savings and the check that was paid to him. He was going to get the car afterward. He had about two hours before his mother's bus made it downtown. They were both going to get the car out sometime before four thirty.

The good thing about Melvin Hillyard was his focus. He had an unnerving look that could not be called just a stare, because a stare had some detectable emotional vein. His had an icy glaze of numbness. He could be talking about anything, but you could not read his attachment to what he was saying. His voice held a distinct monotone; its inflections were somewhere else. Melvin was a dapper dresser, always in a gray or black or brown suit, and was an apprenticed undertaker. This meant that he had seen his share of death. An icy coldness that he carried with him for protection was the only thing left inside him that held the same infant development of his narrowing values. He kind of oozed silently to Solomon and fell like silent hope to a parallel sofa and sat first. The more he went unnoticed to the many whites who were there as well, the more he became the background of the brown and tan and green of the lounge or the impending future. He sat in the same arch and felt the same heat, but was not the same as you. He knew where he was going and probably thought of where you were going as well, and it gave him an apparent absurdness of Biblical right. People avoided him or saw other people avoid him, and did the same in turn. This wasn't hard for the white students, but was hard for the few black students attending classes.

Solomon always found him interesting during the times when he had time to pay attention to him. Melvin saw him and beckoned him to come over and sit. He was like that to most people, beckoning. From him it always seemed intrusive. When he beckoned to come over it could be symbolic. Some people thought that way if they had the time to pay attention. They were the same people who would avoid doctors or run to them because no one else would listen, or the same people who were always unsure or sure of themselves. Not many of the other students he knew were any different. But Solomon was aware when he had time to pay attention.

"So what'cha doing, man?" said Melvin to Solomon. His voice had a squeaky twinge to it and he spoke unnecessarily fast. "What'cha doing, man? 'Cause I don't know what's going on."

The glass doors opened and a whiff of diesel and carbon followed a glint of sunlight into the lobby. Shannon Melanie, a classmate from Solomon's high school, walked in with her big puff of natural styled hair and saw him for the first time since graduation. She was a smart black girl, which meant something at all times in Texas. She was a long way from Bishop College, the only black college in the city in the newly developed homes of the Highland Hills area. For her to come downtown to the mostly white junior college was an event as well. She walked toward Solomon with a purpose in her walk that complemented the oddity of the instance of her presence.

"It's the same, man, the same as always. Taking classes and working," Solomon said. He began to look away from his three areas of concern and stared blandly at no place. For the first time he saw Shannon walking over with a dog-eared rolled-up pamphlet under her arm. She smiled and her eyes gleamed with a recognition of a feeling that was finally understood from a long time ago. Her eyes smiled and then went hard and moist. She looked away, but continued in a rush and finally

JON-MICHAEL HAMILTON

the composure of playfulness came and took over the awkwardness of her moment.

"You know my job is like that too, man. Sometimes there is so much to do and you lose sight of everything else. There is a lot to do, and you'd be surprised at what the most interesting thing about my job is."

"So how are you, Solomon?" Shannon sang. She said this as almost a song as she walked up to them. She started with a smile, but her eyes became serious. She was dressed in wide bell-bottom jeans and a jean jacket, a tight black T-shirt, and a full Afro. Her dark shades gave her the image of a modern intellectual or a brown-skinned Parisian fashion model, or a revolutionary from the West Coast. She could sing, but not like everyone else. Her singing was always controlled without an emotional personality, yet always reaching for the perfection of the note. She could imitate the pure cords or notes in any key from a wind or string instrument with clarity, and that was the confident part of her personality. The other part was that she was very smart and competitive, but at the same time kind and loving and loyal. They were rivals on the academic side, but while Solomon had to work after school Shannon had gone off to Bishop College. She was in her sophomore year and becoming more outgoing, while Solomon was entering his first year at El Centro.

"So, I guess you can't speak to me anymore," she said in a teasing way that still had that same flirtatious high school manner, but more as an echo now and growing more mature with each of her new experiences.

Solomon smiled quickly out of memory, but then lost it just as quickly when his moment came back. She moved with a soft hissing of her jeans in some of the tight places until she came closer and stood directly in front of him.

"Long time no see," he said. His eyes became evasive and he looked away from her. This was when he noticed the way the other students in the lobby and passerby students looked at her with mixed interest. There was the soft murmur of whispered conversation of Texas things and a lot of echoes of "boy" and "what are they planning now?" that distracted Solomon. But it was only momentary, because what his brief experience in jail had taught him was if he didn't focus on what he wanted and

164

what was coming at him, then he could get caught with something that he didn't want, and he shouldn't settle for that.

"What brings you downtown?" he asked with a soft and sincere crook that always caught in his throat when he became earnest or honest. It was always there, but he had thought lately to hide it. He was disappointed that he could not hide it from her, especially since he had just started into his new realization and discipline about not letting anyone know what he was thinking.

"Not from the bus; you should know that much. And not from that Mustang of yours, since you never come around anymore."

"I've been kind of busy and I never can find you on that campus."

"Yeah, you did come down to the South side last year, brother man," she said with a smile. "Well I guess up here it's hard to get lost." She made a backward swinging motion with her arm and followed the gesture to look around the lobby. For the first time she could notice what was around her and who was looking to her with curiosity, and the few with fear. She felt neutral first, and then a faint glimmer of sadness filled her eyes. Her eyes changed back quickly and then she looked back to Solomon.

"How are your classes?" she asked.

"They're okay."

"You were always the one who never could stop talking about new things and what you wanted to do. I guess that year off working was tough enough on you in many ways. But you're looking like you're hanging in there."

"Your hair is so full it's amazing. It looks really good," said Melvin. He slid up closer and tried a conversation triangle. It was rare for him to be seen speaking to any person; two would be a plus to his prestige.

"Yeah, the sister got her do in place as well, but I'm a long way off from where I want to be," said Shannon. "I want it to be tall and mean!"

"Shannon meet Melvin, Melvin, this is Shannon. She's a sophomore at Bishop College."

"Don't come any closer, my brother. I'm not going to be here that long. These formal meetings always try to last longer than people have time for."

165

Melvin stood anyway, smiled, and laughed a forced throated chortle. Because Shannon was tall and slender, they appeared almost the same height. He tried to shake her hand, but she refused instinctively. He moved over to her side and looked to her full Afro.

"Yeah, I hate formal meetings. People get the wrong idea from formal meetings. I'm just talking about your hair, Sister. It's just that sometimes I have to help with the viewing preparations. I've done a couple of guys and one older lady, and everybody wants to look good with a large Afro," said Melvin. He smiled now more with his mouth and not his eyes.

"So, you're in the hair trade, brother?"

"Well, not exactly, my sister. I'm an apprentice at the Trinity Mortuary. I know what you think, even before you say it. It's not that bad. It's just a job."

"Yeah, brother man. Somebody has to do it or it won't get done." She said this as a matter of fact and looked to the doorway. Students were walking in and walking out, and through the doorway she caught a glimpse of two familiar round Afros bobbing outside in a happy rhythm. "Brother Denzil Dowell needs your help," she said, finishing her thought.

"I don't think I know him. Anyway, when I go into a barber or beauty shop looking at hairstyles, they always get the wrong idea, until it's their folks. Then they expect latest styles and everybody wants me to know," said Melvin.

Solomon had heard the story before and interrupted, more not to hear Melvin's again on that day than to do anything else, like concealing Melvin's occupation from Shannon. He had never thought one way or the other, but Melvin took it at just the opposite.

It wasn't the competition for the attentions of a beautiful soul sister where Melvin felt the slight. It was from the misunderstanding of his occupation that everyone that he had met at the college shared.

"Why'd you come here, Shan?" asked Solomon. "You thinking of buying some books?"

"Naw, we got books at our school. I was downtown and thought about you. You know how our moms talk."

"Yeah, they do tell ya everything about what everybody else is doing." He said it in a matter-of-fact tone, but paused and let the implication sink in. It was in that moment when he realized why she might be there.

"But they don't see everything as it changes, and like you always say, we are in changing times. Things got to get better, you always say that," said Shannon.

And it seemed to get quiet all around, and everything closed in and he found his focus that he had used before to get to one of the high points in high school and through to this point.

"And I'll keep saying it until things change."

"You don't make those kinds of speeches anymore."

"I never made any speeches."

"Talking like you wanted to do something about it."

"Yeah, I am. I think."

"Come to Bishop, brother, transfer," she said with a twinge of urgency. "It's not what you think. It's might be what you're looking for."

"So, what's Bishop like? Does it have a mortuary program?" asked Melvin.

"Isn't that like a family business?" asked Shannon flatly and with not as much interest as before. She had had success in the past just stating the obvious.

"Yeah, but why is it like that? Is that some part of the medical field or something?" asked Solomon, now moving away from the moment.

"It's a trade," said Shannon a little too loudly.

"Let's go outside and walk to H. L. Green," said Solomon.

"That's a long walk, but let's go somewhere and talk. I want you to look at something." She used her off-hand to pat on the rolled-up pamphlet under her arm.

"Yeah, I want to go too, but I said I was gonna wait for my professors."

"You'll come back?" asked Melvin to Shannon.

"Yeah, I'll come back, Melvin," said Shannon.

167

"So, I'm not going with you folks this time?" asked Melvin.

"Not this time, man."

"But you'll come back. You'll always come back," said Melvin.

"Why would you say something like that, man?" asked Shannon with a bit of stress in her voice.

"You'll stay at El Centro," Melvin said, just a little too innocent sounding from his voice. It wasn't his normal drabber of a monotone monologue. It had a foreboding stillness of more to be said but wasn't. It had urgency.

"Now you know why no one wants to sit with you," said Solomon. He was moving away with Shannon.

It was close to twelve o'clock, and the sun gave a bleached gauze on the sidewalks because it was August, but not quite autumn or another one of those dry Texas autumn tweeners. All the people came in with a little of the Texas autumn and a little of the summer dryness. The air conditioning was blowing and there was a coolness that gave the lobby the separation that Solomon noticed again and again. In all of that stillness Melvin, was untouched and avoided. Solomon knew about superstitions and black folks, but not superstitious white folks. He thought that if it was said and then heard enough times, then there had to be some truth to the myth. Melvin was a carrier of that brooding legacy of death, and he couldn't really care at the moment.

It didn't help that Melvin was dressed in the tools of his trade, or so was the impression that everyone seemed share who had noticed advertisements in *Jet* or *Ebony* magazine. His suit and white shirt were becoming staples for the advertisement of the trade. No one in the mortuary trade advertised in blue jeans. Blue jeans were becoming the student trademark for rebellion and change since James Dean and *Rebel* and the great Sidney Poitier in *Blackboard Jungle* some ten years previous. Maybe that was why he was avoided? He didn't dress like the other black students, and he didn't act like the other two black students at the school. One thing no one could deny: He handled death. He was around death. He touched past the scarceness of death. And for whatever reason, good or bad, he assisted death in the appearance of life: a cruel treasure, a selfish contradiction for the grieving survivors.

Melvin hated it. He hated the superior attitudes in breath and the whimpered silence in death. He marveled at how some, the many he worked for, held that same attitude, a silent confident strength even in death. It would always show in the cheekbones. How high they were. How shallow was the face around the cheekbones. How much strength was there in the hunger that remained even in the honest pain and even eventually in their death? What made black people feel this way? Strength in hunger and suffering. He would have thought that in death, a sorrow for what could have been would stay on the black faces. He had worked on a few whites, the poor ones in West Dallas, and some of the stuffier ones in the Pleasant Grove area, and their faces were always of contentment—or so it seemed to him. He could see that same contentment in some of the faces of the students who were beginning to gather in the lounge area. It was closing in on the noon hour and a lot of the classes were letting out, and the movement in the entire lobby area began to change with facial expressions that Melvin had seen before.

He saw some frowns and a few stares, but they were in large amounts of looking the other way. Melvin retreated in his shoulders and retreated from the scenery of the lobby and the day. He stood and walked unnoticed toward the rear door of the main street exit and out into the mass sound of transportation as cars drove by with engine noises as the air filled with the electricity of the moment. He emerged into the rear of the school and the faculty and employee parking lot that led across to the cafeteria. He moved to the back and stood quietly. He could hear a few of the cafeteria workers busy clattering pots and the whispered hum of a big blowing fan. He stood out and watched as a few of the workers ambled or stumbled or scurried back and forth across an opened back doorway.

XV

Go Round Go Round Return
September 13, 1967

The beauty of Texas was found in the brutality of the landscape. The flat barren horizon gave most people the vision of vastness, and only the new few over the last thirty years felt the need to compete with the landscape and build something high stretching away from the ground.

It held a shimmer of gray and silver against a starlit sky. A tranquil streaming of red and screams, laughter with hellos shouting back and forth, fun from the participants in their carriages, the long lines of anticipation from below that held the dancing eye, and the held breaths piercing through what was above. It rotated slowly, floating in the air, largely to the left hand of Big Tex as Tex faced downtown and as his right hand beckoned the eastern landscape with minstrel lyrics of a piping song, a child's ditty, that created the irony with the rush of air, and the screams and creaks of metal scraping the elevated tracks of the roller coaster that was further left. From a distance you could see the Ferris wheel moving clearly with the many occupied buckets creaking back and forth with gravity and dangling feet—some happy and some temporarily panicking from the loss of footing. Up close you could hear it more than you could see it, and that is when the heat of the moment would catch you. Everyone buzzing with excitement and anticipation clattering and moving up into the heat of the corn-dog smells and popcorn, and somewhere close was the sweet syrupy smell of cotton candy. The air was like that if you kept your nose up, but if you looked down and accidentally inhaled you could catch the morning dew, soiled now against the makeshift performing stages and the running water from some runoff somewhere. The city needed some type of waste disposal to run downstream to the pond, the livestock, the zoo animals—and of course, somewhere in a crevice in the Fair Park grounds, maybe near the Cotton Bowl, the show horses. The gravity pulled at the wear and tear of progress: toward the waste of progress, to the value of the past.

From Highway 310 and Highway 30, the whole of the state fair looked like the advertisements that promised the year would be the best. Big Tex, the original Dallas cowboy, stood at 52 feet high with his blue jeans, wide-brim white cowboy hat, and red plaid long-sleeved shirt and held a striking contrast to any Texas sky at any time of the day. The structure stood tall and wide-legged in black makeshift cowboy boots that led up to an extended arm and hand and the crazy never-flinching smile that beckoned all the visitors to come in and enjoy. From the side streets and into the inner parking properties was a gathering of expectations from a year of wait and want of release into a celebration of state and just plain fun. The Cotton Bowl Classic was near, and the seasonal gatherings of high school football and college and the Cowboy season danced in the starlight.

Rebo drove past the parking lot shepherds, the dark faces with the clear whites of eyes and the large smiling teeth, and moved the cruiser within with authority. There was so much black from a starlit sky that the air below hissed, and the neon that tried to compete with luminance made all the light sparkle. The cruiser limped in through on the tarmac as it crunched under the tires in rhythm with each brilliantly glossed black stretched lane heading straight into the infant manifestations of black American capitalism and business ownership. There was a low bass note, rhythmic, that thumped through the air from the tires that matched in time with the heartbeat of Fair Park, the gas generators, the electric generators above, and fastened above on the tall electric poles.

Rebo felt his easy breaths ease into the turbulence that burned from a warm place that was reserved for anger. He had seen the Sears girl earlier today, outside on Lamar waiting for her transportation to her home. She was still as beautiful a woman as he had seen in his lifetime, and that made her more. She was the beauty in the heat, the brilliance of light to be cherished and to be held above. She was the beauty that made the image of great cities memorable and possible. He had made a point of seeing her as often as possible since he had first glimpsed her at the downtown Negro rally. Earlier, he had parked the cruiser across from the department store and waited for a glimpse of her again and again as she crossed over into her routine. He should go over and arrest that Negro who drove the Mustang again, but for some reason he had felt uncomfortable about showing her his strength or giving her the knowledge of his pain. The emptiness of not seeing beauty, or seeing it for the first time and knowing it for what it meant to the virgin appreciation of beauty, the touching of beauty in him was something holy. He felt it. It came from the deepest drama of the Texas landscape the invincible innocence of beauty that was deepest in testament, sweltering, untamed, and pawing wildly.

Clearer still were the red lights of the Ferris wheel, a tilt, a sharp glinting slant of yellow, and a drop. The cruiser parked. And before the lights dimmed, Rebo walked out into the night lights with a back-shadowed silhouette, alone, leaving his partner on the other side of the fairgrounds with the instructions to meet up at the pond. Rebo wanted to see the Sears girl while he was alone; he didn't know why. His other conquests had been from his shield and the respect and power that it had given him. The brotherhood that gathered behind the shield was his safety, and familiarity that came from wearing the shield and his buffer between him and everyone else. He could not remember when he had turned the corner from just going through the motions and showing everyone what they expected to see from a policeman to what he was now.

He could remember the first time he smiled when he saw the Sears girl. He could remember the first time he walked into the personal office of the department store and described the girl to the receptionist and finally got her department and name. Dawn was as memorable and liked a person at the store as she was in every place she frequented, from her creaks and yawns that bounced against the glass mannequins of the downtown department stores, the long soft strides down Lamar Street, to the glass doors of El Centro College, and finally sitting quietly and with ease on her porch at the house on Mockingbird Lane. She was quirky and kind of innocent and everyone noticed it and liked it. Rebo saw Dawn as a key to what he wanted to become, what he wanted to be known for doing, and what he wanted to be known as.

Dawn had a presence. She could be anywhere and you could spot her floppy hat resting over her head, more from the Goldie Hawn model of legs and gangly arms and standing like she was bracing against the wind while a room full of white shirts and flowered knee-length dresses and white heels surrounded her. Mind you, you could make her out if she had on the same outfit as the area college girls, the young working downtown girls, or the occasional rodeo attire. She was a breath, and that was always a good thing. She held the light and never wanted to let it go away. Her voice was harsh music with a strain of loneliness that made her stronger, and she held her chin high with pouting lips that were always moist. He could not get that out of his eyes. He couldn't get it out of his mind.

He left Kenneth on the other side entirely and hoped he had at least an hour before he would have to find him and make sure nothing happened. It was an irony that this one black…should have this kind of exposure and protection at the state fair, and he wasn't even a true Texan, but LBJ and damn. It made him second-guess his place in society a place that was his from his teachings and the way he was treated and the way he saw the world. He knew why it mattered. Somewhere inside he would be weak, and no one should know where or why. It was the sign of the truly weak, was what his father had told him on numerous occasions on the farm. "Nothing good comes from the absence of labor," he said. If you didn't earn what you got, then and there it would turn into something else.

His mother didn't seem to know this, but there were no disagreements on the farm. So, her day was as routine as daylight rising and everything coming to life with the light. She was a slight woman. Rebo saw her in gray, always gray. Her silence was gray. Her toil was the gray shades between the edges of shadows and the gripping of light, and her smile was soft and reserved. She was all business in her gray dress and hair up and coiffed, and she was the strength that pushed his father out of bed in those early dark mornings and working for life, and Rebo had just come to realize that. It was the emptiness that he fought when he found that place of honesty that he tried to protect, and he would never let any deceit touch that honesty.

He would be angry if it didn't happen his way. He walked through the fairgoers in a stiff starched dark blue crease with shiny buckles and bucklers. The evening fairgoers were more jubilant, more boisterous than the morning goers, and he felt an air of invincibility from knowing who they were, their tendencies. Walking among them, he could see their happy out-of-town faces, their happy kids, their happy groupings of the intermittent laughter of young people who had more privileges for them than for him, but they were in the big city and could see Big Tex facing the beautiful downtown buildings. It was a moment of realization for him, always, and he reveled in it. The intimidation of a big city on a small-county soul had gradually increased since 1963.

Every Texan had his or her reasons for coming to the state fair. It was the first and only state fair for miles around. People from Louisiana, Arkansas, and Oklahoma and other surrounding states came to the fairground. Not to mention at least one member of each of the 256 county offices in the state were attending the fair, and something from every county was somewhere on the grounds. Everything was on display. The new cars for 1968 were in the automobile display building, and museum art from all over the state had a place as well. Everyone was there to see new things, meet new people, and be engulfed in Texas pride.

"Hello, officer? Can we say that to you?"

"Evening, officer. I'm glad that you are here."

"Officer, if you need to get by me, I'll move and let you go by."

"I want my son to grow up straight like him."

"I want my daughter to marry a man like him."

IN SEARCH OF THE RABBIT MAN

"Dallas is such a big and beautiful city."

"Our officers are the best in the state."

Kenneth walked in from across the street from a northern parking lot. It was a solitary walk. It seemed that the darkness and quiet that held him like a hand was a comfort for him. For the first time as he emerged from the dark was a good thing: the museum, the pond, the many people contemplating if they would be able to buy the new 1968 cars and trucks. Everyone was happy. He walked in as either an attraction to change or a repulsion of change. How should he act alone amid the various out-of-town white faces from the barren counties that had never really seen a Negro officer walking alone, or for that matter at all? His training had taught him of the silence of blue, but not the inner wall or what he perceived as a more secretive level. He had never seen a Negro officer from Chicago there, and he had never seen anyone there who could admit that they thought what he thought or felt, and so much was the distance from the decisions that he felt he could make alone. This place was not like Chicago, where he had felt the freedom of familiarity of so many black faces that grazed on the gray of the concrete porches, paved playground areas, and parks. Now it was a quiet nod to the few that had those friendly, lighted faces and a silent stare to the ground of the few that tried to catch his eye. It was walking with the bearing of authority, and also a survival trait with a sharp peripheral of reading all movements, and then body and knee twitching and hands to a possible Colt sidearm or beer bottles.

"Hello officer! Can we call you that?" was the occasional drunken cackle from a cowboy standing under a bright tower pole light, who had a little too much to drink in him. There was a growing majority that frowned a hard Texas frown on the outward display of that intoxicated resentment in front of their children. After all, this was still LBJ country, and the state fair and a changing Texas were necessary to remain the Star-Spangled State. It was just as good as the St. Louis Fair in Missouri. Most Democrats fought out of a revenge for John F. and a fire for Bobby to win and fulfill the American promise. Others fought out of the shame of the assassination, and others still for the new communication technology from Texas Instruments and for what they did not understand but understood in faith about the change in sentiment in the television telecast—how the kids were growing longer hair and so were the blacks. The big puffy hair and the long drizzly hair hanging down unkempt matched the same smiling smirk of something hidden, but it was really the fact of seeing the change, the immediate change, from months and weeks and days that was the most impactful addiction. Television was as new a drug as the many drugs that were filtering into the psyche of the state.

Kenneth felt a growing confidence, a growing acceptance, and he cast a sharp blue crease through sparkling edges under the Texas fairground lights with a straight stiffness like a knife cutting through so much mud and oatmeal in the falling evening light. Not a true cut yet, but an indentation. His walk was straight and slow and kind and helpful. When he got to the pond, he felt a sadness for the ducks that swam in toward the slowly dying light at the edges of the illumination of the pond, only to return for dried bread bits and leftovers or seed. It wasn't like him to feel this type of sadness or frustration in such a quiet cool calmness of glow. After all, he was from the concrete. Even the tiniest of Chicago children had the concrete knowledge of toughness. They would run in the rhythm of purpose. The bouncing quick paces of movement with the discovery of something new every day gave them anything but the sad solitary face of defeat. It was a spontaneous reaction to the freedom of events and the black people who were seen for the first time away from their neighborhoods. Black faces were seen a lot more, and television had given him his first glimpse for a comparison as he first noticed that he did not see the southern blacks living like the blacks were where he grew up.

Chicago was different. It wasn't the South. More people had a quiet reluctance for the present and a hunger for change. The other young people of different races felt the city change the same way. But in Dallas it was the South. It was the opposite. The blacks that he saw lived in the happiness of the moment and the hopes that the moment would continue. There were the brief moments of happiness from meager earthly satisfactions, because it was a strain to be ambitious. So, no one ever looked up except to a hand that could help them up, and that included religion. The solitude of service, an internal mantra brought up from the depths of slavery, was prevalent and blended so well with the attitudes of the state. It was almost regimental, this attitude of servitude. It was passed down from generation to generation and gave the culture a constant identity, never changing and never causing any changes. Chicago was always changing.

It caught Rebo off guard, but over near the edge of the pool on the farthest side was the Sears Girl standing alone under a big draping willow and tossing bread crumbs to the silently floating ducks. Rebo could see her, rebellious in her solitude like a stranger walking in a bland stoic crowd. The truth is a thirst that you will always have once it leaves you. You can never get enough to get it back. He imagined the look of realization on her face when she looked at him through his facade and could only see the ugly naked hunger of dishonesty. He could see her reacting as the other women in his life had. His true self often repulsed his past friends, and nothing he could do could get them back with their own virginal identities intact. If they came back, they didn't bring their trust, and as those relationships faded into less than friendship Rebo became more and more comfortable with his solitude. It became the job that got him through it. He used the job for everything.

He walked over the few steps close to the edge of the pond and stared at her. He couldn't see much of her because of the hat and large oval shades she wore, and the downward tilt of her head to the pond as if listening to the soft paddle of duck feet through water. But he knew her style and her stance. He recognized the slender hands like long flowers and her pale white skin gesturing like streaming lights tracing her movements as she picked and tossed and followed through to the start of her movement. She was graceful and he was mesmerized by the light show that she generated with each moving breath and angle.

He walked over to her, but could not approach her. He maintained a four-foot distance and tried to survey the surrounding pond area in a vigilant probing. It was too dark for his routine shades, but his visor from his hat was tilted down over his eyes and he felt safe from her. It had just dawned on him in a piercing shudder that he felt guilt when he was near her. He couldn't look to her, so he did not see her walk up to him and look to him through large oval shades.

"Do you see something interesting?" she asked.

"What was that?" he half whispered and half stumbled out.

"When I stand there, I can always see interesting things. I can almost see the whole fairground. I think it's because the trees don't get in the way."

"Yeah, the trees are larger this year. I guess they take to growing like everything else."

He could not look to her, but he liked talking to her. The sound of her voice amid all the other sounds of the day was the clarity that gave the day its meaning. He was immobilized. He fought it with his training. The man became the policeman and the distance in routine became evident. He stood a little taller and squinted his eyes narrower. His breaths became sharper and almost silent, and his features grew thin and sharp.

"I see you're busy," she said.

Without another word she moved away and to the right where she came from and to the other side of the oval. She seemed to wave to some people who were walking past the automobile building. Rebo followed her movement with his eyes and saw a familiar young black man wave back and then move against the flow of the small pedestrian traffic and in pace with her in what Rebo envisioned as their paths intersected on the other side of the trees that restricted his vision. He focused on her for a few beats and then began to move around the oval after her. He walked in her steps with his eyes staring straight and found movement in his peripheral vision. There he saw Kenneth moving parallel to him on the other side of the pond. His walk accelerated by reflex in an impulse to catch up with the Sears girl. Kenneth matched his pace, so Rebo slowed his pace and became more deliberate with the precision of the uniform.

XVI

A Reason to Lie
April 21, 1968
Sunday

The evening sun shone yellow with rays that slanted sharply across the neighborhood. Just like the entire area of the state at this time of year, weather systems would move across rapidly and without any encumbrance because there was nothing there to keep them in place. This part of Texas was flat and void of natural landmarks like mountains or large bodies of water to keep weather systems in place, so each day could be entirely different from the previous but when a system was in, it was in. In April there was some precipitation that could move up from the gulf, but the majority of the systems came from the jet stream and the Arctic flow. While the days of April were sometimes windy, cloudy, or rainy, the evenings were cool with soft breezes blowing like quiet whispers of affirmation to everyone who had live through the showers or winds of March. Sundays were the best days. It seemed like the sun always shone brightly in the mornings and the evenings were quiet and cool.

In the city of Dallas, football was the bread and butter of just about every community. From the north where the schools were plentiful and well-funded, to the east side where the clusters of projects molded the new black voices, to the west side where the older generation found the lazy evenings and sunsets soothing, to the south side where everything was faster and slightly more dangerous for blacks and sometimes whites, everybody loved football. It was the thought of competition and winning that was the water used to clean and cook and refresh and replenish, and it was the clothing that warmed in the cool nights and the balm that healed. Football gave everyone that one moment of equality within the framework of a team when you could play with or against someone from a different background, or have a greeting and converse about your favorite moments from your favorite team. It was the equalizer before everything reverted back to class and economics and education and race.

Mikey's favorite team was the baseball Cardinals, which was a small mistake on his part. No one played baseball in his neighborhood or at his school. It was a question of equipment, which meant bats, gloves, and baseballs, and of course space. The baseball diamond had to be wide enough to hold four bases and long enough to have outfielders, and that was just the start. The game also needed players, at least enough to make the game interesting.

So, Mikey was back to football. His favorite football player was the incomparable Jim Brown, the stunning running back for the Cleveland Browns. It seemed that there was nothing that Jim Brown could not do. He would be seen on the televised games or the sports highlights or the newspapers, carrying the football with players draped over him but unable to stop him. There was nothing he couldn't do. He singlehandedly fought off the mighty Packers and demolished the lovable Cowboys. He was unstoppable, he was stupendous, and when Mikey played football with the older boys, he would pretend to be him.

After dinner, Mikey walked over to Silverhill Drive with his battle clothes on. An old football jersey, blue jeans, and his old sneakers was the attire that he always chose for these occasions. He didn't believe in good luck or bad luck per se, it was only that his mother inspected all of his clothing for wear and tear when washing and actually gave him feedback when some portion of his wardrobe was moving too fast. Plus, he was more comfortable when he dressed in this ratty way, even though his father and mother stressed a neat, professional attire whenever possible.

He would not be the quarterback today; that role was left out for the elementary school players. His role today was running, blocking,

IN SEARCH OF THE RABBIT MAN

and catching whatever was thrown in his direction, and still defending an opposing player in a one-on-one matchup. They would be playing in the street, which was a two-lane drive. There probably would have been more room if cars weren't parked on the curb near the homes of the owners. Most of the homes on Silverhill had enough room for two cars in the driveway lined one behind the other, but sometimes the residents did not want to back out of the driveway. Those few would circle the home, then park by the curb of their home and have their car heading out to Simpson Stuart Road. This gave the residents easier access for their morning commutes. And in this neighborhood, every resident had a commute.

The gang was all there, waiting to start up the game. They were all older than the three patrol boys, and in high school from the eighth to the tenth grades. All had varying degrees of height, weight, and football skill. There was Daniels's older brother Lenny, who was stocky with muscles but slow, and Ronald Turner and Jarvis Walker who were both slender young men with long arms and legs. Then there were the two of the three Michaels, and Wilmer Wilson and his younger brother Gary, who were both about the same height and build. All were waiting to choose sides. The game began with the two tenth graders, Ronald choosing sides against Jarvis. Since Mikey was advanced for his age but still a sixth grader, and Washington was still a no show, Mikey's team would have an extra man. So, it was Ronald, Lenny, Daniels, and Mikey against the remaining two tenth graders and an eighth grader, with Mikey going one-on-one against the eighth grader Gary Wilson. Although short-handed it was still the way it usually matched up.

Two-hand touch below the belt football was the game. It was the sandlot version of the real game, because if you didn't have uniforms for blocking and tackling then the game could save some broken bones. That's what the teachers and other adults said, but maybe they hadn't played the game the way it was played on Silverhill Drive. If the cars that were parked by the curb in front of the homes were the initial obstacles, then the defenders could also make them allies or second defenders against their opponents. A lot of receivers were often caught between a

183

defender and a car. If you bypassed the cars but didn't run straight down the street, then the curb came into play. Even though it was considered out-of-bounds, it was still hell on the ankles and toes and, God forbid, knees. The good thing about falling on the curb was that you could fall on a patch of grass that separated the curb from the sidewalk. If you lost your footing for any other reason, tripped, stumbled, or were just pushed down then the street, that came into play. It was the pavement that got to your knees and hands and elbows. A lot of scrapes and burns for bending body parts were always at risk when they played the civil game of two-hand touch football. It was a good thing that it was only official if it was below the belt. This required a certain amount of dexterity to have the participants reach below the belt on hips or back pants pockets to stop the progress of the ball carrier, but it also created a safe dimension to the game because it avoided the brutality of hands to the face or shoulders or back. This was an easy way to knock a person over and onto the pavement.

The game started with the kickoff, a long high pass from Jarvis to the other end of the street where Ronald caught the ball and started running down the middle of the street with Mikey, Michael Daniels, and Lenny leading the way. The usual soft collision occurred after about ten feet, and the runner was declared down after the blocking broke down with a two-hand touch applied aptly by Wilmer Wilson. Mikey's team went together to a makeshift huddle where they received instructions from Ronald, who gave them out like a seasoned quarterback. It wasn't after every play that they would huddle, but usually on the first play of the game everybody would take the procedures seriously. Later, when the game was going really well, the players would just stand at the imaginary line of scrimmage and run to a clear path.

"Mikey, run ten yards past that Ford and then stop. Lenny, you start slow and then burn down to the end zone. Daniels, you hike the ball and block. If no one is open, I'll throw it to you. On two, ready, break."

The team broke the huddle and lined up alongside the football. Washington leaned over the football assuming the center position, Mikey lined up to the left, and Lenny to the right. Ronald was back a few feet and behind Felder, as if he were in a short punt formation. It was the sandlot shotgun formation, and everyone used it because the rusher—only one—could bypass the center—usually the weakest player—and touch the quarterback down before he could get the pass away to his other players.

Everything was in order. Both teams were gearing up for the first offensive and defensive plays when a car turned from Bonnie View Road and started at the top of Silverhill, would be interrupting the play in a few seconds. Ronald saw this, but decided to use it for an advantage. He called for Daniels to hike the football to him, and Mikey ran a few steps and then saw the car and stopped and moved to the sidewalk. Lenny saw the car and then ran faster, racing straight toward the oncoming vehicle. Jarvis, playing the middle help defender, turned and saw the car and stopped, but Wilmer stayed with Lenny as both ran closer to the oncoming vehicle. Ronald tossed the ball high and expertly away from the car toward the sidewalk, where Lenny turned at the last minute toward the ball and away from the car and Wilmer. Wilmer turned also just as the oncoming vehicle blew its horn and made him stop in his tracks. Lenny continued moving toward the ball, caught it, and moved across the imaginary goal line.

"Touchdown," shouted Lenny with his arms in the air.

"Touchdown," shouted Ronald with his arms also in the air from the other end of the street.

Everyone moved to the sidewalks and let the oncoming vehicle pass by. The lady in the vehicle stared at the boys as she passed by. She was undeniably upset for the delay in her destination. Ronald moved toward the other end of the street, and walking toward him was Jarvis.

"Hurry and move that old car out of the way," said Ronald. "We could have run four plays while she was passing by at two miles an hour."

"That's not a touchdown," said Jarvis. "Everybody stopped so the car could pass by. You should not have even run the play. You know the rules."

"Touchdown, baby. Touchdown. That's all it is," said Ronald.

"You've got to play by the rules or no one will play," said Wilmer. He was moving up alongside of Jarvis. The rest of their team were moving down to the other end of the street to either do the play over or receive the kickoff. Lenny came up alongside Ronald and gave him the football. Ronald began walking away from Jarvis.

"Somebody's got to break the rules sometime, so you should go on down there and get ready for the kickoff because I'm gonna throw it up as high as I can."

Mikey joined his team on the other end of the street. He didn't really like the way the car had given his team an advantage, but he couldn't say much. It was the argument for the older boys to sort out, and anyway, the game had just started. But it did set a tone for the evening. Both teams fought hard on both sides and expended as much energy as possible to achieve their goals. After the touchdown from Team 1, and the kickoff, Team 2 moved down the street with short passes underneath the long passes progressing down to the goal line. This scenario was repeated for three straight scores by both teams.

The method proved both efficient and time-consuming for Team 2. It forced Team 1 to spend a lot of time on defense, where the two sixth graders were at a disadvantage. They were either rushing the passer or covering underneath, and the way Team 2 set up their offense there would be a catch and someone blocking for the pass receiver where the physical advantage was exploited. Mikey and Daniels were having a hard time touching below the belt on many occasions, and this had an effect on their offensive contributions. So eventually it became Ronald and Lenny against the entire Team 2. Team 1 fell behind by one touchdown and then Ronald threw an interception to Wilmer, who ran it all the way back for a touchdown. Ronald became angry with his team, then and began throwing the ball harder to his teammates. Their next drive was unsuccessful as well, and the ball was turned over to Team 2.

The sun was almost gone and the game would end from that signal. Parents would be calling kids home, so Team 1, Mikey's team, needed to take desperate measures. Mikey pressed closer to his opposition, and for the first time felt the urge to do something different. With other times when he played football it was always a game, but this time it became more. Just what, he did not know.

Washington hiked the ball to Jarvis, but this time instead of Daniels rushing the passer, it was Lenny. Mikey knew the switch was going to happen and he was supposed to stay with Gary Wilson, but he sort of drifted down the street angling toward the sidewalk paying close attention to the underneath area where he and Gary were when the play started.

Lenny's rush was unexpected and impressive. He moved quickly to Jarvis, who tried to move away and pass the ball at the same time, something he was not good at. He was forced to his left but tried to throw the ball quickly and right-handed to Gary Wilson. Lenny had both hands up and rushed toward Jarvis. When the ball was passed, he tipped it and it floated harmlessly toward the street. Mikey stopped in his tracks and moved to retrieve the ball before it hit the ground. He caught it and began to run in the other direction toward his goal line.

Jarvis realized his mistake and began to move toward the ball immediately after he threw it. After the interception, he adjusted his path and began to chase Mikey down the street. Mikey heard his teammates shouting for him to run faster, and he began to try as hard as possible. He knew someone was moving up behind, but he thought it was Gary Wilson. If he had known that it was the larger tenth grader he probably would have screamed and dived to the grass out-of-bounds, but he ran on.

He moved up toward the McFadden house, a white brick with blue wood trim that marked the goal line boundary, when he saw the second-most amazing sight of the week for him. It was a young black man sitting Indian style in the front yard of the McFadden's home. He was wearing an old green army shirt and pants and had his bare feet crossed. He had a large Afro that jutted out, a rope of some kind tied around his head, and a large full beard that covered his face and most of his neck. And lastly, he had dark mirrored shades covering his eyes. His facial expression was blank but serene. His hands, although gloved with cut-off finger slots, were flat on his knees with palms pointing up toward the sky. The front door to the home was open and there was loud rock music blaring from it. Rock music on Sunday was considered a blasphemy, yet there he was listening.

Mikey was startled by the sight of the young man and inadvertently slowed down. This gave Jarvis the opportunity to catch up with him and grab at the football that Mikey was carrying under his left arm. Jarvis finally got a grip on the football and pulled against Mikey's pulling arm. This caused Mikey to stumble across the goal line and into the grass that was out-of-bounds, but also caused the ball to plop up into the air and float over into the yard where the young man was sitting.

"No touchdown! He didn't have the ball when he crossed the goal line! No touchdown! No way!" shouted Jarvis.

"Touchdown, man! Yeah, touchdown! Way to go, Mikey! Touchdown, baby, touchdown!" shouted Ronald. He and Lenny ran up to the goal line. Both were dancing and happy.

Mikey lay in the grass for a moment and then traced the flight of the football with his eyes. He turned his head to get the full picture of the ball, the yard, and the young man. He half expected the young man to break the tie of the two opposing views of the play. The young man did not move. He continued his stoic posture almost like a statue. Mikey did not know what to make of the young man's lack of interest in football.

"Did you see the play?" asked Mikey. "Did I make a touchdown?"

By that time Ronald, Lenny, and Jarvis had moved up alongside Mikey, who was still lying in the grass.

"Hey man, don't talk to him," whispered Lenny, urgently.

"Yeah, man. Just run up there and get the ball," said Ronald.

"Naw, you can talk to him," said Jarvis. He moved to the sidewalk. "Hey can you throw us our football. We know it's not a touchdown. I caused a fumble before he went across the Goal and it accidentally flew into your front yard. If you don't want to toss it to us can we get it? Maybe you don't like football?"

The young man did not move. The music continued. The home, apparently empty now, was the modest abode of Francis McFadden, a fellow ninth grader, her mother, and another sister. There were rumors of an older son, Darius McFadden, a good and happy student and athlete at the high school. He had graduated earlier and was drafted by the military, but that information was sketchy and with a lapse of three to five years tended to make the credibility of any story more rumor than fact. There were rumors of his involvement in Vietnam and other rumors of the Black Panther Party, and then finally the rumor of hospitalization from a war injury. No one knew for sure, and few people ever mentioned him. In fact, his presence in the neighborhood would be a rumor if the boys had not seen him for themselves. Darius stayed to himself.

Jarvis moved forward and then stopped abruptly. He turned to Mikey, who was still lying on the grass out-of-bounds and watching the episode unfold.

"Mikey, you should go get the ball. You fumbled it," said Jarvis.

"You go and get the ball, Jarvis. You caused the fumble," said Ronald.

"Yeah, man. It's a touchdown, anyway, and you are just trying to run the time out. It's almost sunset and we'll have to stop the game," said Lenny.

"Yeah, Jarvis. You know that we are going to stop you and make another touchdown," said Ronald.

"Mikey should go and get the ball. That's what he gets for fumbling. This is how you learn to hold on to the ball."

Jarvis said this with a sneer, which was always taken as a dare, although most dares are given to disguise fear. Jarvis was one of the older of the players and he knew this was the best way to keep face. He had heard the rumors about Darius and didn't really want to press him. He remembered him from football when he first started watching it, and the same touch football games that he played with Darius when he was actually Mikey's age. Darius was one of the guys he would always watch, and who had said these same words. He had never known him well, but he hoped that repeating the same words that he had heard Darius say would startle some recognition.

"You're always making up things to get your way. You should go and get the ball," said Ronald.

"Well man, if we don't get the ball the game is over, so we win again."

With that. Ronald approached Jarvis and they stood face-to-face. The rest of the boys were walking up to the goal line and waiting for the outcome of the argument. This would determine the day. Darius McFadden sat quietly, as if he didn't notice the argument.

"If you didn't cheat on that first touchdown, this would not have happened."

"A touchdown is a touchdown. Your team has to find a way to stop us."

"And we did. I guess you haven't noticed that we are ahead, man."

"Well, when you get the ball, we will show you how to win, you loser."

"Who are you calling a loser, you last-place cheater?"

Mikey felt this could go on until sundown. He decided to make the sacrifice for the game and go and get the football. He stood and walked toward the grass and the football that was five feet away from Darius McFadden. Mikey moved closer, and with each step hoped that the young man would stand up and toss him the football. The argument stopped and all eyes were on Mikey as he got closer to the football and Darius McFadden. With each step that Mikey took, the silence seemed to grow more prominent.

He was about three feet away from both the football and Darius, standing right between both, when he paused while trying to decide whether to approach Darius with a formal greeting or grab the football and run back to the street. Without warning and with fluid movements, Darius rose from his Indian squat to full standing, like a streaming watering sprinkler turned on for the first time.

Mikey stopped in his tracks with his mouth open, trying to find the right words. He stammered a bit and then stopped and stared at the face of the young man. Standing now, Darius was much taller than Mikey, but surprisingly much thinner. Mikey could now see his hair under the hat, an uncombed Afro that had specks of lint and grass in it. His clothes were military green and baggy like a movie uniform, but different and somewhat dirtier. His shoes were combat boots that were once black and needed polish. Before Mikey could say anything, Darius turned and walked briskly into the house. As he walked his shirt moved up with his movements and briefly revealed an empty knife sheath. Then he was gone into the house with the front door slowly closing.

"Go get the ball," shouted Ronald.

Mikey, still stunned, paused for a beat and then moved up to retrieve the football. He reached it, and when he picked it up, the music from inside the home stopped. With the ball in hand, Mikey started for the street and the other boys, but he kept his eyes on the front door of the McFadden house.

"It was a touchdown, man," said Ronald.

"It was a fumble out-of-bounds. No touchdown…no touchdown… First down on the goal line, and we'll show you a goal line stand like you've never seen. You're just afraid to try against our defense," shouted Jarvis.

"Touchdown, man. Touchdown."

The two leaders continued their argument, with neither giving an inch to the other. The sun settled in the west and the home and streetlights began to illuminate a sleepy hamlet that was waiting for Monday morning.

"Wilmer…Wilmer, I know you and Gary can see those street lights!" shouted a voice from the front door of a home down the street. "Bring your brother and your butt home. You know you're not supposed to be out at night. Anything can happen to you."

The boys listened to Wilmer's mother's shouts and promises of punishments from the distance, and all at the same time exchanged looks of realization. Fleeting thoughts of their own admonishments that were coming soon surfaced, as did still deeper thoughts of the unknown and the still unanswered questions about the body that had been found in the past weeks. They exchanged good-byes and all moved silently to their homes. The farther away they got from each other, the faster they walked. Mikey, with the farthest to go, started a fast trot to his home.

XVII

April Showers
April 22, 1968

"So, he's like half-man and half-rabbit with large furry legs and a human head, shoulders, and arms. He's got on a torn T-shirt, too. Some say he's a white man, but others say something different, like he is a light-skinned black guy, and no one has been alive long enough to say for sure. He has large teeth and large ears, and the ears are half rabbit and half human so he can hear you move and understand what you are saying at the same time, and he can run fast and I mean really fast. You could be running at full speed and he could just bounce a couple of bounces and catch up with you, and you will be running and he will be bouncing ever so softly and you can't escape him. He makes this springing sound when he bounces after you like brink-brink, brink-brink! And you can't get away, as hard as you try and as fast as you run, and you can scream and scream but he will still catch you. And then he will land on your neck and bite you and bite you."

"Stop saying that! There is no such thing as the Rabbit Man. Isn't that true, Yolanda?" pleaded Jackie Brown. There was an obvious twinge of fear in her voice and her fingers were clenched tightly with her knuckles showing paleness.

It had rained again that morning, so the school recess was canceled. These were the quiet yet interesting times when the boys would run to school in their yellow raincoats and try to splash in every rain puddle on the way home. The girls were dressed in yellow raincoats with matching hats and pulled-on galoshes, but they were actually ferried back and forth to school by the mothers. They were always dry, their hair was always neatly manicured, and their raincoats were always neatly folded and lined in the back of the classroom. The boys had their rain jackets hanging above a trash can atop a broom in a corner near the broom closet, hoping that they would be dry by the end of the school day.

At least the patrol boys still did their duty in the rain. They didn't run up the flag, but they did direct traffic and allow the crossings of the younger students. They hung their wet coats in the back closet away from the coats of the other boys, and they hung proudly as badges of honor. This difference made it difficult to have civil interactions between the two groups, and eventually one would get on the other's nerves.

Aside from the schoolwork competitions in math, English, and geography, the guys usually stayed away from the girls and vice versa. The boys were always too busy talking about football and physical competitions, while the girls talked about music, clothes, dancing, and cooking. With the indoor recess an imperative, it was only natural for the two groups to overlap in the close confines of the classroom. Michael Washington was talking to Marvin Gooden about all of the rumors of the Rabbit Man and his exploits, but Yolanda and the other girls could not help but listen in. The rumors of his origin stretched from one extreme to another starting with, "He's a freak of nature who was abandoned as a child," to "radiation experiments made a madman of him."

Mikey thought, this was the longest Washington had spoken to anyone since his dog Tippy had been found dead in the tree line near the school. He also remembered that this was the same story told by Lenny, the owner of the convenience store across from the E-Z shop. Lenny's shop, "The Five and Dime" was where everyone in the neighborhood went to tell and hear stories about the current things that were happening. The Rabbit Man story had been told almost word for word about three years ago, to many adults, including Mikey's mother. Mikey overheard her after she had told his father. When Mikey had repeated the story to his father, he initially told him that it was a lie, but later told him that he had heard it as well and that it was a Jewish folktale told by an old Jewish man. His mother said, "As if being Jewish had anything to do with it," because she had heard of it a second time, but it was from the elder ladies at the church.

This was the first most important affirmation from the Wisdom Wiser's that Mikey had heard. The entire neighborhood gave the Wisdom Wiser's the stamp of approval. If they repeated it then it must be true. Then with a wink that Mikey's Mom didn't see, his father agreed that he had heard of it as well from the church and that the Rabbit Man lived in the woods where the trail led from Bishop Heights to Highland Hills. It was further rumored that the Rabbit Man came out at night and that Mikey had to be home before dark. Mikey would always make a note to be home before dark. This was a long time before they found the dead body in those same woods. After that, it never came up again in Mikey's home unless he was late. It was then when his mother would only say during a long drawn out "Okay!" in a you-know-what-will-happen-to-you tone. And after he became familiar enough with the tone, then she would only use a look that said the same thing.

"That's probably what happened to Tippy. Isn't that right, Mikey?" asked Washington.

Washington was becoming more desperate in his actions and a twinge of urgency surfaced in his tone. His eyes pleaded to Mikey to confirm his suspicions. Mikey found himself in the uncomfortable dilemma of whether to side with his best friend or continue his logical position of never committing to anything without evidence. He had learned that from his father, but his mother was blunter about the situation. She would say, "People lie to you, sometimes just 'Cause they can."

In a way this was confirmed by Mr. Campbell and the math lessons that they had learned after lunch. It was probably because numbers could not lie. And that's what his insect collection was all about. He used that logic in his exploration and capture of the insects that he would find around his home, and he would also use that same logic when he had his arguments with his sisters at home when they would try hard to have their way. That same logic became a way of life for him, a pattern of behavior that instilled confidence in the people who wanted him to side with them. He had no evidence for the Rabbit Man's existence one way or the other, and he didn't know what to say.

"Isn't that true, Mikey! Tell them that it's true! Tell them that is what happened to Tippy! That he got cut down the middle by the claws from the Rabbit Man. That he was torn down the middle and he was still alive." Washington began to get frantic. There were tears in his eyes.

"He's right, girls, he's right. It had to be the Rabbit Man. It could be no one else. Tippy was a small loving dog that never bothered anyone," said Mikey. Even as he said it, he could not believe that he was saying it. He hoped that he was saying it with conviction and no one would doubt him, but as he finished and before he could inhale, he felt Yolanda's eyes searching his face.

"Mikey, if you believe that, then you should do something about it! That's what you patrol boys do. You go out and solve problems and protect everyone," said Yolanda.

She was trying to recite the patrol boy's motto as best she knew it. She had never been privy to it. Her voice was soft and she tried to imitate the sweet-sounding voice that she had heard from a television actress. That voice was always used to persuade the boys to do what she wanted them to do. It was like Cat Woman from *Batman* or Miss Kitty from the television show *Gunsmoke,* or maybe the character in the show *Honey West*. She loved Honey West, the female private detective.

She liked all the stories of women that persuaded men to do their wishes. Even in the Bible she was interested in Jezebel, who tried to change a kingdom, or Delilah, who brought the strongest man in the land to his knees. Yolanda would ask her mother about those women, but tried not to make it too obvious so she wouldn't attract too much attention to her interest from her mother or the Wisdom Wiser's, that group of elderly ladies that had the answers and the premonitions for everything. It wasn't the bad that the Bible ladies had done, it was more the fact that they could do something that no one thought they could do that interested her. It was just another way for women to be strong.

It wasn't just the honest, hardworking, God-fearing strength of a woman that mattered now. Everyone called her Bone Girl because

JON-MICHAEL HAMILTON

she was always right. It was also the smart, beautiful, and extremely persuasive woman that was changing the world now and that's what she wanted to be. She didn't think that she was beautiful. She really didn't know what beautiful was or meant, but she believed that if it were necessary for her with this new strength, then she would become it.

"Mikey, you should go out and get to the bottom of the mystery and put everyone at ease. We all would appreciate that, and it would make Michael Washington feel happy and it would make me so happy."

"No one cares about you, Bone Girl," said Michael Daniels. "Mikey should go out and solve this mystery for Tippy because Tippy was just a poor innocent dog who never hurt anyone."

"Yeah. Didn't that dog try to bite me that day I was walking on Silverhill and I was trying to give you back your stupid comic book?"

"Tippy was going to bite you because you are a Bone Girl and dogs like bones."

Just as suddenly as the intensity grew it got very quiet, and everyone knew as if in a reflex that rippled from student to student that Mr. Campbell had reentered the classroom. It was kind of early for him, but he walked in with a bustle of energy. On days like this, like the snow days in December and January and the other days when it was too cold for recess, he would let them have the entire recess without interruption and sometimes a few more minutes. Now he walked through the doorway and beckoned for Michael Washington to come over to him.

Washington stood and went to the door and they both went back out into the hallway. The students stopped what they were doing, leaned an ear in the direction of the hallway, and tried to listen in, but Mr. Campbell whispered softly, calmly, and quietly, and no words were overheard. Only Yolanda remained in her in her seat, facing Mikey. She was unmoving and disinterested. She knew what was being said without listening.

"Mikey, what about what I asked you?" Yolanda challenged. When Mikey heard her, he knew that she understood what was being said in the hallway, and this was a type of diversion. With that, he understood what she meant as well.

196

IN SEARCH OF THE RABBIT MAN

"What can I do?"

"You can find out if any of the rumors are true."

"What about if it's dangerous?" Mikey said. He said it without thinking, and regretted it immediately because he realized for the first time that he didn't know what he could do or what to expect. He had never thought twice about the Rabbit Man, but now with the rumors about the dead body and finding Tippy torn down the middle he wondered for the first time what it was he could really do. After all, he was just a sixth grader. What could he do?

"You can always run away, Mikey. You can just see it for the first time and come back and tell us and we will believe you. That will be enough because you are just a sixth grader. You can tell the big boys and they will do something, or you can tell your father or Mr. Campbell and you know they will do something. But you are a patrol boy and we want to believe you. That's all we want, is to believe you."

Somehow, everything seemed to get more serious. He looked at Yolanda and her face was the same, with the same big Bone Girl eyes and the same skinny Bone Girl jowls and chin and the same Bone Girl body, but it seemed everything else became more serious. Mikey sat quietly for a moment and it seemed as if the entire class was looking to him. That was what Yolanda did so very well. She would make a speech in front of everyone that would be like a challenge, and then everyone listening would wait for a response. She would pick the best times to do this, and he really couldn't hate her for it. In fact, he sort of respected her for voicing her opinions. She was the opposite of him and he respected her.

But what could he do about the Rabbit Man question? If he followed her suggestion it would seem like she was ordering him around, because she put it that way. In reality it was a good suggestion, but she had suggested it. What difference did that make? It didn't matter who suggested it as long as it was a plan. It was a plan.

Mikey begin to speak, but at that very moment Mr. Campbell came back into the classroom followed by Washington. The good thing about Mr. Campbell was that no one could ever read his face or understand what was underneath the medium Afro, bushy mustache, and thick

197

sideburns, and no one would ever know what it was he was feeling. He would have that same happy expression as soon as he began to speak to his students, and then whatever happened before was over and the new was beginning. He walked in and stood before the class and waited until Washington returned to his seat. Then he began to speak.

"Okay class, you must have forgotten what we've decided to do on the days when we can't go outside. Does anyone remember?"

The students were caught between the crossroads of a possible disobedience or plain neglect of a classroom protocol and so they remained silent. Mr. Campbell smiled a light smile, then went to the file cabinet by his desk, opened it, and then pulled out a small case that contained a phonograph player with a 45 spindle on top. He set it on his desk and then went back to plug the extension into the outlet.

"It's time for the four Temptations," he said, facing the students. A few yelped with joy, some groaned with relief, but Michael Washington, Michael Daniels, and Marvin Gooden all looked to Mikey with the same measure of apprehension.

"Let's go, guys. It's time our four tempting Temptations," said Mr. Campbell again. "Go on to the back and get the routine ready. I'll start the music when you are ready."

The students clapped with encouragement, and even Yolanda smiled a bit. Marvin stood first. In his heart he considered himself the best performer. He would do the Easter plays at his church, and whenever it was time to say a speech or do any production he would volunteer. This started as a dare between chess matches with Mikey, and after the first run-through he knew he could be good at it. What was most important was that he liked to do it. No one was really singing, and although he could hold a few notes on his own, he found that the pantomiming of the song was an art in its own right. When it was his turn to sing, he would put on his best airs with the facial expressions and gestures that matched the words. He easily became the lead singer of the group.

The others followed, and for the first and only time acquiesced to his leadership. Michael Washington followed without as much enthusiasm, and then Michael Daniels, and finally Mikey, while everyone waited with growing anticipation of the performance. Mr. Campbell stood ready at his desk with the small phonograph already turning and warming up. The small 45 single was already spinning around, and the whole contraption gave a hiss from the one built-in speaker and a scraping sound from the revolving single.

The guys huddled in the back and then Marvin got four raincoats from the back-closet area and brought them to the huddle. The guys huddled even more and then emerged at the same time from the huddle wearing the raincoats, only the coats were worn inside out. This broke up the slick yellow outdoor appearance and gave the boys white jacket arms with dark backs and fronts. It gave them the color cohesion that looked more like a planned performance than a recess distraction. When they tucked the collars in instead of out, the wardrobe was complete. The girls yelped with glee and the rest of the class gave a smattering of applause and desk pounding.

Mr. Campbell continued to move the few desks away from the front of the classroom and made a makeshift performing area. When it was complete, the boys moved to the front of the classroom and took their positions facing away from the rest of the students. Mr. Campbell moved to the desk and started the phonograph and then moved away and to the back of the classroom.

The music started and all four boys begin rocking their shoulders left and right in sequence to the rhythm of the beat. Then one by one, they turned and faced the class. They were only supposed to lip sync, but Marvin would never listen. In the past he had always been the alternate patrol boy, but never really a patrol boy. He could never have the input about safety for street crossing even though he was trained like the rest, just in case. But he would blast the lead lyrics over the record every chance he got. He was a good singer, this the boys would admit, but the fact that they were only lip syncing put them in the spotlight as not real singers. Like all the new Afro-wearing blacks were saying, how important it was to be real.

This took something away from the experience for Mikey. He felt that everything that he had done up to this point was real. Assuming the danger from wasp stings and mosquito bites and still collecting all of the insects for his research displays was real. No one had anything to match his insect collection. And if they tried, even Marvin came up woefully short. Mikey had never liked to pretend anything like going to church or playing the piano or eating squash. He was always serious when he had to do those things, and the key was to not let anyone know that he hated to do those things, because people would watch him more closely when he did those things, those adult things. All the girls in his family knew from the way he did things if he liked to do it or was just pretending. It seemed to be the female practice to determine whether a man was serious or pretending. That's what his father would say when his mother's sisters, his aunts, would gather around with his uncles and talk about what men and women should do. That he didn't like to pretend, or more importantly, when he wasn't real was something that Mikey had struggle with all the time.

Mikey was twelve years old and he really wanted to pretend and be a kid and play and not take everything so seriously, but everything was becoming so serious. Everybody was frightened because of the dead body, and then Tippy died, and it seemed that everybody was talking about the Rabbit Man again. In a way he envied the army guy who sat in his front yard in an Indian squat for half the day and never talked to anyone.

Mikey wasn't paying much attention to the song and eventually missed a step. Daniels and Washington looked to him at the same time with the same glare. So much for the dancing. He grew more attentive and began to sing in the direction of Yolanda. This was a way to become more serious, although Bone Girl would never believe that he was singing to her.

Marvin was a good singer. Marvin was the lead singer, and unfortunately the only singer in the group. He could sing like the people on television and like the singers who performed the Christmas songs that he had heard before, like "Rudolph" and "Frosty" and "The Little Drummer Boy." He could sing those songs with feeling and a range from a young bass to a full tenor and make the songs sound like the real singers. He loved a lot of things; maybe the Archie songs and the *Charlie Brown Christmas* songs but his favorite was *The Red Baron Song*. No one wanted to sing that song.

The rest of the class began to use his specialty, his love, against the rest of the patrol boys. Marvin used this as well, because he was an alternate patrol boy and not really a normal patrol boy. When it was time for the lead singer to sing the solo, he would step away for the group and try more of the gestures and the facial expressions, and it felt good for him. This was when and where he separated himself from the rest of the patrol boys—when it was time to sing a solo, any solo, but mostly when the entire class was witness.

So, maybe Marvin was an awkward football player, and he was slow with the flash cards, and he was slow with the science, and he was slow with the states…but aside from the football, he was second for boys only to Mikey in science, and in flash cards, but not in math. Well, maybe just a little in math and numbers, because football had been reduced to numbers, and how much you weighed, and how tall you were, and how fast you were, and how strong you were. Those boys did not really know what football was really all about, and his father had told him what football was really about because his father wanted him to be more. But who really cared about football anyway?

But Marvin could sing and he could hold the notes and make them sound like the original singers, and he did not have to try too hard. He loved it most when he had bested Mikey. Those were Marvin's own words, and what he would say to Mikey when Mikey had won a chess match: "You've bested me." Sometimes he would ask for another game, and he would always try to double his rooks on any row to win and Mikey would try something different. He didn't think all of this at one time, but it was there whenever he needed it. He would always remember what Mikey had told him that his mother would say on these times when everything counted for something: to do what you do best and forget about the other people. He kept that in mind and he moved forward and belted his lyrics loudly over the music again.

Jon-Michael Hamilton

"I've got sunshine on a cloudy day.
When it's cold outside I've got the month of May.
I guess you'd say
What can make me feel this way?
My girl (my girl, my girl)
Talkin' 'bout my girl (my girl)."

Mikey always tried to say "Bone Girl" in the chorus, but the task was to mask his voice so no one could determine who said it, especially Yolanda. He would not do it early and he would not do it too often, but he would do it at least three times in the song and make sure Yolanda heard it. When the other boys heard it, they would not know who sang it either, or if they did, they wouldn't say.

Mr. Campbell could never tell who had said it, and he didn't really care. It was a harmless attempt to attract a young girl's attention, and if it got bad then he would say something, but these were his kids and he had them all day and he knew who their parents were. Nothing strange had ever happened in this neighborhood or at this school until lately. He was from Chicago and he knew what was bad and what was good and what was dead and what was dying. He had learned at home what dying was, really, and he could say he argued or reaffirmed what dead or death really was.

He had taught in this state for ten years for the school district and four years at this school. He was glad to be at this school with the young black children and the new black community that had never heard of a dead body or even a dead bird; they always had a young innocence in everything that they would do. It was like everything was new to this community. He was there to get away. He needed to move from the clutter and bustle of Chicago. To move away from the pressures of living without innocence and seeing and knowing everything too early.

He heard Mikey sing to Yolanda, a little off-key, and he knew it was best to say nothing and let the environment determine the norm for the behavior. He remembered the song and always thought the Temptations were the best group that he had heard in his lifetime. That song was about his wife and what she wanted and what they were trying to build, and this was his balance, he felt, from his caring and caring too much. He wanted to be a good teacher, and the best teachers knew when to step back and let things happen and when to step in and make changes. The question was always about decisions, the right decisions, and whether to step in or not.

To the audience the patrol boys worked through the number with the same ease as before, and they were thoroughly pleased with the distraction. The good thing was that Washington was acting interested again and not moping around with his grief and sadness. Daniels and Marvin Gooden were happy as well. Even Mikey got into the whole number. The boys finished with a bang and a bow and applause, and everyone reluctantly went back to the lessons. The best way to end this day after the English lesson was with the geography flash cards. It was no reason to waste the energy of a good applause.

XVIII

The Timing
April 22, 1968l

It was so much like music, to make the day better. It was like sunshine fighting through a still gray sky and touching the horizon with long fingers and pausing the sunset. There was music for every occasion; that's the way Mikey looked at it. It wasn't just snowy glimmering Christmas music with bells jingling and people laughing, or anyone's birthday music. It was like shiny and glittery light streaming across the snow and shimmering across the pavement and off the downtown buildings at night like the just-as-bright moonlight, and telling many things in hidden voices, so much more. It wasn't just the musical cadence of "Red Light, Green Light Go" anymore, in the spring moonlight when the happy voices of family and love would seep out into the night like a warm caress of love and everyone is there and everyone is all right. But it was the day, a new day and the day after the rain.

The 45s and the larger LPs were giving everybody the sounds of the day. The AM stations and the new FM—or really, the only FM—was sending music to the antennae of everyone's cars and home radios and to the guys lucky enough to be walking around with transistor radios in 1968. It was still 1968 and was the sounds of James Brown, the Four Tops, The Spinners, Aretha, Smokey, the Supremes and the Tempting Temps for his neighborhood. And yeah, within all of the various harmonies and soloists and tenor's pitches was the sound of the beat.

When Mikey first heard the sound of the music it was always something to make him stop and think, or even watch the ways people reacted to music. He could see his mother and sisters move with quick stilted movements that soon led to smooth swaying and rocking and giving in to a wave that always swayed back in time, still singing to the music.

His mom was a churchgoing woman, and music and the piano were in their home as well and as long as the church had been in their family. It was not like the church was foreign to their house, because Mikey's grandfather was a minister. Even though he didn't know him, his shadow seemed to be there. Ministers were important, that's what his father always said. His mother said it as well, and so everyone would hear the practice of church songs in the evening up to Sunday, when they would sing. Mostly his mother who sang, because Te'ah really couldn't and Dottie just wasn't old enough and Palmer would not even try. He could still hear the piano music and the rehearsed church songs that came from his grandfather because they were church songs, and the only notes he liked were the lower notes that seemed to keep everything in place. Just like a heartbeat.

Heartbeats were very important to Mikey because they led back to science like everything led back to science. Michelangelo could see that everything had a sort of time to it, like the insects he followed and somehow caught because he could judge their time, feel their time. Time was like a pause that you could feel or not feel but would notice nonetheless. And in church, time was like a movement or a wind, or a loud thump. The spiritual music that people would clap to was in the church, always someone patting a foot to the time and the beat, and grandmothers rocking, and girls nodding their heads, and Mikey finding himself watching everything. The slow songs were the easiest to keep time with because even if they were slower, they had the same amount of time as the popular fast songs. It was always more to them, more ways to count because you had to work harder and find the count.

When Mikey became older, he began to categorize and add worthwhile things to his regular routine. He would listen to a song, and if he liked the way it sounds, he would remember it on the day and time when he had heard it and would test himself later when he heard it again and add it to his routine. Music became another thing like the insects he collected, and the math and science lessons he had learned and categorized, and the stories and newspaper articles where he had read about the Cowboys and the Browns and the Packers, and the best players and his favorite characters and lessons and numbers and bugs that were from numbers from pages and that became numbers to keep in place. The beat became a number within his numbers that seemed to give him the audible balance to his pictures and his collecting and categorizing that could overwhelm a sixth grader who always watched. But the beat was there, like a tick of a clock or the slight whizzing of a Texas breeze that would blow like breath and shake everything the same way with the same bump every time, and then stop like an inhale and bring silence and keep time and give the day meaning.

The day finally ended and the rain stopped with more of an absence than a ceasing. It had moved away. At three o'clock the sun peeked out through some of the clouds in a patch of the sky and there were no arguments about the Patrol Boys status, who would work and who would not work, or why. After the music, the Temptations number, and the flash card game—where Yolanda and the girls eventually won again with a lot of celebration—the routine solved itself. Michael Daniels decided to let Marvin have his turn, and while he watched he took the opportunity to critique Marvin on his street-crossing duties and his flag-folding duties and even the way he wore his belt. Since the belts were adjustable, with the width around the waist and the length of the shoulder strap, it was important to know and to show how far down the waist belt hung on the waist, how the shoulder strap ran across the shoulder to the waist, and also how tight or loose the waist belt was cinched. Washington helped with a mock inspection of Marvin before and afterward and it became all in good fun.

Washington said, "Even if your name isn't Michael, you're looking good and you're gonna do a good job."

This took the sting out of the day's disappointments for Washington, and perhaps for everyone who had felt that searching for the Rabbit

IN SEARCH OF THE RABBIT MAN

Man was a life-or-death struggle. And it wasn't much of a life-or-death struggle after Bone Girl and the girls won the flash-card contest again. "Who really cares where Topeka really is anyway?"

It wasn't a life-or-death struggle for Marvin either, because his name was not Michael. There were already three Michaels in the classroom and his name did start with an M, so that made it close enough, he felt, so everyone should have forgotten by now. Marvin stood there looking out for validation like he had always done before, for someone to say again that he was okay. If it came from anyone other than Washington in the group, then it would be okay. But it only came from Washington, and Marvin was an outsider and needed validation again from someone outside of the group. It became obvious to everyone that was watching. Someone outside of the group would, should, or had to.

Mikey was stoic and aloof, a spectator to the event. Everyone had walked, run, or were taken away from school like Yolanda and her friends, and this was the way, his father and his uncles and all the men had said it would be. Sometimes when things were over, it was best if you were not the last person there, especially if you couldn't take responsibility for being the last person there. This was anywhere.

It started with a conversation with Mikey and his father after a Sunday evening at Grandma's. They were never the last to leave, but for the first time Mikey felt it was for a good reason. Grandma's, Mikey's mother's mother, was where Mikey's mom's sisters, the aunts, would bring their husbands. It wasn't animosity; it was just good competition.

The boys returned all of the patrol belts and the flags to the principal's office, and with the same camaraderie waited to gather their books from the pile that had been there waiting like so many blocks on the side of the desk of the principal's secretary. They had thought about fooling her, Ms. Pardee, with a game that they would play of trying to remove the books without her notice. She was young and very cute, Mikey thought, and had an easy smile, and always had good humor about the game. This time she wasn't paying much attention to them. She only listened intently to the telephone that she held up to her ear. She had a worried look on her face and tried to get the boys to wait

207

until she finished with her phone conversation. What was being said forced distress from her, so it must have been school information? It was probably something about books or a trip to the Dallas Symphony, which was starting its season again.

At any rate it had to be something boring, thought Daniels. In a hurried scoop he gathered up all the books for the boys and started out the door to the hallway. When he raced down the hallway, he heard the other patrol boys pattering behind him. When he exited the school and down near the flagpole, he heard the boys urging him to "slow down, stop, and stop playing."

He reached the crossing and darted in front of a worried mother and daughter in a purring Ford, who had just begun to move from the stop sign and into the crosswalk. They stopped abruptly, and while the mother's face had a reprimanding scowl the daughter's face showed glee and mirth for the moment.

Reaching the other side, he finally dropped two books, Marvin Gooden's *Chess Moves Made Simple* and his natural science textbook. Gooden bellowed in genuine pain as he watched his precious books fall down to the wet pavement and so close to the drainage ducts that lined the curbs in intervals and welcomed rushing streams of runoff. Daniels finally stopped on the other side of the street and laughed and shouted encouragement and begged the boys to come across and join him. Mikey, Michael Washington, and Marvin stood on the other side. Washington laughed, for the first time in a long time it seemed. Mikey was glad to see Washington returning to his old normal self, so he laughed also.

Marvin took the opportunity to close ground on Daniels. What he intended to do he hadn't really thought about clearly. He only wanted to grab his two favorite books, one the key to finally besting Mikey at chess, and the other his first love and a stepping-stone to space travel. Marvin ran across the street about the same time as an oncoming City of Dallas water and sanitation truck turned the corner and barreled through the crosswalk. The horn blared loudly as two men in white uniforms peered behind cigarette smoke and reflected sunglasses. "Git out of the way, boy," shouted the driver.

IN SEARCH OF THE RABBIT MAN

Marvin dived back in the direction that he had come from and was barely grazed on his shoe by the truck bumper. It knocked his shoe off, which went tumbling down the street and finally came to rest against the adjacent curb. The shoe, a black dress one with laces, rested right side down and would need drying and cleaning. Marvin landed in the wet grass just in front of Washington and Mikey. He would need cleaning and drying as well. The sanitation truck continued through the crosswalk and seemed to accelerate through the surrounding homes until it vanished from sight.

Daniels was stunned. He stood across the street and mouthed some unintelligible sounds. He held the rest of the books in place only because he could not move. The lady in the purring Ford, Mrs. Blakely, a neighbor who lived on Silverhill and a few houses down from Washington, gasped and then jumped from her car and ran awkwardly toward Marvin. She was a small thin woman, but not frail. She had a frenetic strength that complimented her various arm and facial expressions, and of course her shrieking voice. She got halfway there and then ran back and stopped the ignition of her car. It belched, and then quit, and then there was a silent pall that dropped over the street.

There were muffled sounds. The fast and soft clacking footsteps of the woman from the car as she rushed over to Marvin. The soft moaning of Marvin as he slowly realized that his clothing was spoiled, that his shoe was further down the street, and that his precious books were still lying near the curb across the street and quickly becoming more ruined with each passing moment. The soft breaths from Mikey and Michael Washington as they watched the effects of a playful excursion gone badly. The look on Daniels's face, still happy, still hoping for validation of his actions.

It was then when Mikey sensed something was wrong. What? He did not know. It just wasn't like Daniels to hold on to a joke for too long. Usually it would be over when he came to street. He never would have run across the street before. It was part of the patrol boy's motto and in the handbook. Too many things could happen that weren't good if you ran across the street. It was something that they would urge the young kids to refrain from. And then he had dropped Marvin's books and left them in the street and laughed again. It wasn't normal. But then, the past weeks weren't following the normal pattern.

Mikey stood on the sidewalk and watched as the patter of shoes came closer.

"Holler, holler, lie down and holler," said Mrs. Blakely as she walked briskly to Marvin. "Scream, lie down on your back and scream. I'll call the police…just lie back and scream and cry. You boys over there come over and help him."

She stood over Marvin and bent down to try to touch him or hold him down, because at that moment Marvin jumped up and began dusting his clothes off.

"Stay down, you silly boy. You could really be hurt! You boys should be more careful. This patrol stuff is a dangerous job, running in front of cars and hoping they'll stop for you and your little belts and hands. You could really get hurt. Just stay where you are."

"Please, Mrs. Blakely, I'm not going to lie in this wet grass. I'm all right…I just want my shoe. It must be around here somewhere," Marvin said.

"I saw it fly all the way down the street. It's down there against the curb," said Washington. It was the first time that he had witnessed anything like this or had the chance to say anything about it. He wanted everything to sound honest and be accurate. It was his way to be helpful. "Honesty is helpful" was what his father would always say to him. "It was in the air a long time like a pop fly, and it turned over and over and then came down. It bounced a little and then landed by the curb."

"You've said that before," Marvin shouted as he peered down the street. "My father will be here to pick me up in a few minutes. Let's look for it." He could not withhold the urgency in his voice. Horseplay of any kind was something his father had always warned against: "It never leads to anything positive."

Mikey and Daniels moved down the street, with Daniels moving faster. He knew exactly were the shoe was. Marvin stayed behind, and for the first time looked over to Washington. Michael Washington watched and saw the pain of Marvin's face. He smiled again, but didn't know why.

"I got it!" shouted Daniels. He ran back to Marvin and gave it to him. Marvin finally exhaled a long sigh. Mrs. Blakely felt better. She saw the relief on Marvin's face and this gave her a bit of respite for the moment, as well. She went back to her car and closed the door. Sitting in the seat with her hands on the wheel and her head turned, she gave Daniels a hard stare before starting her car with a loud burp and a cloud of white smoke. After some delay, she finally drove off.

"Stop playing around and bring the books over!" shouted Mikey.

Michael Daniels was reluctant for a moment, but finally resigned to comply. He ran back and picked up the fallen books and started back over across the street. His head was down to give the appearance of contrition, but on his face and hidden from view was a long tight smile. He tried hard to hold it in, but as he got closer the larger it became. When he reached the other side with the books he looked up and smiled now, to all the boys.

"Man, did you see that? Boy that was fun!"

Mikey and Marvin and Mike Washington looked to him with as many different reactions as there were boys. Mike Washington had a look of wonder on his face. He felt the act was incredulous at best and just outright stupid in the least. He looked with arched eyebrows and a mouth slightly opened at the lips, and for some reason began to breathe through his mouth. He would only do that when he became excited or overly happy. Marvin had an angry look on his face: his mouth taut, his cheeks flushed, his head held high, but his eyes strangely calm. And even his fists had been clenched, but were unclenched in a moment of respite. Mikey had the strangest look. It was a look of soft watery eyes and with slight breaths, his lips pursed and hidden from view. He spoke softly in an exhale: "Let's go home."

And that was it, a silent ending to the escapade and the short walk home. Mikey and Washington and Daniels joined together and walked across the street while Marvin walked back to the front of the school where he would wait patiently for his father. He was looking dejected

Jon-Michael Hamilton

when he walked up to the school and sat down on the step and looked through his books. Waiting by the door was Ms. Pardee with her hands on her slim hips. She leaned down to Marvin, who moved away and could be seen by the other boys turning his head from side to side to communicate *no*.

The patrol boys walked down the inclined Tioga Street that led away from the school, across their home street, and to the large cross street that led out of the neighborhood. The homes in this section of the neighborhood were all brick with wood siding and trim and asphalt roofs, and all had trimmed front and back yards. Not many were without backyard fences, and the homes that stood out from the rest were noticed. The kids from those families acted differently or were treated differently by the children at school, and teachers were alert to incidents of mistreatment from both sides. As a patrol boy, Mikey was privy to this type of information. Mr. Campbell felt that all the boys should be aware of personal problems that could create classroom or playground problems. It seemed like such a small thing to be treated differently because of where and how you lived, but Mr. Campbell had said that that was the way it was, so Mikey tried to be aware of both sides of the argument before he formed an opinion.

The boys walked along the sidewalk with an awkward silence, which seemed to exist more and more since Washington's dog, Tippy, was found. The times before, which weren't often, Mikey would tease Washington about Tippy and how much he depended on the small dog for his happiness. It was Washington's responsibility. Now when the silence came it seemed to be an unwelcome reminder of the past discussions and playful teasing; all the more reason to find something new to talk about and all the more reason for the awkwardness.

As the boys turned onto La Grange Drive, they came face-to-face with the ice cream truck speeding away. It seemed that the driver must have just finished a stop, because a group of kids were standing near the street in a small huddle. Mikey remembered the last episode with the ice cream truck and how the kids from Silverhill and La Grange Circle had chased him down the street with rocks and bottles. It was the same truck and must have had the same results from possible customers. The truck had some of the same dents and scratches and now mud balls across the sides and back, and the driver stared straight ahead with his jaw set in an angry clench. The boys smiled and Daniels took it in with more enjoyment than the others.

He said, "Why does he keep coming back? No one wants to buy that lousy ice cream. I mean, who would want anything from him?"

"Yeah, he keeps trying though," said Mikey.

"Why do they treat him like that?" asked Washington.

"Someone said that he was trying to give some girls free Popsicles after he took a bite from the tops of them."

"Did he take the paper off before he took the bite?" asked Daniels.

"What difference does that make? I wouldn't want one from him if it wasn't a whole Popsicle," said Washington. The boys were coming up on the huddle of kids still standing near the street. It seemed that they were standing over and looking down at something. Mikey recognized all of the boys from the elementary school. Some were in the other sixth grade class that would play every day on recess. They were the same boys who never could keep their shirttails tucked into their pants during the school day. It was Donny Edmonds and Larry Stranger, and a few girls like Penny Goodwin and Lucy Brown.

"You don't like to share. That's all there is to it, Michael," said Daniels to Washington. He laughed loudly and looked to Mikey to join in.

Washington said, "If you receive something from someone, it should be the whole thing and not just a piece of something."

"Haven't you heard, it's the thought that counts? That's what my mom always says," said Daniels. He was enjoying this exchange. It made him feel good again. It made him feel like he felt when he snatched Marvin's books and ran away.

"My mom says, never take anything from someone you don't know," said Washington. He stopped walking and almost shouted. Mikey kept walking. He was more interested in the huddle of boys then the playful argument. He arrived at the huddle and looked down and had the same hushed reaction as the other boys. He could see now that Donny was angry. Larry, seeing Mikey walk up for the first time, also became angry.

"What do you want here, Patrol Boy?" said Larry. It was more a statement than a question and Mikey wondered if he should just walk away. Daniels and Washington finally made it to the huddle and both boys looked down and gasped at almost the same time.

"Whose dog is that?" asked Washington. "It looks dead just like my dog."

Donny said, "It's my dog. I mean, I found it one day and it just stayed with us in the yard and in the garage. I didn't even name it."

Donny's yard was one of the few yards in the neighborhood without a fence. It was a sprawling yard and one of the largest in the neighborhood. It was sometimes used for football games in the summer, and kickball when the girls joined in, but now had a small scruffy mixed-breed collie dead on the edge of the grass. There was some blood, but the animal looked peaceful with its paws in pairs stretched out in front and its hind legs tucked in close to its belly, almost like it was sleeping.

"I guess the patrol boys are going to report this to Mr. Campbell too. Just like everything else."

Mikey ignored Larry and said to Donny, "Maybe you should tell you father. He'll know what to do."

"My father doesn't care about the dog. He told me to let him run away because it cost too much to feed him. He said dogs need special dog food and not just bones from the table, so I would hide him and give him some of my food. He really did like macaroni and cheese." Donny knelt down beside the dog and touched his paw.

"Maybe you can tell one of your brothers," said Mikey. Donny had two older brothers who played high school football. They were big guys who already had sideburns and mustaches.

"He doesn't have to tell anybody," said Larry Stranger. "It's just a dog that he found. It not like anybody bought it or anything."

"What's that got to do with anything?" said Washington. He moved to the circle and stood face-to-face with Larry Stranger. "Dogs don't have to be expensive. If he didn't bite anyone, and if he licked your hand and played with you when you couldn't go anywhere or stopped people from fighting, then he would be all right. You don't know anything about dogs; that's why you guys always lose the football games. Ain't that right, Mikey?"

"You damn Patrol Boys think you know so much!" said Larry.

"He's cursing," said Washington.

The girls begin to move away, and for a moment Larry and Washington stood face-to-face. They both stared long and hard to each other, and then Donny stood up and walked to his home. He walked with a determined look and smooth confident strides to his garage. He was inside for a moment and then returned with a brown pillowcase. He moved to the dog and scooped him up and into the case, and carried him away to the two large tin family trash cans that were stationed behind the house and on the edge of the yard facing the alley. He walked over and put the pillowcase into the trash can, closed the lid, and went inside his home.

"I'm going home," said Washington. He turned to leave and Mikey and Daniels followed, leaving Larry and the other boys standing behind in silence.

The End of the World
April 22, 1968
Monday evening

"Damn patrol boys! Is that what he said? Lord have mercy…Who was out there when he said it? Was there anyone around to watch you boys? I told you to come straight home and don't waste time talking to those boys down the street who love to have their shirttails out. They never go to church and they just do as much sinning as possible. Lord have mercy."

Mikey's mom was home from work at her usual time of four o'clock and in the kitchen preparing dinner. She always planned for a five-thirty dinner, so the day would finish at the dinner table and then the cleaning and preparing for the next day would begin before television time. Her routine was engrained to the children's routine now and it was best for the children to remember that.

She had a big bowl of potatoes soaking in water and was starting to peel them with a much-too-large knife as she spoke. She handled the potato peeling smoothly and used a circular motion with the hand holding the potato and straight expert precision with the hand holding the knife and peeling the skin. She placed the peeled skin on yesterday's newspaper, which she had set on the adjacent counter. She still had on her work clothes at home, a cafeteria worker's light blue smock and brown hairnet. She even had the white shoes in her attire, the shoes that Mikey would help wipe clean on the weekends.

In Search of the Rabbit Man

She was a tall woman whose Native American ancestry showed more than her African ancestry. She was almost five feet eleven inches tall, with long brown shoulder-length hair. She had large hands and feet for a woman, and that was not the most unique aspect of her appearance. She had high cheekbones and a straight nose that gave her face a noble look, and her skin color was more reddish than brown. Mikey liked her professional look and always tried to help her with her evening preparations while the girls, Palmer, Theodora, and Dottie were in their rooms doing homework and girl things. They were probably doing more girl things than homework because when Mikey went in one day, he saw them looking in magazines and practicing makeup and dress-up.

"You should pray, Michael. You should pray for all the people who don't understand how-to do-good things for the Lord." Mikey only nodded. It wasn't that he didn't believe in the teachings of the Good Book; it was just hard to pray for people who insulted him. He would never tell his mother that, but he had told his father who had told him never to tell his mother. "Why start an argument if you can avoid one?" was his saying.

It was all part of the service community which his father and mother were a part of. His father and mother had been in many situations where avoidance was the best prescription for success. Even if it was 1968, not long ago, before the marching and Dr. King and the civil rights struggle, blacks had to live with one eye on the road and the other eye watching everything around them. In fact, they lived with the label of Negro or colored as opposed to black, and took many criticisms without any opportunity to respond. His father had said words to this effect and had said specifically that in those days taking it and praying about it was the only answer for situations like that. But that was a long time ago, was always Mikey's reply. His dad didn't agree and did argue the alternative.

"We found another dog, Mom. It was Donny Edmonds's dog and they found it in the grass on the side of their house. We saw the ice cream truck pass by before we got there."

"Well, you know not to eat any ice cream from some truck. You know it will spoil your appetite for dinner."

217

"I wouldn't eat any ice cream before dinner. I don't have the money for it, but…"

"I heard this man was trying to give people free ice cream after he had tasted it himself. You had better never let me hear about you taking ice cream from that man. I will tan your hide and then tell your father and he will pound you."

She had finished peeling the potatoes and gave Mikey the newspaper that held the skins to throw into the trash. After washing and rinsing them again she moved from the sink to the counter and began to dice them into cubes, and then tossed the cubes back into the bowl with water.

"Mikey, reach up to the bar and turn on my radio I hope no one has messed with my station."

Mikey knew that the end of their conversation was near, but he didn't want it to end. Eventually the music would play, gospel music, and then his mom would begin singing, and while the mashed potatoes were simmering and the roast was shimmering and the greens were greening and the corn bread was breading, she would soon move to the piano and begin playing. The house would be filled with gospel music and the girls would really try to study then to keep from being asked to come out and join in with the singing. Sometimes it would turn into an old-fashioned choir rehearsal with music books and musical selections and coaching. Luckily, Mikey thought, he sang off-key and always too loud.

Mikey moved to the radio and turned it on, but also turned the volume down low so he could be heard.

"This makes the second dog, and with the dead body, something must be going on around here. Do you think the Rabbit Man is doing this?"

"You know what I think about the Rabbit Man. If you don't pray enough, well then, bad things always happen."

"You think we should pray more…?"

"Boy, shut up and listen. All of this is in the Bible in the book of Revelation, and if you would read it you would know what is happening. If a great man like Dr. King can be killed, then the world is living in a sorry state and there is not much else you can do but pray and hope that your slate is clean so you can go up to heaven when the day comes."

In Search of the Rabbit Man

"But shouldn't we try to find the Rabbit Man?"

"Who've you been talking to? If Mr. Campbell is giving you this nonsense about finding strange people and things then I am going to make you quit the Patrol Boys;"

"Yolanda said that someone should do something. Even the police came to school and said we should watch out for strange things."

"Yolanda from up the street?"

"Yeah."

"Didn't you boys used to call her Bone Woman or something?"

"Bone Girl? Mom, you don't remember. We've talked about this before. I've never called her that. It is always been Michael Washington or Daniels."

"Boy, you got a good memory. But, why do they call her that?"

"They say because she is skinny and she is always trying to do what the boys are doing. She wants to be a Patrol Boy," said Maxi. She finished the potatoes, drained them and then walked around from the kitchen to the dining room. She went to the piano, which was an upright model placed against the furthest wall from the kitchen. Above the piano, an unfinished picture of Jesus Christ was placed. It was a larger version of the picture that was in the family Bible and was Mikey's father's artistic effort. It matched color for color and line for line, except the face was unfinished. Big Teddy had said that the face was the hardest thing to complete. "Who really knows the face of Christ?" he said. When Mikey was younger, he thought that this was the strangest thing his father had ever told him, but that was before he started doing his own investigations of everything.

Maxi stool by the piano stool, lifted the top seat, and pulled out two of the songbooks that were inside. She began to look through the first but continued to listen halfheartedly.

"And you think that's bad because she wanted to be a patrol boy?"

"I don't care, but it is strange that she is the only girl who wants to do it and the rest of the girls are okay with what they are doing."

"And have you seen many strange things?"

"Yeah, every day we find something strange," said Mikey. His voice took on the pleading sound that he always used when he felt he couldn't explain himself clearly. It seemed that whatever he said, his mother always had some kind of answer. She finally looked from the songbook to him.

"There is nothing strange, Mikey. You're just growing up and seeing new things, and I know one thing for sure: I can't hear my music. Boy, you must've turned it down so I could listen to your nonsense. Now turn it up. If you want to talk about this, talk to your father when he comes home."

"And that would be...?"

"Come here for a second." Mikey moved from the day bar and the radio and over to his mother. She stopped playing and reached to his head and ran a hand over it and felt his hair. He tilted his head down, looking at his shoes. She then brushed his face with her fingers tracing from his brow down the side of a cheek to the point of his chin. She then lifted up his chin and looked into his eyes.

"Your hair is really getting long. You know Mama likes your hair cut short. You'll look like those important young men on television with Dr. King and those important ones at our church. Always so proud and polite and doing good things for people. One day you'll be a young usher with the young adults on Sunday. You know it makes your mama happy when you do what is right. On the weekend when you see your father, you must tell him to cut your hair. Everything will be okay if you have some patience and let the Lord fix it. Now go see what your sisters are doing and tell them to come here."

Maxi sat on the piano stool and placed the books on the stand and rolled back the piano top. She brushed her fingers across the keys and began to play softly. She started a soft hum that soon escalated to a mild chorus.

> *"Jesus will fix it by and by,*
> *after a while,*
> *Jesus will fix it by and by..."*

Mikey moved to his sisters' room, knocked, and then went in. The music from the outside whiffed into the room for a moment and then muffled as the door closed. Palmer, who at a young age looked most like her mother, was lying on the bed on her back and peering up through a magazine that was held above her. Theodora, nicknamed Te'ah, was sitting on the other bed alternating between listening to Dottie read her favorite book, *The Dark Pony*, from the chair at the dressing table and looking into the mirror behind Dottie and combing her hair. Te'ah always spent a lot of time looking into the mirror. She had many different hairstyles, and since she had her hair cut short just above her shoulders, she would practice the different styles. One was when the hair was combed all to the back, another was parted on the side, another was parted down the middle, and another was combed to the front like the Beatles singing group. Those were just a few favorites. When she moved into the Diana Ross and Aretha Franklin style she would start incorporating flips and waves. As a beginning sophomore in the fall semester, she started practicing the more stylish ways, but tried carefully to keep them all hidden from her mother's preview.

The bedroom was spacious and was really the master bedroom for the home design. There was a tiered bunk bed for Dottie and Palmer and a full-sized bed for Te'ah. There was also a white chiffon dressing table with a vanity mirror and matching chair with white pillows tied to the frame for comfort. There was a big dresser with five drawers for undergarments and summer wear that stood adjacent to the big double closet. In the closet were various hats, Sunday dresses, shoes, jackets, and other assorted costumes for young females. There was also a bookcase for schoolbooks and magazines, and piled neatly in a back corner in a box were teddy bears, stuffed animals, and dolls. The room also had beautiful green and white curtains that adorned the two windows that faced the street and side view of the home. The room also has its own bathroom facilities with shower, which Te'ah monopolized in the mornings before school. And finally, the most important thing that graced the room was samples of the girls' schoolwork pinned up on the walls with stickpins. Above Te'ah's bed were her dress and skirt designs that she had created in her first year sewing and design class. There were also clipped-out pictures of black models from *Ebony* magazine wearing everything from dark and sultry bare-shouldered evening dresses to the very smart mini-dress and the fashionable women's pants suits. There wasn't much room for any of the other girls' work above the wall where her bed was placed.

The other bare wall that was adjacent to the toy box was where Palmer's and Dottie's works were placed. Palmer had an assortment of items. There were some pictures from *Jet* and *Ebony* of musicians. Her favorite was an old picture of Little Stevie Wonder, and of course there were the Supremes, the Temptations, and the Impressions. She also had a real song sheet with music and lyrics that her father had brought home one day. It was a James Brown song, very rare and not found in many if any stores. It was maybe something left over from one of the ninety-nine cent concerts that Mr. Brown was known for. After all, everyone chartered a bus from their hotel to the performing center if they stayed in a hotel and stayed overnight.

Dottie's room area was sparse, and because of the crowded space there were not many items. She had small pictures of horses that she had drawn in her recreation time. She loved ponies and horses and drew them running and grazing and standing, rearing up with hooves striking at air. Some were stick-figure horses and others were her adorable adolescent creations. Her favorite was the paint-by-numbers picture that she had received on her most recent birthday, of two horses on a hill and sharing a tree. She had painted one horse black and white, a pinto, and the other red with yellow hair. It was supposed to be a palomino.

"We found another dead dog today," said Mikey. He walked in and stood in the middle of the bedroom.

"Ugh," said Palmer. "Don't come in here talking about dead dogs and things. We don't want to hear it. Keep talking about that grossed-out mess and I will tell Mom."

"You really found another dead dog, Mikey?" asked Dottie. She looked up with all the excitement of a preschooler on a quest for backyard artifacts.

"If you want me to listen to this story you'd better keep reading and not pay any attention to Mikey," said Te'ah. She always used the stern voice with Bonita, which was helpful when it was reading time for the second grader.

"You know Mikey is always finding stuff," said Palmer. The eighth grader looked up from the magazine for a moment, then looked back to it. "Go outside and find some more bugs, Mikey."

"Yeah, Mikey," said Te'ah. "Go find anything that you want, but please…leave us alone." All the girls begin to laugh at the same time, but Mikey held his ground.

"They're saying that the Rabbit Man killed all of those dogs."

"Who's saying that? You little sixth graders don't know anything. I heard that it's probably some crazy hobo man having fun, or probably some crazy man killing all the black people's dogs," said Te'ah.

"Then what about the dead body in the trail?" asked Mikey.

"At my school, Mikey, the high school, they are saying that the man fell out of an airplane when he was trying to go to the plane's restroom. The stewardess did not report it because she didn't want to lose her job," explained Te'ah with some seriousness.

"Yeah, Michael," said Palmer. "I believe that the man fell out of an airplane and everybody forgot about him."

"Yeah, so get out of here or we'll tell Mom that you are trying to scare us!"

"Yeah, scare us!!"

Mikey slowly backed to the door of the bedroom and then opened it. The music wafted into the room with vocal and piano vigor. The room became filled with it, and Te'ah looked to the clock that was on the dressing table. Her happy expression changed to one of regret. Dottie looked down and closed her book. Palmer dropped the magazine to her face, feigning snoring. Mikey continued to stand at the door and looked to Te'ah. Te'ah stood from her seat and moved to the closet. She opened the sliding door and began to rummage through the dresses and coats. The music and vocals began to get louder as their mother felt more of the gospel spirit. It was a telling sign for Palmer, who finally removed the book from her face and sat up on Te'ah's bed.

"We know we should go and get it over with," she said to no one in particular. Dottie closed her book with some reluctance and stood from her reading seat. She began to walk to the door.

"Okay," Te'ah said reluctantly. She slid the closet back and started toward the door and Palmer as well. Mikey moved out into the hallway and held the door open as the girls moved out and toward the dining room area and the piano.

"Mama's boy," said Palmer.

The girls walked in single file out to the dining room and Maxi playing at the piano. She continued to play. They lined up behind the piano stool and looked over her shoulder to the songbook on the stand. Maxi played and began to sing, and the girls joined in and sang the song just as loud as the walls would tolerate but down the street some of the neighbors heard and welcomed the normalcy of the evening routine.

XX

The Inventions
April 22, 1968

A "mama's boy" was what Palmer called him, and this bothered him somewhat. There was still some time before dinner, so when Mikey left the girls' room with this in his head he went to his room and pondered her disparagement. He was always more comfortable in his own surroundings, and this was the place where he got his private thoughts straightened out. His room, which was a reflection of his personality, was sprawled in minor disarray of the usual array of items: his collection of animal books, his Encyclopedia Britannica volume with the letter "I" which had a great section on all the insects of the world, and a college science book that his father had brought home after someone had left it on the bus. His father, Big Teddy, had waited the mandatory week for someone to claim it and then brought it to Mikey, who jumped at the chance to read it and he did as best he could. It was a cursory science book that contained a combination of earth science and some natural elements. It was just enough information to get the average student interested. Mikey began to use it as one of his reference books, but of course there were no answers to the questions that had been surfacing these past few weeks.

A mama's boy was about the worst thing a girl could call a boy. In fact, it was understood between the genders that to be called a Mama's boy was the sole insult that a girl could use that would humiliate and at the same time challenge a boy to become a man. It was supposed to be the type of son who would stay at home and help out around the house, in the kitchen, with the house cleaning and washing, and gossip. The son would also know something about the daytime soaps like *The Guiding Light* and *As the World Turns*, and *General Hospital*. While boys could call each other "coward" and "chicken" and "frog legs," those insults could be easily overcome with just one action: standing up to the person who was saying or doing the insulting. But how could you stand up to a girl? In fact, it was rumored that the only way you could stand up to a girl who called you a mama's boy was to rush up and kiss her on the lips. That was what the older boys up the street had told Mikey and Daniels and Washington during one of the rap sessions after a football. "Just rush up and kiss her on the lips and don't run away. Just stand there, and if she doesn't leave then kiss her again." And rumor had it from Junior Thompson that girls would call him that just to receive a kiss. It seemed that as you got older things changed, thought Mikey, and that was all he thought about that.

But what could you do if it was your sister? He felt that he wasn't a coward, or at least he wasn't overly afraid of many things after he overcame his fear of the dark. He had accomplished this by himself, alone and in his room. It was one lonely late night when everyone was asleep. His father had said a few days earlier that his nightlight had burned long enough and it was time for him to find a way to overcome his fear. He tried, slowly, first looking at his hands in the dark and then his feet, and then his books, walls, windows, clothes, and then his door and beyond. It was slow and painstaking when some nights he found himself trembling in his bed with his hands clenched into small fists and his eyes tightly shut. He had known for a fact in those days that he would not make it through the night to the next day, and he had prayed a lot then, but when he began to use his senses, he slowly deduced that everything was safe. Not only would he look around for movement, but he would also smell the air for difference. He had trained himself to recognize the difference, first trying to find his own soapy smell for his night bath, to the cleaning solvents used in the next rooms, to the lingering aroma of dinner, and then finally when his window was open and the night air would creep in he would search for the smell of the grass and rosebushes and the always-humid night air. Soon he became very good at discerning the different smells. Of course, this was at his home and surroundings. He had tried testing his skills at school and at church with varying degrees of success. It seemed that church was easier than school.

There were other sounds, the hardest to overcome. It started with the hiss of silence like so much oxygen that could not help but make sound by standing still. Mikey reasoned that if oxygen was floating, then there was movement and therefore it made sounds to stay afloat. When he identified that sound, then he would move to the next sounds like his sister's sleeping breaths, his mother's wheezing breaths, the distant sounds of the home settling from so much movement and piano playing, and then the night breeze starting in the backyard and caressing the trees and flowers and then moving across the home and on further down the street, down the block, through the city.

He could hear the sound of his father's Plymouth Fury III returning home from his second shift driving for the city bus company. He could hear him walk in and could trace his steps to the kitchen where his dinner plate and ice tea were out and prepared by Mikey's mother. He could hear him chewing and drinking, and sometimes hear his mother get up from bed and join him at the table, and there would be laughter and then soft talking and happiness. Mikey's father was proud of his job and always beaming with confidence from his successful day. Mikey would sleep with that same good feeling of success and a job well done with his accomplishments at school.

He knew that success in getting evidence about the Rabbit Man would come from effort and collecting information, then planning, then experimentation, and then finally conclusions from the findings of this process. He had spent time observing the entire insect population in his neighborhood and at school, as many as he could find, and reading up on them before he went out to collect them. After doing so he would log them into his tablet journals, which had now become four small volumes with the beginning of the new one, and kept them secure in the shoeboxes under his bed. It was solitary work, but was necessary if he wanted to achieve his goal of being a scientist like George Washington Carver or becoming an astronaut and going up into outer space.

Now was the time to apply that process to the Rabbit Man. So far, he was only a rumor who no one had seen or lived to tell about, but there were signs of his existence. Things were dying around the neighborhood, and no one had a clue or idea of how this was happening. This meant that no one would do anything about it. The simple thing to do was to find evidence to show someone so a plan could be put into place to catch him.

Mikey started a new journal with this information. After skipping the first three pages that he designated for summary, he selected three other pages for the important categories. He wanted to make a quick list for these categories, so he thumbed the top page of each and gave each the headings of *Rumors, Real Things,* and *Fear and Strangers.* On the page with the heading of "Rumors" he began to jot down the names of the people who had that type of information: the people who were spreading the rumors and the people who were reliable for information about the Rabbit Man, whether past or present. They included Lenny, the Five and Dime store owner, and Ms. Bruce, the cashier at the E-Z Shop. Then there was Yolanda "Bone Girl" Jackson and Junior Johnson from up the street, and soon there would be more names with short paragraphs about the information that they had.

On the next page, "Real Things," Mikey listed the times and dates of the events that had happened and as much factual information and outcome that he knew of. At the very top of this page was where he listed the body that was found in the woods on the trail that led from Bishop Heights to Highland Hills and that seemed to start this whole series of deaths. There were the two dogs that he listed, but that was it. He realized that this page needed more work and investigation.

He decided to list everything that he heard about that had died in the past two weeks on this page. That meant going back and asking more questions and reading more newspapers in the news sections, and not just the sports section. There could be more dogs or cats or even people that had died in the surrounding neighborhoods that he had neglected to recognize. They could also be attributed to the Rabbit Man's presence. He had to go somewhere when he wasn't in the woods by the trail or on the other side of the high school.

And lastly, there was the page that was labeled "Fear and Strangers." He knew that most people in the neighborhood were now more afraid of strangers after the death of Dr. King than before. This list included the two policemen who were new to the neighborhood and now using the fire station as a police substation. There could be more policemen, but these were the ones who came to the school and these were all he knew of. It wasn't that they were policemen that caused the fear, Mikey reasoned. It was more that they were new to the neighborhood.

Using this reasoning, Mikey felt comfortable listing the ice cream man and the Vietnam vet as strangers. He would also support and add to this page with interviews from classmates and adults or anyone who could provide information. But what about Hercules McElroy? He was new to the neighborhood and was a very different type of person. In fact, all the people who were associated with Hercules McElroy were different. He decided to put all the people who were involved with Hercules McElroy on the list. That included the three thin dark-skinned men in black and the thin dark-skinned man with the rings and the suit who was driving the car. He seemed to be in charge of the entire group.

Mikey finished the notes in his tablet, closed it, and placed it on his bed under his pillow. He felt a sense of pride from his review of successes and his initial preparation before undertaking the task of finding the Rabbit Man, but he knew he needed more. He knew that his senses would work in his search because they had worked before and because they were a hereditary trait found on his mother's side of the family. Mikey's great-grandmother was a distant relative of the old Natchez Indians who had inhabited that part of Texas and Louisiana before the American settlers took over, and Maxi wasted no time in reminding him of this. The stories always started with Maxi's father, or Mikey's grandfather, the tall and angular brownish red-skinned man with the large knuckles on his hands, who could run for days, loved baseball, and how much he loved life.

Grandfather Brannon was well over six feet and had a silent but sure way about him. Mikey saw him when he was older and withered from years and the wind, but the stories told by his mother of his adventures always made him larger than life. From his life as a railroad hand to his bar-fighting exploits, the stories were whispered by uncles at Mikey's grandmother's house.

But when Maxi told the stories, she would always digress to Great-Grandmother Erma and her journey to Texas where she had nine male Brannon children. And how Great-Grandmother Erma and her people were abruptly displaced or migrated from their humble beginnings and scattered throughout the country. And how Great-Grandmother Erma lived one hundred and three years.

It gave Mikey a new understanding of life and a different opinion about the movie westerns that he would watch on Saturday afternoons— and, of course, a new side to root for. It did not matter if they won or lost the game; it was to observe the lifestyle that the Indians led in the midst of the great westward movement of the Americans. He liked the tepees, the bandannas, and the weapons. In fact, the only weapons that he admired were the slingshot from the Bible story when David slew Goliath, and the bows and arrows that the Indians used. He reasoned that these would be the easiest to make and still be effective in a hunt or mock combat.

When Mikey was younger, and before the patrol boys, he had designed, made, and used these weapons when he and Daniels and Washington had played war. Their weapons of choice were spears and rocks. One time, Daniels tried to make a catapult, but the projectile always went straight up and then straight down on the person who tried to use the ill-conceived contraption. The Indian weapons were so much easier to construct and so much more effective than anything they could attempt to duplicate. Mikey realized that he still had the designs in the box of journals in the closet. It would take a short time to find them again and review them. They could prove to be helpful in defending himself against the Rabbit Man if the thing pursued him after discovery. After all, based on the rumors, the Rabbit Man could bounce and hop faster than most kids could run.

And with all the activities and abilities that the Rabbit Man had, he must have had a home that he went to when he needed to rest or hide from everyone. If not, then where was he in the daytime? Mikey reasoned that it might not be the normal type of home. It could be a cave or an abandoned barn or shack. He would have to map out the neighborhood and identify the possible daytime hiding places. There were many areas in the neighborhood that he should investigate. He took out the large drawing paper that he kept under his bed and began scribbling and sketching.

First, there was the trail area leading to Highland Hills where the body was found. As much as he hated to admit it, this should be the number one place to start. The good thing was that the new fire station and the policemen that came there were on Bonnie View Road and were facing the vast field area behind Daniels' house that stretched all the way to Simpson Stuart Road. This was another two-lane north-south road that cut through the undeveloped land that was behind the big field west of Mikey's home. The road stretched all the way from the Lancaster Kiest shopping center to Lancaster City, a city south and on the outskirts of Dallas. Another area was the field behind Yolanda Jackson's home. It was very flat and easy to investigate. He had played football on that field last summer. There was the wooded area behind the high school. This was the area that had the creek and the animals, and was the least explored. He had heard tales about raccoons and other wild animals in that area, and tiny lobster things with pinchers that lived in the creek, but he had never been there. He would have to muster the courage to go there as soon as possible. There was the haunted house, where the old witch lived. This was the home that he could see from his front porch when he came outside and looked to the east. It was large, with maybe four bedrooms on the top floors alone, and old white wood framing with molded green panels and trim. It was a house that had been in the neighborhood long before the neighborhood became inhabited with the new families and the owner, a much older woman could be seen sometimes in the evening sitting in her rocking chair on her large porch. He would only go to that house late at night, and then he would only get close enough to just listen. He really didn't want the witch to catch him.

He finished sketching the locations on the crude makeshift map and labeled everything as near as authentically as possible. Then his plan began to come into focus. If he could just locate the Rabbit Man at night and follow him to his home or nest, it would be a success. Then he could notify the right people and they could decide what to do with him. He would have to be careful because the Rabbit Man was killing things, if not just dogs then maybe the body in the trail and who knew what else. He would need the weapons for protection.

His next task was simple. He would have to find a way to defend himself. Whatever way was possible was the best. He rummaged in the closet for the book where he had drawn designs for the weapons in the mock combat games, found it, then made way for the garage where all the tools and supplies were kept. He would have to move past the music and the singing of the girls, and hoped to avoid the scrutiny of his sisters.

He exited his room and moved down the hallway with his head held down and determination on his face. He walked past the group of singers without anyone saying anything to him. He made it through the kitchen and to the back door to the house that led to the garage. As he touched the knob of the door and turned it, the music stopped.

"Don't go too far and forget about dinner," said his mother. "I don't want to call out to you, and we won't wait for you. Is that clear, Mikey?"

"Yeah. I'm just going out to...."

"I don't care. You know what will happen if you are late

1967

I Say a Little Prayer
November 18, 1967

A Saturday morning. The television set, a big portable, sat on an end table near the front window for a better reception for the rabbit-ear antenna that sat atop it, but not too close to the window where it would tempt someone to lift it and run. The fear of an easy theft was always the continuing truth that formed the personality of the projects. Some of the folks, like captive cats, would prowl against the edges of the fence of their boundaries while other folks, the homemakers, fought to keep a lasting loving Christian lifestyle that complemented the reflection of good Christian values and stayed in place. But the hunt was always too great for the cat, and while the restless continued to stretch the extent of their boundaries, those who failed to escape turned inward to prey within. The friction that resulted from this opposing of values was the movement in the projects that gave the projects their life, just like any other place with people who enjoyed the energy of choice. Some people trying to get out, some people trying to get in, and some people just trying to make a home. It was a community with rules, some unspoken, just like any other community.

The television had stories about people trying to get out and people trying to get in. The shows about the cowboy days, the old west, the Westerns that reflected what was valued most in Texas: the freedom of the cowboy tradition. The good clean tradition of what was right and what was white. How everything happened well for the good. How clear it was to see who was good and who was not.

Solomon grew up playing cowboys and Indians and saw the allegory to Christianity or the retelling of Christian stories in the Western traditions that were shown at the drive-in theaters. The vast Western landscapes from John Ford and John Wayne black-and-whites contrasted with the startling clarity of the reds and blues in the drive-in classic *How the West Was Won*.

But there was an absence of blacks in the Western movies. After all, Solomon did grow up in Dallas where there were the football Cowboys playing just last year against the powerful Packers from Green Bay. There was Bob Hayes and others, which was a big thing since no blacks played football in the NCAA's Southwest Conference. The only school in the conference from Dallas, Southern Methodist University, was also white and private, and glad to snub the state-funded schools with their mastery of education but still competed for the big athletic prizes. That included the big Cotton Bowl powerhouse, the University of Texas in Austin. They would come to the fairgrounds and play against the Sooners from Oklahoma. There were black guys playing for the Sooners. And then there was Jim Brown. Jim Brown went to Syracuse in New York, and Solomon knew about New York from the Harlem Renaissance. He never dreamed that it was a whole state, even after he learned that it was. The city was almost synonymous with the good things that happened in the state. In fact, if it wasn't near or in the city, it wasn't of interest or mentioned.

The quiet teachers who understood this refrain of commitment whispered echoes of bright new ideals through thirsty hallways of growing young minds against same such thoughts of rejection. But never in the classrooms of Texas were those thoughts repeated. The curriculum, as at the Abraham Lincoln High School on the east side of the city, should be regimented by grade, by district, by county, by state. Some of it was progressive such as *Huck Finn* or *Uncle Tom's Cabin*, and some was conservative such as any Texas history book that was filled with the state's history as well as the story of the westward movement. This one reason became the focal point for the black intellectuals, and for that matter, the civil rights movement. Whatever the acceptance of song or Rochester in society was then in opposition to what became the disadvantage of substandard education and substandard living conditions. That's what was said in lecture halls of law and black colleges, and in so many words on the televisions and in some new songs.

Television could not help but show the change in attitudes and the efforts for equality. *American Bandstand* had a few black people dancing to songs on it, and then there were the black entertainers who seemed to make life easier because they were doing so well and everybody liked them. That was the transparency of the values of the country shown on a national level, from the mystique of "Ask Not What Your Country Can Do for You…" to "I am somebody." Because that was what was important to black folks and just about everybody else: somebody to like you. It seemed that everything was all right or getting all right, and folks just needed to find their way. Television became the plateau of ideas for everyone, and sometimes no one, but most people were watching it and more people were modeling behavior from it.

Solomon played chess, so he noticed the change in the television programming. He used to watch the Westerns and he loved them. He had the cowboy hat and the cap gun six-shooters and two-gun holster because it was a layaway bargain and it was the only thing sold. Solomon loved it. And he played with the kids who loved it in the "poorjects" as well, because everyone wanted to be alike because difference was treated differently. Solomon conformed, but still grew quiet and tall with the television that grew just as quiet and tall. Sometimes he was in jeans and a white shirt because it was the closest, he could get to the civil rights marchers who had on black church pants and white shirts with the collar-buttoned top. When he was a child he was in the Western outfits with the white collars and cuffs and plaid shirts, and learned to square dance in the elementary schools and loved it.

But like all chess players, he changed with the movement. He watched the girls change from the long-skirted Christian values to the short mini of the mod generation, and then the new musical values of love that were expressed in song. Black girls looked so different in the mini dress, especially if they had the Afro and the attitude to go with it. Natural meant so much to the Afro and the emerging black socially enlightened graduating class. Makeup was considered for whites and black was considered beautiful, but it was hard to find black girls without makeup on television. Solomon started turning the channel first to watch the girls, then to watch the noise, because that was the strength in the change. The noise.

Shannon Melanie was like that, a beautiful black girl with an Afro and smooth brown skin like cocoa butter. She had a mean Afro, thick and black and stretching out to the sky. He had seen her a couple of times lately, and she was a different kind of girl. She was strong and unafraid like his mother used to be before the projects had beaten her down. She had to protect everything, especially since there wasn't a man around. Solomon's father was a memory, having died in a mysterious way in the wrong part of town. The projects were like that. Men died, vanished, or just plain ran away.

His mother started strong, throughout all the places that they had lived. Rockwall was in the country and the projects were close to the city. The city meant jobs while the country meant chores. She had reached out and brought her family and wound up in the East Dallas projects. There were worse places for a mother without a husband and two small kids. His mother was strong then, for a long time, and that was what he saw in Shannon when he first met her in his sophomore year in high school. She was unafraid.

Solomon sat in the living room watching the television. He was alone in the apartment. His mother had long since gone to work by bus, which was her routine. She was big on routines, and she had taught him the value of routine. She said routines told a person that they could trust you, regardless of who they were. You were considered harmless if people knew your routines. She had learned it from her days of picking cotton in the cotton fields from around Rockwall county and other fields further east, and some further south moving toward Houston. Solomon's routine had changed. He was no longer an office dayworker at the Sears department store. He worked second shift and his academic ambition was somewhat stifled. Day school was different

In Search of the Rabbit Man

from night school, but he didn't know why. He sat in front of the television watching the news.

More importantly, television brought the Vietnam War and the draft, which was something different from the cavalry and the Indian wars. There was no charging on horseback or marching soldiers going uphill or downhill with cannon fire like the movies. Even the World War II movies didn't look like the films from Vietnam. Solomon didn't know what to think of it. If he were drafted, what would it mean to him?

There was Muhammad Ali. There was his refusal of the draft that blended into the Islamic movement as well as the civil rights movement. His statement had illuminate so many newfound black religions for the black community, and some were so different from Dr. King's thoughts that people found the person who they were in their decision making. It showed blacks in erect postures with shoulders high and heads high and silence and mystery. Television had people like Walter Cronkite talking with faces and people talking over pictures, telling you what the pictures were about in voices over some ambient sounds of the battles of Vietnam, but the Baptist faith was just as loud. You could hear the singing from the church walls, and the gospel, and the plans for tomorrow, and make decisions any time on a Sunday morning until around four in the afternoon.

Shannon felt that the war was a bad thing for black people. A lot of the students at Bishop College felt that way. There were student meetings to continue the communication with the other all-black colleges in the country. There seem to be a black college grapevine that was either directly or indirectly connecting the schools together. *Ebony* and *Jet* magazines supplied the news for blacks, and both magazines interests were the black American way of life. The movies, the music, the people, the college news, and the black American businesses were the occasional topics of interest, and the students read and reacted. Styles were changing and people were changing, and what the television missed the magazines caught. Shannon was also there and changing, Solomon thought. The more he saw of her the more he felt her comfort in the midst of argument. She lived for the argument just like the music and just like the times.

The students at El Centro college were just the opposite. They were for the good of the country, and anything the American way of life would do would have to be right.

Solomon had to move. He had to get up, but nothing was making it easier. He could not trace the moment of his descent into this gray area of thought because he could not determine the moment that brought him here. He could feel the walls climbing in. Footsteps. New restrictions that he had never noticed before were everywhere, and he did not know what to do or whom to trust. The sunrise was the same, amber light creasing through a blue-sky backdrop against the tan fields of soon-green Texas grasses. But he had to move forward. He needed a sense of freedom because the past was a landscape that he had grown up with and shared with others of his peers of the temptation of freedom and space.

He thought of Dawn and the movement of choice. Her choice always surprised him. Why did she respond to him? Why did she confide to him? The more he found out about life and the way things were, the more he felt the significance of her choice and the freedom. He felt the responsibility of his choice within her choice, because without it her choice was worthless. He could become worthless as well within the weight of her choice. He guessed he liked her, but he knew for a fact that he never wanted to see her in pain.

He moved from his seat and turned the television off, and then moved to the door and out. The Mustang in the parking lot sat idle and gray in the dying evening light. He looked to the back window, empty still from the lack of glass, and the exposed the cold interior and bucket seats. A costly result of the towing from downtown that day when he sat in front of Sears and waited for Dawn. He had met the officer that he had seen at the fairgrounds that day. A day when he was waiting and the policeman approached the car for the first time ever in the two months since he had started taking Dawn to her home. It was the same policeman from two months ago, and he just didn't have his papers that day. He was taken to jail and the Mustang had been towed. When he had gotten enough money and his mom had gotten her papers from her mom down in Rockwall, Texas, then he went down to the city storage. The back window was shattered and glass shears were on along the edges. It was not a gunshot because the glass was inward with no exit. It was from a large hammer that battered the window in with anger. It had taken a while to get all the glass out, sweeping and brushing and flicking and moving the backseats out. After he had finished it took a moment for the realization to creep in. He didn't have the money to replace it, and it was just a big gaping hole on the back of his car.

November was the start of the cold months so he had a leather jacket and wool hat on, and his same Stevie Wonder shades that he had worn in the summer, but he was now tracing a fall fifties look. This was from Dawn's influence. She really loved the loneliness of the fifties. The first teen films were like that. The moment where no one cared about anyone.

He drove to the interstate heading into downtown, and the city skyline at a gleaming sunlit ten o'clock gave the blue gleam of promise to the ongoing blur of the Mustang. The highway blurring, the white lines, other drivers, other cars, the whirl of wind inside the car louder going out the back, the gray pavement, downtown and then the wisp of the off-ramp and the screech and smells of Main Street when the buses creaked from both sides from inbound and outbound. He drove on past the incline of the convergence of the highways into the downtown drag. Main Street and its attractions and coldness loomed west to the always-ominous JFK assassination point, and then out and away from downtown.

Dawn was like the morning and what was right in the world. She had proud features, a smooth neck with a nice nose and dark double Italian lashes that draped down like long dark flowers against her eyes. She had a pouting smile and a Mona Lisa grin, and that was what you had to watch out for. Her eyes crinkled with her grin and that made the grin even more mysterious, as if she knew all the answers and that made her better than everyone else. She was often misunderstood, and that was the demon in her eyes.

She stood in the light in front of the Sears building with the big floppy and that much disdain for the routine of the city. People passed

JON-MICHAEL HAMILTON

by her, cars and buses and more cars moving slowly through the arteries of downtown, and she held her silhouette against the wind like a modern art piece in a storm. She paced back and forth, under the floppy hat, and sometimes she sat. She had come in for her check on her off-day, not because she needed the money, but because it was an excuse to hang out with Solomon. He was coming by to pick her up and take her riding down Mockingbird Lane, and then on a ride to Lee Park before the full winter came in and quieted the noise. The winter was always so quiet.

She needed her freedom to move about her world at her own pleasure and her own pace. This was an old thing building on a new thing, starting as far back as Maryland and her decision to come to Texas. She saw boundaries as minor contrivances. She talked to whom she wanted and when. Her choices were considered as an East Coast bias, so they were overlooked unless she broke the big Texas rule about race-mixing and line crossing. Or, unless she broke her generation's rule that had no rules about race mixing and crossing lines. Talking about her generation.

Solomon drove the battered car down his usual route to the Sears building on Lamar. Dawn was standing outside in her usual large floppy hat, even though the temperature was changing and fall was giving way to winter. Soon it would be colder, and December was around the corner. The weather would be nothing special for either because both were used to weather changes and both were looking forward to it, but this would be the first winter of their friendship. While Dawn took it in stride, Solomon felt a warm kinship. Family was a big thing for him.

He pulled to a side street and waited for her to walk to the car. He could not trace the moment when this friendship changed and evolved into what it was now, a symbiotic relationship where she would tell him all about her problems and fears and he would listen and try to solve them. He never once thought that her problems were beyond his ability to solve. They were the familiar family problems, and he felt the distance that her family was apart had brought this on. There was the boyfriend problem where Dawn could never find the right man to treat her the way that she could reciprocate in turn. And then there was her fear of being alone. Her anger brought this on from the orphanage.

Solomon could soothe her anger, reassure her of the bright side of things, and always confide that her family missed her as much as she missed them. That was his occasional benefit. He was deemed a problem solver. He could see taking control of his life with this new prescription for solving problems, any problem, as long as he had the opportunity to work them out exclusively. It became a defining part of him. It felt good to have this new type of control.

Maybe this was the attraction that he was developing with Dawn. A deepening of understanding and dependence that could not be clearly defined but seemed to still be there after everything else was said had a lingering effect after she became quiet. Her fears and frustrations subdued. Her optimism refreshed.

"Babe, I got your spirit. They'll try to take it away from you. But I got it." Solomon told her this when she was down. She was down a lot lately. She began to react to the anger in the media and it was more than the civil rights struggle. The music she listened to said a lot about her disappointments and how life should be.

Her mood was down now. He leaned across the passenger seat and opened the door and she got in. Her smell was fresh like flowers and it always filled the car with an intoxicating fragrance. It was some rose flowery stuff that just lingered, and Solomon began to enjoy the fragrance. She loved flowers. Roses were her weakness. The colors that she wore said flowers. She was always richly colored in dark greens and browns, whether dresses or blouses, and she wore dark solid colors and she even made pants look good. She could make jeans look good as well. And she could be the dark-haired flower child, dainty and not angry, on one day and be a young "That Girl" the next day. She was just trying to find her way.

They drove away from the building and headed through downtown to their usual route to North Dallas. At the on-ramp from north to south, Solomon made a right to the south on the interstate instead of a left. The horizon moved steadily. The colors seemed to fade. Although well into morning, the sky became gray from the stacks of smoke from the Proctor and Gamble soap factory. The gray white puffy clouds gave the air a unique arid pungent odor and the land became flat with nary a building of banking or business to be seen. To the left the landscape made of more of the wooden two-story warehouse structures and barns that sold the liquor, feed, or lawn products, and to the right the city development. Urban sprawl and the new black neighborhoods that stretched further south with a new gleam. Solomon drove the speed limit down the interstate and they began to notice the traffic. Second-hand trucks hauling used furniture and cars loaded with large black families with small children with plaited hair all moved in a procession south. The children stared at Dawn in the passenger seat. Everyone passing by took a second look at the floppy hat and the white skin underneath in the car with a young black man driving it until they saw the windowless back of the car. Then they nodded and looked away.

Solomon noticed the looks and he felt a familiar empathy for Dawn. How awkward she must feel away from all the white faces downtown or in her own neighborhood. He saw in her eyes the same look that she held for him when he would take her to her home. She would touch him then. She would give him strength and confidence in her way. He reached to touch her hand and squeezed it and gave in turn.

The turnoff was an exit and a gas station off the interstate that suggested that Simpson Stuart Road was a connecting artery to other roads leading north to downtown. Highlands Hills was the unnamed neighborhood because of the high sloping streets leading up to a main artery and the quaint homes that stretched through the landscape. A new and prosperous black neighborhood sprawling in the hundreds sat opposite the only black college for miles. The first thing you could spot after exiting the interstate is the football stadium. It was circular fence that began on the right at the edge of the visitors' bleachers and ran across to the ticket holders and the main parking lot; the home team field house began on the edge of vast grassland so it stood out over the first hill.

The college had all the trappings of a healthy collegiate lifestyle. Driving beside it you could see the dormitories, the buildings of education. Through a curving entrance you could see the main building and the expansive chapel. Bishop College was another all-black college that needed religious contributions to sustain it. The chapel held a church clergy that held religious professorships from other black universities and was a testament to the civil rights movement. Chapel was held every day and as they rode into the inner circle that led to the faculty parking lots and the chapel services lot, Dawn noticed the rosebushes that fenced the street away from the chapel. She loved the red of the roses even under a Saturday sun.

The traffic of the day was becoming dense. Cars were being detoured to the grasslands that Solomon and Dawn had just passed, and they were also being detoured from the entrance out and away from the school. The road was being blocked off with white sawhorses and funeral motorcycle escorts. The whole campus was preparing for the Tigers Homecoming parade. The school's marching band, all the frats and sororities, floats, the campus officers and dignitaries, and of course the beautiful homecoming queen would parade up Simpson Stuart and turn back when the parade touched the intersection of Bonnie View.

Solomon and Dawn left the Mustang in one of the makeshift parking lots and began walking up through the gathering crowds of people. On one side of the street the college students were all lined up and waiting to cheer for their favorite part of the procession. On the opposite side of the street were the lines of neighborhood people, kids, mothers, old ladies, and high school–age teens who came out every year to watch the parade.

Solomon and Dawn walked side by side like friends out for a stroll on the college side of the street through the gathering students, without so much as a stare at Dawn's white skin and Solomon's blackness. They could blend in for the first time and relax and walk like normal people. They would stop and peer over a shoulder and even push through the crowd. There were other white faces, a smattering of them, and some local clergy giving support, businessmen, and maybe a shop owner. They moved up as close to the mini shops as they could. The parade trek started from the entrance to the football stadium following Simpson Stuart Road to Bonnie View Road and back. On the return route, the opposite direction on Simpson Stuart, coming back was the side of interest. The E-Z shop sat at the corner of the intersection and a long way behind it was another new neighborhood, Bishop Heights, named because of the elementary school. Immediately behind the shop was a wooded area of trees, a creek, and long grass flowing up and swaying with the wind.

Clouds moved in quietly and blocked out the sun. The parade started with a banner carried by two of the NJROTC students indicating that Bishop College's alumni, staff, and student body were celebrating their fifth annual homecoming with the marching band and drill team leading the way. The two drum majors, very animated, pranced back and forth on the two-lane road and ogled and teased the little children and students who were enamored with the uniforms, large hats, and high black boots.

Then the cars began to roll by in a slow procession. New convertible Pontiacs from David McDavid Pontiac with signs attributing the donation of the vehicles passed with slow rumbles and horns to the onlookers. Inside each convertible sat the campus dignitaries, the president of the school and his wife, the provost and his wife, the class officers, and then finally the homecoming queen. They all waved to the community that they had adopted, and the community waved back in an affirmation of a change for the betterment of black people in the city.

But homecoming is about football as well, and the team creaked by on a big flatbed truck at an easy pace with their jerseys pulled taut against their arms and chest. After they passed, bringing up the rear was the marching band and drill team from the visiting team, Prairie View A&M University from the Houston area. Their presence, their style, and their precision promised a great band battle at the halftime show.

The trek back to the campus had the same fanfare for everyone as before. There was more waving and cheering and laughter from both sides of the street, which foreshadowed an impending eruption of happiness for the afternoon and evening events. A few of the young people and the college students fell in line behind the Prairie View band and begin marching on the return path to the college.

Dawn was mesmerized with the parade. It was her first experience with a black college homecoming parade and she was swept away with the energy of the moment. She found herself falling in line with the other people and marching to the beat of the visitors' drum cadence. Solomon went with her, and followed her down the path to the college. He felt the same sense of happiness that he saw on her face and he enjoyed the moment of her happiness. They followed the band, crossed the front parking lot of the E-Z Shop, and trekked back to the campus, singing and cheering just like everyone else.

Rebo stood on that side of the street up front at the beginning of the intersection. His cruiser was parked in the parking lot of the shop. His eyes were shaded under reflecting shades and his cap was pulled snug against his brow. He saw Dawn from the distance, her white skin and floppy hat standing out against the animated black faces and he watched as she danced behind the band. As the band turned on their return march, he let Dawn come abreast of him and shadowed her movements. She didn't notice him. She marched happily and danced and waved her hands to the sky. For a brief moment she looked just like one of the hippie students in San Francisco's drug community. He had seen other such animations from the film footage in his perpetrator awareness classes on how to identify the changing problems that could occur in the community. He knew she was employed. He knew she lived with a retired lady who once was a silent actress. He knew she liked to be around blacks, especially the one black kid that he had arrested. He knew she had smiled at him once.

Rebo paralleled her movements, and as she marched, he walked. He pushed through some of the onlookers, matching her step for step. He attracted some attention, but he was an officer in uniform so his behavior was excused as perhaps routine security measures. Rebo saw the parade differently. The many black faces marching in rows gave him the same impressions that he felt when he watched the civil rights marches that were constantly being televised. He didn't see the importance of the parade except to get a lot of black people together who could probably start fighting against whites. After all, the civil rights marches were about revenge against slavery. That's what he felt. What other reason could there be?

The parade continued on. The lead procession was down the hill and turning in to the stadium gates. Dawn was caught up in the moment and she continued to dance and follow the visiting band down the hill. Solomon walked by her side, somewhat subdued to the excitement. Rebo paralleled them both, step for step, feature for feature, but looking straight ahead and down the hill.

XXII

A Cold Desire of Heart
December 14, 1967
Thursday

Christmas season in Dallas was when the cold comes in from the north. The sky turned a deep blue gray and you could smell the moisture in the air. Sometimes it snowed, like this season's snow with soft flourishes that made a soft blanket. The days became shorter and the nights longer. Strangely though, the downtown area became more alive during the Christmas season. This was when shoppers coming from the surrounding counties on long shopping trips to purchase from the big city's wares and stores filled the evening with the joyous good cheer of the season. They walked under long streaming Christmas lights that traced up and down and across the middle lanes of the two main arteries of downtown, Elm and Main Streets. Both streets traced east to the highway and west to the college and in front to the large tree that was adorned with red and green Christmas lights and blue blinking bulbs that gave a twinkle to the night.

The thirty-foot evergreen had a coursing of snow that stretched across its small shoulders and fell powdery to its sloping skirt, and gave the evening an amber gleam of dying sparkles and growing nightlights. Dawn always loved this time of year. This was when everyone seemed a little happier and people were always brisk in manners and glances and quick smiles and always approachable, with approachable hands. She was working late partly because she wanted the money and partly because this was her time of year. She could not be home on these days and nights, with the amber glow of sunset's gleam against the skyscrapers of downtown Dallas. The way the sunset could be seen dropping between the buildings and running past them to the stretching landscape and with the snow silently melting with the dying sunset gave downtown a sense of movement, a sense of dying, and a sense of living.

She had felt this imbalance before when she was alone in an orphanage in the long sloping hills of upstate Maryland. School was no prize for her. She had friends but had always kept a pace that was protected, and no friend would come there because she was there, placed there by her early experiences growing up alone. She had a calmness of security in her aloneness. She had been there before and she could return anytime, because saying good-bye soon became easy. The sunset was just a long quiet good-bye.

She walked outside the store as often as possible when she accepted these hours, to catch the sunset and the saying of good-bye. Her world was so organized, so controlled with her keenness for disorder, that her movements, although routinely predictable, became boring. When it came to her occasional co-worker's routine, they had a curiosity for the more changing times and the glitter of money in the downtown area, she went unnoticed as an oddity. Her wants and needs were still a mystery to them. She took the role of outsider in stride because it was so normal for her.

She sat on one of the twin benches and gazed at the Christmas tree. For the first time in a long time, she had a dress on. An in-season blue wool knee-length dress hugged her inside a wool blue pea coat. She also had on high seasonal brown boots kicking softly against pieces of snow and the grit that was always on the concrete.

She remembered the times when she was a child in the snow-covered hills of Maryland, where everything was white and green and Christmas cheer was in the air, and she would kick her boots softly against dirt or snow or grass or pieces of grit that was always on concrete. Life was always about making decisions, and she learned this fact too early in life—what hurt her and what made her happy. This gave her expectations. She anticipated avoiding or numbing herself to the hurt and looking forward to the happiness. She had to learn to hide her happiness because others tried to use it or hide it from her. She had to see their side of the conflict because there was so much conflict for a person growing up alone that to survive, she had to empathize. It made her independent, and with each day of survival it gave her the confidence of expectations.

She stood now as a brisk cool wind whistled through dry leaves and caught her at her waist and fluttered off into nothingness. Her hair, shorter and darker now, clung tightly against her neck and gave her a mod British look that blended tightly to the department store rest areas. She walked forward to the now-lightening streetlights and the dazzling office lights of the hotels and banks, and downtown came alive with her steps. She walked out and turned and walked straight to her destination and the rest was routine. She knew what was around her, so she rarely looked in a single angle moving in the same direction.

She looked up and down slightly, and as if in a natural motion found a reason to look left and right and she saw you when you looked at her from your car or from a building elevator or from a restaurant awning. And she waved out of the manners that she had learned, and walked with such purpose in her destination that she creased through the air as motion to stillness. And you found a way to be near her. Some way, any way, was better than no way.

You arranged your breaks when you could and drove the patrol car close to her vicinity and looked out and lied about your breaks and vicinity breaks. You fought to be alone on patrol on second shift, and you finally got that promotion to corporal around the time of the state fair, and so you took it in stride, this routine of concern for her. You watched her at the fairgrounds and downtown and at the home where she rented a room on Tuttle Creek drive. You could see her in the wind and the evening sky, and everything that was right or could be right and something to fight for. It gave you a crisp sharpness of substance against the illusion of routine. More is what is denied you and not what you can't create, and the sunset held the same promise. You could see so many sunsets because without her there were already so many. You couldn't count because you don't trust yourself. You and the numbers become a blur. Stuff is happening around her and you can't keep track of the changes. Is she right for you?

She saw the officer and looked away as naturally as a breath of air. She walked past his eyes and to the bus stop, where she waited for the 55-Lancaster bus to come by. She stood and looked away intentionally in avoidance, but was aware of her surroundings. When the bus rolled up and stopped with a squeak she waited and walked through the open doors. She sat in the middle of the bus, and was able to face the front of the bus and the exiting side doors with the ease of a shift of her chin.

The bus traced down Lamar, crossing Commerce and Elm, and then headed to cross the facade of the college. She rode in silence and watched as a few other riders joined the rest of the occupants moving to the heart of downtown. The bus stopped just before turning right on Main in front of the college. She walked and stepped off and into the night air and sounds again and felt the elegance of the city as the quickly dying light gave way to the sparkle of the night lights. To see people in this light defused the harsh daylight of anger of so much aloneness and softened the demeanors of the folks that were out bustling to and from their destinations.

She crossed the intersection of Lamar and Main and moved with all the other pedestrians to the front corner of the college. It was after seven in the evening and the amber glint fought a losing battle against the growing shadows along the corners of the building, and there was the usual amount of traffic at this time. Students coming and going to and from classes, and the gatherings of lingerers sometimes huddled in bunches, touching with the dying heat of the day.

She felt comfortable among people of her age with the security of opinion and the growing means to express it. It was in the music. The words. The pictures. It was in the way her generation dressed. The freedom in the way they wore their hair. It was always about someone having a good time or someone making a statement against having a good time by the ones with the short hair. It was an opposition of

In Search of the Rabbit Man

social class structure, but it really became about the values to live by because that was where the most determined influences hid and gained momentum.

Dawn liked all music, all words, and all ballads of love and life that told a story of struggle like her own life. Dawn became a type of explorer of the way things were and whose opinion was right for the moment. There was Beebe, with her twenties experiences, her Hollywood movie experiences, her Depression era experiences and her later experiences, living within the fear of the destructive power of the atomic bomb and the bomb shelters that everyone seemed to passed on and along until it became the national attitude. The atomic bomb became something to argue against. It became a generational chasm, the atomic bomb. "President Johnson should drop, should not drop the bomb on Vietnam!"

The statement took on a life of itself like a great growing wave of emotion. The statement turned into a question of pride in certain areas and a statement of shock and fear and sorrow and pain in others. Dawn was empathic as she was taken on by all of the currents of the tide. Some days she was so keen to the issues of one side of the current, but quite easily she could turn to the opposite current like a sailboat taxing and making no headway. She needed a lot to keep her steady and she found it in the people around her. Socially, she looked down instead of up and listened to the voices of her generation and got past the Southern bias to the eastern coast people.

You saw this early because since the first time you had seen her you could never stop watching her. She was crying that first time. She was crying about some disappointing thing from someplace that you didn't know anything about, and you approached her. She was with a friend. She was crying and she couldn't stop and you felt so helpless. You saw her beauty in her strength to do something you could never do. You could never cry. You could never cry for any reason, and it became a task to see if you could. But you could never make it. Something always stopped you. You watched it, her face with smooth high cheeks, a small proud nose, and deep brown brows, and adored it and wondered the limits of it.

253

And then she looked at you. She wondered who was coming near her, so she looked at the movement and it was you. She caught your eyes and you didn't know what to do with that contact when it touched the place that you kept concealed. You looked into her eyes, a deep dark brown that you fell into and were treading easily to stay afloat. It stayed with you until now. You watched her walk from a distance, not able to get closer or further away, unable to come to any kind of resolution, so you watched with a crease of pain that scratched across your forehead and diagonally across your eye and across your cheek to rest. It made your eyes blink uncontrollably sometimes, and sometimes you could control it. But you had to keep watching her.

Dawn took a seat on a bench under an elm tree and shuddered briefly against the cold wooden planks. She was waiting for Solomon to take a break. She knew he would come to the campus and maybe they could catch up on some things, especially since he had been working and going to day school this entire semester. Things were so different now. He had always been quiet, but now he was moodier with deep bouts of silence followed by spells of anger and then silence again. He would return from the silence with an off-topic comment about how beautiful the city was and all the opportunities that were changing the way people lived. And then back to the silence. It was strange that she was not afraid of him. Maybe it was the orphanage experience helping her to realize that his anger was not directed toward her. She had seen this and she had done the same. She had used those same words to sway that feeling of helplessness when she faced the fear of not belonging.

She realized early that life was different, and being watched by teachers she held it inside until she found a way to articulate a comparison. It was later, at college in one of the brief psychology classes she phrased, "It's like a deep, deep hole of mistrust and the fear that it brings," and that same silence and then anger and then silence again she felt. She loved the rustle within the silence and the movement of space of air and sound in the silence, and from that she could hear everything. The scattered leaves, the gasps, the whispers, the wind, and the sounds that everyone hears and everyone takes for granted as the normal bustling of people she saw as patterns of movement. Because she felt like an outsider, she could be an outsider and observe the patterns of movement without anyone detecting her curious passion for understanding.

She saw the officer following her. He was out of uniform, as he had often been lately, and when she always looked up and saw him look away or beyond or directly, she knew him. She had known that he had been there for as long as she was where she was, and she became curious as to why anyone would be curious about her.

Briefly but long ago, she began to recognize the meanings of different looks when she first felt the eyes of the overseeing teachers and caretakers in the orphanage behind their evasive looks. She learned how to read people from the repeated looks and the different looks. What was the true intention behind the actions that the eyes could never conceal? She saw it as an orphan with the other kids. How people learned to use the power of influence, or not use it at all and still luck out. To get adopted by anyone was sometimes luck, and sometimes listening to the always-optimistic teachers and caretakers became the same monotone.

She was a white child with brown hair. She was thin but not frail. She was quiet but not shy and "that could become a problem because it sometimes keeps people at a distance." She had been told that by one of the many voices at the place, or leaned to articulate that in retrospection. At any rate, she used her actions in the flow of life, which she became aware of at an early age. She was never totally against the grain, complaining, rebelling, or giving a dramatic reaction to the routine of the orphanage, but you would notice her going within the flow of life as routine but at her own pace. She was careful but deliberate and learned early not to believe in luck.

Every time you saw her, you saw her within the fabric of what was soon becoming the pulse of the city and of your life. She was at the NAACP meeting downtown on that Saturday in April, with the Lee Park crowd that fancied a good time at the park, and that homecoming parade in the black part of town just this past November. She was not a troublemaker. She just seemed to watch and enjoy things, and it was a lot like she was a visitor from some other planet or country who knew an inside joke. She wasn't a troublemaker, but she had a way of being around the trouble spots of the city, and it got your interest as much as your dreams.

You could see her in your life like the wives of the other married officers, doing the things that they do and seeing her going through the pace of their lives her own way. You could be included in the barbecues on the Saturdays when all the married officers got together and talked to each other about their children, their bills, and their other common endeavors. You could see her walking with you on a quiet Sunday morning out at Bachman Lake, or even going to a Cowboy game and losing her head in the cheering and excitement. You could also see her quiet and fierce with eyes of iron-hard stares pushing herself through the fabric and making her opinion known without words. You saw that in the way that she showed pride in her happiness and her lack of fear in losing it. She was recklessly happy at the wrong times; when the other white girls would retreat into their Texas roles, she would emerge and somehow challenge a man with her manner, her tone, and her facial expressions. You never saw her batting her eyelashes at anyone or silently looking down from a compliment. Her straightforwardness was alarming, was something you had not experienced from any woman before, but somehow it was familiar. This was what you thought your mother would have been like when she was younger. This was something that had made your father work harder and try to build a life around as he had done with your mother.

Dawn moved to one of the outdoor benches in the break area of the college. She didn't like the attention that she would receive inside, and sitting in one of the lounge areas made her feel more comfortable. She had tried the lounge areas with Solomon, and it had not gotten better but worse. She knew the history of Dallas and the conservative attitudes that led to white flight or fright and the economic classifications that further segregated, but she ignored it for the sake of her generation. She continued to push within the movement of the fabric of her generation and she sometimes stood out. But she always felt that her efforts were misinterpreted. She didn't talk to many people. She had her own circle to talk with: the people she trusted, like Beebe, and Solomon, and her mom and dad. But she found herself being selective about the topics that she shared with them.

She sat at the bench with a chill beginning and she shivered slightly in satisfaction and hunched her shoulders closer together with her hands in the pockets of the blue pea coat. The officer came over, seeming to come over from the shadows, and stood before her. He was holding two cups of lightly steaming coffee in his hands and had a lopsided grin on his face. He was all Joe Cartwright with traces of dark hair, eyes, and brows, and even the slumping shoulders, but she remained impassive and almost impolite. She knew that if she acknowledged his greeting then it would forgive his spying and his being at the same places she had just happened to be. She had never liked this type of attention to her whereabouts, and whether she having a good time or what she was just doing from moment to moment was always a movement in her life that she had never truly accepted. From the orphanage to the adopted parents to her teachers in school to college and now at her job, she had found coldness in her heart that she could put away and live with the happiness of the day, of the moment, but still find and hold the coldness without too much difficulty. It gave her a confidence that she had to conceal, so she explored in a neutral flat tone.

"You've found the evening coffee."

"Yeah, it's just around the corner from the school. I know a guy that works there and it was easy...It's hot chocolate. Would you like a cup?" he said in an innocent Southern drawl.

"And you have two," she said just as flatly. She looked away and tried to remember her politeness. Maybe that should have been a question, but she knew she was at a perceptible disadvantage. She was alone and this was the tone that she decided was best.

You watched her get on the bus. She looked good doing the usual things like giving coins to the driver, or combing her hair, or walking with food in her hands, or concentrating on a paperwork problem

257

from her job, or reading the newspapers. She looked best when she was learning. She was beautiful. She had a facial expression of concern that seemed to focus her nose and her eyes, and she would purse her lips all toward the item of interest. Then realization would hit, and her smile and her nose would move up and slant evasively to the left and she would give a short laugh. You loved her laugh; even though you'd never shared one you loved to see it, and, if possible, to hear it.

You got closer. You would move alongside her in one of the downtown stores where you had left junior officer Conway in the lurch alone and sitting in the cruiser. You loved the way she looked in a dress in the summer. The little sun dresses of different bright colors that all had the same Barbie-doll quality. And the way she would wear her hair, sometimes down and sometimes up in a swirling swish whenever she took off that big floppy hat. You could imagine her in a professional skirt or long straight-leg pants and blouses like the Laura Petrie or Marlo Thomas look when she was in the back offices where all the decisions were made.

You didn't understand the hat. How could an out-of-place thing such as a hat give you any insight to a person's values? You were right when you realized that this was Texas and you were a policeman, and that element of observation was from your training that had been drilled into you right after the assassination of President Kennedy. You remembered it most from your Jack Ruby experience, watching hats and other accoutrements of identity. You didn't understand her hat or why she wore it. You understood the significance of the hat. It was an identifier of a mod-generation person who could be involved with drugs and unrest in the community. One of the many moving gypsies that seemed to migrate through the state.

After two years of an increasing flow of different faces identified, your job evolved to more of a trail hand and census taker commenting through the network that decided to move them on to California. That was what happened during the Midwest drought you accepted. That's where all the weirdoes were steered, or people who wanted to change the Texas way, the people who just couldn't accept the Texas values.

IN SEARCH OF THE RABBIT MAN

But with Dawn you saw a difference. She never stood out too much in all of the places that she attended that were talking about change. She never actually said anything that you could recall, and she was always polite. Yeah, it was that hat and that black guy that she liked and had been around so much until you arrested him. He was not around her at all afterward but sometimes people and distance in the area at the same function separated him. But you still had to see her. You followed her from school, but you didn't get on the bus. You had your truck so you ran to it when she got on the bus. You guessed the college and so you raced her there and got chocolate and walked up just after she sat down.

Dawn thought about accepting his offer and immediately recognized the turning point in this encounter. If there were any relationship it would be similar to a relationship of the wind to a standing tree. Who had the roots of repetition and who had the freedom to move up and stretch out into the sky? What did she want and what could she learn from him? Would it change her? She let him stand there for a beat and then she looked to him.

"That's very nice, but I'm waiting for my friend," she said. "He should have been here by now."

"And I've got to drink all of this hot chocolate by myself?" He smiled a crooked smile. "Just take a sip."

He sat at the other end of the bench and placed both cups down between them and held them in place.

"You better take one before it falls. I can't hold 'em much longer."

She saw the grin on his face now more evident, and she felt all of the discomfort that he had given her as taunting to who she really was or what she really felt. She looked out for a beat, then looked to the left and the direction that Solomon usually would walk up from. She looked down and took one of the cups.

"Thanks for the chocolate." She stood easily and took a sip. "I must be going. I see my friend over there."

She waved to a girl whom she had known from the store and her previous visits to the school. The girl was moving inside and to the ladies' restroom. She was from the religious side of Texas and was always

259

eager to talk with Dawn. Walking at a normal pace, she moved away and alongside Rebecca Greenly and they both walked side by side to the ladies' restroom.

You sat quietly at the bench and after a while began to feel so alone. You sat there, and for the first time listened to the sounds of what was actually surrounding you. The fluctuating banter and chatter of the college students, and the swish of the evening wind, which could have been from automobiles and buses passing or doors closing or people walking by, gave the evening its lure. It gave the moment a pattern of movement.

XXIII

Solomon: I Second That Emotion
January 17, 1968
Wednesday

Ever since the arrest back in August, you had been changing. You could see it when people pointed it out to you about the tone of your voice now, and your choice of words and the way you would drift away in mid-conversation, but you could not put a finger on the exact moment of change. The change was a reaction from somewhere inside that came forward to offset the pain without knowing, without hesitation, and without regard for anyone else. It was only for you, from you.

Sometimes it would come when you looked at the busted-out back window of the Mustang. You couldn't put cardboard there to replace it because you would not be able to use the inside rearview mirror that helped you see what was behind your car. Plastic would not hold long, regardless of the tape that you used to hold it in place. On a good wind it would blow and blow and eventually blow out flapping by pieces against the tape that always gave way. You could not put a new window there because you did not have the money, and your insurance company would not fix it because it happened when the police towed and stored it in the in-pound. You had very few options for this pain. Yeah, yeah, yeah.

You had thought about this but never really told anyone about the choices. A lot of people seemed to know about your situation but must have always found a way to conceal it. A lot of people would ask and give their opinions without asking specifically what had happened, and some of the more vocal ones were found at your job. You hated this. Now you were on the evening line in the back loading and unloading in the blue uniform pants and shirt on a probationary basis and not inside working the inventory numbers as before. You knew you were lucky to have any job at the company, and the warehouse was a good restart. It seemed like all eyes were on you as you went through your routine of lifting and waiting to follow instructions and have someone befriend you without prying into the reason why.

You felt you needed to protect Dawn and you wanted to keep her out of the conversations that people were having about your life. You became evasive about her and more and more alone when that was what all the men wanted to talk about. Yeah, you were hiding something from them because you had lost trust in these people, or they hadn't earned your trust. You saw this as the essential pain for you, not being able to trust anyone anymore except your mother and sister. But somehow it seemed to hurt to only trust them and leave them out of your relationship with Dawn. This was another source of pain. Yeah, yeah, yeah.

You were born in Rockwall and you had a childhood girlfriend. You were always walking hand in hand in elementary school and you would try to protect her. You did not know the extent of the relationship with Dawn nor see confirmation of it in the usual relationship exchanges. Your experiences were childhood at best and then even later the condemnation of easy women. It was a southern Baptist attitude that gave the family its value. So, sex was something special, like procreation with your wife and was folly when you needed it for pleasure from the condemned.

Somehow Dawn was different. You always felt she needed protection and you were glad to give it. But it wasn't like the protection that you gave your mother and sister. They were always their own people, expecting him to fill the role of the oldest male in the house routine. Protection was so cheap. Protection was so inexpensive.

In Search of the Rabbit Man

Dawn's protection stemmed from an entirely different perspective. She needed to talk. She needed to be listened to and heard as clearly. She needed understanding and someone to talk to. You did not know why she picked you, but you felt happy for her choice. You did not know that you were putting your heart into it until it was too late. You realized this when you could not explain why you wanted to be around her within her emotional dialogue. It was not for passion in the sense of boyfriend and girlfriend, but more so a feeling from someone who wanted to make someone else's life easier. This was not paternal, since you had no experience with a real father relationship. You considered her as an equal in the reciprocity of emotional exchanges so frequent that it became commonplace to hear her spout her opinions about things and the times and the city where you both lived. She did give you her fears and her regrets and her deepest pain, and you felt that was a balanced exchange because she knew you were catching hell as well.

She knew you were all alone at work, singled out because you were the only one of your kind moving through the Texas educational opportunities, but she never pursued any dialogue with your experiences. She must have felt confident to have confided in you about her own emotions, because she did and yours could remain private. You liked that part of the relationship. The implied alikeness was stronger and somewhat more spiritual and went without saying much, but it was always there from the very beginning when you first met her and it went a long way toward building trust with her. Yeah, yeah, yeah.

You took your break alone and outside and away from the others. A few walked by and said hello, but no one tried to join or accompany you, and that wasn't anything new. A warm baloney sandwich was your evening meal, and you ate it without tasting it. You were reading Dickens and understanding it for the first time. Pip, the lonely one. The innocent one. You had to read as much of your class assignments as possible on your breaks because the day classes are more challenging and because the other students have more time to study. They seemed to be more prepared and the classes moved faster. Their brains moved faster and they could start with the topic and be prepared for any feasible opinion about the topic, and most importantly get the approving nod from the professor. Being able to speak in the classes was a must-do and you had to know what to comment about before you could say anything. You couldn't think like that, but you had not been able to think like that about the topic because you had other things to think about like that for other topics. But this was not a place to talk about those topics that were seen in your community. And they were there, your classmates, in the topic of the day in the course. The classes had a rhythm, a sound, a pattern, and these were just the word classes. Yeah, yeah, yeah.

You read and chewed the baloney sandwich, and then it was time to go back to work. You did not read enough during your break and you did not know if you would be able to read any further tonight after work. You did not eat enough, but you could eat something anytime. Dawn talked a lot about leaving the city and going to California now, and the University of California Berkley. You listened. And thought about California.

"You guys need to unload this truck, here. Come on, let me show you where it is."

A linesman barked the instructions, and you and Winifred Jones followed him out onto the loading dock. Winifred was the slow-thinking son of the foreman, Big Will Jones, and he was teamed up with you for some strange comedy that you could not perceive as balanced light-hearted comparisons that they kept away from Big Will. Winifred was loud and had a strange overly Texas twang in his pronunciations of words, and you joined in on the laughter at least one time. And at least one time you spoke up for him and brought a startled look from everyone. You have been teamed up with him ever since. And there were laughs and slogans and brain jokes about smart niggers in everyone's breath and you just looked the other way. After all, you were not the only black person on the dock, and not one other person took the leadership in the situation so everything fell back on you because you were in college.

You both followed him back to the docks and watched as the freight truck lifted up the sliding rear door. Boxes of boxes of shoes were straddled on palettes from twelve feet high and as far back as ten yards of freight space. You selected a dolly and rolled it up to the back of the truck and begin placing six boxes at a time on it. If you had been allowed to operate the forklift then you could have removed the items one palette at a time, but this was a typical job selected for you and Winifred so you began the work in silence. It was tedious and time-consuming, and you enjoyed the seclusion of it.

Dawn talked about California and the Ashbury Park district in San Francisco and the Black Panther Party movement in Oakland. She spoke about changing times and the changing music and how Dallas was slow to see and acknowledge a different opinion about how life was changing. And how, while the choices were not crystal clear, there were choices to be made and not to be given. You listened to her talk about moving away and trying a new start, finding new work, making new friends, and learning new things. You listened to her glisten and gleam with happiness when she explained about finding education opportunities in other states and other countries, and how the Dallas community college system was kind of behind the other cities and states. She made it sound so clear and easy for you and how it would be easy to pack up in the Mustang and head out to the coast. She had money saved up and she made it seem so easy. You could always come back to Texas.

The work was moving slowly and you could often work in silence for hours now since your incarceration. The biggest shock with your stay in the city jail was how easily you fell into the solitude of work and how satisfying it was to keep quiet and not reveal your anger or sadness to anyone. Dawn had shown you pictures of the Black Panther Party members under their black berets with the impassive blank expression on their faces and the cold stares out into nowhere. Now you could understand that look and feel at certain times, and not feel it but still have it. They had a look of determination that was so uncommon for black people to show to whites through any public venue.

The two newspapers of the area, the *Morning News* and the *Times Herald*, and the city television news programs found any type of information as new and disseminated it to a split audience. You would watch the topics that were shown and then use the college library for news from other states for a different perspective. It wasn't that Dallas was biased. It was just that other papers sometimes got more in-depth within the events, and the events were so far away from Dallas that different views of the same topic probably weren't relevant to the local papers. But the network news programs started showing more detail and information about the war, and about drugs and music, and the generation movement and what was going on in the world. The network news also showed Dr. King giving speeches and marching and standing up for black people all over the South. You began to look for that in other people away from the churches, because it was always there in the churches, but seeing everyone else condemned for looking too determined was something you wanted to see challenged.

Melanie gave you volume 1 of the *Black Community News Service* back in August and you read it and asked the same questions about Denzell Dowell. You felt that the people you were coming in contact with weren't asking those types of questions because everyone had their own questions. At the Sears Roebuck store and at El Centro College, you didn't see that many black faces so you were always alone. Your world was working and helping your mom, even though she didn't want you to. She wanted you to save your money so that you could finish your education with as much ease as possible, and then leave the projects. She wanted you out of the projects at any cost, and to go out into the world and see more and more of what was good in it. Her housekeeper job and your help gave the family a chance to live without stealing, and that was what your mother was most proud of.

Your mother was like a lot of the good Southern God-fearing women with families that found their behavior comfort within the lines of a black leather worn Bible. The good deeds and good lessons were learned from the fragile pages and given to you in portions and portions and then understanding of the portions. She was proud of your behavior and your example of continuing to push forward always forward in your education, in your ambition, and in your relationships. She always said good things about whites and would never let you disparage them in her presence. Her religious teachings always reminded you of the good Christian way of doing things. You knew what she would say about your choices. Just like what she said about the jail time and when she went with you to get the Mustang from the impound yard and found the window busted out.

After you paid the money, you both went over to the car and your mom took out the Bible and begin to pray from Paul in Romans 12, pleading for change in people first and then their lives in appreciation of God's gifts. She also thanked God for Dr. King. She said it aloud in her prayers to God, and the yard attendant in his booth, a tow truck driver, and an officer standing outside the booth heard every word. The driver laughed and the attendant joined in, but the officer did not. He stopped all of the humor of the moment with a loud clearing of his throat and a step into the attendant booth. After that movement, everyone in the booth bowed their heads in reverence, respect, or fear. It was a moment of humanity that was almost lost when you found yourself falling into your solitude of disappointment, and it always brought you out. Just like in the Bible.

Your mother would also read Proverbs and to you. She would tell you about the son of King David and his rules of behavior in life. This was the discipline that she always wanted you to try to emulate. She wanted you to follow the rules of Solomon as much as possible. But it was you who decided to go to the next book in the Bible and read about the adorations of love that were expressed in the Song of Solomon. You became interested when you found you needed some other way to thank Dawn for her help.

But more recently it was harder to find that moment of humanity amid all of the puddle of moments that were always surfacing now. You had known the policeman who arrested you because you had seen him before when you were driving the Mustang in the projects. He had followed you a couple of times and stopped you once or twice when you were driving home from college. He was a patrolman in the projects, so it was normal. You saw him following you downtown at the college at least once or twice, but since the courthouse was there as well it seemed normal. The Lee Park concert, the NAACP meeting downtown, the fair park, the fairground parking lots of the Texas–OU Cotton Bowl game, the Bishop College homecoming, and now downtown on his lunch breaks when you met Dawn somewhere and talked all seemed a little too much. But you did not know what to do about it.

You read volume 1 of the *Black Community News Service* more often now. You read the same pages over and over and you thirsted for more knowledge about change. You went to the school library to read more about black people in the out-of-state newspapers and you saw the anger of the times. You also saw young whites marching with Dr. King and more blacks listening to rock 'n' roll, and you thought there was a chance for change every time you saw and read about it. You watched *American Bandstand* like so many other people your age, and saw a difference in that show and Ed Sullivan's show. You saw dancing and liked it. You watched change through happiness, and you watched change through anger, but you never saw it when it happened and no one was there to see it. No one ever did. You thought you should show your emotions on your face, but you never could and had not yet.

Sometimes Dawn would wait until seven in the evening because she would be working late as well, and sometimes you would leave early to take her home because you had had enough of work. You were working five hours a day now, but you could leave early for homework. The company had a business policy about college that was practiced in the Midwest and that you fell under as well, thanks to Dawn's concern and ingenuity, and you politely used this information to your advantage. You didn't know why the company still believed in you, but you wanted to remain humble so you didn't inquire. You appreciated Dawn more and more because you could do things around her and see movement in things that were being done around her. You loved her way of thinking and how she made everything that had happened against you a problem to be solved and an obstacle to overcome. There was no quit in her.

Maybe that is what love is, you thought. Maybe love is always present but never looked at until the need arises. Love is that comfort

In Search of the Rabbit Man

area in life that gives a person a dream and a plan and the confidence to make the dream come true, and somehow you could reason that Dawn was that person for you. Dawn was the embodiment of what you wanted love to be in everyone's life. She was immune to color or the other opinions that everyone else seemed to be formulating, and she was innocent in doing so. She was like a refreshing spring breeze touching everything but never fastening to any particular object or event. She was an idea of life and a choice, a decision because you realized for the first time that her life was her own choice and decision, and in that vein her own freedom. You had the strongest feeling that Dawn would never be alone in life, yet never fasten to life like you could do, but knew it wasn't a disadvantage for her. She could be standing alone, and this was where all the people would soon gather to accompany her or be there in the vicinity of her presence for the interest of the moment. This was a gift that was given to her and she used it modestly by always having at least one person there to privatize her moment and keep the other onlookers away. Yeah, yeah, yeah.

The unloading was ending now, and you had beads of sweat across your brow and on your neck. You worked hard, almost alone, as if in penitence for some deed that was misinterpreted or was an outright sin. You worked hard in hopes that people would forget your problems, but human nature has a strain of self-preservation that sometimes becomes the act of "putting your brother down beneath you to elevate yourself." It seemed like the more you worked the more attention to yourself you uncovered. Always standing out in everything that you did was the one element in your life that would make leaving easier. Going someplace and starting fresh and new with the innocence of the moment and the new impressions that you could make from that moment was the most enticing reason for going to California with Dawn.

XXIV

Rebo: Chain of Fools
February 16, 1968
Friday

You had come to the end of the line with your frustrations. You were driving downtown in your cruiser in the afternoon, and you realized that it was harder and harder to see Dawn. It was as if she were hiding from you, and the more you looked for her the more helpless you felt. It made you regret the times you were nice to her and a perfect gentleman. Life was not about choices but about decisions, and you had not made the best decisions when it came to her. You wanted to be nice to her and have her accept you into her heart, and not capture her and ignore her feelings for the sake of a union within your world. She talked to you sometimes and she was polite and direct. She did tell you her name, but it was not a submission; it was more an identification of who she was. She was like the break of a new day and every time you saw her something inside of you would creep forward like an early breeze that brought you the first fresh smell of morning. She caused coolness across your cheeks and you were becoming more awkward around her.

The bad part was that you saw her in everything, and this was enough to change all of your opinions about what you valued. She gave you the impression that she was aware of everything on the liberal side as well as the Texas value system and had her reasons for reacting to both. You wondered if she had found that balance of not offending

In Search of the Rabbit Man

either side while not defending either side. The more you watched her, the more you learned about people.

You were trying to change. You were starting to read more and you had your hair cut like Brando in the movie *On the Waterfront*. You still had your cowboy boots, but you didn't wear them as often and you began to show more patience on your job. You hadn't accosted that many black winos in the past months, and after you received your promotion you had more freedom at work and more time to cruise around alone and perhaps see her walking outside or sitting somewhere on a break. You knew her routine and the times for her movements, and you got good enough that you could position yourself at the places of her comings and goings. You could see her usual exit points from the building and the places that she would go on certain days and at certain times. You could be there watching and making sure that everything was okay with her, and it gave you a chance to see her. When she would walk with her unassuming confidence you would marvel at it. She was quiet and confident. She was mesmerizing in her own way, you thought.

You turned on Akard Street and began the routine circle back to the heart of downtown. You wanted to see the usual shops again. You had called dispatch earlier and informed them of your lunch meeting, so you were free for at least another thirty minutes. You were reluctant to get out and walk around. There were people watching the patrol car, and if you stopped anywhere someone would pass by, see your car, and report to dispatch for a problem at the location. Dispatch would call you and ask for your location. When you circled you could always say that you were spending your lunch helping out.

You wanted to find her and tell her about your change of opinions. You wanted her help in understanding this new way of thinking that you were ready to explore. You were just seven years older, yet it seemed like one hundred years or one hundred miles of distance between what she valued and what you were trained to value. She must have been brought up by some liberal-minded people to be able to make up her mind about trying new things. You couldn't imagine where she came

JON-MICHAEL HAMILTON

from because she was living with a lady who had been an actress in California, but she was without her parents.

You were trying to change. This added to the frustration. You were a sergeant now, and it was only one way to think. The blue way was the brotherhood that you could rely on, and everything else was just an illusion. The blue way was enforcing the rules and maintaining the order in social interactions, and there was no reason for negotiations. The blue way was a life choice, a lifestyle, an attitude, a twenty-four-hour concentration, and an ever-present perspective. It had to be that way if it was to be honest to the people and for the people. The blue way was a belief, and something to believe in, because the more you put into it the more you got from it. The blue way was only second to the Bible and the Christian faith in a Bible-Belt state, and a lot of times the two were intertwined when you and everyone else followed the Ten Commandments. That was the first thing that you changed about yourself. You began to believe in the blue way as a parallel to the religion that your mother and father believed so feverishly in. You even thought about Dr. King's views on that same religion and how maybe things were changing. You saw the difference in your father and mother's religion and what Dr. King was talking about, and this was a new sign of frustration.

On Elm Street you saw a young woman standing alone on the sidewalk looking in her purse. You gazed through the cruiser, and the more you looked at her the more it seemed that she was looking away from you and into her purse. You strained to look because the woman looked a little like Dawn, and she would look away to avoid any contact with you. You continued to look and tried to take in any detail that could tell you one way or the other if it was Dawn. You tried to see her hands. Her hair was different, but that could be her new style. It had been a long time since you had seen her. Her shoes were like the ones that Dawn was comfortable with, and her body type was similar.

You quickly circled the block over to Main Street and then back to Akard and then back to Elm. The young woman was still there looking into her purse, and you strained again to see her face as the cruiser came abreast of her. Now she looked down and you could not make out any features of her face. You tried to see if the woman had the same proud nose that Dawn had, or if the woman had the same beautiful high cheekbones. You tried to see if the woman had the same pout of lips and an always-creeping smile in the corners of her mouth. You pulled the cruiser over to the curb and exited with the door open. You walked briskly to the young woman, but by that time she was moving into the doorway of the Sanger Harris store. She had her back to you now, and her light blue dress flowed easily in the street breeze.

She was inside the store and moving to the cosmetics counter, and you were walking up behind her in your full regal blue and sergeant stripes across the sleeves of your shirt. You could feel the Sam Brown straddling your waist and your walk was a jaunt and sway that complemented the weight of the belt. The young woman was talking to a salesperson about some lipstick samples, and you moved right beside her to measure her height in comparison to your own. The woman still ignored you, but the salesperson, an older woman, looked to you and smiled.

"Hello, sergeant. Are you looking to purchase something as a present for a special someone?"

"Yes, I do have a special someone in mind." Even as you said it, your voice broke off into a deep croak. The young woman still looked away and you felt a pull of anger in your gut and you didn't know why. The young woman had done nothing to you and you still could not tell for certain if she was Dawn or someone else altogether.

"If this young lady could turn around, I could tell if I wanted that brand of lipstick for my girl." You said it as a hopeful request in your most inviting voice with a pleasing smile on your face.

"I'm sure this young lady will help with your request," said the salesperson. There was a long pause and the young woman turned and faced you.

The first thing that you noticed was that the lady was almost pink, like she had never ever been in the sunlight. He knew that Dawn was almost tanned from her love of the outdoors. The woman's hands were pink and older for her face. She had to be older than you by two years. You could feel your face betraying your enthusiasm and you didn't know if you could save the chance meeting. You could feel the disappointment creeping up to your eyes and prying at the edges of your smile. You fought to keep your shoulders straight and back, and you were careful with your hands so you put them behind your back. But the most telling sign was the instinctual push back that you tried hard to control. Your entire body bolted back a half inch and strained, but found you at a losing cause and it was noticed by the woman.

"I think the officer wants another brand. This might not be what he needs for his companion."

The woman's perception of the moment saved you further embarrassment.

"Yeah, she is a little different from you. She might like redder on her face than the other color. Maybe I should let her come here on her own and find her way around these things." You gave your biggest smile then, and it worked. Both women smiled a little more than needed and gave you your exit. You gave them a wave and walk out of the store with long purposeful strides that caused all waking traffic to give way to your steps.

Outside at the car you could hear the dispatch squawking for a response. You had been away for maybe five minutes, but already one of the walking patrols had noticed your car pulled over to the curb in front of the store.

"Car 1027, no problems. Just stopped in on a suspicious character walking into a store. Returning from lunch break in ten, over."

"Car 1027, roger that. Ten four."

You started up the car and sat there thinking of your next possible options to get her in your life. You wondered if it was this hard for your brother or your father. Everything always seemed so easy for them. While it always seemed that you were in the middle of everything that was happening bad, their lives were so normal and moving in the right direction. Maybe you wanted more? Maybe you questioned more?

You start to pull away from the curb and you saw an old colored woman walking up to the cruiser waving an envelope in front of her from side to side. She was hunched over from age and moving at a slow pace with an old brown walking cane helping her on her way. She must have been approaching you since you made the radio call. You opened the door and moved out and onto the sidewalk and waited for her to come to the car. You knew you should go over to meet her as you would with a white woman of her age, but something kept you fastened in your tracks. You remembered how you reacted when the black boy came to the impound lot to get his car and how his mother prayed and you made the other people show some respect for her pain and faith. You couldn't understand why you could not do the same thing now and move forward now, but you stood there through years of history and your Bible training and your family training. You waited on her, which seemed to take longer and longer.

You could see the face of the colored woman clearly now. How her dark features were etched with lines of submission and pain and her lips pursed with determination for her task in spite of the physical discomfort of just walking forward. You saw her hair, curled and black and under an out-of-place Sunday bonnet that sat a little askew atop her head. You saw her white sweater draped over her shoulders and her faded flowered dress that came down past her knees. You saw her legs, old crooked branches covered with tan stockings, and at the bottom were thick white ankle socks tied into the thick soles of white orthopedic shoes. You saw the other walking traffic moving past her from behind and passing her going the other way and ignoring her task. She continued to move toward you with the waving envelope in her dark hands. Somehow this was one of the Bible images that you had imagined when you read the book of Exodus—or was it by chance a remembrance from the movie *The Ten Commandments*?

"What can I do for you?" you asked halfheartedly.

"You are the officer that knows the young white girl?" she said with a little difficulty. You saw the spaces from the missing top and bottom front teeth and a big pink tongue working hard to keep the saliva from spilling over onto her lips and chin. She took a clean white handkerchief from a large black plastic bag and began to dab her forehead and the corners of her mouth.

"This envelope is for you to read on your on-time."

You started to tear it open and read it then, but the old woman stopped you.

"No! Don't read it now. It's from heaven and it is something that you should read later when you can really understand it," she said. She turned around and walked back the way she came from, with her cane picking its spots and the bag bouncing with her steps.

You got back into the cruiser and placed the envelope in the passenger seat. Church people were always coming up to the police and giving them things to read, and it seemed to increase with Dr. King and all the unrest he was causing. You didn't know why colored people wanted the same things that white people wanted. It was obvious that colored people didn't know what to do with it if they got it. You thought about your father's farm. Now what would a colored boy do with a farm like that? Your father had told you that they would probably let everything go to shit because they didn't have the know-how or desire to work it. They would probably spend the work time eating watermelon and drinking and dancing. And everyone knew that they were not going to get up early unless someone made them. They were just like animals. You were taught this and it was hard to dispute it. You hadn't seen anything to change your mind. What did Dawn see in that simple skinny colored boy?

You put the car in gear and pulled away from the curb. You thought of the worst sins in the Bible and you knew that man was not supposed to mate with animals. Sleeping with a colored woman was fine because it was just something that you were throwing away, but a white woman sleeping with a colored boy was a blasphemy. It all had to do with the receptacle of life. No colored boy could throw away a white woman, because they were the bearers of the children for white people. If that happened everywhere then it would be Babylon all over again. Your father had told you that his father had told him and on and on up the family tree. He said that God destroyed the tower to separate people because people would not work if they were the same. He said that his father's father had taught him that the main reason people worked and lived better was to prove that Babylon was destroyed. People were supposed to be different with different languages and different customs and different values and colors. You could change for Dawn, but she would have to change for you. She would have to have a good explanation about her friendship with the black boy, and maybe it was the explanation that would change your way of thinking about everything. Things were changing all over the world, and while the Bible should be stronger there was more evidence that people were outgrowing the ways of the Bible. You found this out by reading the newspaper and spending time in the library. The Vietnamese didn't seem to be reading the same Bible. The Germans were Christians, but their actions were trying to recreate Babylon, or, for that matter, ancient Rome. This was the opinion that the librarian offered.

You turned the cruiser left into the underground parking lot of the county building, gave the attendant a mock salute, and then found a parking space reserved for special vehicles. You were about to leave but you saw the envelope. You decided to open it and read it.

Hi

Stop trying to see me. I am not interested in you at all!! I do not appreciate your advances. If you continue to try to contact me I will go away and you will never know where I will be. I am not your friend.

Dawn

You read the letter twice and felt your whole world collapsing like all the air leaving a balloon. You could see all of your values and beliefs questioned by this one rebuff. In another time before your enlightenment you would have found a direct way to convince her, but even then, you knew somehow that would be fruitless. You needed something to convince her that you were sincere about your enlightenment, and you needed to tell her quickly. The more she rebuffed you, the more you wanted her.

You folded the letter and left the car and walked to the door to the elevator and stairs. You wondered if anything could help you show her of your life change. You decided to take the questions to the librarian later when you left work today. Somehow this intelligent woman would know what would make Dawn, another intelligent woman, change her mind.

XXV

**Dawn: These Boots
March 19, 1968**

"So, you're finally going out to California," Beebe said to you. She was standing in the dining room with her usual black dress draped across her thin frame and her loafers rooted on a circular rug. The sunlight was splashing in through the open curtains, and particles of dust and wisps of cigarette smoke were dancing through the rays. She was swirling around to an old Jimmy Dorsey tune playing softly and with her energy, coffee, and a cigarette, she was ready for the morning issues. She didn't ask it and you didn't expect her to. You had talked with her about leaving and now it was all planned. You walked down the stairs in your favorite jeans and sneakers with a red blouse and matching headband that kept the hair off your ears.

"Sit down on the sofa so I can talk to you. How long before you start out?" she asked in a raspy morning voice. She moved to the phonograph and removed the stylus needle from the LP, stopping the music. You went into the kitchen and poured yourself a cup of coffee and came back and sat at the dining table away from the cigarette smoke. She sat on the sofa and beckoned you down beside her. You resisted by a wave of your hand, and stayed at the table and took a sip of the coffee.

"The mountains are going to be beautiful, Dear," she said. "Pictures in every corner of the sky are the things that I miss most. I just can't get used to all this flatness and weeds. I guess it goes hand in hand with the silence here, but in all fairness, I love the silence here."

"I am going out in the evening and I guess the bus will try to make it all the way through."

"You won't see anything at night but trucks. You think you will be okay? Buses break down, you know."

"I'll be okay."

"You're going to take a cab to that address I gave you when you get to San Francisco. Don't try the streetcars until you get to know them. I've already called my sister Belinda and she will watch out for you until you get started in Berkeley. I still think you should wait until the summer."

"I'm going there early because I can find work more easily, and I want to see some things before I decide what I want to do."

"You're twenty-one and you're still looking around for the right thing to do with your life. You're a lot like me. When I was your age, I wanted more than just a marriage," said Beebe. "But when I found the work in the movies there was nothing else, I ever wanted to do." She reached over to an end table and with the cigarette flicked ashes onto the ashtray.

"It's not marriage. It's just that things are different and I feel different about some things and the same about some things. It just seems natural to want more then what's in front of us. Everybody is asking for something different," you told her.

"Yeah, in nineteen and twenty-eight I was three years younger than you and wanted the whole world to stay the same. Two years later the world changed and everyone was complaining. Be careful what you ask for."

You took another sip of coffee and leaned back into the chair. You looked to the curtains and could see a fine breeze beginning to blow through. You contemplated before you spoke, but then said it as flatly as you possibly could. "The world is changing and the universities are where the changes are starting at. There is so much free thought out there that everyone is exploding with ideas. I don't want to miss any of it."

"The movies were like that in the thirties and forties. There were so many new ideas that every month there was so much to watch and choose from. So many different types, and they got better every year. Then color came and even now there is so much that is new and different. I guess I know what you are feeling. I couldn't wait to get on a chorus line or to audition for a speaking part."

You drank your coffee and let the morning sounds wafer over you. The soft chirpings of a distant black bird on a telephone wire, a few dogs barking at a big trash pick-up truck that was rumbling down the street, a push mower clipping grass in the distance, the crinkle of curtain lines in motion from a sigh of a morning breeze, and finally the sponge of silence that now filled the dining room. Beebe was quiet now with her eyes closed and the reflections of her memories now etched across her face. You could use those same muscles, but now was the time you sought confidence and you only got that from your judgments of the present.

You felt you were losing your sense of independence by leaving the Sears job, and although there was correspondence with Berkeley you would still have to wait until summer before everything was settled. Meanwhile, you couldn't wait to spend time exploring San Francisco and maybe other parts of the coastal areas. With all the different people and races and ideas mixing together to make the area an adventure in every corner and every day, the move was bound to be exciting. That was the true meaning of happiness. The freedom to come and go as you pleased and interact with any and all persons that you were inclined to entertain or learn from. You found that this was an idea that was not shared with much enthusiasm from the people you knew, or for that matter from the older generation. That was why you got along with Beebe so well. She understood freedom.

You finished the coffee with one lasting sip and then returned the cup to the kitchen. Beebe was still caught in her reflections. You wondered if she would be okay without you there to listen to her advice.

"I'm going outside to read, and then later upstairs to finish packing."

Beebe smiled a tiny smile but didn't move. Her eyes remained closed. You walked over to the stereo and restarted the LP. The Dorsey tune started up again. You walked past her and went outside to the backyard. There was evergreen long-blade grass stretching and swaying in the morning breeze. There was a buzzing sound of morning bees and wasps in flight, moving from one elephant-eared plant to the next, and there was also a small batch of purple gladiolas reaching out to the sunlight. The sky was filled with puffy white clouds, and you couldn't wait to sit at the gazebo and digest some poetry and then look up to the clouds to see what shapes gathered around your world. The cloud shapes could range from happy farm animals, or large droopy-eared rabbits, or big soft islands of faraway lands, to frightening big-fanged prehistoric exiles or menacing fists depending on your mood.

The gazebo was a happy place with a small merry-go-round feel to it that always made you think of happier days. That's why you loved it so. It had a tin, American flag–colored, umbrella supported by a white middle table pole and four other red, white, and blue support poles that were spaced around the circumference. Four wooden benches that were also arranged in a circle on the floor edges accompanied the wood floor. It was the most interesting and your favorite place of the house, not because of the patriotic theme but because of the dancing shade from one side to the next throughout the day. You had spent a lot of time there and it was one place that you would miss.

You went out to it, picked up the book of poetry, and thumbed through the pages to your favorite poem. The words meant so much to you because it gave you the same moment of realization that you felt when you became on your own at the orphanage. How "Face to Face" made you see the true intentions of people. How "Adrienne" words had made you feel the stark terror of survival with one line, one thought, and one truth. How you wanted to move away from that truth because maybe you just hadn't found the meaning of truth in people, or maybe you had and it was so disappointing.

"And each with his God-given secret," you said aloud.

People had their own selfish desires and you had yet to find the true selfless person that you strived to be. Your stepmother had often echoed that sentiment in her own way when she would say, "Pain makes everyone selfish." She told you this to comfort you on a long lonely night under a Maryland sky when you were both alone and your stepfather was working late. You later found out that it was something that she used to comfort herself with and you could not share in that axiom anymore. You didn't know that much about her pain or if she had any. It seemed like she had everything that she could have ever wanted in life. An attentive husband who watched and waited on her every whim and want. She also had a beautiful home in a state that had some of the most progressive attitudes in the country. She was beautiful; even though the outfits she selected for herself were not designed to be eye-catching, you could still see her natural attractiveness coming through. Still, those were her words and you needed your own words to give you comfort for your own pain.

Your pain had to be different from hers. Your pain came from the early realization of not being wanted. It was more than a feeling. You could remember the visiting days at the orphanage when potential parents would come to the offices and request to meet a few of the kids who were there. You remembered what it felt like when you found out what the whole thing meant. You asked one of your teachers and she had responded that the thing was called an interview when people wanted to meet you and see if they wanted to be your parent. And then you felt the weight of that knowledge at the age of six and knew what it meant to others and how it made them act.

There weren't as many kids who were the same age as you as there were younger kids, so the reactions were varied. A few had the sense of hopelessness that restricted their actions and made them walk with the greatest of disregard for human activity. These were the ones who either became the teacher's pet or the teacher's pest because there had to be an order for attention when one person is responsible for giving it. You didn't want to be one of those kids who waited around and depended on the attentions of others. You had to be doing something, and the more you felt this need the more you became confident with your own choices and the freedom that you experienced. After all, everybody wanted to get away from this place.

Your solace for the pain came from the loneliness of your voluntary isolation. Not because you were alone, but because you chose to be alone

JON-MICHAEL HAMILTON

instead of hurting another person. When you first became familiar with the pattern of behavior and the subtle influences that could not help but motivate the other children, your reaction was bad. You found that out with the few toys that you had to play with that were considered your own. How sometimes a rival for attention would always have your toys when visiting day was a few days away. This was how you found out that you were attracting attention. It seemed like there was always a competition to be the first and most loved in the orphanage, because first and loved meant the best. Your first fights were had in reluctance because you could not understand that if you did not have a desire to be the first or the best that did not mean that you were not in the competition or considered that you were by the others. Later the fights became easier for you as you got better. You could fight for a long time and never get tired, and you could win every fight by pushing the other child down. That would end the fight. Until one little girl practiced something that she had seen on television. She hit you with her little fist with tried to imitate a punch from a Popeye cartoon. You hit her back harder and hurt her and felt good about doing it. That was when you decided to stay within yourself and not let anyone know of your inner desires. Your isolation was your first selfless act and also a way to express your freedom.

Your individuality came from that part of your life so your pain came from the time when you could not experience your freedom. You made a point of concealing this because the less that was known about what you cared about, the easier it was for you to keep it. Your independence and individuality were some of the selling points to potential parents for children of your age. No one really wanted a six-year-old baby. Parents wanted six-year-olds to be somewhat precocious but not arrogant, independent but not too individual and thoughtful. Somehow these were the qualities that you practiced all the time, to be independent and to keep your freedom. Even now you wondered if you were good with concealing your desires for your freedom.

The move to California was a chance to see how life on the other coast was. It was not as farfetched as your move to Dallas where you didn't have any friends and only a recommendation from your father and mother to some family friends and then finally Beebe and this gazebo. She had left the door open for your return, if you didn't like San Francisco or Berkley. But you were looking for happiness, and the same happiness that everyone had taken for granted had eluded you. The for-granted feeling that you would have someone beside you who would share in your dreams and desires and never question or try to change the way you think or feel. That did not seem like so much to ask. It seemed so easy for everyone else to find this thing in life. San Francisco could be the beginning or the ending of the search, but you would start there and let the fog from the ocean roll in and stick to everything like so much wet cotton, and you would accept the judgment of the fog if you were not alone. You could also accept the judgment of a time to move again and continue your search if it was not the place for you.

Maybe this was how pain made you selfish. It gave you the strength to keep moving, keep searching, and keep the fire burning inside of you so that you could continue on your trek of life searching for understanding and a place to belong beside someone who truly understood you.

XXVI

A Death in the Family
March 22, 1968

"So, I've decided to go out to California with you. What do you think about that?" Solomon asks. They were in the Mustang heading away from Dawn's home in Turtle Creek. Dawn had a large bag and a small bag nestled in the backseat of the car and Solomon had his bags in the trunk. They were both in jeans, and Solomon had on his favorite blue sweater while Dawn had on her dark blue navy pea coat.

"I'm going to catch the bus just like you and ride out and see the country. It should be good for me as well as you."

"What about your job and school? What about your family? If you are going on the bus with me, what will happen to your car? I don't want you to do anything hurtful because of me." Dawn spoke with a nervous fever. Solomon could not help but smile.

"What's so funny?" she asked.

"I have never heard you ask so many questions. You must really be worried. I've thought about this quite a bit. I have my transcripts, and you know that finding a job is going to be easy since I have a letter from Mr. Taylor introducing me to another Sears or any big department store. I have money saved up that will help me get by, and Shannon is riding with us to the bus station to take the car back to my mom tonight. That's why we are going to the college now. Everything will be okay."

"I'm not that concerned with the money. I have money and you can stay with me at Beebe's sister's home. From what I'm told, she is a lady that stays alone and could use the company. I just don't want to see you hurt your family."

Solomon let out a little chuckle again and Dawn looked to him, hurt first, then smiled and looked out the window. They were entering on the 75 freeway and heading to Interstate 45 and Bishop College. The March evening had lowering temperatures and the wind blowing in from the back window did not make things better. Solomon turned the heater on and up and the blower from the fan hummed against the rustle of the car's passing wind.

They traveled in a nervous silence with both now realizing for the first time the enormous decision that they were making. For Dawn it was nothing new to start over again. She had honed this talent in the orphanage and followed her instincts so far. With each new endeavor it became more and more important to be right about her decision-making skills. Throughout all of this she had never been responsible for another person's life and she didn't know how to begin now. She did look out for Solomon at work and did deflect a lot of the negative rumors that seemed to come to him after his arrest. But this was done in the context of a co-worker and the security of a home and job. Now that would be in question for him, and she was now entering an area where she had no real experience. She rationalized that it could not be any worse than it was now. She might even see the change as another chance to learn something from people.

Solomon was ready for anything now. His arrest was something that he wanted to put behind him as soon and as far away as possible. After seeing the change in him, his mom and sister wanted whatever was best for him to bring him back to his old happy self, and if this is what it took then they were happy with it. He had no real friends to leave behind, and even Shannon could see the move to the West Coast as a plus for her, knowing of a person moving closer to the movement. She had all kinds of suggestions for him about helping and joining the Black Panthers in Oakland, and she also said to stay in touch because she and her classmates were planning to make a trek to the movement grounds in the summer. Everything felt right.

289

"I don't want to have a car out there yet; I mean not until I know the city. I'm going to use the city transportation first, and if it becomes necessary then yeah, I'll go get it. I want to move close to the college. I want to walk in the sunshine on a big college campus," he said. "It should be so easy."

Solomon was talking, but not necessarily to Dawn. One of the first truths that his mom had taught him a long time ago was that everything that was said aloud meant more than just thinking about it. It was just like when you're saying your prayers. They are always best replied to when they are said aloud. Like when they got the Mustang back from the impound lot, a lot of loud praying and planning. He had to learn to stop doing this in the projects or at school or at college, and especially at the job he was leaving behind. He had to learn to keep his thoughts to himself and not let anyone know his plans. No one heard it from him that he was going to California. They just knew that he said he needed more time for his education and that he was taking some time away from the job. Solomon and Dawn drove the rest of the way in silence, watching cars pass by in the southbound traffic congestions and seeing the green landscape pass by with a few industrial buildings sprinkled in along the way.

Rebo drove his truck down Main Street to the southbound on-ramp and slowly merged into the traffic. There was a large flow of cars moving and the Ford truck movements were sluggish. It was an old black 1950s model with the gearshift handle choking around the collar and a slow-catching clutch, but Rebo loved it like a trusted friend. It throttled on in first gear and then Rebo shifted to second and found the flow of the traffic bunched into a speed crawl of twenty miles an hour under the pace. In the past he could have just flashed the lights on his cruiser and made headway at any pace that he desired. But now he was without those types of advantages and he was becoming more accustomed with the normal driving practices.

It wasn't a big surprise to his superiors that he had resigned from the police force. They felt that the stress was getting to him more than the other officers his age, but they were still disappointed that he would leave. The captain took his badge and gun with reluctance and advised him to revisit his decision after six months away from the job. Rebo walked out of the office without ceremony and with a sense of relief and happiness for what could happen tomorrow.

He spotted the broken back window frame first, and then the blue-gray color of the Mustang. It was moving at a slow deliberate pace with two occupants sitting inside and staring straight ahead. His heart rate immediately picked up. There was so much to apologize for, and inexperience with never ever apologizing for anything before gave him the twinge of a nervous twitch pulling away from the corner of his right eye. He often had that tendency now when he began covering new ground in his life. It was more than just changing the music he listened to, it was the food he selected as well. Or the places that he began to go for his food. He could not go to the same hunts as the officers and he didn't eat at the same times. He was dressed differently as well, so it was hard to blend in at those places. Fast food became his primary subsistence, but he also learned to shop at the markets.

He tried to read Kerouac's *On The Road* but settled for trying hard with Miller's *Tropic of Cancer*. He tried to learn something new every day. He began to question authority subconsciously with his choices, and his eyes always held a questioning gaze. He wanted to apologize for his treatment of the colored boy. He wanted to stop saying "colored boy" and start saying "black boy." That would be a start. Maybe that would be something that Dawn would respond to. She was so liberal minded that it had to have an effect on her. He wanted to see things the way she saw them, and if it were better than his experiences then he would change for good.

He followed them with about two car lengths behind but always kept the Mustang in sight. The landscape moved slowly. It was unchanging throughout the seasons and held the same green luster through summer, fall, winter, and now the eve of spring. To his right the Proctor and Gamble soap factory churned the same billowy smoke residue from its processing and production furnaces through the twin concrete stacks, and from behind his head the slowly vanishing downtown skyline now became smaller with lights stretching up to the sky. The sunlight dwindled steadily on the right side of his face and his eye.

The old Ford churned on toward the night and a new beginning for him. He couldn't wait to catch up with them, but he had to be sure it was in the right moment when he approached them. He speculated on their destination and guessed that it must be the black college. It didn't matter where; he would get her attention some way wherever they were going. He would tell her that he agreed with the way that she thought about some of the things that she cared about and that he would begin to change. He wanted to tell her that it was because of her that brought out this change in him. He hoped that his appearance and actions would say more than the words he would speak, but she had never responded to his actions. He really didn't know what she responded to, but now he was willing to try anything.

They were coming up on the Simpson Stuart exit now, and Solomon slowed the car down and eased into the right turn. Dawn was sleeping lightly. She had that rare quality of being able to sleep during the most stressful times. After, she would awaken with the most wide-eyed optimism and approach the day with an innocence that was refreshing to everyone around her. Her eyes blinked twice with the deceleration of the car and she brought her head up from the headrest. She never yawned, but smiled, and then Solomon knew that she was alert and ready for everything.

"We are gonna drive up to the dorms and see if Shannon is ready to go with us."

Dawn was quiet but she acknowledged with a smile and looked out the window at the upcoming football field. The campus looked empty on this side; spring training for football was still two months away and no one was in the area. The lights were out, but the field was still illuminated by an eerie light from some indistinct source. The sun was in full set now and the nightlife began to come alive in the area. A stream of red taillights ran down the street as an assortment of vehicles traveled to the homes that were lined up on the right side of the street.

IN SEARCH OF THE RABBIT MAN

Rebo took the same exit but kept his distance. He had no reason to be on the college campus and he did not know exactly what to do. If he stayed on the street, he could lose them leaving from another exit. If he went into the campus the truck would stand out, not to mention his white face. He was stuck within a problem that did not have an immediate solution. For lack of a better decision he pulled the truck over to the side of the street and waited in contemplation. He began to second-guess his decision to follow the Mustang. He looked into the rearview mirror and gazed at his face, his eyes, his new haircut, and the new him. He took stock of his new blue cardigan sweater and the red and white lapels that covered his neck from the shirt that was underneath. This was definitely a different style from his usual lusty cowboy plaid shirt and Lee jeans but not close enough to what he was going for, a preppy white college kid. The last he had seen when he passed by El Centro College was how they were all bundled up in white shirts with black ties and pants like the protesters and civil rights marchers. He might have changed, but he didn't know if he was prepared for any conversations about that issue. This is why he needed Dawn so much. She could tell him how to think.

The Mustang pulled alongside a small three-story building. Standing outside and under the lights were two large Afros side by side. Shannon and her boyfriend Thomas Clark, a very light-skinned black, were waiting for the Mustang to roll to a stop. When it did, they went up to the passenger side door and Thomas opened it. He climbed in the backseat and sat behind Solomon and set Dawn's large bag upright on the seat where it separated him from Shannon, who slid in behind Dawn. When everyone was settled, Solomon put the car in gear and drove away.

"The West Coast is where it's at, man. Everything is happening out there," said Thomas. He and Shannon were sporting the matching jean jackets and bell-bottom jean pants. They both had on high ankle boots and had a different rhythm to their movements and words.

"Yeah, I'm gonna drive back downtown to the bus station. We are heading out tonight," said Solomon.

293

"If we are going now, I want a red soda," said Shannon. "Drive up to the E-Z Shop. I can run in and buy one."

Solomon gassed the car and let it follow the winding road back out to Simpson Stuart. He made the right turn and headed in the direction of the market.

The traffic leaving the campus was sparse, and Rebo easily picked out the Mustang as it turned right and headed west and up the homecoming parade route. He put the truck in gear and followed along. He had no idea where he was going, but even from his distance he could make out two large hair types in the backseat. He didn't know what to expect, so he was glad that he had his long-nose .38 revolver underneath his seat. He felt comfortable with any situation, even though he knew he could never let Dawn see him use it. It was only for protection, and just in case he needed it.

He saw the Mustang make a left on Bonnie View, which really turned out to be a U-turn back onto Simpson Stuart Road. The Mustang turned quickly into the E-Z Shop parking lot and stopped. Rebo missed the light to U-turn as well and waited until the next opportunity to turn. This seemed like as good a chance as any to talk to her. He would ask to speak to her alone and then tell of the changes that he had made in his life.

"Let me out so I can get some soda pop," said Shannon. She slid out past Dawn, who was now crunched up against the dashboard. "Come with me, sister. We may as well get something for the men as well."

Dawn smiled and got out and joined Shannon, and they walked into the store together. Solomon and Thomas stayed behind.

"Dawn seems like a cool sister, brother man. She must be down for the cause," said Thomas.

"Why would you say that?"

"She's here with you and making the move to the West Coast at a time when we really need communication from everywhere."

"I never looked at it that way. I think she's just doing what she has to do to be happy."

"Don't we all. But what about you, bro?"

In Search of the Rabbit Man

"I need to make a move. Dawn says that the education is better on the West Coast. She says there are more four-year colleges then here in Dallas."

"Yeah, she could be right. All we have is Bishop and SMU, and no one has the money for either without the grants and loans, or of course family money, like SMU. I'm from Arkansas and there are not many there either, maybe two in the whole state."

"Why not come with us?"

"Bishop is not bad, and it is the last black college going west. Houston has two black colleges, but Dallas has one and so there is more to do here in the city."

"Like what?"

"Aw, bro. Like helping out in the community. This is an all-black community right here and it is quiet and affluent with hardworking people. Not many are educated, but there is always the future."

"Thomas, man, what are you studying?"

"I'm into sociology, bro. Fourth year, man and then maybe a master's at Spellman in community activism, law, or political science. I'm into it, bro. We need all types in the movement."

"Yeah, brother. I know what you mean." With that said, Solomon got really quiet. He heard the door of a truck slam hard and loud first and then saw the white policeman walking away from the truck and moving to the doors of the E-Z Shop. He recognized the cop, even though he did not see him in uniform, but he knew it was not an accident that he was there. He looked over to where he the slam came from and remembered seeing the black truck on the highway in the rearview mirror of the Mustang. He thought it looked out of place heading into the black neighborhood, but disregarded it for the task at hand. He moved from the Mustang with a fast pace and left the keys in the ignition. He paralleled the officer's movements in walking to the doors of the E-Z Shop.

Out of the corner of his eye, Rebo saw the young black boy moving at about the same pace as he and angling in the same direction. He thought about talking to the kid and starting with his apology to him

295

Jon-Michael Hamilton

first. It would be a step in the right direction, he felt, but it would be stronger if Dawn saw him do it. He quickened his pace to almost a trot, and when he got to the doors Dawn and a girl with a large Afro came out of the store holding two paper bags, one with a big chip bag peeking out of the top and the other with something heavy, like bottles.. Dawn saw him and then saw Solomon moving up as well. She thought instinctually to avoid any confrontation for Solomon by first dropping the bag and then turning and running to her right, heading to the darkness behind the store. She moved quietly but fast, and was around the corner before anyone could react.

Shannon was shocked and almost dropped her bags as well. She was caught between retrieving the items that Dawn had dropped and following her. Before she could do anything, she saw a white man cross her path and running in the same direction as Dawn. After that, she saw Solomon following in a sprint in the same direction as Dawn and the white man. She did not know what was going on.

"Solomon, Solomon, where are you going, bro? Where is everybody going? Thomas! Thomas! Get over here quick!! Come here quick!!"

Thomas pulled forward from the backseat and moved out of the open driver's side door of the Mustang. He quickly came over to Shannon.

"What is happening? Where is everybody going?"

"I don't know. Let's put everything in the car and wait."

"Shouldn't we follow?"

"I don't know. We should move to the car before someone calls the police."

Dawn turned the corner and ran out in the darkness. Behind the store was a vast grassy area with large trees that stretched up to the moonlit night, and she headed into it. The terrain was uneven, with fallen branches and tree stumps, but it had a worn trail leading into it offering concealment and escape. She took the path in stride and began running while ducking down under low-hanging branches and sidestepping tall drooping grass. The path was wet and slippery, but she trekked on deeper into the woods. From the distance she could smell and hear running water and she headed in that direction. She kept her eyes open wide while looking for a hiding place to duck into and double back. This was a trick she had learned a long time ago. She knew that if she could become quiet in her steps it would work better, so she began to move lightly but still fast. It could fool the officer, perhaps. She did not know that Solomon was following as well.

This was not the way Rebo wanted this to happen. He did not want to chase her or frighten her. He thought about stopping and turning around and waiting for another chance, but he knew it would be harder and almost impossible to approach her ever again if he could not explain his intentions now. In his mind, in his heart he was caught between being aggressive in his chase and being passive and apologetic. He wondered why it was so important to convince this girl of his change. He wondered if this was love.

He ran on and saw her vanish down an incline into the dark. He heard someone coming up behind him and knew it was the black boy. He did not want to confront the kid, and he wondered why he did not want to. He entered the incline and slowed his pace. He found a stopping point off the path standing by two tall trees. The boy entered the path, winded and frantic and searching with wide eyes. Rebo stepped out with his hands held up.

"Slow down, boy; I'm not trying to hurt anyone."

The kid swung a fist at Rebo and connected on his jaw. It was a good punch, but it was a punch from a nineteen-year-old and Rebo recoiled and hit the kid first in the stomach with a left and then to the jaw with a right and knocked him out cold. The kid lay sprawled out in the grass but was unhurt. Rebo leaned over to be sure, and then began his search again for Dawn. Somewhere she was moving into dangerous terrain with only moon illumination. He felt a little desperate with the way things were turning out. He had hurt the kid again, and this time without really trying. He began to run almost blindly now. He thought about calling her name to reassure her. Maybe this would work.

"Dawn," he started in almost a whisper, but got louder. "Dawn... Dawn, I just want to talk to you...Dawn, come out."

Dawn was hiding in the grass right before the creek crossing. She had put a loose log right across the path and had tried to cover it with some grass. It was a makeshift trap, but it was designed to trip him and give her time to backtrack to the car and the bus station. It was an incline with a few large slippery rocks embedded in the mud of the trail, and she had almost fallen with the tree branch. She heard him and held her breath while waiting for him to start down the incline.

Rebo became frantic now. He thought maybe something had happened to her and it would be his entire fault. This was not the way he had planned it. He saw the trail leading down to the creek and started as fast as he could. His intention was to jump over the creek with one leap by stepping on the grass that was before it. He could save time with this maneuver, and it was something that he had practiced in rookie training and chase scenarios with his newly hired officers. He approached the grass with all his weight and felt his foot and balance give way. From the moment he was upended feet first until the time his head hit the rock behind him, he felt this was all the wrong approach but it was very funny. It could be something that they could talk about later in their old age when they would sit around and listen to music and drink lemonade and watch the sun set. It could be something that they could share with their friends and their children and their children's children.

The back of his head hit with a thud and a crack and he saw beautiful white stars dancing before his eyes. Everything slowed down then. He knew he was bleeding and he tried to stand, but couldn't. He looked over to his left and saw Dawn hiding in the grass. He tried to move his feet to slide over to her, and he did use his left hand to pull at some grass and it gave him more leverage for the movement. He began to slide off the trail and into the tall grass, and with each pull, each push with his right hand and both feet, he became weaker. He wanted to talk and to tell her of his change. He wanted to sleep and tell her tomorrow.

Dawn emerged from her hiding place and lightly but quickly ran back up the trail. She thought he would be getting up at any moment, and so she didn't look back. She came to Solomon, still sprawled out on the side of the trail and knocked out. She ran to him and held his head up.

"Solomon, oh Solomon. This is my fault. This is all my fault. You shouldn't have followed me. You shouldn't follow me."

She was crying and shaking him and he began to regain consciousness. He looked up to her and the first thing he could do was smile and then he began to move his jaw to talk.

"Non…Non…sense. We are friends. We are friends going for a change in our lives."

"Can you get up?"

"Yeah…yeah, I can get up." He rose to a sitting position and looked around and then down the trail. "Where is our friend?"

"He fell down back there, but he could be getting up any minute now. Let's get back to the car and catch the bus out of this city."

"Yeah. Let's catch the bus."

They got up and retraced their steps with Dawn holding Solomon steady out of the wood and back to the front of the store. No one seemed to notice them as they walked in the parking lot and back to the Mustang. Thomas and Shannon were sitting very quietly in the front seats of the car. They both got out and got into the backseats. Solomon and Dawn returned to their seats.

"We should move that black truck so it will be harder for him to follow us," said Solomon.

"Let's just go," said Dawn.

"No. Solomon is right. He could come out of those woods and follow us downtown," said Shannon.

"We don't even know if the keys are in the thing."

"I'll go and see," said Thomas. He got out of the car on the driver's side and moved over to the truck. He got in and started it up. He found a truck drivers cap in the passenger seat and put it on while tucking his black Afro underneath. It gave him a different look altogether. From a distance he looked like he belonged to the truck. He gave a salute and put the truck in gear, and headed out to Simpson Stuart Road. Solomon started up the Mustang and followed the truck. Solomon knew they were going downtown, and that would be as good a place as any to leave the truck.

XXVII

The Search
April 26, 1968

There was no light more beautiful than the light that was found in the midnight sky of a Texas spring. When the stars were up high but still so bright that it seemed to bring the sky down and closer to the quiet homes and the people and you could reach up and poke one and watch it fall if you had a long enough branch from a cottonwood tree, then the night had so much innocence and quiet mystery, and made a young man feel as if anything was possible. The moonlight of a full moon splashed through the crevices and corners, made the few streetlights useless, and gave everything that bathed under it a shiny look, as if it were in a downtown Neiman Marcus department store window during Christmas and everything was new to the touch. Neiman's was the Dallas equivalent of a Tiffany's department stores but it may as well be the top of a mountain to the people in Mikey's neighborhood because of the prices. Still in this light, all the homes on Mikey's street that lay underneath the sky sat in uniform long patches of red and tan brick and green grass yards with one large tree in the front yard that waited patiently for this light, and then began to glisten with the cool soft comfort of peace. The animals were always asleep in their trees and bush, and when you listened closely to the homes that faced each other along the long winding street you could hear the soft purring of breaths and snores and the releasing of the day's tensions, adventures, responsibilities, and happiness.

Mikey emerged into the Friday night light after his father had returned from work and everything was quiet and still. Big Teddy had dinner that was left prepared by Mikey's mom and retired to a night's rest from an exhausting day of driving the patrons of the city without so much as a word to Mikey or his sisters. Mikey was supposed to be asleep but of course he wasn't; he was just feigning sleep with the lights out in his room and his eyes closed to look as normal as possible. After retrieving his supply bag from the garage, he had slipped quietly out the back door, which he had to leave unlocked for his return. As an afterthought he had removed the trash from last night's dinner and placed it into the cans in the backyard. Somehow, taking responsibility for the household chores made him feel more at ease with his decision to venture out into the night. Even though he felt his task was noble, he still had to come to terms with his deceit, his keeping his plans from his mom and dad.

He moved out into the night and to his first destination with a lighter burden. In his bag were his makeshift weapons. He had molded a few arrows from branches from the peach and plum trees in his backyard. He had to be very careful in the future if he wanted to continue to use those trees for weapons. They were the easiest to notice because they were his father's favorites. He had given Mikey the responsibility of their care and welfare. Mikey was supposed to prune away dead leaves and branches and make sure the trunks were not crowded. It was with this reasoning that Mikey only took two branches from each tree. He sheared the leaves away and sharpened the edges by rubbing them on the concrete porch of the backyard. The last step was to fasten soda pop bottle tops on the edges by bending them in half with pliers and hammering them snug with the ball peen from the tool box. The bottle tops gave the arrows more weight, point, and strength. He also fastened cardboard edges that he had collected from old milk cartons and held them in place with kite string. This gave the arrows a slight precision in the direction they were aimed, which he needed if he wanted to hit anything.

The problem was anything past ten yards would cause the design to lose its effectiveness. And that was when he had tried the design two years ago. In his haste to gather information about the Rabbit Man he rushed in his preparations. He didn't have time to test or perfect his design. He needed evidence. But instead of going out with no protection at all, he decided to go out with what he had. He felt he needed weapons because no true adventurer entered any place without them. The Indians always had them, and even Kirk and Spock needed them.

Another thing he did not consider was the brightness of the night. When playing games in the summer like hide-and-seek and games of tag and night dodge ball, he had never considered how bright the night sky could be. When you are out having fun with friends you don't notice things like that, but when you are actually sneaking and seeking out something that no one should notice or perhaps approve of, then you became aware of the night lights. He tried to look the part in the night, with his bluest blue jeans and a blue button-collar long-sleeve shirt that was more accustomed to Sundays as opposed to a Friday night walk. It was the closest he could find to all black.

He walked past the large mimosa tree that stood watch in his front yard and then out onto the sidewalk with his blue ski cap pulled over his ears, and he noticed for the first time that he was the only thing moving on the street. He felt for the first time that his movements would upset the natural routine of the night. He noticed the silence and now felt alone. Every home had its own peaceful tranquility and he became aware of the disturbing calm of the night.

Somewhere deep in the back of his mind he reasoned that this was the effect of all the events that had taken place in the last two weeks. The death of Dr. King and the riots, the body in the trail, and now all the dogs that were found dead and split open down the middle had somehow changed things. The neighborhood had changed, the people had changed, the attitudes had changed, and finally trust had changed. That was it. Trust in the neighborhood had changed and everyone was suspicious of the new things that would occur in the neighborhood. Mikey wanted everything to be normal again, to be safe again, to be trusting again, and this reinforced his resolve to find some evidence of the Rabbit Man.

He became stronger in his being, and while his footsteps became softer and more careful, his commitment became stronger. He virtually tiptoed down the sidewalk trying to be as quiet as the night, but he could not escape the lights, which became more evasive in the silence, but he didn't care.

It seemed his movements became more pronounced, more disruptive with the absence of anything else moving. Nothing was stirring, which gave a grave resemblance to a Christmas Eve night. In fact, for the first time what became clearer to Mikey was that this was a direct reaction to the April events and the televised protesting and violence from around the country. It wasn't an official curfew, but there was a reluctance of nightlife in the neighborhood. Maybe it would pick up after the spring semester when the students were released for the summer, but this was a Friday night and no one was outside on the left side of midnight. There were no teenagers talking, or music playing, or laughter heard in the night.

Of course, there was a new police substation further down Bonnie View near Loop 12 Road, but he reasoned that it was there for the benefit of the neighborhood. As he walked under the streetlights, he became more aware of the pained silence and the imposed trepidation of his own movement as if he were walking in a still pool of water and didn't want to disturb the peaceful leaves and life that waddled in it. When he reached the second streetlight that stood on the corner of Donnie Edmonds's home, he remembered the scene that had happened some eight hours earlier. The place had returned to normal. There was no lingering evidence of the slain dog and this dismayed Mikey in a new way. He didn't know what to expect but he did expect something, maybe a trace of blood, or a collar or a dog bowl or something to show that the animal had meant something to someone. Instead nothing was present to remind anyone of the pain that Donnie had experienced or that his friends had experienced through him. He intentionally crossed the street and proceeded on the other side so that he would not disturb any lingering echoes of sadness. He was like that when it came to death. Reverent. He didn't have much experience with death, but he would always pause at any last resting place and would never trample over it. This came from both his mother and his father and his Bible school teaching. Somewhere in the Bible the Christians had shown a reverence for the last resting place of people. He just included the slain dog by extension. He could not see himself walking over anyone's gravesite and he would not begin on this night of adventure. He felt that if he did everything the right way, then his luck would continue and everything would be okay. It would take some luck to achieve what he hoped to achieve and then return before his parents awoke the next day. What was in his favor was that the next day was Saturday morning and a good day for sleeping late.

When he turned right on Tioga and up the incline toward the elementary school, he could hear the inclement traffic behind him. There were some travelers moving down Bonnie View Road and destinations through and away from the neighborhood, but no one turned up or down Tioga Street, so he walked with more ease and freedom in his purpose. As he grew closer to the school, he realized how lifeless it was without the noise of the students and the teachers and the classroom lights. And this was Mikey's first great realization. The darkness that surrounded the school after hours was haunting. It seemed that the starlight and the moonlight had no effect on the now-lifeless building, and it even looked lower, like it was sinking into the ground at rest. The flag was long since put away and the wind took the same recession from the grounds. Everything that could have shown life now hung or draped or slumped.

Mikey intentionally walked in the shadows alongside the school on the Tioga sidewalk until he came to edge of the second building and the beginning of the recess area and football field. He felt that the starting point for his adventure should be where Felder's dog, Tippy, was found so he quickly darted from the sidewalk and across the playground with a brisk trot. He began to make better time when his eyes became more accustomed to the darkness, so he soon reached the area where a fresh scoop of earth and grass had been removed. He concluded that this was the location where Tippy was found because the custodian had come out with a shovel when it happened last week and the grounds still hadn't recovered from the deep scoop of earth removed along with the frail lifeless pet.

Mikey stopped before stepping onto the death marker and looked around in all four directions. To his right was the street and sidewalk from whence he came, behind him was the school, in front was the grassland leading for miles and miles to the next neighborhoods of Lancaster and Alta Mesa, and to his left behind the high school was the creek and wooded area that little was known about. This seemed the best starting point now because it was the hardest to reach and the easiest to conceal things in. It seemed logical that someone could hide in those woods in the daylight but come out at night to roam around the neighborhood when everyone was either working or in school. Mikey forgot in his reasoning that tomorrow was a weekend and it was no need for whomever was hiding in the woods to come out in the daylight so they could easily be hiding in the woods, even now.

He began to move to his left in the direction of the woods with slow deliberate steps. He could feel the grass crumple underneath his footsteps and could now hear a slight breeze rustling across the tips of the highest grass and at the edges of the woods as he got closer. Closer still, now he could smell the branches and leaves of the large cottonwoods and red oaks and the brisk smells of the cedars that now obscured the forward movement as far as he could see. He could now see the large trunks and branches jutting up and outward, and if not for the massive overflowing of leaves he could have seen the starlit ink-filled sky. Now there was an imposed darkness beyond five feet.

As he walked into the darkness it became clearer and more visible, and it seemed that the grounds underneath the trees had their own way of staying short and maintain the appearance of being well kept. Maybe some grazing wildlife had wandered through, or maybe the lack of sunlight helped to hinder the wild growth that could have happened if left untended, or maybe someone did come here with shears or push mowers to snip and clip and maintain the balance. Mikey did not know, but it did not hinder his quest for answers.

Sounds came to him from the darkness. There was the rustling of a night breeze, gentle with intermittent breaths in the night, and then there was the sound of night crickets calling out to their mates, the incessant shrilling that would die down and then begin again, and finally the soft trickling of water rushing by from some far-off creek. Mikey moved in the direction of the sounds and now began to smell the moisture in the air and the scent of wet leaves and grass. Through a clearing the ground began to incline upward and then down with such an abrupt decline that he almost lost his footing, but stumbled awkwardly to the edge of a shallow creek.

As he looked into the creek, he remembered this location from a story that was told on a past summer night by Reggie Turner or one of the other older boys who lived on the street. Those boys had talked about skipping school and going out to fish for crayfish in the spring of last year. The way they had told the tale it seemed as if it was a faraway place with hidden secrets and lazy afternoons. As Mikey stood on the edge and watched a fallen leaf stream past him and bubble into the settling pool that started the smaller sewage runoff, he realized that it was only a makeshift place of recreation like so many in the underdeveloped places that surrounded the neighborhoods.

Mikey knelt down by the creek and took an arrow from the old army man pack and poked it into the water. It was deeper than he thought it would be. After reaching down so deep that his hand was in the water halfway to his wrist, he swirled it around until wispy gray mud clouds came up to the surface of the water and the tiny creatures with the tiny lobster claws came up and swam around, wondering what had disturbed their late night silence. If they were angry, Mikey really couldn't determine, but he did watch a few of the more adventurous ones swim out to the dark muddy bank and begin to slowly crawl through the mud and crumpled grass forward and toward him.

He wondered what Yolanda would say about these little creatures, away from their home, and investigating the disturbance that he had

IN SEARCH OF THE RABBIT MAN

caused. She would probably say that it had something to do with the natural order of things and how everything had the same curiosity about sameness and differences and any disturbance was worth investigating, regardless of the circumstances. She would say that it was a part of life and survival, this quest for sameness. And while these tiny angry creatures with the tiny pincher claws had the need to crawl out from their muddy darkened abode and to the shore of the creek with no sense of fear, Mikey realized that this was something that he could do. He could find evidence of the Rabbit Man and bring it back to the others and give everybody something to move toward. To move to the sameness as before now became the overall goal. Before the body and the dogs and the rumors of the Rabbit Man and the fear and the closed-off that everyone gave to everyone else in the neighborhood was something to move away from. Then it became clear. And what vanished was the underlining guilt of his adventure. And what vanished was the undermining fear that lingered underneath his bravado and his daring and his curiosity. All he needed was a place to cross the stream. The tiny crayfish continued to crawl up the bank and toward Mikey. He looked down at them and fought the urge to strike one of them. That would not be right. He was the intruder in this habitat and he must make the adjustment.

He looked long to his left and then looked downstream to his right. He spotted what appeared to be a shallow area that also had the edges of both sides of the creek reaching close as if trying to touch. On the other side of the creek was a large oak tree whose trunk sprouted up over twenty feet and then had large branches that pierced out into the night. The roots from the large tree dug down deep like long strong fingers, and one stain, brown and black from dirt and age, wandered out and down to the creek's edge. This was the cause of the extension from one side of the creek to the other. Mikey moved to that place along the creek line and briskly jumped across to the other side.

He lost his balance for a moment and almost fell over on his side but crouched down on all fours, regained his balance, and crawled up to the other side using the extended root as balance. When he reached

307

the flat area of the other side he stood up and realized that in his haste he hadn't brought anything to wipe his hands. His hands now covered with mud posed a problem. If he allowed the mud to dry, he was afraid it would make his weapons useless. He had to find a solution.

He remembered the times when his father had soiled his own hands from changing the oil on their sedan, or had actually gotten mud from their own rosebush or backyard garden, and how he would wipe his on the corner of the grass or someplace that was easily replaced in the yard. Mikey used the same technique and moved away from the large tree and further into the darkness of the other side. He returned to all fours and began to wipe his hands on the grass. He started to move forward with each wipe and before he knew it, he had moved some fifty feet away from the tree.

He continued to wipe his hands but stopped when he heard a loud shout. It was coming from a pass that was covered with trees. The shouts continued and were short, as if commands were being given, and then there seemed to be sharp replies but words were obscured and nothing was definite about the sounds except the direction that they came from. Mikey moved in the direction of the sounds slowly at first, and then faster as they grew louder. He was moving up an incline and the trees were clearing with each step. As an afterthought he tugged on a shoulder strap of his backpack and immediately felt reassurance. His makeshift weapons clanged with the sound of that reassurance.

Before the trees parted, Mikey could see lights splashing over a vast grassy expanse that appeared to be sitting atop a smaller sandy tan diamond-shaped area. But both areas were flat and Mikey had seen areas like this on television when he had watched the World Series last year. It was a small baseball field, complete with two dugouts, but there were no players.

Mikey stopped at the edge of the clearing where he was still concealed by the shadows of the trees. He looked down to the more distant dugout where the grunts, groans, and shouts were coming from and saw the shapes of men caught in a struggle of some type deep within the dugout.

He looked to the left of the dugout and for the first time saw the flashing lights of the two police cruisers parked over home plate and still shedding off steam trails from a hard-fast drive. There were four officers surrounding one large man while three more were sitting with their hands behind them on the home dugout bench. They were looking down and slumped and were very quiet.

Off in the distance Mikey could see a familiar big white convertible covered in mud and sand and turned inward at an awkward angle; the doors were spread out and open like big white duck wings stretched out and pulling through the rippled waters of a pond, and the occupants spit out like so much after wash. When he got closer, he saw the haste and neglect of the occupants as they departed the vehicle, and the disrepair of the doors. His father would never allow this to happen to their car.

Near the convertible stood Hercules McElroy, surround by four officers, his shirt torn down the back and front but still hanging by the waist showing his glistening skin shining in the light and his magnificent stature unmoving, undaunted by the overwhelming odds, and his cold stare of escape still glaring brightly through the night air. The officers had as much conviction in their task, whatever that was, and their stares matched his with the intensity and determination of a bricklayer in stopping Hercules's movements as they circled and surrounded him in the four corners of a clock. Their faces were just as wrinkled as his in the menacing frowns that men make when they have a straightforward decision for the violence of survival, not thinking of the aftereffects but only the outcome. Winning in this struggle brings past experience, past history, past lives and responsibilities, past decisions all together in a split second that gives the surveyor of this wasteland a reason to submerge into this cold hard silence and not find a way out before the stay, the end of this split-second time, when this moment-by-moment time is over. That is the key to winning, to stay until it is over.

McElroy watched his combatants through squinting, angry eyes that were staring straight ahead, but he reacted like he could see more. They had narrowed until the blacks were the only glint showing after the glint of his strong white teeth and quickly flaring nostrils. His arms were spread out and marking the movements of two of his aggressors, but his two hands were relaxed, which seemed like a gesture of beckoning to the officers who were at arm's reach. His feet were spread in a wide stance but crossed over to move toward the combatants at the edge of each hand. When he got near either one, he would use his fingers to jab at the eye sockets of the officers. When he would return to his center he would rotate like the hands of a clock and face the officer that he had struck at while holding the other two at bay and at arm's length. His weakness was his back, but he seemed to be aware of it because he would always rotate from 90 degrees to 180 quickly as if someone were trying to sneak up from behind him.

Mikey had never seen anyone move with such grace and determination in his life. He tried to recall movies or cartoons or any of the older boys who would have possibly described Hercules's fighting style and realized that no one had ever mentioned or pretended to know anything quite like this. But the best thing was while it looked so different, so foreign, it was so logical and effective. He smiled for the first time that night as he realized the simplicity of the movements and how it kept the officers at bay. He would admit for the first time later to anyone who would listen that he had no special sympathy for Hercules McElroy in his struggle against the police officers; in fact, he recognized two officers from the school assembly and the two others were from the police car that was often parked in the customer lot of the E-Z shop, except McElroy was something new to this environment and Mikey was fascinated by the effectiveness of the movements. He began to stand involuntarily with his hands still on his knees, reacting to the awe of the moment. He probably would have moved closer into the lights of the baseball diamond but felt a hand grab his ankle and pull him back into the darkness.

Darius McFadden, the high school football star and now quiet Vietnam veteran, pulled Mikey down and back into the darkness of the woods. Mikey moved with a rush but let out a little yelp before he vanished and escaped the attention of the officer who was facing Hercules McElroy. One officer turned his head and shoulders back and took a glance in the direction of the sound. Before he could turn back completely, Hercules McElroy struck. He moved to the officer with an open hand and gave the officer a full hand shove directly from his chin to his nose that sent the officer backward in quick shuffling movements and sent him down. His feet caught one behind the other on the back of a heel and he tumbled down and away from the fray. McElroy gave him a final look and seemed to brace for the remaining officer's onslaught. Two rushed to him from the three o'clock and the six o'clock positions and McElroy centered and fought off both positions with a two-hand thrust that caught them both flush with a middle knuckle to the forehead. This sent the two down in slow slumping humps that folded like cardboard boxes.

Mikey struggled in the moment. He wanted to watch what was happening to Hercules McElroy, but he could not struggle against the stronger hands that pulled him away by the ankles. He struggled to understand why Darius would pull him away. Was this help or harm? Before he could free himself from any of the consternations, Darius placed one finger to his lips and shushed him. He then beckoned him away and back through the trees. Both standing upright, they began to run, with Darius leading and taking quiet looping strides through the woods and across the field and to the lights of the two schools. Mikey was behind, not able to keep the pace that Darius had. He noticed for the first time that although Darius ran with speed and purpose, he also stayed in the shadows alongside the trees and dark sides of the buildings. They ran in silence as two silhouettes bouncing away from the watchful eye of the moonlight. Mikey ran in the same footprints as much as possible and finally caught up with Darius at the corner of Tioga Drive, where in one direction was La Grange Drive and the other direction was the undeveloped fields that stretched to the Alta Mesa neighborhood and the new houses that were being built as an add-on project to the neighborhood. Darius stood in the shadows and shushed Mikey to silence.

Turning the corner and passing through the same crosswalk where earlier the patrol boys had helped the students cross the street was an old black-and-white police cruiser creeping through at a snail's pace. Mikey's heartbeat started a loud pounding that he was sure was overheard by everyone. They were standing at the edge of the elementary building on a corner and would have to move to the light in the back of the school that illuminated the two buildings.

As the cruiser moved closer Mikey found his movements harder to manage. His legs seemed stiff and could pop at any moment. His breaths became louder and he thought they were as loud as the wind. His eyes were large and he remembered the cartoon about scared black people whose eyes revealed their presence when the lights were out. He shut them and dropped down to his butt with his knees pulled close to his chest. He was out of sight and in the shadows, and he only listened and waited for the inevitable commands from the officers.

He heard the rustling of footsteps moving away from him. He looked in the direction of the sound and saw Darius in full flight and taking long strides across the front of the school and turning left to the field as he crossed Tioga. The police cruiser sprang into action as it did a three-point turn and gave chase to the vanishing figure of a trained soldier. Mikey was ignored, or saved, he didn't quite know which for sure. All he knew was that the coast was clear for his return to his home. He quickly stood and darted away as the police cruiser turned the corner of Tioga in pursuit of Darius as he darted away as a single silhouette of the night.

The Question Hours
April 27, 1968

The days seemed to move slowly now, and the answers to the questions were windswept further and further away like leaves caught in a tiny elusive dust storm. It was a cool quiet Saturday. Mikey was outside in the backyard sand pit with his G. I. Joes and some smaller army model soldiers playing combat or mystery or just plain hero. On the outside he was setting up mock combat on a chessboard plane, but inside his head he was thinking about the past events. He was no closer to solving the origins of the body. Who was it and where did it come from? Who was responsible for the deaths of the animals in the neighborhood? There were birds and cats that were also found dead, but had been overlooked. Finally, where was the Rabbit Man hiding?

This feeling of helplessness was not new for Mikey, but the futility of his efforts was something that he was not accustomed to. In fact, up until now he had always had success from his efforts, and this gave him the confidence in his independence, his uncanny ability to act on his own with little or no help, but this was changing now. The only thing that he could do, what he had been taught to do by his father and his surroundings, was to try harder in his efforts. That is what the civil rights struggle was all about, and in some way, he saw this as his part. Even though Dr. King had been assassinated there was still talk on the radio, on the television, at school, and at his church that the movement and the struggle would continue.

But there was one other question he had to answer. How was it so easy for him to run away from the park when the police were beating Hercules McElroy and his assistants? Darius never said anything that night. Darius never talked to anyone. Mikey could not tell his father because he was somewhat hesitant toward Dr. King and the fight for Civil Rights and would never understand why Mikey would even sneak out at night to find evidence for what was at best a rumor. Mikey had heard discussions between his father and mother about the movement and his father's reasons was always clear. A man who worked for the city could not be protesting and marching for a cause if he wanted to keep his job. A man with a family can't take the same risk as everybody else. And lastly, a man who wants things in life can't let everyone know what he's thinking. Talking to his father was not his first choice.

Mikey wanted to tell his teacher, but the times to talk to Mr. Campbell were when the student had the answers and not searching for the answers like he always made the students do. Mr. Campbell had a way of staying out of the students' life decisions, and there was no guarantee that it would not get back to the mothers. Mikey was trying to keep the girls out of it. This was the man that his mother saw as the teacher to all. After all he had taught both of his older sisters.

Mikey could rationalize the answer as if the hero understood the odds and regrouped for reinforcements, because this was something that John Wayne and all of the other heroes would always do. In fact, there were not many instances where heroes were there to face the opponent unarmed and against weapons. The Western heroes could always shoot their way out, and the best or fastest gun was on the side of right and usually won. In the military movies it was the American way of life, and that was always right in comparison to the other countries of the world. In the Biblical movies it was the Christian way of life that was right, and that just surviving against the Roman way of life was how you became a hero. You could run or you could die, but as long as you stayed Christian you were a hero. Whether it was a military or Western movie, the overwhelming odds in combat could not compare to two unarmed black men against five armed policemen. And what could

Mikey do? He did not know the situation. He did not know if Hercules was right or wrong. There were too many questions to be answered, but the main question was why everyone was in the park area where Mikey thought he would find some trace of the Rabbit Man. So luckily it was from some ingrained instinct for the young to match the movements of an elder person, and when Darius decided to leave Mikey decided it as well. But since Darius never talked, Mikey did not know if this was a religious way of winning or not. Mikey had no confirmation of his decision, and so it did not feel right inside. It was another unanswered question.

Darius was a Vietnam veteran who was home from the war for some unspecified reason. This was what the rumors had said. Mikey did not know that much about him, but from his demeanor and his overall appearance of kindness he could not see what the dread and fear that the rumors had started were all about. Mikey's knowledge of Vietnam was a lot that he had read from the *Weekly Reader* news pamphlet that was delivered to the sixth graders at the elementary school. Inside the ten pages were stories about world events and stories about the American way of life. The *Reader* also had crossword puzzles and vocabulary words. It was sometimes more current than the history that the sixth graders were confined to, and for that reason Mr. Campbell used the pamphlet as a current event item.

But even the *Reader* was tame in comparison to the television news broadcast about the war. It became a contest for the three major news channels to have at least some footage of the war every day, and Mikey enjoyed turning the knob from CBS to NBC to ABC right before or after the dinner hour. Of course, it was dependent on his mother's mood. At first everything was of interest to everyone and his mom even watched with a bit of mirth and interest in the live reports and the chopping sounds of helicopters landing or taking off. That was until the Vietnamese New Year and the Tet Offensive.

The story of the offensive started on January 30 with pictures of the war until his mother started monitoring the viewing of the news hour. Mikey listened to and watched the talking faces of Walter Cronkite,

Jon-Michael Hamilton

Chet Huntley, and David Brinkley expound with a narrative on the conflict supported by the graphic films of American soldiers being injured and moved away by helicopter. That was what caught Mikey's interest, the grainy images of deep green jungles and marshlands with soldiers who were on their own quest harsher than the terrain that Mikey was engaging on his quest. It got to a point that every time his mother heard the sound of chopper blades from the television she would drop whatever she was doing, come from whatever room she just happened to be in, and change the channel of the television to an independent network that had family viewing. But Darius had been in Vietnam and no doubt in some of the war, so he must know what he was doing when he fled when the police arrested Hercules.

Mikey began to move the G. I. Joes to the most tactical position in the sand pit from a position that he remembered from the movies like *The Sands of Iwo Jima* or *Pork Chop Hill*. This was when the heroes had to take the high ground to win. There was no question about their goal. Moving the G. I. Joes to victory was an easy task as well, but he needed to move them into his real-life scenarios and see if an answer became just as clear.

He needed to write down what he knew about the questions in order to organize the possible answers. He stopped moving and stood up over the sand pit with one of the figures in his hand. Looking down on his combat construction he began to visualize an altogether different pattern. He walked over to the top left corner of the sand pit and placed the figure in and drew an X in the spot in front of it. He went back to the combat position and picked up three more figures and then repeated the same steps in the other three corners of the square pit. After he finished, he stood away from the pit and folded his arms behind his back and took in the entire pattern.

The neighborhood backyards were all aligned with gray metal fences and clotheslines with shirts and pants and towels flapping softly in the breeze. This was a pattern and shape of a community with answers to whatever questions would come up. Everyone in the neighborhood strived to live the same way because this was the measurement for success. Every family had just about the same income and material possessions, and every family had about the same number of children. This was a subtle way of ensuring that everyone started on equal ground and emerged through a better way of life on their own merit. But the questions in the neighborhood upset that equilibrium.

Mikey went back to the sand pit and picked up a handful of the model soldiers. He went back to the top left corner and replaced the G. I. Joe with three model soldiers. This represented the dogs that were found in the field in proximity to his home. He went across the pit to the top right corner and placed a full figure G. I. Joe on the sand, face down. This represented the body that was found on the trail. He walked across the front of the pit and back to the model soldiers. He picked up a large handful and placed them in the front left corner with five facing three. This represented when and where Hercules McElroy was arrested.

He stood away and looked at the pit again. He tried to think of where the Rabbit Man could be hiding. Not where the body was found, because the police had looked closely in that area for anything of interest. Not in the park where Hercules was arrested, because the police were there as well. The only two places that were of interest were where the dogs had been found and the front right area of the neighborhood. In fact, the front right area was never explored. It started with the old witch's house and then went to a winding grazing land for horses, and then finally to an old brick house with a well and a barn. These were all good hiding places for a half-man half-rabbit killer. This was the place that he must start his new searches.

Yet how would this help in the civil rights struggle? What could this add? What would be the outcome for his search, his discovery? He could see himself decisively locating the lair of the half-man half-rabbit and leading the police to the spot with a bright smile. He could see himself pointing it out and watching as the police captured the animal and took it away. He could see the celebrations in the neighborhood as a huge mystery would be uncovered and lifted from the shoulders of the men and the rumors that had haunted the many children finally could be put to rest. There were times when children could not even go to sleep at night or play in certain areas of the neighborhood, and if they were out late, they would race against the sunset to their homes for their own safety and the sanity of their parents. That would stop. Children could walk home and parents could relax and give them more freedom. Children could see the night lights and the fireflies, and play red-light-green-light-go under the moonlight.

Still, how would his capture of the Rabbit Man help in the civil rights struggle? Mikey first thought, what was the movement about? He had heard from his teachers and the radio and had read in the newspapers that the movement was about equality for black people in the South and all over America. He had heard of some places that did not allow black people to enter because of the color of their skin. He had read about the Jim Crow Rule in Alabama and Mississippi and the other Southern states where the Civil War was fought, and had wondered how that worked in Texas.

It was true that he had never been out of the neighborhood unless he went to his grandmother's home in Rockwall, so he did not know anything about not being able to go to places because of skin color. Even in Rockwall it was only his cousins and other black people, and he did not see that many white people. If he had to, he would confess that his real exposure to the civil rights movement was from television coverage. As early as 1966, Mikey could remember watching coverage of the protests and the speeches and the arguments for and against the movement. He could remember the pictures of Dr. King and his impassive and determined look as he walked through the storm of protest. He could remember the protesters being accosted and washed away by fireman water hoses, bitten and snapped at by police dogs, and pushed and shoved to the ground by angry police officers. These pictures were the most violent images on the television. The images were more violent than a John Wayne movie. The images were more violent than a Cowboy football game. The images were more violent than the old boxing footage of a Cassius Clay match. He was still called Clay in Mikey's home because his father Teddy did not approve of the name change of the boxer. Teddy thought that the Muslims in Chicago were troublemakers, just like Dr. King was down in Memphis and just like the new Black Panther Party out there in Oakland, California. Mikey's father Big Teddy Malone thought of himself as a conservative Texan who had faith in the status quo. Mikey just quietly disagreed with him.

If someone from the community, the black community, helped capture the Rabbit Man then Mikey felt that a certain amount of pride would be given to the community. He could see the civil rights survivors, Dr. King's followers, coming to the neighborhood and marching in celebration, and the community would have proven that they were equals by putting an end to a scourge of the community. It would be a big plus for everyone and it would be something that Mikey knew he had to accomplish if he wanted answers to all the questions that had been plaguing him lately.

He stood over his sand pit construction and pointed to each location, quietly mouthing the labeling for each position.

"You should finish your homework before Mom comes home," said Theodora.

Mikey's oldest sister walked up behind him just as quietly as his own thoughts. He startled more from embarrassment than fear and thought to shield her from the sand pit to hide his secret plans.

"Oh, you're still out here playing G. I. Joe. You know you should do your homework before you come out and play these war games. And why are you out here by yourself?"

"It's not just games, Te'ah. You just don't understand what I'm doing. I'm just…" Mikey started defensively. He wanted to explain more, but stopped. He knew Theodora had a way of finding out everything that he was doing and he was not ready to share it with her or anybody. Someone like his parents could easily put a stop to his entire plan, and no one would win when that happened. He could not picture anyone else taking the risk to solve the mystery.

"You're just what? What, Mikey? If you don't know, you should come inside and do what you're supposed to be doing and no arguments."

"Yeah, you're right."

JON-MICHAEL HAMILTON

Mikey turned and walked past Theodora in quick light steps that left light imprints against patchy blades of grass. Theodora watched Mikey, and then turned back and looked down at the mismatched design of the toy soldiers in the sand. She gave a breathy sigh and wondered why little scooter head boys played in some of the strangest ways. When she played Barbie dolls that long time ago, she would have never dreamed of playing with them in all of this sand and all alone. She gave another sigh, turned, and walked to the house.

Mikey returned through the back door of the house, right past Theodora, with a writing tablet and pencil in his hand. He walked back to the sand pit and began to transfer the design from the pit to the tablet. He worked quickly, writing down the information and scribbling notes by each design. He had his own symbols and he used them just in case someone, like his mother or one of his nosy little sisters, found another way into his room. He finished his writing and began returning the toys back inside his carry-out box with a faster pace than before. He wanted to finish up and head back into his bedroom. He also wanted to be inside when his mother came home to keep everything as normal as possible and all suspicion away from his next excursion.

XXIX

The Witch Hunt
April 28, 1968

Church was over. The Sunday worship was over. Mama Maxie had finally stopped playing the piano, singing with her girls, and let the spirit rest into a quiet Sunday night. Everyone was finally asleep. Mikey went out again, through the back door of the house and into a full moonlit night. The air was moist and cool and filled with the night sounds of chirping crickets, buzzing night beetle bugs flying and bumping into street lights, and in the trees the shrill sporadic sounds of cicadas beckoning out and beyond for mates. Outside on the side of the back porch he picked up his concealed bow, arrows, makeshift quill, and one of his father's emergency flashlights smuggled from a kitchen cabinet drawer. This time he wanted to stay away from the streetlights in the front of the house so it became easy for him to decide on the use of the alleyway as his exit. He knew there were problems with this choice, but he wanted to take the chance. Plus, it would show if his practice had paid off on how quiet he could be in walking and exploring.

It was a real test. It was after one in the morning and everyone should have been settled in for the night. The alleyway was a long concrete paved road that separated the bellies of all the backyards from the adjoining La Grange Drive and Silverhill Drive, and for some reason each backyard had some of the same warning elements. A few had running porch lights, and another few had dogs lurking and bedding in for the night. Mikey knew that the key to his success was to make it down the alley to Bonnie View without waking a single dog.

He had on his dark blue Lee Jeans with a pair of soft black Converse sneakers tied tight and draped over from the cuff less straight legs, a black turtleneck *I Spy* sweater snuggled up on his neck, and long sleeves that covered past his wrist to the middle of his hands and held tightly by rubber bands that stretched across his knuckles and palms, and a black Rocky the Flying Squirrel cap covering his head and ears and snapped under his chin. He had his makeshift quill on at an angle over his left shoulder, across his shirt to his right-side waist and held in place by the makeshift bow and fishing lines. The arrows inside the quill were held in position by wrapped and slipknot-tied black telephone wire. He had three pairs of long white socks stuffed in at the bottom of the quill to keep the arrows in place and a sock in his back pocket holding his house key in place. He took the flashlight and placed it on the belt that cinched his jeans in place and on his right side like a handgun holster.

He moved slowly and quietly, trying to stay within the shadows, and crouched over while moving to the back gate. This took him all of five minutes, as he made sure every step was as quiet as possible and every movement was pronounced and not wasted. He was holding the quill steady with his off-hand, an arm behind his back, and his left hand pointed forward for balance and the stillness of the movement. It was like the game Red Light, Green Light, as Mikey's movements were steady, but he was still aware of other movements around him. It was still a quiet and sleepy night and any out-of-place sound would carry.

He finally made it to the back gate and was crouched over where his head was at the same height as the gate. This helped to mask his movement and his position. He stayed there at the gate for a good two minutes and continued to listen to all of the sounds of the night. He heard a slow sleepy car creep down Bonnie View with a purring engine and soft creaking spring shocks that tried to hold the body steady. He heard the buzz of a television still on from a station signed off for the night. He knew that the test pattern would be on until the person who fell asleep in front of it woke up and turned the television off. He heard a soft breeze whistle quietly past the tin trash cans that a few homes had out and lined up outside at the back fences waiting for the trash pickup in the morning. Some people would have to wake up early and put their cans out by the fences before they started their day if they wanted their trash picked up. He heard the purr of a few stray cats with all four paws on the can tops, pacing and trying to pry the cans open while scavenging for food. He could smell the trash from the cans and a moist heavy air starting to settle down with dew for the morning.

He placed his hand on the gate handle and slowly lifted it up, trying to avoid the squeak of metal moving up against metal. He watched the cats to judge the sound of his movements. One cat looked up into the air and Mikey froze quietly in his tracks, waiting until the cat again found interest in the trash cans. His movement was smooth, and after the handle slid up he paused and then knelt down to the bottom of the gate and lifted it up by the bottom rail slowly, slowly, and soundlessly until a small oblique about a foot and a half wide was exposed so he could easily glide through. He stayed crouched over and closed the gate the same way he had opened it, only a little bit faster.

Now walking on the concrete quietly was his next concern. He turned and walked briskly first and made good time with his pace, but after a quarter of the way through the alley he almost lost his balance, scraped his sneakers against the concrete, which sounded a little like scraping sandpaper loudly, and then the quill and arrows rustled just enough to attract the attention of one of the sleeping dogs. It was a crossbred terrier mutt that was tan with white paws and collar and could yap and bark with a sneezing yelp.

He began to walk faster, and to trot. But he woke the dog that was two backyards ahead and on the other side of alley. The brown floppy-eared hound retriever barked with a *woof, woof* and ran sluggishly to the edge of the fence. Mikey would have to get past him. Perhaps there was one more dog that would be aware of the racket that he was making.

Mikey started running loudly first, and then when he got into his stride, he began to soften his steps up on his toes. He made it past the hound before the dog could get one bark out, and this caught the last dog off-guard, who could only growl through the wire rectangles of the fence. He made it past the backyard dogs and immediately began to slow and stop and darted to a trash can shadow that sat by a fence. His breaths were heavy at first, but quickly slowed as he remembered to breathe through his nose. He didn't want to take a chance of running out of the alley with a car passing by. It would attract the attention that he did not want. Before he reached the sidewalk, he would have to appear to be composed in case he was detected by anyone. His breathing was slowing down very quickly, and he was composed very quickly.

He crouched down again and then went to one knee and listened in the night for any movement or sounds that could be coming from the street. Bonnie View was the main street that led into and out of the neighborhood, and was the only road that a police cruiser would routinely use in going to the park or to the school. There was a strong possibility of their presence and concern in the neighborhood; this he understood from the arrest of Hercules McElroy. He only wanted to get across the street without alerting anyone. He waited in the shadows for any sign of movement, and then slowly stepped forward to the edge of the illumination from a streetlight that identified the Silverhill street sign. He waited again and heard a door open from behind him in one of the backyards. He didn't look around, but he knew that the dogs were not the only ones awake now. He could hear the buzz of a back-porch light turned on, and someone standing on the porch ready to admonish whichever dog had awakened its master. He did not move. He lay close to a fence and was concealed from the dogs and that meant no one else would look in his direction, but he was ready to dart out and down the sidewalk if he had to. He would walk down the sidewalk until he knew that it was safe to run across the street.

He waited in the shadows quietly, and he finally heard a loud yawn and the shuffle of bedroom slippers turn and then a door close. He could feel the quiet blanket of the night come down again and a stillness that was only upset by an occasional breeze that brought the trash can smells to him and past him to the direction he needed to go. He took a step forward, and another and another until he could lean his head forward and look both ways down the sidewalk and still have his body concealed. It was the dead of night and nothing was moving. He had heard television thrillers use that same description, and he smiled a little bit for the familiarity of the description to his surroundings. Somehow this gave him confidence with his actions, so he became daring and gathered himself and ran across the street with a bolt of energy. It was still quiet, and the only thing that he could hear was the *rub rub* of his footsteps on the street as he crossed it, and then the rustling of sandstone gravel on the other side as he stepped on it, still moving to the trees and grass that caught up quickly as he moved to the woods.

Inside these woods was different. He had never been in this part of the woods and up until now had no reason to be here. If he had never looked at the model from the sand pit, he would have continued to overlook this area of the neighborhood, primarily because it did not have a sidewalk. It was the one thing that separated the old neighborhood from the new. On one side of Bonnie View Road was a sidewalk that ran from Simpson Stuart Road all the way to the park, and on the other side it was foot trails and gravel shavings that lined the road. Away from the road was the Methodist Church, a tar street that led to two old wooden houses, and then further down there was one big white wood house that was designed like the Addams Family house. This was his destination on this night. The Addams Family house was where the neighborhood witches lived, and he wanted to take a look over there for any places that the Rabbit Man could be hiding. If anyone was helping the man-animal, it had to be the old woman and her odd daughter. No one ever went up to visit them, and there was always some type of strange-colored smoke escaping the fireplace.

He walked further away from the road and the lights and began to pick up dense undergrowth and tall overhanging trees. He moved slowly and tried to move quietly, but the terrain was new to him so he began to trudge through weeds and long grass. He went in the general direction of the witches' house and hunched over and listened to whatever sounds he could pick up. There was an old hoot owl sitting up high on one of the tree branches, hooting down like a lookout for the residents of the woods. In the tall grass to his left, something slithered away from him and then slithered back and stopped. There was buzzing over by a large pile of trash and then twice a large mosquito flew by his face and was shooed away by his hand both times.

He continued to move in the direction of the white facade in the distance, becoming closer with each step that he took. Finally, he saw the edge of the section and a clearing and the house, moonlit and nestled quietly up ahead. He stopped at the edge and looked before moving. There was an old water well that looked in good use, with a pretty sturdy rope rolled up on the painted white crank and a clean bucket attached and sitting on the brick walls that circled it. Over and near the back of the yard was an old sawhorse resting and a few planks sitting on it, and a few more in the grass. Over to the right of that was a big tree stump cut smoothly and used as a wood chopping block. On the side of the block were a big sturdy ax and a number of chopped wood pieces and a few other whole logs that needed splitting and chopping. Away from the wood block was a wire chicken coop with sleeping chickens and a rooster sitting atop and alone at one of the egg-laying berths.

Along the edges of the house and below two windows with shutters closed was a lawn sprinkler attached to water hose that was rolled up with care and a garden rake leaning against the side of the house. Connected to the back of the house was a wooden patio with an elevated wooden floor and two beams running from the top, supporting a wooden overhanging awning. They went down to the ground and were held in place with cement. There was a three-foot elevation that would allow a young boy, a dog, a wolf, or any assortment of crawling creatures the freedom to live and roam or hide underneath the patio.

He crouched lower and tried to look through the overhanging patio deck to the other side. He expected to see light on the other side, and this would tell him if there was anything underneath. Indeed, something was blocking the light to the other side. He ran up to the side of the house and lay down flat under the window. He took out his flashlight and put it in one hand and began to slowly crawl forward to the point where the patio deck began and the house ended. There was light in the yard but he was close to the side and in shadows. It was important that he did not make any noise. Chickens could create the loudest racket with clucking and pecking, and if the roster crowed then Mikey would have to run back into the woods very quickly.

He came to the edge of the house and turned his head to look underneath the deck, but still could only see the darkness. He pulled the flashlight up to eye level and shone it underneath the house. He could make out a pile of old clothes or canvas or a blanket stuffed underneath the deck and not moving. He could see past the pile to the other side now, and saw another structure that could lead to an attic or storage room. For a moment he wondered if he should crawl underneath when he saw the mound underneath the deck move away from the light and begin to scurry out from underneath.

Mikey turned off the flashlight and watched as a figure crawled out, followed by another. He watched as the figures bolted upright and ran away from the light, straight back past the chicken coop and into the woods. The chickens began to flutter and cluck, which was not an uncommon occurrence for them so they quickly settled down. The house remained quiet and nothing stirred. He retraced his steps back into the woods and listened for the direction of the two figures.

He waited until he was sure and began moving in the direction slowly and still in the woods, as quietly as possible. There were more tall trees with high cover but they were sparse and spaced out and this made his movements easier. He could still hear the footsteps of the running figures slowing down and becoming softer, and he continued to move in that direction. He could see patches of the sky now, clear and starlit. The moon was moving away and the night was cooling off but he still felt a little warm. The turtleneck shirt and jeans were good but the Rocky Squirrel cap was becoming warm around his ears.

Mikey had been at this trek for more than an hour and he could feel some relief that his efforts were paying off. Following these figures was a new thing, but they could lead to the Rabbit Man. He guessed that the figures were men by the way they moved, and no lady would be under a porch at night unless it was something that the older boys were whispering about. It still seemed kind of late for something like that, unless they didn't have a home to go back to. This was another reason to follow the figures and answer some of the questions. He lifted the earflaps from the cap and fastened the strap around his head and continued walking.

Mikey came up to another clearing, and he smelled smoke first and then heard voices. He stopped and hid beside a large tree and listened. The voices were men, laughing, lighthearted and joking, and seemed to be greeting someone, or admonishing them for coming in late, or stepping over them to get to the fire.

"Did you get any chickens?"

"Hell naw, someone came and shone a light under the porch where we were hiding."

"You think they will call the police?"

"Hell, I don't know. I just don't know. We did git some corn and two apples."

Mikey stayed by the tree and waited until everything seemed to settle down. The talking continued for another five minutes and then stopped. He waited another five minutes by the tree and then moved away from it very slowly. He saw another tree before him and he moved to it, a little closer to the voices, and he saw the smoke from the campfire for the first time and knew that the men were hobos traveling from the train tracks that were on the other side of Highland Hills and past Bishop College. He had heard about these types of men from his father. Dressed in hand-me-downs or old discarded or any kind of clothing they could find or steal, they lived from moment to moment and scavenged off the land with who knew what dreams they were searching for or running from. Big Teddy always said that these were the men who were afraid of settling down and were therefore cowards. Big Teddy always said the measure of a man is from the roots he puts down. Mikey watched them, not to defy Big Teddy, but to put the picture with the words. He knew that if he saw them, he would agree or disagree but never openly defy Big Teddy.

There was another tree further down and a little off the line of moving closer, but it was a way to face into the direction of the camp and not look over their shoulders. He moved out and away from his tree and the camp and circled the last tree slowly. When he came up beside it, he looked around the tree and into the camp quickly and saw one of the men sitting up and looking at him.

This man was dressed differently. He had on a blue cardigan sweater that look new and was underneath his old raincoat and hat. Mikey was crouched down, but still had to look like a little kid, so he took off running away from the camp. He ran zig and zag through the woods and stopped after passing a number of trees to hear sounds and if anyone had followed him. The night grew quiet again. He began to walk back on his way to Bonnie View and felt that his quest tonight had brought him one step closer to answering the questions of the Rabbit Man and where he might be hiding. He would get back to his notes and write down what happened, where it had happened, and who was involved. He had found out some things about the witches and how they lived. They were just like normal happy people who were living life the old Texas way. But they had a problem under their porch. People were hiding under there. He thought that he would write a note telling them and leave it in their mailbox as soon as possible.

He came out of the woods about the same place that he went in and saw the alley looming across the road. He went up to the edge of the road and looked both ways. The roadway was clear, so he bolted across it and stopped at the entrance to the alley. Coming down the alley was a police cruiser with lights out and causing a stir with the dogs. Mikey turned and ran toward Silverhill Drive and turned left into the street and started running down the sidewalk. He listened while he ran and heard the police car engine rev up and the car drive fast through the alley. He knew he could not make it all the way to the end of the street and the start of his street, so he began looking for a place to hide. He could not go down the alley because the dogs would surely bark. He had to find a hiding place quickly before the car turned the corner and began searching the street. He ran quickly to the side of the Smith

JON-MICHAEL HAMILTON

family house and lay down flat in the shadows and the grass. He heard the police car turn the corner and rev the engine as it came down the street. The car slowed down as the search began and they had a spotlight on the driver's side of the car. He saw the light shine on the sides of the Smith's and Washington's houses, and somehow just missed him lying in the grass.

He heard the car move away and brake loudly a few yards down the street. He heard the car doors open and footsteps of officers striking the street and then the sidewalks. He heard them talking to someone. He got up and went out to the street and saw the patrol car parked across from the McFadden home. He saw the officers trying to talk to Darius as he walked to his front door and opened it and went through it. The officers went back to the car, got in, U-turned, and then drove the car away with tires burning rubber in the street. The car passed him without even a look in his direction. The police drove away and turned left and screeched away from the neighborhood. He didn't know what to make of this, but that would be one of the last things he would be thinking about on his way to his home and to his bed. He had enough information for the night.

Yolanda
April 29, 1968

For the first time Mikey had overslept and missed his mother's wake-up call for school. He had a breakfast to go, which was something that his mother frowned upon but Te'ah made it possible to escape her inspection. She told her mother that Mikey was slow because the girls were taking longer in the bathroom this morning. It was something about her hair that Te'ah had to get just right so she covered by saying that she was really the hold-up in the shared restroom mirror. It was the only room in the house where the light was just right for combing and bending, and all the girls followed Te'ah's lead.

His mom placed the egg portions, bacon, and toast on plates on the dining room table and then went back to her own bedroom to prepare for her morning destination. Te'ah pulled Mikey's plate next to her own and Palmer's and made a sandwich with the toast, placed it in wrapping paper, and then brought it to Mikey's room with his lunch pail. If the food was missing then his mom would conclude that he had come down, ate, and left. He was still sleeping heavily and resisted Te'ah's first and second shoulder shakes, and finally shook awake with a startled look on his face. He needed a shower and toothbrush so he raced to the bathroom and started a rushed shower and brush. He made it out the door with clean jeans and shirt, the same Rocky Squirrel hat and pair of Converse sneakers, and the lunch pail with an apple, baloney sandwich, and an extra egg sandwich smashed inside.

331

JON-MICHAEL HAMILTON

The morning subjects were a daze of words and calculations with the same rhythm as before, but he was not the leader in answering the questions in Texas history, mathematics, or in his favorite subject, science. He did not avoid any questions when they were presented to him, and answered them just the same way as before but he did not volunteer any answers without prodding. Yolanda had probably the best day of her life. She was the star today and led the class through the morning subjects and Mr. Campbell had to acknowledge that something was wrong with Mikey's participation from his lack of competition with her or this part of history, math and science subjects were something that sparked her interest. Usually they would both have the right answers to the questions for all the subjects; only Mikey's responses were first because he came up with the answers faster. But Yolanda was relentless. She could take the baton and run past everyone in the class. She was already the leader of the girls at the school and a few of the boys were timid enough to follow her or sing her praise and she continued to gain prestige at the school and in the neighborhood. Unfortunately, she was not a patrol boy and Yolanda felt that the most prestigious responsibility at the school was to be a patrol boy. Two weeks ago, her mother had talked to Mr. Campbell about her being a patrol girl and it probably would have happened in spite of the objections of the female teachers. The girls and boys were separated in the recess activities in the fifth grade and the mothers and female teachers agreed that this was in preparation for the girl's upcoming adult life. In the sixth grade the girls would not play want to play football, baseball, or basketball and this was about the time when kickball and dodge ball became sissy sports so the girls were left to their own devices of jump rope and jacks and Dream Date. But Yolanda was relentless. If not for the Patrol Boys being replaced by adults, she would have most certainly changed the opinion of the teachers and the boys. Someone had complained that children standing in front of moving cars with only a hand out and a stop sign to signal stop and a patrol belt to identify the authority was not the safest thing that a student should be doing with their time.

IN SEARCH OF THE RABBIT MAN

The lunchroom was the same bustle of grades sitting with their teachers and enjoying the activity as a class. The time was broken down into two lunch periods with the first through third grades enjoying the first twenty minutes and the last forty minutes for recess while the fourth through sixth grades enjoyed their fourth period of classroom instruction and went to lunch after the younger grades had completed their activity. The routine was reversed when the younger grades went back to their classrooms for their fourth period of instruction and after that hour the entire school was back on the same bell schedule. Lunch was a very controlled activity with the teachers continuing to monitor and govern the student behavior at all times. The little elementary school with the all black student body had a lot to uphold and a lot to prove and the teachers never let the students forget it. It was a relatively new school just like the community and with the changing times it seemed that all the eyes of the city were on it.

Mikey hardly touched any of his food. He nibbled on the egg sandwich, rewrapped it and put it back into the opened pail before taking out the apple and taking a few bits from it. The other Patrol Boys, all gathered together at the table, passed looks of agreement when they noticed how Mikey was withdrawn throughout the morning and felt that he shared their own apprehension about the outcome of the accident and who would be punished if any were passed. He wanted to sleep and had already decided to stay in the classroom during recess and lay his head on his desk. He had to tell Mr. Campbell a lie but he felt that it was worth it. He still did not want his parent to learn about his searches in the neighborhood because he would have to face condemnation from the Bible as spoken by his mom. The Bible would be her tools of admonishment and of course the verses and lyrics from the piano and songbooks. It was best that he told Mr. Campbell that he had a slight head or stomachache and would feel better if he just put his head on his desk.

His plan worked rather easily. After walking back from lunch in the single file the students were dismissed for recess. Mr. Campbell took out the football, board games, jump ropes and his whistle and watched

333

as everyone briskly walked out and onto the playground. Mikey stayed behind and took out his planning tablet to look over his notes and add the new information from last night. The witch's house and the hobo camp were the new topics of interest but he would think about that later. After completing the note writing he folded up the tablet and used it as a hard pillow

He dosed off quickly and began to fall into a world of brightly multicolored plants and a large lake with trickling brooks searching away from the lake and fresh water running from it to all the surrounding plants and trees. He was there alone and, in the distance, away from the lake he could see a sparkling rainbow glistening like so much floating happiness and a constant sunset that rained an amber glimmer within all of the clear light. He was so comfortable with his surroundings and in the dream, he began to walk toward a large bulb of light that was to the right of sunset and became larger than a bulb and more like a small fountain of light and seemed to make the other lights less interesting. It was the light of knowledge and he somehow felt that this light would answer all of the questions that he had uncovered since the dawn of his curiosity and his most recent unanswered questions. He began to walk toward it and at first it was easy to move toward it and the surroundings moved with his progress but then he got to a point where the light seemed to be moving away and the surroundings began to move in the other direction. He looked behind him and saw nothing first but heard the piano and the Bible lyrics playing loudly and his mother calling him. But she wasn't calling him because she was singing a song and her voice on a separate interval was calling out to Adam and to remember the destruction that was brought to the world for his folly. Mikey could feel himself slowing down and almost stopping but heard a piercing voice that was in front of him and somehow coming from the light say to him to keep moving, keep moving, keep movement moving, keep the movement moving. He began to walk again and saw the surroundings move to his sides and behind him. He could see the light becoming the only light and dimming out the other lights but giving light to the plants and trees and brooks and the still blue lake like so much food passing to each living thing and making it bigger and brighter and stronger. He felt in his head the answers were right there at his grasp when he would reach the light so he continued to walk forward and there were sounds and so much music that was different but was music and he could see the notes of every kind of music and it became the same kind of music and it became all emotion and all emotion became the same. He began to see a lot of different books about a lot of different things, and a brand new set of the Encyclopedia Britannica filled with pictures and facts and places and things about this planet, and he also saw the insects that he had investigated that were flying or crawling around happily about. He could see the birds that he had tried to recreate by drawing in colored pencils from memory and categorized and he heard in the distance the cartoon hopping sounds of a large rabbit somewhere out of the light but coming toward the light as well.

Also walking toward the light was a girl and in his mind, he heard the name Bone Girl echo from his fellow Patrol Boys' voices and knew that Yolanda was moving toward the answers as well. He felt in his mind how normal her routine was and he accepted that she was on a quest but a different quest all together and he welcomed it. As soon as he saw her, he heard the whispers of the Wisdom Wiser's', and their monotone proclamations of what happened to people in their purview and what was learned from what they did and what was done to them for what they did. For the first time she was smiling at him and not being competitive and he saw that her arms were outstretched and her palms were flat and she was asking for something. He noticed for the first time that he had the tablet of research of his quest in his right hand and a pencil in his left and he felt how normal it was to walk toward her as she was now in the light. He felt how normal it was to give her the tablet and he heard her say that it was all right now, you can wake up now, and it is all right now and you can wake up now.

"You can wake up now, Mikey, she said. Mikey you better wake up the recess is over."

Mikey looked up and saw Yolanda standing at his desk. He noticed for the first time that she had on a new pair of glasses. These were of the new style and a soft brown color that looked darker against her skin. She looked different, more modern and good. She started to move away from him and back to her desk. He saw that she had his tablet in her hand and saw her hold the tablet under her arm to hide it from the other students and Mikey as well. She went to her seat and sat and placed the tablet on her lap and began to take out her own English book and began to glance at the reading assignment. Mikey stood as a reflex and began to walk to Yolanda's desk. At that moment Mr. Campbell came into the classroom.

"Okay, Michael Malone is up. Must be feeling a little better?"

"Yeah, a little bit," said Mikey.

"Your team could have used you today. Did you guys win the football game today," asked Mr. Campbell. He looked to Michael Daniels and Michael Washington.

"Naw, they just barely beat us today," said Washington.

"I guess you guys could have used your star quarterback."

"Okay, let's settle down. It's good to see everybody back and in his or her seats getting ready for the reading. *The 500 Hats of Bartholomew Cubbins* is going to be a good story today and we will pay attention to rhyme."

Mr. Campbell looked straight to Mikey and then moved to the wall cabinet to put the recess items back and lock it. Mikey froze in the moment. He had the choice of going to Yolanda's desk and asking for the tablet but he didn't know how she would react. She could make a commotion at any time and everyone in the classroom would become more interested in what was in the tablet then what was on the walls of the classroom. All the multiplication tables and numbers that were on the wall just to the left of the entrance and the alphabets that lined the walls above the windows that were just opposite of the entrance would be ignored.

Mikey decided to move back to his desk just as Mr. Campbell moved back to his desk and they both sat at about the same time.

Yolanda could strike a pose and an attitude that everyone would recognized from what they had seen depicted on television and how similar her actions were and how familiar she could be to the strong confident black woman who always knew how to handle the situations that they were faced with on television. But her best scene or attitude was when she began to become one of the Wisdom Wiser women. This was the attitude that was beyond mother with her primary concern as the family and moved more toward the big picture attitude of a politician or someone that people listen to. But many people could separate that attitude from Yolanda's original attitude as only a matter of magnification. She was still young and not naturally loud and taught to have manners so when she became loud everyone thought of her attitude for the Wisdom Wiser's. Yolanda could see the big picture very clearly at all times and whether her advice was correct in what a person does in the big picture was a matter of opinion.

The lesson continued throughout to the end of the day and Mikey felt an apprehension for his confrontation with Yolanda. First, he would have to separate from his friends, the last patrol boys. It had been awkward after the patrol boy duties were relieved and the boys walking straight home now because the excuse to stay a few minutes after school was not an easy remedy anymore. It was like an early good-bye every day for the group and the diminishing of the group closeness because everyone in the neighborhood went directly home after school and began watching television or doing homework. He wasn't ready to show the patrol boys his notes because in the past it just never seemed right to show them and now it didn't seem to be the most important thing for them as it was for him. The best answers for that dilemma was to not walk with them on the way out the door and try to walk with Yolanda to her mother's car.

There were only a few exits so when the final bell rang the entire elementary school students rose from their desks and began walking through the doorways, the hallways, and the sidewalks. Mikey stood up and walked straight to Yolanda. She had a few books in her arms for homework and atop the books was Mikey's tablet. He was surprised to see that she waited for him and they began to walk out of the doorways together. When they got to the sidewalk Yolanda stepped off and onto the grass. Mikey followed her.

JON-MICHAEL HAMILTON

"I read your tablet, Mikey. Is all of that true?" she asked.

"Naw, it's just something that I made up. I'm writing a book like the encyclopedia. Just about our neighborhood."

"An encyclopedia about Bishop Heights and Highland Hills and the Rabbit Man. I think this tablet is true."

"Well, stop talking so loud and attracting everyone's attention." He looked to her with pleading eyes. She looked at him as if she saw him for the first time and her whole face softened and her eyes glistened.

"I think these are some of the craziest little notes that I have ever read. It seems like something you would find in the encyclopedia or even a newspaper. I think it is very good, Mikey. I think it is good."

She gave the tablet to Mikey and began walking down the sidewalk again. Mikey fell in step beside her.

"I didn't show this to anyone. I didn't think anyone would understand it."

"Yeah, I understand it. I just don't know why you are the person doing it. They should hire a private detective or someone to do what you are doing. Just like they do on television when there is something to be found."

They were coming up on Yolanda's mom's car, which was parked on the road with the motor running. Mikey grabbed her arm lightly.

"Don't tell anyone about the tablet. I want to keep it a secret until I know what to do."

"There's my mom; I have to go now. And I won't say anything, but everybody should read this tablet. Maybe some of the questions would be answered. You know, more people should think like you, Mikey. Everyone would feel safer."

Yeah, Mikey thought. He watched her walk to the passenger side of the brown Buick and get in. The car putted into the line of cars that were moving away from the school. He had never thought to hear something like that from Yolanda and it's true he expected the worse. He felt relief on so many levels and it felt good for one reason and it felt good for another.

338

XXXI

A Convenient Scapegoat
April 29, 1968

The evening was shaping up with a cool embrace, glistening amber cast a bronze glow and the beginning of long shadows drooped off and into the east. A wisp of clouds in the west trying to obscure a blinking sunset gave the sky the final burning image of a fallen day. Everybody was out doing their usual touch football pastime and all the past disappointments and memories were put on hold for the sake of the game. There wasn't much else to do on a Saturday evening but pass the ball and catch the ball, run and keep score on Silverhill Drive while the smaller kids and the girls stood on the sidewalks and in the grass and watched the boys run back and forth on the street. Even Darius McFadden had his usual meditative position in the middle of his front yard in the grass. These were the actual dreams of the future. Who would be Jim Brown and who would be Don Perkins and who would be Cornel Green? Mikey would run and catch with the best of them and for the moment, the body, the Rabbit Man, Hercules McElroy and all of the dead animals in the neighborhood could be put on hold.

There were squads of three against three and Ronald Turner, a high school freshman, was the quarterback for both and leading both groups down the street with an objective balance. He only threw you the pass if you had an advantage like you were wide open or if you were like Mikey and ran faster than the coverage. The ex-patrol boys, still a team, were on one side while the other neighborhood boys from a couple of streets over manned the other squad. The score was tied as fitting and both sides were winding down with the exhaustion of the contest. There was time for one last pass. The boys took their positions leaning and straining in expectation. Ronald called the professional like signals and awaited the snap of the football in the shotgun formation. Before he could get to his last numbers the neighborhood dogs started barking and a blaring siren stretched out and bled into the air. Both squads stopped and looked up in the direction of the sirens.

Turning the corner from Bonnie View to Silverhill was the first police car with a screech of rubber, a loud revving engine, lights flashing and the siren loud and invading the tranquility of the street. The boys moved to the sidewalk and watched as the car move past them and toward the McFadden home. Mikey followed the car with his eyes to the McFadden home and saw Darius react by standing up and running to the side of his home. Instead of running away Darius climbed up to the roof of his home and sat atop it in the same meditative Indian squat. A second car soon followed the first car with lights and siren flashing and screaming. A third car arrived from La Grange Drive an intersecting direction and they all stopped in front of the McFadden home. The dogs stopped barking and the only sounds heard were car doors opening and closing. Two officers from each car got out one with a megaphone in his hand and when the other five got out, four with riot shotguns at the ready and one who went to the trunk of the car and retrieved an M1 rifle with a scope. The officers had the grim features of impending action, the narrowing eyes of determination, the thin-pursed lips of a snarl, and the tight stiff movements of anger. Mikey recognized the features as well as the faces of some of the same policemen who had surrounded Hercules McElroy that late night at the park.

The boys were caught in the action of the movement and found themselves being drawn closer to the three police cars and the Vietnam vet who was now sitting atop his home in his meditative Indian squat with a black bandana tied across his forehead. Darius did not look at the policeman and by now the officer's, signature, reflecting shades were glinting occasionally within the dying sunlight. The neighborhood girls came out of their homes and began to huddle together and Yolanda, with her hair out in two big afro puffs on both sides of her head, no glasses, and with blue jeans and sneakers on for the first time, walked over to the bunch. She soon became the leader of the bunch. The sirens had also penetrated the peaceful home interiors and now parents were coming out of their homes on Silverhill and walking toward the police cars. It soon became a modest crowd of parents, teens, and children with only mummers and whispers asking the questions that no one could answer.

The sergeant with the megaphone looked up to the veteran of the last war sitting impassively on the roof of his home. He directed three officers to go around to the backyard and the two sides thereby surrounding the house. The officers took their positions with riot guns pointing up to the roof. The other two officers took positions in the front yard with the officers with the scope rifle now pointing at Darius. The sergeant walked to the front of the house and rang the doorbell and then knocked on the door with a firm authority. The door opened and Darius's mother answered in a plain brown dress and apron. She was a youngish Christian woman in her fifties and although proud sternness was in her shoulders fear became ever-present in her eyes. Not many people in the neighborhood had a true confidence in the police especially since their growing presence was more apparent when the body was found some three weeks ago. She opened the door and stood out on the porch with a large family Bible in her hands. Coming up from behind was her daughter, Francis McFadden. She was in the same class as Roland Turner and Mikey's sister, Te'ah.

"What is it officer? Why are you here at my home and in my yard?" She said this with fear growing in her voice.

"Mrs. McFadden is it? Is your husband here? We're here to arrest your son," he said. Although his words were apologetic his tone was not.

"No, my husband is no longer here, sir. You say you are here to arrest my son. What did he do? What could he have possibly done? He just got back from that place overseas a month ago. What could he have done? He hasn't been out of the neighborhood."

"He has been here long enough and we've had reports from your neighbors and some of the shop keepers about his behavior toward them. I'm just telling you we have to take him with us."

"What about his doctor?" asked Francis?

"What does a doctor have to do with this? Is there anyone else inside?" asked the sergeant. He was becoming impatient but it became clear that he was trying to show some restraint. The crowd was growing behind him and around the house and the voices begin to echo the words of Mrs. McFadden and her daughter.

"What doctor?"

"Yeah, I remember something about a doctor was helping him," said another.

"Why is he up there on the roof?"

"He must think he's back over in those jungles, man."

The sergeant turned to the crowd and gave them a stern look. He saw one officer taking aim through the scope with the rifle at the vet on the roof and the other backing him up with a riot shotgun looking at the crowd and then looking to the roof. The sergeant looked back to the two frightened women on the porch.

"Is there anyone else inside the home?" he asked again.

"No, sir. It's just us three. We are the only ones here," Mrs. McFadden said.

"You must leave the home immediately. If you need to call someone ask your neighbors if you could use their phone. I can't let you go back inside. It's not gonna be safe."

"What do you mean, not safe?"

"Who are you, young lady?"

"I'm her daughter, Francis. I live here too. Darius is my brother and I know he did not do anything wrong, officer. Why don't you just talk to him?" Francis was trying to be calm by the excitement in her voice became contagious to her mother and the crowd.

"We'll do that. Meanwhile, why don't you go over to someone's home and call the doctor," said the sergeant.

"The number is inside in our information book. Let me go back inside the house and get it," said Francis. She looked to the officer with pleading eyes. "I won't touch anything. I swear. I'll just go inside and get the book and come back to be with my mother."

The Sergeant stood impassive and stared to Francis and then stared through her as if she wasn't there. He turned and signaled for the officer with the riot gun to come forward.

"Go inside with her and make sure she gets the book and nothing else."

Francis went inside with the officer following her with his shotgun at the ready. Mrs. McFadden stayed on the porch with the sergeant and paced back and forth nervously. The crowd continued the murmurs and the officers stood ready for any surprises. Darius stayed on the roof under the now dying evening light. Francis returned with the book and stood alongside her mother. The officer led them away from the house. When they got to the yard Mrs. McFadden looked to the crowd and saw the looks of sympathy and a few with anger that were looking past her and to the roof. She followed their stares and saw her son on the roof for the first time. She shuddered and tried but couldn't suppress a cry.

"Oh, son. What are you doing up there? Please come down before you hurt yourself. Please come down." She turned to the sergeant and touched his shoulder and tried to touch his hands while pleading. "Please help him. He is not a bad boy. He's just changed so much since he got back from the war. He is not a bad boy. Please call his doctor. He is not a bad boy."

"Go over to the home of one of your neighbors and call the doctor. I'll try to talk him down. But if he has any weapons it going to be hard. So just go and call the doctor."

With that said the Sergeant led them away from the home. He went back and sat the megaphone on the hood of the car and retrieved a pair of binoculars from the seat.

"What can you see so far?" He asked the officer who was looking through the scope. He placed the binoculars to his eyes. He took a long look and could see the Vet sitting quietly on the roof with his hands

343

folded across his waist. He had not moved since he had sat on the roof and the policemen arrived.

"He's got something around his waist, a belt, military, with a hostler. Could be a gun or knife. I need a better position to see," said the officer still looking through the scope.

"Stay where you are, I'll go and talk to him." The sergeant let the binoculars hang from his neck by the straps, grabbed the megaphone and moved away from the car and to the yard. He pointed the megaphone at the roof and spoke into it.

"Darius McFadden, can you hear me? Can you hear me? You need to come down from the roof of that house. You need to come down and join your family."

Darius did not respond. He did not move. He sat on the roof and the light was dying quickly. The sergeant considered the use of the car spotlight and flashlights for his officers. He also considered the options for going up to the roof and taking the man in custody. He knew the longer this took the harder it would be to resolve it. The crowd was growing larger. His officers were becoming more and tenser and the evening was quickly turning to night. He went back to the car and told the trail officer to pass out flashlights to the three officers who were surrounding the house. He got on the car radio and informed the dispatch of his situation and requested a fire engine truck with ladders. He also requested for an ambulance just in case the situation went bad. With all things in order he went back to the yard to try again.

"Darius McFadden, can you hear me? Can you hear me? Son, you need to come down from the roof of that house. We know you did a good thing for your country. We also know you didn't do what people are saying you did. Come down and tell your side of the story. You need to come down and join your family."

The mother and sister came from one of the houses and moved into the crowd. Mrs. McFadden was crying but Francis was strong and held her mother tightly and upright. The crowd began to splinter into different opinions and the murmurs began to grow louder.

"He needs to come down from there. He is making our neighborhood look bad."

"He was always a troublemaker ever since they moved here from South Dallas."

"South Dallas people always do crazy things."

"It was the military that made him that way!"

"Yeah, it was the military!"

"The military made him crazy!"

"The police have no right to make him go up on his roof. If they leave him alone, he will be okay."

"He never bothered anyone that I know of."

"This is what happens when a black man comes back from the war. That's why I never would go even if they begged me."

"He should not be making his mother go through things like this."

"He never went to church since he's been back from that place."

"The Lord is punishing him for killing those people over there. The Lord don't like people killing people for whatever reason."

"They said he's the one's been killing all the dogs in the neighborhood."

"The Lord protects the meek and the weak on this earth."

"Amen!"

"Amen!"

"Amen!"

The dogs started barking again. Another siren could be heard from a distant point on Bonnie View and growing louder, coming closer. For the first time the crowd noticed that two police cars had set up a roadblock at the intersection of Bonnie View and Silverhill and no cars were allowed to come down the street. The roadblock parted and a long fire truck turned the corner and slowly rumbled down the street with its horn blaring and its siren screaming. The truck moved straight down the street and parked with a hiss of brakes in front of the McFadden home. Two firemen jumped from the truck and with ladder in hand waited on instructions. Another fireman emerged from the passenger seat and walked over to the sergeant.

JON-MICHAEL HAMILTON

"I don't see a fire. But I see why you might need a ladder," said the Fire Captain.

"Yeah. If you guys put it against the side of the roof we'll go up and get him."

"Is that the only way? It looks like you got too much of an audience for this."

"I don't know. Maybe they will learn something from this. Everybody's got to learn sometime. It's getting late and I've got to do something. It's going on two hours. Where is the ambulance?" asked the sergeant.

"Who knows? It was requested. I heard it over the radio. It may take a longer time to come here. We don't have too many in this area."

"We'll wait a little while for now. I don't know what will happened with him on that roof."

The sergeant walked away from the yard and moved to his car. While facing the crowd he began to look around for the family members. He saw the mother crying and the daughter holding her and standing away from the crowd. He saw the hatred in some of the faces and the fear in some of the other faces. He saw the boys staring in amazement and he saw the young girls becoming more and angrier. The night was in full bloom and the sky, clear, was filled with stars and an amber half-moon. The homes alive with lights now had every porch light lit up and a few of the closest homes had people in lawn chairs out in the yards. He decided now was the time to end this if he could. He turned and walked back to the Fire Chief.

"Have your guys take the ladder to the backyard. We are gonna end this now."

The sergeant walked around to the side of the house and then moved to the back corner and beckoned the officer in the backyard. The officer in the back came over.

"You two are gonna go up and get him and no guns. You hear me! Just the "night-sticks" if they should be necessary. You're covered from the street. Stay in sight. Just grab him and cuff him. We'll get him down with the ladder and take him to the substation."

346

The sergeant walked back to the yard, looked up to the roof and placed the megaphone to his lips.

"Darius McFadden, two officers are coming up to help you get down from there. We don't want any problems so you'd better not give them any problems. Just come down quietly."

The sergeant gave the okay sign to the officers who were ready to climb the ladder. He went back to his car and gave the ready sign for the officer who was peering through the scope of the M1. The trail officer stood by the driver's side of the Sergeant's car and had his hand on the vehicle spotlight. The Sergeant opened the passenger door of his vehicle and stood with one foot in the vehicle and the other on the ground with the door still open and separating him from the home.

One dog, a she started barking when she saw the firemen holding the ladder steady as the first officer climbed up to the roof of the house. This caused the other dogs in hearing range to bark as well. This is the way the officer's movements were documented in the community. Darius moved for the first time in hours. He turned his head sharply to the left and in the direction of the new scraping sounds on the roof. He moved his hands from his waist to behind his back with his palms lying flat on the roof.

"Knife on the waist belt, on the left," said the officer behind the scope. The sergeant cursed under his breath.

The officers came into view now, standing up as bookends to the veteran. You could see their lips moving but the sounds were obscured by the growing noise and excitement. Both officers pulled the nightsticks from their Sam Brown waist belts and held them at their sides. The officers were still giving instructions to the veteran because their lips were moving more pronounced now. Darius stood now with his hands at his side. The trail officer turned on the vehicle spotlight and pointed it to the roof. The splash of light bathes the veteran with a blinding white heat and he flinched for the first time. The movement startled the officers and both pulled the night-sticks up and above their heads preparing to strike. Darius turned toward the movement and away from the light and could see the officers about to strike. He instantly moved his left hand up and away as a guard against a blow and his right hand moved across his waist toward the knife that was now visible to the crowd from the spotlight. There was one shot. The first and only shot of the night and it silenced everyone. The dogs stopped barking. The two officers flinched and then crouched away from the sound. The Sergeant blinked and then looked to the back of his car. The trail officer flinched, blinked, and then pressed the palms of his hands over his ears. The crowd jumped and cursed. Mrs. McFadden screamed. Frances cried.

"No, no, no…My baby!!! My baby!"

"Why did you do that? Why did you do that?"

The veteran snapped with the impact of the bullet. It hit him below his left shoulder and center chest and tossed his body in a sickly, death dance around like a top and then down to the roof in a lifeless heap of twisted arms and legs. The body rested and slowly began to slide down the roof toward the front yard with the hands ironically reaching up to the peak of the roof.

"Grab him!! Grab him!! Take him to the ladder and to the backyard! Take him back there!!" shouted the sergeant.

The officers moved from the startled daze, quickly now, with the commands from the sergeant. Both grabbed the sliding outstretched hands and pulled them back to the peak and to the other side of the roof. A trail of blood became evident now streaking down the roof like a red paint stain and then finally the black chino shoes vanishing from the crowd. Like the last light at a movie theater, the trail officer shut off the spotlight and the crowd were left staring in disbelief at the roof and the starlit sky as if it had never happened.

"Go inside to your homes now. Go inside or I'm going to give you tickets for unlawful demonstrations. Go on home now. The show is over," said the sergeant.

And then it was all over, like so much routine. The officer with the M1 placed the rifle back into the trunk of the sergeant's car and retrieved his riot shotgun and a big olive-green blanket. He walked around the back and into obscurity as he blended in with the rest of the officers. Everyone began to leave. The patrol boys walked their separate ways. Mikey and Yolanda walked back over to La Grange Drive and then to their homes. They walked together in unison first but then separated when she came to her home and said a soft "goodbye," and he turned and walked further down to his home and down the hill into the silence of a cold, uncaring, but familiar night.

EPILOGUE

In April's Last Breath
April 30, 1968

The early morning sprinkle subsided and Mikey took his anger, his disappointment, his love, his fear and felt it all on the handle of the shovel and pushed the spade up through the first fist of grass that angrily gripped in clinging clutches of moist mud clumps. It was the heart of Texas; the moist soil when the time was right, just after the rains had soaked the thirsty lands and creation was in the air. It was a moment just like after a death and the ripple of a newborn in the lives of the few who had once felt the loss and needed the new life. From the rains residue you could see dead insects who were caught unaware, ants and beetles and lightening bugs in intermitting rivulets running down the curbs to the drainage vents and from the many homes with the outline drainage vent tracing up along the edges, passing around the edges of the roofs and always to the backyard that had the sand mound where X marked the road to China. He had calculated this spot with weather reports and longitude and latitude measurements from the globe in his geography class. After the first shovel full he discarded the grass over his shoulder with an over emphasized huff. He wanted to go under the sand at an angle then tunnel straight down to the other side of the world from his point using his compass. The sound of his work carried through the early morning and mingled with the far croaking of a night frog leaping to shelter against the rising sun and the early chirpings of a single blackbird perched high and looking down in solitude from a telephone wire and the occasional clatter of pots and pans from Tuesday morning breakfast. Light pierced through the horizons, through the overgrown weed stalks and the sloping grasslands of the park, the vast field that separated the Heights from Alta Mesa, the windows of homes that reflected the glancing sunlight as spotlights of hope on driveway shimmering Dodges and Chryslers, an old Plymouth, to a Corvair and VW Beetle and gave the appearance of quiet accomplishment. The neighborhood. Now awaking, dogs barking in the morning as a serenade of movement that erased the outlines of silence to breathing to movement to reaction and interaction. Morning, and not so early morning anymore invaded in moist light, a shimmering afterglow and cleansing that revealed a little boy, small with a large man-sized shovel flicking dirt up and around and behind in soft pelting whistles.

Mikey took his anger, his disappointment, his love, his fear and felt it all on the handle of the shovel and pushed the spade up through the first indention of the crawling loss of flesh of heart that angrily gripping in dripping clutches of moist soil now seeing his goal in his mind's eye for the first time, China. He could see himself walking with the Chinese people in quiet unison, in the white martial arts jumpers with the white headbands and the belts tied tight. He would become an expert like Kato from the Green Hornet and he would be content and silent but explode with yells and kicks and win. He would let everything go just like everything had left him.

The Patrol Boys were a distant memory. They would not finish out the semester. The end of the responsibility was not as uncomfortable for him as losing the sense of authority was. The other students had taken for granted that what the Patrol Boys said meant something and held the same weight of authority as the people who had put them in charge. That authority was gone. The people in charge had changed the assignment for safety reasons. Someone had reported the accident and the ruling went strangely in favor of the ice cream man. It seemed that the patrol boys were interfering with a business and the driver had the right to make a living. Leave it to Yolanda to find the rumor of that decision from her usual means of knowledge. Although quietly absent from the community gossip her mother was quite active in the knowledge of rumor that ran through the Wisdom Wiser's and into the community. Mr. Campbell talked to the guys quietly and collected the yellow belts and sadly placed them in an office cabinet and locked them away.

"It's not in the *Morning News*, son," said Big Teddy Malone. He walked out of the house and to the sand box. He was holding the newspaper in one hand and smoking a cigarette in another. "But I guess that solves that problem though, about the body and all that mystery you were so interested in. People have been calling all night and I know your mom told you before you came out here."

Darius was shot and carried away last night and no one really knew if he were dead or alive. The rumors all over the neighborhood had preceded whatever official news report that was forthcoming. It surfaced all night, over-night, in the form of phone calls from neighbors, that he was suspected and shot for possibly robbing the stores in the small shopping center. The knife, the K Bar that he had been caught with could have been the same weapon that had been used for killing all the dogs that had been coming up missing, and he was probably responsible for the body that was found on the trail. It was easy to conclude that he was indeed the Rabbit Man.

"It seems like you can't trust those army people. They say they teach them to be crazy like that. He always wore those sunglasses. He always looked angry. Son, always let them see your eyes. You learn a lot about people when you drive the bus, and you got to let people see your eyes. That way, they won't be afraid of you," he said. "When people are afraid of you, they won't hesitate to hurt you."

Big Teddy stubbed out his cigarette on the heel of his shoe and tossed the butt out and onto the alleyway. He rolled the newspaper up into a small baton and used it as a pointer. He moved up to the edge of the sand pit and pointed down with the newspaper to the hole that Mikey had completed so far.

"You're gonna dig your way to school today? Well, the only thing you can find by digging in that sand is nothing but a hole in the ground. You ought to cover it up and build on top of it. I can put some swings right here for your sisters." He was wearing his second-best pair of dress shoes and the moist grass start to glisten against the leather. He had moved into the pit and began walking around the wood planks that aligned the pit into a square. From the moisture his shoes began to clump with sand on the side. He stopped and looked down at one of the corners and stomped the sand down with his heel. "You like swings, don't you, and a slide? This is what I was intending to do when we got this sand."

He looked up to Mikey and waited out his angry evasive glance until Mikey finally looked up with a glistening disappointment in his eyes that he felt inside.

"You can play G. I. Joe over there in that patch of rosebush." He pointed toward the fence that separated their yard from the neighbors' yard. Six feet of the fence was lined with manicured petals and budding roses that were opening up to the sunlight. "Just don't touch the roses, boy. Your mom will kill you if you hurt a single one."

He walked around the sand pit one more time and then once more but counting his footsteps each time.

"A swing set and a good slide and maybe there is some room for a jungle gym for you. You like to climb, don't you? It will probably keep you off the top of the house climbing up and looking around at the neighborhood."

He finished his squared walk and then moved over to near the rosebush area. He left footprints of sand finally falling off the sides and bottoms of his shoes.

"Come over here and take a look."

Mikey walked over with the shovel draped over his shoulder like a soldier walking a perimeter just like on the television show *Combat*.

"I can get some bricks from this guy I know at work for a good price. We can line off the rosebushes from the rest of the yard and put and your mother will come out and dig around it and make the dirt fresh and easy to water. What do you think about that?"

"Sounds like a lot of work."

"Well you have never been afraid of work, have you?"

"No, I don't mind working."

354

"Yeah, I know that's the way you are."

Big Teddy kicked the edge of the grass where he wanted the bricks to begin and the grass to end. "You will start digging here and follow this line to the end of the bushes. It's going to look good. Now, look over here."

He walked over away from the rosebushes about seven paces to where he stood between the sand pit and the rosebushes. He planted both feet on a particular spot and made an X with one. Mikey walked over with the shovel still on his shoulder and stood beside him.

"This is where I am going to put the barbecue pit. I am going to get enough bricks to make one. I saw one at the store and I am going to draw the design on paper and measure it with the bricks. It's not easy but there is a guy at my job who can help me check the measurements."

Mikey looked down and moved over to plant the shovel on the X spot in the grass. He traced a big X and the placed the point of the shovel in the ground and then put a foot on top to drive it into the ground. As soon the blade went into the ground then his father moved away.

Big Teddy moved over to the big double exit gates at the edge of the fence. He started there and then began walking to the furthest edge of the fence about two feet away and then turned and walked toward the house. He was counting his steps as he walked and when he counted twenty or so feet, he made an abrupt right turn, marked it with an X with his feet and then started back toward Mikey, still counting. He made it twenty or so feet from his turn, marked it with an X and then started back to the back fence. He was disappointed when he didn't come to twenty feet with his final measurements but shook it off with slight head nod and a side whistle from his lips.

"We'll go back and get that later. Come to think of it the frame planks will have the same length as the proper markings for end planks. Come over here and look at this."

Mikey walked over to his father with the shovel clear of dirt and again on his shoulder. The sun began to rise in the east, maybe two hours or less away from 9am, and fought against the nice puffy white clouds that were scattered across the sky. A slight breeze blew and flapped some hanging shirts and a pair of pants from a few backyard clotheslines that neighbored their home. For the most part they were alone and all the other neighbors were inside and doing their early morning routine.

"Right here will be our outdoor garage. It's going to be the same brown as our house but smaller so I can park the Plymouth and the tools and lawnmower. We can also put the trashcans in it because it will have a garage door that will lead to the alley. It's gonna have a door that will open on this side facing the house and maybe a window."

"We going to do that all at once, Dad?" asked Mikey.

"Nope, not all at once, but I'm not finished." He began turning around slowly and using his hands to hold and shape things in the air. "The floor has got to be concrete so it will hold everything in place and the mud won't get on everything, like your bicycle tires. You can put your bicycle inside alone with the wagon and your sister old tricycle."

Mikey began walking around within the interior of the rectangle that his father had marked off. Big Teddy inhaled deeply and held his hands up to the sky and then brought them down slowly while exhaling loudly. He walked around again slowly this time and taking a different look from every circumference direction and grew taller with each step. He came to the imaginary door and walked through it and counted off ten paces toward the house. He stopped and continued to face the dining room window and the far dark brown wood wall of the house.

"A patio. That's what we need right here. A patio where we could all sit under the shade in the backyard as a family and enjoy our own entertainment. Leave the shovel and come over here and take a look at this."

Mikey put the shovel down and walked over and beside his father. Both looked at the back façade of the house.

"The patio floor will start at the porch and then move up about three feet and then straight across to the end of the wall. It's going to stop about four feet from the fence. It's gonna be concrete with one brick side over there."

Big Teddy pointed to an imaginary line that started four feet from the side fence to their left and then moved his hand, palm flat, down

356

to about three feet high, paused and then begin talking with feeling and both hands in the air. He looked like Moses parting the Red Sea, or at least a man who was mustering a lot of pride for his presentation.

"This is about all the high it needs to be. I'm going to get one of those tinted patio tops and it will give us some shade. We are gonna get patio chairs just like at the beach in Galveston and put them back here so everybody can come out here and have barbecues and birthday parties. We'll have the swings for your sisters. And I can bring the radio out here anytime. It gonna be great," said Big Teddy. He rubbed his hands together and looked out to his backyard.

"But what will we do with two garages, Dad?"

"Oh, I didn't tell you that I am gonna change that into a party room with a bar and with its own refrigerator. Me and your mom have friends, you know."

Big Teddy turned back and faced the house.

"Yeah, I know," said Mikey. He retrieved the shovel with one hand and then followed his father's sightline to the back façade of the house.

"I'm gonna put three bar stools over there and by the bar and people will come in and listen to music and dance a little bit. You know me and your mom can dance a little bit and your mom loves to dance."

"Yeah, I know."

"It's gonna be what I always wanted to do," said Big Teddy. He looked up to the morning sky and smiled for the first time in a long time.

"So, what are we gonna start first?"

"I don't know. Let's go inside and talk to the rest of the family. You can take the day off from school. Today will be the start of something big."

THE END

CPSIA information can be obtained
at www.ICGtesting.com
Printed in the USA
LVHW040956121120
671367LV00012B/351/J